Tia

The
Broncbuster

Mike Flanagan

Cumberland House
Nashville, Tennessee

The
Broncbuster

To my son Dusty
who inspired me to write
and to God
who gave me the ability

Published by Cumberland House Publishing, Inc.
2200 Abbott Martin Road, Suite 102
Nashville, Tennessee 3725.

Jacket design by Bob Schwalb,
Schwalb Creative Communications.
Jacket illustration by Bob Schwalb,
Schwalb Creative Communications.

Distributed to the trade by
Andrews and McMeel
4520 Main Street
Kansas City, Missouri 64111-7701

Printed in the United States of America
1 2 3 4 5 6 7 8—00 99 98 97 96

Prologue

Standing behind the bucking chutes in the Houston Astrodome, Clint Paxton said a silent prayer, as was his habit.

Finishing with a silent Amen, he turned, placed his right boot on the fence railing, and adjusted the strap on his spur, his gray and blue fringed chaps falling around his legs. His eyes lingered on the Rafter TP brand sewed in bold white leather on the outsides of each leg, and a lump came into his throat. He fought down the feeling that threatened to overwhelm him and turned his attention to chute number three as one of the chute hands slammed the sliding gate closed behind horse number 135, Thunder Alley.

Clint picked his saddle off the ground and hefted it up on the platform that ran behind the chutes. Helpful hands took the saddle and placed it on Thunder's back as Clint climbed onto the platform.

The crowd of men, most of whom were contestants who preferred to watch the action from behind the chutes, moved aside to allow him room. Leaning over the chute rail, Clint adjusted the saddle until it fit the withers of the horse to his satisfaction. Then, nodding to the hook man, he waited as the girth was retrieved from beneath the horse by a long wire hook and raised to where the latigo cinch could be run through it.

Clint looped the latigo through the girth and pulled it tight, then handed the tail to Lonny Travers, a long-time friend and fellow saddle bronc rider. As Lonny tightened the cinch, Clint positioned the saddle to be sure its position was right. When he was satisfied, he nodded to Lonny and waited for him to pull tightly on the latigo.

Thunder blew through his nostrils in a rolling breath and stepped forward in the confines of his trap, but other than that he made no move to escape. He was a seasoned pro at this game and knew that he'd soon have his chance to deal misery to the man above him.

Satisfied that the cinch was tight enough, Clint took the tail, looped it through the "D" ring, and secured it through itself with a loop. Lonny handed him his halter, a heavy wide leather headstall with a long, thick rope rein attached. Clint slipped the halter over Thunder's head and buckled it securely, then checked the rein once more to be sure it wasn't frayed. This was the third time he had checked his equipment that day, a habit instilled in him by his father, Carver Paxton.

Clint turned his attention to the arena and the ride that was taking place. Gary Burgheart had just completed a ride on a large Palomino horse named Sundown, and the pick-up men were moving in to assist him in his dismount. As Gary slid across the back of the pick-up man's horse, the judges turned in their score to the arena director who added them together and called them up to the announcer and rodeo secretary.

Clint lowered himself into the saddle as the Palomino was led from the arena by one of the pick-up men. The announcer was calling out Gary's score.

"Ladies and gentlemen, we have a new leader in saddle bronc riding. Gary Burgheart just scored an eighty-eight on that ride."

The crowd's response was enthusiastic. Applause, whistles, and yells were directed at Burgheart as he made his way back to the bucking chutes. They reached a crescendo and slowly died away.

"Going to be tough to beat," Lonny said to Clint as he bent over Thunder and adjusted the halter and rein.

"It was a good ride on a good horse," Clint answered as

he placed his feet in the stirrups and brought them up over the points of the horse's shoulders.

Adjusting the stirrups on his high-heeled boots and taking hold of the bronc's rein, Clint threaded it through his hand at a predetermined length that would allow Thunder to lower his head, but not so much that Clint would not be able to use it as leverage to hold himself in the saddle.

The rodeo announcer, a professional in his own right, was just completing his oration on the standings thus far. As the arena was cleared and the pick-up men took their places, he announced Clint's main event.

"And now if you'll turn your attention to chute number three, where Clint Paxton will be coming out on horse number 135, Thunder Alley. Clint is presently sitting third in the standings for the year and has drawn the horse that was voted bucking horse of the year in 1995. This should be a great match between two great athletes." As the announcer's voice continued, Clint tuned him out, concentrating on the horse before him.

"You're on, Paxton," the gate man announced as he placed his hand on the gate latch. Clint took a deep breath, raised his left hand, and nodded. The gate swung open.

Thunder Alley hesitated for only an instant before turning and hurling his fourteen hundred pounds into the open arena. As the horse's front feet hit the arena dirt, he ducked his head and sent his back feet into the air until he was as close to vertical as possible without tipping forward.

Clint leaned back against the cantle of the saddle, pressing himself against the stirrups and preparing himself for what was to come.

As Thunder's hind hooves landed on the ground, he bunched himself and leaped into the air, kicking out front and back feet and clearing the top of the bucking chutes. Clint's spurs had been over the horse's shoulders, but now they raked down the sides and up to the skirt and cantle behind him, only to return to the shoulders as Thunder hit the ground once again in a bone-jarring, stiff-legged maneuver that rattled every bone in Clint's body.

The next four jumps were straight out of the textbook, allowing Clint to score points for spurring and providing the opportunity for him to show his skills.

Thunder Alley bucked straight away, head down, back legs kicking high into the air with the force of a tornado.

Clint's spurs were in perfect time with each jump the big horse made, raking from shoulders to the saddle cantle, only to return to the shoulders as the horse's front feet hit the ground.

After four straight jumps, Thunder changed tactics, leaping into the air and changing directions before landing. Thunder turned away from the rein side of his body, a trick designed to throw a rider off balance; but Clint had seen that move before, and he locked his left spur into the horse's side and waited for him to straighten out, only to have it back over the point of his shoulder before he hit the ground.

Eight seconds into the ride the buzzer sounded, ending the portion of the ride to be scored. Thunder, a well-seasoned saddle bronc, ceased his bucking and began a slow lope around the arena. Clint grabbed the pommel of the saddle and hung on as the pick-up men moved in to assist him, one hazing the large horse as the other moved along side and allowed Clint to dismount onto his horse, not an easy maneuver. Being professionals, they made the move look easy.

As the pick-up man slowed his mount, Clint slid easily to the ground and began his walk back to the bucking chutes. Walking with his head down, he barely heard the applause and yells from the crowd as he passed in front of the grandstand.

"That ride, ladies and gentlemen, shows you why this young man is now sitting in third place in the national standings. We'll have the judges' score in just a moment, but let's pay off that great ride with another round of applause to show our appreciation."

The crowd responded as enthusiastically as before, and Clint grinned up at them, thanking them in his own quiet manner.

"Ladies and gentlemen, we just received the scores from our two judges, and Clint Paxton has just moved into the lead here tonight with an unbelievable score of 92."

Already excited to a fever pitch, the crowd went wild again as Clint reached the chutes and accepted slaps on the back and congratulations from the other contestants. Gary Burgheart held out his hand in sincere congratulations. "Great ride, Clint. That ought to move you up in the standings."

Clint smiled as he shook the man's hand. "Thanks, Gary. I didn't think I'd beat your ride, but old Thunder really turned it on tonight."

"That he did," Gary smiled, "but it took a bronc rider to stay with him."

Gary's smile faded, and he looked at the ground, then back at Clint. When he spoke again, the emotion was plain in his voice. "I was real sorry to hear about your dad. He was a good man and the best rider I ever saw. We're sure going to miss him."

The lump returned to Clint's throat. "Thanks, Gary. I appreciate all the support you guys have given me and Carrie."

"It was nothin'," Gary said. "Sorry I couldn't be there for the funeral, but I was up in Durango and didn't hear about it until it was too late."

Clint grinned, "I understand. Dad would rather you be ridin' than hangin' around watchin' them put his body in the ground anyway."

Gary chuckled. "Yeah that's the way I figured he'd feel about it. I reckon he was up there watchin' me come unglued from old Dynamite that day anyway."

"You can bet he was," Clint agreed

Clint made his way to the back of the chutes, where he picked up his saddle and gear bag. Lonny was there as he headed out the back gate.

"You headed to Denver?" he asked as Clint walked up.

"Yeah, but I got to stop over at the ranch and meet with the family attorney. I'll be there by Thursday mornin'."

"You be careful then, and don't worry. I'll keep Charlie company till you get there."

Clint smiled as he walked through the gate. "I appreciate that, Lonny, and I'll be sure to tell Gail and your kids what a fine fella you are, too."

Clint heard Lonny laugh as he made his way to the Ford pickup he'd left parked in the contestants' parking lot. It was a six-hour drive to the ranch, and as he pulled out on the interstate he began thinking about the Paxtons.

Clint knew the complete history of the Paxtons and the rodeo blood that had been bred into each of them. They had continued to add to and improve the Rafter TP ranch operation, generation after generation, using the skills Will Paxton had first learned in Montana in the 1800s.

The stories about Clint's great-grandfather, Will Paxton, and the other Paxton men, told mostly by Janet Paxton, had kept Clint and his sister Carrie entertained for countless hours. As a boy Clint had never tired of hearing his grandfather talk about the adventures of Will Paxton and Tye Garrett.

Tye Garrett was Will Paxton's teacher, mentor, long-time friend, and partner, which explained why Will's son had been named after him.

Clint's mother had died of cancer four years earlier, suffering through a long illness that had left her with little dignity. But she had clung to life up to her last breath.

Janet Paxton had been a Christian woman in every sense of the word, and it was Carver and her faith that had shaped Clint's life, preparing him since early childhood for the life he now led. It was the only way of life he had ever known or wanted.

Clint smiled as he thought about his mother and father and the stories of their early years.

Janet Paxton had loved her children with a passion surpassed only by her love for her husband. She devoted her life to their upbringing and care, but her sun rose and set with Carver Paxton. His love was the same for her.

Even though Janet and Carver Paxton's love had been

strong from the beginning, the road had not been easy for them. Their courtship had been a whirlwind affair to say the least. Janet Paxton, formerly Janet Greely, had fallen in love with the tall cowboy who had come to El Paso to compete in the rodeo, and he had fallen head over heels for the city gal with the long blond hair and blue eyes who had smiled at him as he came out of the restaurant. Boldly he'd asked her name, and when she told him, he asked her to be at the rodeo that night because he was going to be riding for her. Carver had always said it was the best ride he'd ever made. He won the saddle bronc riding and placed second in the bareback riding. Janet lost her heart forever, even though watching him ride had made her nauseated from fear and worry. Her illness did not prevent her from going to the dance with him that night, and four days later they left town in the dark of night, after sneaking her out of her father's house by way of an upstairs window and a neighbor's borrowed ladder. Three hours later they woke up a sleeping justice of the peace in a neighboring county and became Mr. and Mrs. Carver Paxton. The following day they were at the rodeo in Amarillo, where Janet became ill again while watching Carver ride.

Carver brought her back to the Rafter TP after three weeks of traveling the rodeo circuit. Janet had lost weight and couldn't sleep for worrying about Carver risking his life. He kept assuring her it was all right and he wasn't going to get hurt, but his assurance did little to calm her fears, especially after a horse had fallen with him in Santa Fe. He had escaped unharmed and was awarded a re-ride. Janet had run under the bleachers to hide her embarrassment at losing what little she had on her stomach.

Tye and Charlotte Paxton accepted Janet instantly. Neither said anything about her delicate nature over Carver's riding. Charlotte's motherly attention even calmed Janet's fears temporarily.

Carver practiced in the open arena every day, while Tye Paxton looked on, giving advice and pointers to his son. Janet couldn't bear to watch. She remained in the house with Charlotte and helped her cook and clean, waiting in anxiety until Carver came to the house. The audible sigh of relief when he walked in the room did not go unobserved by Charlotte, and she continued to worry about her new daughter-in-law's anxiety.

Carver continued to take his bride with him as he traveled from one show to the next, and Janet continued to worry, becoming nauseated each time he rode. Only during the trips back to the ranch did she have any relief from the constant nausea, and it was during one of these visits that Carver decided Janet should stay behind while he traveled. Janet halfheartedly agreed, thinking maybe it would be easier on her if she wasn't there to watch. That proved not to be the case. She worried even more. To make matters worse, she started worrying about other things as well, such as what was he doing? Was he with another woman who was stronger than she was? Would he still want her when he came home?

Despite Charlotte's constant reassurance that Carver was fine, Janet remained depressed and listless until he returned. She never allowed him to leave her alone again until after the first child was born. By the time the second one was born, she had accepted the fact that Carver was going to continue riding and she was going to stay home and care for the children, only going with him when there was a rodeo close enough for her to travel there and back in a day's time. She still got ill every time she watched him ride.

Janet became totally devoted to her children, allowing them to consume her time and her thoughts. Even though they were the center of her attention when Carver was away, she never allowed her affection and love for them to replace the love she felt for her husband. Their love for each other had grown even stronger over the years as was evident by the looks and touches they gave each other when they were together.

By the time Clint, their son, was old enough to start riding rough stock, Janet had resigned herself to the fact that he was going to follow in his father's and grandfather's footsteps. He had talked of nothing else since he was old enough to sit in a saddle. She had hoped that maybe he'd want to rope calves or wrestle steers, but the yearning to ride rough stock came at an early age in the Paxton family and she knew she could do nothing to stop it. So she accepted it gracefully and allowed him to follow the rodeo circuit with Carver until at the age of thirty-nine, Carver hung up his spurs and stayed at the ranch.

Clint had known his dad had several good years of riding left, but he had also known what having both of them on the circuit was doing to Janet. The ranch was doing well, and the family long ago had ceased to need his winnings from the rodeo circuit. Carver and Clint didn't ride to keep the ranch going. They rode to keep themselves going. It was in their blood. It was their life. They lived to ride, but Carver gave it up for the woman he loved. He figured he'd had his time, and now it was time for him to give to his wife. He never showed any remorse at quitting, but Clint knew it was the most difficult decision his dad had ever made.

Clint's thoughts were pulled away as he thought about the meeting tomorrow with Harvey Watkins, the family attorney.

He was supposed to meet with Clint and Carrie to go over some details about the ranch. Clint had dreaded this meeting since Harvey had first approached him. He knew there were problems with the ranch and had some knowledge of them, but his dad had assured him there was nothing to worry about. But then, his dad wasn't supposed to have died in a car wreck, run into head-on by a drunk driver.

Clint reached the outskirts of Houston and set the cruise control for seventy. As he drove along Highway 290 heading to Austin, he wondered about the legacy he had been left. Where would the Paxton name be when he was laid to rest? Was he strong enough to stand against those who would take what his family had worked generations to build? Whatever it took, he would handle it the way his grandfather and father always taught him: head held high, back straight, and actions bold. That was the Paxton way.

Chapter One

Will Paxton carried the pail of dirty dishwater to the ditch behind the cook shack. As he watched the water pour from the pail and disappear over the edge of the canyon, he wondered again how he'd wound up in Montana working as a cook's helper on the Triangle T Ranch.

The sound of a horse's squeal and the crash of four hooves landing with an impact that vibrated the ground brought Will back to the present. Turning toward the corral, he saw Tye Garrett on the back of a line-backed dun, reins pulled tight, his spurs raking the horse's side in perfect rhythm with every jump.

Tye Garrett broke all the horses for the Triangle T. In the two years Will had been there, he had watched with fascination as Tye rode the rough string, breaking the horses to be used in the day-to-day ranch work.

Breaking horses was not a full-time job on the Triangle T, so when Tye wasn't busy with the new remuda, he was with the other hands, working cattle, building fences, putting up prairie hay, or helping with the gathering and branding, until there were colts old enough to break or the ranch foreman, Charley Hicks, bought a new string of unbroken horses. The demands placed on a working ranch horse required replacements on a regular basis.

Tye's broad shoulders stretched the denim shirt tight, as his arms strained against the pull of the reins. His six-foot frame was lean and fit. His face was browned by many hours of working in the sun, making him look older than his twenty-three years.

Will climbed the fence to watch, mesmerized by the battle taking place before him. The dun was using every trick in the book to lose the man on his back. Leaping high in the air, he'd turn all four feet almost to the sky, twisting his body in the air, then righting himself before coming back to earth with a stiff-legged, bone-jarring thud. Meanwhile, the rider on his back clung to the reins, raking the horse's sides with each lunge. Will could not see how it was humanly possible for anyone to remain astride a horse that could buck the way this one did, but Tye not only stayed aboard, he made it look easy. Will could swear Tye had a smile on his face during the entire ride.

The battle lasted for another five minutes, then the dun, after one of his sunfishing slams back to earth, stopped, head down and breath coming hard. Tye allowed the horse to breathe a moment, then kicked him into a lope around the corral. He loped him around twice, then turned and loped him in the other direction, finally coming to a stop in front of Will.

"Ya wanna ride him?" Tye asked.

"Sure," Will said with such eagerness it brought a smile to Tye's face.

Will was climbing down from his perch on the fence when an angry voice reached his ears.

"Will ... Will Paxton, where in the blazes are ya? I'm gonna tan your hide when I catch ya, boy. Lazy no-account kid. Can't get an honest day's work outa ya fer nothin'."

Will looked up at Tye, regret written all over his face. "I guess I'd better get back to work. Can I ride him some other time?"

"Sure ya can," Tye agreed with a grin. He watched as Will climbed the fence and headed around to the front of the cook shack. That was a good boy, Tye thought to himself. He deserved better than to be workin' for that lazy, no-account cook. He had seen Will at night, when he thought no one was watching him, sneak out and ride the horses in the corral. The boy had a natural ability with horses, and the horses trusted him. That spoke a lot for the sort of person he was, and it made an impression on Tye. If a horse trusted a fella, then it was a pretty sure bet he was worth his salt.

The year was 1872. Will Paxton was in his sixteenth year, nearing seventeen. He had the lean look of youth still about him, but he carried it with agility and none of the clumsiness that sometimes plagues the young. He had been working as a cook's helper at the Triangle T for the past two years, since leaving his folks' farm in Kansas to follow his dream.

When he left the farm in Kansas, he'd left with holes in his overalls, food enough for two days, and a single-minded goal. He was going to be a cowboy, riding the range, following the cattle drives, and riding the rough string.

This had been his dream since he'd read his first dime store novel. His father had tanned his hide good for reading what he called trash and lies, but even the whippings hadn't quenched the fire in Will's soul. He scrimped and saved every penny he could to buy another novel.

His dreams might have died a natural death, as dreams so often do when confronted with hard work and disappointments, if it had not been for a chance meeting with a gentleman by the name of Curly Woodson.

This took place after school one day as Will was returning home. Will was late due to the garter snake that had been found in the teacher's desk. Although it could have been placed there by any of the twelve boys in the school, Mr. Henry affixed the blame to Will, and not without good reason since Will was usually the instigator of such pranks, even carrying out most of them on his own.

On this day Will had been detained after school to wash the wooden floor of the one-room schoolhouse.

Will would have preferred a whipping to menial labor, but Mr. Henry never whipped his students. Rather, he chose to keep them late after school. By arriving home late, the errant child was automatically guilty. The only question remaining was, of what crime?

Having two brothers and one sister in school with him, Will knew his father would hear about the prank before he was through washing the floor. He also knew he would get the strap laid to his backside, then the lecture for his soul. He was never sure which of the two was more unbearable.

After scrubbing the floor with halfhearted wipes with the worn-out mop and dirty water for the required half hour, Will was excused. Mr. Henry knew there were chores at home for the boy.

On his way home Will met Curly Woodson.

About a mile from the Paxton farm on the main road running from the small farms scattered around the area to town was a small stream. As Will approached the stream, he noticed a horse picketed under the shade of the large oak tree. The tree itself grew beside the road and was used by many travelers as a resting place, offering a cool reprise for the weary and water for the livestock.

Will was watching the horse as he continued down the road toward home. It wasn't until he was abreast of the tree that he noticed the prone figure lying in the shade.

Cautiously, Will approached the stream, keeping his eyes on the figure under the tree. Upon further inspection, he noticed the man had a Stetson hat pulled over his eyes. His head rested on the saddle.

Will had every intention of passing the stranger by and continuing on his way. He already was in trouble and he didn't want to add to it by dallying, but as he prepared to cross the small rivulet of water, the stranger spoke, causing Will's breath to catch in his throat.

"Howdy, young fella'. Where ya headed?"

Will whirled, looking at the man who by now was tipping the hat back on his head and sitting up.

"Home," Will answered weakly. His knees were shaking slightly.

"Live around here, do ya?" the stranger asked.

"Yes sir, just down the road a spell," Will answered, motioning in the direction of his home.

"You reckon a man could get somethin' to eat there? I

ain't had nothin in my stomach for two days now, and my belt buckle is startin' to rub my backbone." The man stood up and looked down at his stomach.

"I guess so," Will answered hesitantly, knowing both of his parents were good Christian people who'd fed weary travelers before, but he knew they wouldn't take kindly to Will bringing home this stranger.

"Well, let me get my hoss saddled, and we'll ride over and ask your folks. Worst they can do is say no." The man picked up his saddle and started toward the horse.

"By the way, my name's Curly Woodson. What's yers?"

"Will. Will Paxton," Will blurted out, watching the man saddle the horse.

"Pleased to meet ya, Will. Come on. Ol' Smokey'll ride double."

Will walked cautiously over to the horse as the man mounted and extended his hand to him. Will climbed up behind Curly, feeling the sharp backbone of the horse digging into his backside, evidence that Smokey had missed a few meals as well.

"Are ya a cowboy?" Will asked innocently.

"Yep," Curly answered. "I been in Texas workin' on a spread down there. I had some business in Missouri to take care of, and now I'm headed back."

"Wow!" Will exclaimed. "That's what I'm gonna be, a cowboy. Are there really Indians in Texas?"

Curly chuckled. "Yep, there's Injuns there alright. I've killed a passle of 'em, but there's still plenty left for ya."

Will gulped. He couldn't believe his luck. Here was a real live cowboy, and he was taking him home with him. He forgot all about the whipping he'd get when he got home. Here was the real thing, not something out of the novels he'd been reading, but a real live cowboy.

Will's mother listened quietly as Will introduced Curly. She looked neither approving nor disapproving as she listened to her son describe Curly as a "real cowboy" who was headed to Texas. Her expression never changed as Will sheepishly admitted to inviting Curly to eat with them.

"Of course you're welcome to eat with us," Martha Paxton said, the sigh of resignation audible to them.

"Put your horse in the barn, Mr. Woodson. Will, you get down to the field and help your pa."

The meal that evening was a combination of frustration and excitement. Will's constant questioning of Curly about the places he'd been and work he'd done monopolized the conversation and exasperated Will's father, who continued to give him disparaging looks throughout the meal.

Afterward Curly and Will's father sat on the front porch in the two worn rocking chairs, talking about the weather, crop conditions, and the state of the country.

Will sat listening respectfully as his father and Curly talked. Once, during a lull in the conversation, he tried to steer the conversation back to Curly's exploits, but his father's stern look persuaded him to remain quiet.

Due to the large number of Paxtons—six children, Ma and Pa—and the size of the house, Curly spent the night in the barn.

"I'm sorry we ain't got no room in the house, Mr. Woodson. I'll have Mrs. Paxton rustle ya up some extra blankets," Will's father had said.

"There's no need in that," Curly objected. "I'll be fine with my roll. After sleepin' under the stars, that barn will seem like the finest hotel room in St. Louis. I'm much obliged to you and the Mrs. for feedin' me and lettin' me spend the night here."

The next morning Curly was gone before Will arose. The disappointment at finding Curly gone before he had a chance to talk to him again left Will in a solemn mood for the next week. He went to school, did his chores, and helped his father and brothers in the fields, but his heart wasn't in it. The only thought that occupied Will's mind was Curly and the life he led as a cowboy.

* * *

A week later he packed his few belongings in a worn-out case, took enough food for two days, and headed west. He looked back once to see the farm before it was hidden by the rolling hills, then turning back, he headed down the road, carrying his dreams with him.

Will had tried to find work on every ranch between Kansas and Montana, but the story was always the same. No one wanted to hire a fourteen-year-old kid with no experience. Fortunately, the ranchers were willing to feed him before he continued on his trek, which prevented him from starving on the way to Montana. He didn't plan on winding up there. It just turned out that way.

Finally he had found a job as a cook's helper, the only position he'd been offered since leaving Kansas. He had gladly accepted the job. It may not have been what he had expected when he left Kansas, but it was a job. And he ate regular.

Thinking back on it, Will figured things could have been a lot worse than they were. At least he was working on a ranch, and the way he looked at it that was better than being on the farm in Kansas.

Will wasn't worried about being in trouble with the fat cook, but he needed the job, even if it only paid ten dollars a month plus room and board. Besides, he didn't have any-where else to go. The way Will figured it, at least he was working on a ranch, and he might just learn enough to make a ranch hand one day. He worked hard, kept his ears open, and asked few questions, learning early that you learned more by listening and watching than you did from asking.

Will worked from early morning till late at night. He was up before anyone else, including the lazy cook. He started each day stoking the fire in the large wood cook stove, laying out the pots and pans Cookie would need for the morning meal, and gathering the eggs from the hen house that would be used for the meals that day. Eggs were a real treat on a working ranch, and it was said that many of the hands who worked there did so because of the eggs they were fed for breakfast every morning.

Once Will had gathered the eggs, he would knock on Cookie's door, which was a room off the kitchen, and roust him from bed.

Will slept in the bunkhouse with the hands, but since he was up before they were and usually went to bed after they did, he didn't get much time with them.

Will always dreaded waking the grouchy cook. He'd never met a person who complained so much. Cookie would start in first thing in the morning complaining about how dirty Will had left the kitchen the night before and continuing to find fault with everything he did all through the day. He even complained about the number of eggs Will collected, as if it were his fault the chickens only laid one egg apiece.

Will worked hard throughout the day, serving the ranch hands as they ate their meals, keeping their coffee cups full, and bringing more food as they emptied their plates. Keeping twenty-odd plates filled kept Will running.

One thing Will learned shortly after starting to work for the Triangle T was that cowboys could put away the grub. Cookie always said, "A cowboy ain't nothin' but a appetite with a horse 'tween his legs."

Once the meal was over, Will went to work washing dishes, cleaning the long tables and benches where the ranch hands ate, sweeping the floors, chopping wood, and filling the wood box for the next meal.

While Will was busy with his chores, Cookie went back to his room and closed the door, leaving the clean-up work to Will. While this irritated Will, he was grateful to be out from under the constant complaining and harassment of the fat man.

By the time Will finished his cleaning and preparing for the next meal, he had little time to himself before he had to start over. His only break from the daily grind was when the whole outfit was gone, usually during branding time or the spring gather. Then the cowboys just packed a couple of biscuits and some beef jerky to eat until the evening meal. Will had begged the ranch foreman, Charlie Hicks, to let him go along. He even thought the man was going to relent, until the fat cook had intervened and said he needed Will there to help him.

"Sorry, kid," the foreman had said, "Maybe next time."

It had been the same every time, but Will didn't quit trying. He was determined to find a way to prove himself as a hand.

Will was the last one to turn in at night, after making sure everything was clean and ready for the next morning. Then if no one was around, he would head to the corral to catch one of the horses. He had started out riding in the large corral, but as time progressed he had taken to riding in the open pastures. He didn't know what would happen if someone caught him in the act, but the thrill and pleasure he got from the horses far outweighed the risk. He had decided he would continue riding until someone stopped him. He had learned to ride on his father's farm in Kansas, but riding the slow plow horses was a world apart from riding a working cow horse. Riding the wiry cow horses took some getting used to, especially since he rode bareback. He did not dare to risk borrowing a saddle from the tack room.

Will loved the feel of the horses under him, and they seemed to respond to him as if they knew what he was thinking. When riding, he forgot about the hard work of the day, the lazy cook, and the constant harassment. This was his time, and he let his dreams carry him away as he rode. He did not know how he was going to do it, but he knew that one day things would be different. Little did he know things would change sooner than he expected.

Will's second greatest enjoyment came from listening to the stories told by the cowhands as he waited on them during the meals. He listened as they talked about the horses they had ridden, the tough cattle they had worked, trail drives they had been on, and the men they knew. Will liked all the cowhands, and for the most part they were friendly. All, that is, except a man named Slade. Garth Slade hated his given name, and he swore he would beat anyone who used it in his presence.

Slade was a large man, standing six-foot-two and weighing over two hundred pounds. He wore a black drooping mustache that added a sinister look to his appearance, and he was constantly stroking it and twisting it, making it curl on the ends to add to the effect.

The evil looks Slade cast at Will every time he filled his plate or coffee cup sent shivers down his spine. And whenever Will heard the call, "Hey, Dish Boy, bring me some more food," the hair on the back of his neck would stand up on end.

Even though he was young in years, Will recognized Slade for what he was: a man who took his pleasure from bullying those who were weaker than he. He preyed on anyone who was intimidated by his size and menacing looks, and once they caught the brunt of Slade's sadistic humor, they were regularly tormented by the man.

Slade's cruelty was evident to any who inspected the horses he rode. Each carried scars from his Mexican spurs. Will had put salve on the cuts several times on his late-night visits to the horse corral.

The spurs were large rowells, sharpened to razor-sharp points. Slade enjoyed using them to inflict maximum damage and pain. The story had circulated around the bunkhouse, when Slade was gone, about how he had almost killed a man in a fight, using his spurs to rake him while he was down.

Had Will known how Slade would play a major part in changing the course of his life, he might not have harbored such hatred for him. But Will despised the man and swore that somehow he would even the score for the tormenting he took, and for the horses as well.

* * *

The fork in the road for Will began one morning after breakfast.

As the men finished eating, Will placed their plates in the large wash tub as he did every morning. He placed the last plate in the tub, lifted it off the table, and carried it by the handles to the kitchen, his arms straining under the load. Slade was sitting at the end of the long table, and Will had to pass by him. With an evil grin spreading across his face, Slade stuck his foot out as Will walked by. Loaded down with the tub of dishes, Will could not see the extended foot and tripped over Slade's' boot. Will's feet became entangled as he stumbled, trying to right himself, but to no avail. He fell headlong, sending the dishes crashing to the floor as he brought his hands down to brace himself against the fall.

The sound of breaking dishes and Slade's laughter brought Cookie hurrying from the kitchen, cursing Will as he caught sight of broken dishes scattered across the floor.

Will's face was burning with fury as he lunged to his feet, facing the laughing Slade. No one else in the room laughed as Will stood there shaking with rage. He looked into cold black eyes, the grin on Slade's lips taunting. Will knew Slade wanted him to say or do something that would give him cause to strike back.

Fighting back the urge to hurl a challenge into the grinning face, Will bent and started picking up the broken dishes. His face burned hot from the anger he felt.

"What's the matter, Dish Boy, can't ya walk?" Slade mocked, laughing loudly again.

Even though the urge was strong, Will knew better than to say anything. Slade wouldn't hesitate to use his enormous size and strength against him. Though anger burned through him like a hot iron, Will wasn't going to lose his head and get himself into something he had no chance of winning, but he vowed someday Slade would pay.

With the cook yelling at him and Slade's laughter burning in his ears, Will picked up the fallen dishes and headed to the kitchen, the cook right behind him.

Slade was still laughing when a voice from the far end of the table brought instant silence.

"Leave the boy alone!"

Though it was spoken softly, the threat behind the words was unmistakable.

Slade's laughter died instantly. Jerking his head so he could see the end of the table, he stared at the man who had given the order.

Tye Garrett sat at the end of the long bench, his elbows resting on the table, holding a cup of coffee in both hands. He did not look at Slade as he brought the cup to his lips and slowly sipped the coffee.

"Ya say somethin', Garrett?" Slade asked, glaring down the table to where Tye sat.

Setting his cup down slowly and turning to meet Slade's glare, Tye spoke in an even voice. "Yeah, I said leave the boy alone."

"And what if I don't?" Slade taunted. "Ya gonna do somethin' about it?"

Tye stood up and, without taking his eyes from Slade, walked the length of the table until he was opposite him. Leaning over and placing both hands on the table, he stared at Slade and spoke again in a quiet, even voice.

"Ya bother that boy again, and I'll show ya what it's like to be treated like one of yer horses. I'll take those spurs off ya and use 'em to peel your hide." After a brief pause to let his words sink in, he continued.

"If ya think I'm bluffin'," he paused again and stared into Slade's eyes, "ya just try me."

Slade looked into the cold gray eyes across the table. What he saw there unnerved him. There was no doubt in those eyes, only the assurance that Tye believed he could do exactly what he had threatened. Slade had been in many fights. He even enjoyed fighting. But he always had been the aggressor, intimidating smaller men until they did something foolish. Then with pleasure he had beaten them unmercifully. But even though the man standing before him was smaller than Slade, he was not weak. He obviously meant what he said, and he knew he could back up his words.

Slade sat there for several seconds not saying anything. He had enjoyed his status as a dangerous man. Now he was in danger of losing that status. If he backed down under the threat, no one in the room would fear him, and he needed that fear to feed his ego. That was why he cut the horses he rode. They soon came to fear him, and he fed on that fear like rain to the prairie. The more fear he created, the more he needed. But this man standing across from him wasn't afraid. He was threatening him over a cook's helper, and he either had to call him or back down. Either way, Slade felt he was going to lose.

"Well now, Garrett," he said with a sneer on his lips, "I didn't know the kid meant so much to ya. Why if I'd known ya was so fond of cook's helpers, I'd of gotten ya one for Christmas."

Tye didn't say a word as he continued to stare at Slade across the table, waiting for him to play his hand.

"All right," Slade said, the sneer leaving his face. "If he means so much to ya, I won't pick on him no more. But don't push me, Garrett. I might just decide to use ya for spurrin' practice."

Tye smiled for the first time, but the smile didn't reach his eyes as he said, "Anytime ya feel lucky, Slade, just look me up. I'll be more'n happy to give ya the chance." Tye pushed away from the table and started to turn away, then, as if a thought occurred to him, turned back to Slade.

"One more thing. If I find any more spur marks on the horses yer riding, I'll see to it that ya wear the same scars they do." Not waiting for a reply, he turned and walked out the door, leaving Slade glaring at him behind his back.

Will had heard none of the exchange between the two men. After slamming the pan of dishes on the counter, he stormed out the back door, fuming with anger. He leaned against the horse corral thinking about Slade and the things he'd like to do to him. All the men had seen what had taken place, and in his mind he was sure they thought him a coward for not doing something. He was certain Slade would have jumped at the chance to beat him, but sometimes the pain from a beating wasn't near as painful as the pain of humiliation. Even Tye had seen him back down. Will was wondering what Tye thought about him, when a hand came down on his shoulder. Thinking it was Slade, Will swung around, fists cocked and ready.

"Whoa, partner," Tye said, holding his hands in the air.

"Looks like yer ready to pin someone's ears to the ground!"

"Sorry, I thought ya was Slade," Will answered, looking at the ground, feeling the shame and embarrassment wash over him again.

"I know it probably don't help much, but ya did the right thing in there. Slade was just lookin' for an excuse to jump on ya, and ya cheated him outa that. That's the smart thing to do."

"Yeah," Will said with sarcasm, "but now everybody thinks I'm a coward."

"Are ya?" Tye asked.

"No! I'm not afraid of him!" Will said it with such force that Tye couldn't help the smile that formed on his lips.

"Well, as long as ya know that, it don't make no difference what anyone else thinks. But if it helps, I don't think yer a coward. I think ya got a good head on yer shoulders, and ya kept your cool. That says a lot for someone yer age. I know men older'n ya who wouldn't've shown as much sense as ya did in there."

"Thanks," Will said, feeling some of the anger leave him but still burning over the thought of being humiliated in front of the other men.

Tye looked at Will, knowing how hard it was on the boy. Sixteen was almost a man out here, and Will needed to be accepted as a man. Acceptance was a hard thing to come by when you spent your time working in a kitchen, washing dishes and waiting tables.

"I been watchin' ya ride out at night," Tye said. "Ya catch on quick, and the horses respond to ya. Ya got good balance, and that's important if yer gonna ever make a good horse wrangler."

Will's face turned red as Tye spoke. He didn't think anyone had seen him on his late-night rides. The alarmed look on Will's face made Tye smile again.

"Don't worry, I'm the only one that knows about it. I've also seen ya doctorin' the horses that Slade rides. I reckon anyone who'd do that after workin' all day can't be all bad."

"One of these days I'm gonna give Slade a taste of his own medicine! Anyone who'd do that to a horse ought to be horsewhipped," Will said, the vehemence plain in his voice.

"Ya'll have to get in line to do that," Tye said. Will looked at him questioningly, but he said no more. He knew better than to ask.

"I was wonderin' if ya might want to help me with these broncs? I need someone to ride 'em for a while after I get most of the buck out of 'em."

Will looked at Tye, not sure he'd heard right.

"Ya want me to ride horses for ya?"

"Something wrong with yer hearing?" Tye asked, fighting to keep a straight face from seeing the excitement on Will's face.

"Uh, no, it's just that, well …" stuttered Will, "what about Cookie and the kitchen and all?"

"I already took care of that," Tye answered. "I talked to Charlie, and he said ya could ride for me early in the mornin' and after meals. Ya'll help Cookie serve the meals, and when they're over ya ride. Cookie's gettin' too lazy anyway." Tye looked thoughtful for a moment then said, "Sure is gonna make him mad, though." Then, as if dismissing the thought, he said. "Well, how about it? Ya wanna ride or not?"

"Sure. When do I start?"

"As soon as we tell Cookie about the new arrangement. Ya can start with that dun over there," Tye replied, pointing to a horse standing in the corral. "Let's go tell Cookie so we can get started."

"Yahoo," Will shouted, grinning from ear to ear. Tye laughed and said, "I hope yer this excited a week from now when yer backsides are hurtin' so bad ya need a feather pillow to sit on. Ya may wish you were back in the kitchen helpin' Cookie."

"Never," Will answered. "I don't care how sore my backside gets."

Chapter Two

Cookie didn't take the news well. He cussed and ranted for fifteen minutes about how good he'd been to Will and how he couldn't understand why Will would run off and leave him. When Will and Tye explained to him that he'd still be there to help during the meals, Cookie cursed even more, saying that was the easy part. He would have to do all the hard work by himself, and that wasn't fair. He continued to cuss as they turned to leave, and both Tye and Will had to hold their grins until they got out the door.

Will followed Tye to the barn.

"First, we've gotta get ya an outfit. There's some extra saddles in the barn. Let's see if we can find ya one." Then looking at Will's old farm boots, he said, "I got an old pair of boots I'll let ya wear. They may be a little big on ya, but they'll be better than those old clodhoppers yer wearin'. I'd hate to see ya hang yer foot in a stirrup. Ya'll have to ride without chaps until we can get to town, and I don't want ya ridin' with spurs until ya get a little experience on these broncs."

They found the extra saddles in the tack room. Tye picked out one with a high cantle and large swells. The stirrups were small and wishboned, made for riding bucking stock. He talked to Will about the gear as he carried the saddle to the corral.

"This is a good saddle for ridin' broncs. If one of 'em starts buckin', the high cantle will keep ya from slippin' off the back, while the high swells will help hold yer legs in when ya squeeze. The small stirrups will help keep yer feet in without slippin' through."

Tye threw the saddle over the top rail of the corral fence and, after cinching it down to the fence pole, told Will to climb aboard. Even though he wondered what Tye was doing, Will didn't ask. He climbed the fence and sat in the saddle. Tye started adjusting the stirrup height until he had Will's knees slightly bent when he placed his feet in the stirrups.

"That's to help cushion the shock to yer back. If yer stirrups are out all the way, ya can't put weight on yer feet and legs to take some of the joltin' off your backside and spine. Now, let's saddle that dun and see how ya do."

With Will holding the halter lead and keeping the dun calm, Tye placed the saddle pad and saddle on his back, talking to him and soothing him all the while. Even though the dun flinched several times while Tye was saddling him, he never jumped or shied away. Will credited this to Tye's soothing voice and easy handling. Once he had the horse saddled, Tye replaced the halter with a hackamore with large, braided mohair reins. Tye explained the reason for using a hackamore was that the dun hadn't been broken to a bit yet. The hackamore would put pressure on the bridge of his tender nose, and the large reins would make it easier to hold.

Once the hackamore was on, Tye led the horse off a few steps and rechecked the saddle.

"Some horses learn real fast to suck extra air into their bellies when ya cinch 'em up. Then when ya get on, they let it out and yer sittin' there with a loose saddle, which ain't a good thing to have. Always lead yer horse off a step or two and check yer cinch before gettin' on. Well, he's ready. Come on."

Even though Will had dreamed of this moment, now that the time had come, he couldn't stop the butterflies in his stomach. He'd never ridden anything but broken horses. This was a different story altogether. He walked up to where Tye was holding the dun.

"I'll hold him while ya get on. Hold the reins and grab a handful of mane with yer left hand and the saddle horn with yer right hand. When ya swing on, do it slowly, but all in one motion. Don't hesitate. Sit down gently."

Will followed Tye's instructions and was soon sitting astride the dun. He could feel the horse quiver beneath him as he settled himself in the saddle.

"Yer the first person besides me to ride this horse. He's not used to yer weight, and he's nervous. Take the reins in both hands and keep them tight. He may try to buck when I turn him lose, but if ya can keep his head pulled up, he won't be able to. If ya let his head get down between his legs, hang on for the ride. Ya ready?"

"As ready as I'll ever be," Will answered with more confidence than he felt. Will had ridden the horses on his father's farm, and the ranch horses in the corral, but nothing had prepared him for what happened when Tye let go of the dun's head and stepped back. For a few seconds the horse just stood there. Then, realizing he wasn't being held and there was a different person on his back, he ducked his head between his legs and proceeded to leave the ground.

Will was unprepared for the horse's power. The reins were nearly pulled from his hands as the dun ducked his head. Tye's words rang in his ears as he flew through the air and landed face down in the dirt of the corral. He came up spitting dust and whatever else was in there.

Tye leaned against a corral post, chewing on a sliver of wood. "Ya all right?" he asked as Will got to his feet.

"I think so," Will answered

"Well, go catch him, and let's try again."

Will managed to hem the dun into a corner and finally caught him by the reins. Mumbling about the horse's ancestry, Will led him back to the middle of the corral, where Tye stood waiting for him.

"Ya only made one mistake," Tye said

"What was that?"

"Ya got on 'im," Tye replied, with a serious expression on his face.

Will looked at Tye with disbelief, then began grinning as he saw the lines on Tye's face relax into a smile.

"Well, I think I just learned the wrong way to do it. Any pointers on how to do it right?"

"Yep, next time stay on." Tye took the reins from Will.

"Thanks, I'll try to remember that," Will answered with sarcasm.

"Ya just found out what kinda strength this horse has, but ya have the advantage. Ya can outthink him. If ya can't hold his head up, use yer head and body. Hold tight to those reins to pull yerself down into the saddle, and squeeze with yer knees and legs to hold yerself in. Use the swells of the saddle to help hold ya in. If ya let yourself flop around like a sack of potatoes, yer gonna get throwed. Any more questions?"

"Just one," Will said, swinging into the saddle. "Is it my imagination, or has Cookie's disposition just gotten better?"

Tye broke into a laugh as he stepped away and let the dun have his head.

The horse didn't hesitate but immediately ducked his head between his legs. Will was ready this time, and instead of allowing the reins to be pulled through his hands, he hung on, preventing the dun from getting his head to the ground. Even though the dun was able to buck, he couldn't get his head far enough down to turn it loose as he'd done before. He did manage, however, to deliver some good stiff-legged, bone-jarring bucks that knocked the wind out of Will and left him gasping for air. His tight grip on the reins and the squeezing of his legs made a great difference in the ride this time.

After traveling the distance of the corral, the dun allowed Will to pull his head up. Will loped him around the corral and brought him to a stop in front of Tye.

Tye's face was unreadable as Will sat there trying to catch his breath. He had relaxed his hold on the reins, and the pride in making his first ride was evident in his face. The next thing Will knew, he was flying through the air, headed for the corral fence upside down. He struck the fence about half way up and slammed head first into the ground before coming to rest in a heap. The last thing he remembered was Tye taking off his hat as if to scratch his head. The next thing he knew, he was on a keg of dynamite.

"Ya keep gettin' bucked off that horse, and I'm gonna have to start him all over again. Yer gonna teach that bronc bad habits if ya keep that up."

Will wasn't listening to Tye as he tried to rise out of the dust. When he finally got to his feet and could focus his eyes, he looked to where Tye was picking his hat up off the ground in the middle of the corral. It looked as if it had been stepped on a time or two, and it took Will a couple of seconds to make the connection between what had happened to him and Tye's hat being in the corral.

"Ya did that, didn't ya?" Will asked, disbelief in his voice.

"Yep!"

"But why? I'd ridden him. Why would ya want to make him buck again?"

"I didn't want him to buck. I wanted ya to learn a lesson."

"What lesson is that?" Will asked, still not believing what had happened.

"Never relax on a bronc. If ya let yer guard down, he'll know it. Always be ready for the unexpected. If ya'd been ten miles out on the range and a jackrabbit had spooked him, ya'd be walkin' back now. If ya was able to walk, that is."

"Couldn't ya have just told me that? Did ya have to make yer point at the expense of my body?" Will asked, rubbing his hip where he'd struck the fence.

"I reckon ya wouldn't have learned the lesson as well if I'd just told ya. Remember, out here a horse can sometimes mean the difference between life and death. A man on foot could be in serious trouble. Don't take anything for granted where horses are concerned."

"Or cowboys bearing gifts," Will muttered, still rubbing his hip

"Ya catch on fast." Tye grinned at Will, who didn't feel like grinning at the moment.

"Let's go again," Tye said.

Will groaned as he walked over to the horse. By now the dun had gotten most of his buck out, and after a few crow hops around the corral, he allowed his head to be pulled up. Will stopped him in the middle of the corral and watched Tye closely, not relaxing his grip on the reins.

"Ride him out in the horse trap until lunch time. By then I'll have another one ready for ya," Tye called as he headed to the horse corral, his lariat in hand.

When the sun was directly overhead, Will rode the dun up to the gate of the corral. Tye was saddling a large bay mare, a beautiful animal, standing just over fifteen hands and weighing about thirteen hundred pounds. Will had watched Tye ride the mare once before, and the sight was something he would not forget anytime soon. He had ridden her bucking and squalling to a complete standstill. Even after he had totally exhausted her, she wouldn't give in to the man on her back. Instead of stepping out when he touched her with his spurs, she sulled up and wouldn't move. Tye had dismounted and led her back to the horse pen, where the horses to be broken were kept.

Will knew he was in for another show, but remembering his lesson from earlier in the morning, he dismounted and put the dun in a holding pen before climbing the fence for a better view.

Tye didn't need any help mounting the horses he rode. He held the halter and rein with his left hand, keeping the head pulled around to him while he used his right hand to grip the saddle horn and pull himself up. When he was mounted and set, he would let go of the halter, keeping the horse's head pulled around with the rein. He would then play out the rein, allowing the horse to have its head.

Will held his breath as Tye mounted the mare, talking gently to her as he did. As he let go of the mare's head, she reared straight up, front feet pawing the air. Will sat rigid, fearing she was going to fall. Tye leaned forward, holding the reins and grabbing a handful of the mare's mane. After what seemed like an eternity to Will, the mare came down to earth, driving her head between her legs as she did. Her front feet had no more than touched the ground, when her whole body shot skyward. She twisted her head around to her back feet, a move designed to throw the rider off balance, then straightened to come back to earth with legs stiff and back arched. Will watched in fascination as Tye raked his spurs from the mare's shoulders to the cantle of the saddle with each jump she made. Never had he seen a horse that could jump as high as this mare could. Every time she came down, he could see the muscles in her legs and chest tighten, as she prepared to launch herself into the air once more. Each jump easily cleared the top bar of the corral, and each crash back to earth was enough to lay a man up in bed for a week. But Tye rode as if he was part of the horse. Every time the mare changed tactics, he was ready for her, never anticipating but always ready. Will thought the ride was about over when the mare, instead of bunching herself for another jump, relaxed her muscles and lifted her head, then without warning fell over on her side. Will held his breath, expecting Tye to be crushed under the weight of the falling horse, but at the last second Tye jerked his foot from the stirrup and held it out to meet the ground. This maneuver allowed him to step off the mare as she fell. Holding tightly to the reins, he kept the mare's head pulled back and around, preventing her from rising to her feet. As Will watched, Tye slackened the rein holding the mare's head, allowing her to rise. Gathering her hind feet beneath her, and with her forefeet out in front, the mare began to rise. At precisely the right moment, Tye leaped into the saddle and rode the mare up, finding the stirrups as she regained her footing. When her head went down between her forelegs, Tye was seated and ready, but the battle was over. The mare's jumps had lost most of their steam, and each time it took her longer to gather herself for the next one. Finally, with a final lunge, she stopped. Legs spread and chest heaving, she stood there. Tye waited until she got her wind, then touched her lightly with his spurs. This time, instead of sulling, she stepped out at a trot. Tye plow-reined her around the corral twice before stopping her and stepping off. He patted her neck and rubbed her head, talking to her all the while.

Will climbed off the fence and waited for Tye to walk over. Blood was dripping from his nose, and he looked as if he had been in a fight and come out on the losing end.

Tye handed the reins to Will and sank down against a post.

"I'm glad they're not all like her. I'd have to find another occupation if they were."

Taking a handkerchief from his pocket, he wiped the blood from his nose and the sweat from his forehead.

"That was a great ride," Will exclaimed, the excitement of watching it reflected in his voice. "I wish I could ride like that."

"When I get through with ya, ya'll be a better rider than I am."

Will didn't respond to Tye's statement. He couldn't believe he'd ever be as good as Tye, much less better.

After helping Cookie with the noon lunch, Will returned to the corral to find Tye already had saddled another horse for him. This one was a large, red gelding with four white stockings. Broad across the chest and hindquarters, he was built for speed and endurance. Will had watched Tye ride this horse twice earlier, and he liked the way he carried himself. He didn't buck hard, like most of the other horses, and he bucked in a straight line, with smooth, steady jumps. Once he brought his head up, the fight was over. He would lope around the corral, responding to the commands given.

"I want ya to take good care of this horse," Tye said. "He's one of mine."

"One of yours?"

"Yep. That's my deal with Cal Jenkins, the owner. I break his horses for 'im, for ten dollars a head. And he lets me keep my horses here and break 'em along with his."

"How many horses do ya own?" Will asked.

"I've got about fifteen head here," Tye answered as he rubbed the horse's neck.

"What do ya do with 'em?" Will asked, not realizing Tye owned anything more than the clothes on his back and his riggin'.

"I break 'em and sell 'em," Tye replied. "Then I buy some more. I'm always lookin' to buy some good brood mares. I got about thirty head of good blooded mares on a little place south of here."

Will stared, shocked into silence. He had no idea Tye was anything more than a broncbuster working for wages. It just went to show you, you never really knew about men in the West. Will had heard stories of men who worked the cattle drives or on ranches for forty dollars a month who were doctors, lawyers, bankers, or businessmen from back east who had given up their practices to come west. Some were looking to make their fortunes; some were just looking for the excitement; and some were running to escape whatever was behind them—business, love, or, more often than not, the law. Whatever their reason, all had one thing in common: they all had ended up pushing cattle and enduring the hardships and dangers that went with the job.

Will mounted the red horse, while Tye held his head. He wasn't able to keep its head up, but he did manage to follow the instructions Tye had given him earlier in the day, staying aboard as the horse bucked the length of the corral. When he reached the fence on the opposite side, he lifted his head, and Will loped him around the corral twice. Stopping him in front of the gate leading out to the trap, he dismounted and led him through. Tye watched as Will remounted and started across the pasture, a thoughtful expression on his face as he watched Will rein the horse around and ride off. After watching for a few moments, Tye grabbed up his lariat and hackamore and headed to the horse corral.

Will rode two more horses that afternoon, then went to help Cookie prepare the evening meal. The fat cook was in an unpleasant mood and continued to find fault with everything Will did, but Will was determined not to let him spoil his mood. So he smiled every time Cookie began to complain, which infuriated the chubby little man until he became so angry he stormed out of the kitchen, hurling insults at Will as he went.

When all the hands had finished eating, Tye walked back to where Will was washing dishes in the large tub.

"When ya finish with them dishes, meet me at the barn."

The fat cook was sitting on a stool by the back door, slowly peeling potatoes and glancing at Will occasionally with glowering looks meant to spoil his good mood. Even though it was only early April and the evening air was cool, Cookie's shirt and apron were soaked with sweat. Upon hearing Tye's instructions to Will, he stopped peeling his potato and pointed his knife at Will.

"He ain't 'goin' nowhere 'till he chops wood fer the wood box, cleans the tables, and mops the floors."

Tye walked up to the cook and stared straight into his eyes. "Maybe you didn't understand me this mornin'," he said, "when I explained how things was gonna be. Will here will help ya serve the meals. After that he works for me. If you got a problem with that, talk to Charley. I'm sure he'll be more'n happy to straighten things out fer ya.

"Will, I'll expect ya in five minutes. Don't be late." And with that he stepped past the cook, who was sweating even more now.

"Yes, sir," Will said with a grin as Tye went out the door. He couldn't help smiling as he thought about the change his life had taken since morning.

"Ya better wipe that smile from your face, you ungrateful little snot," Cookie hollered at him. "I've treated ya like ya was my own son, and this is the thanks I get fer it."

"Cookie," Will said, "if I was yer son, I'd run away from home and change my name. Yer just mad cause yer gonna have to work for a change." The contempt in Will's voice came through as he addressed the man.

"Ya better watch your mouth, boy! I'll beat the livin'

daylights outa ya if you get smart with me." Cookie's face turned red as he glared at Will.

Will dropped the pot he'd been scrubbing back into the tub of soapy water, then threw the dishrag after it. Turning, he faced the man who had threatened him.

"Ya ever lay a hand on me, you tub of lard, and they'll be needin' a new cook around here."

Cookie lumbered off the stool he was sitting on and walked over to Will.

"Ya've gotten real high and mighty since ya got Tye Garrett lookin' out for ya. Haven't ya, boy?"

"I don't need Tye Garrett to help me take care of ya," Will replied, stepping closer to the fat man before him. "If ya think I can't handle my own affairs, start the ball rollin' and we'll see where it ends up."

Cookie stood there for a few seconds staring into Will's eyes, expecting him to look away, but Will met the cook's stare with a steady gaze. He wasn't afraid of him, and he wasn't about to be pushed around by him. Failing to see fear in Will's eyes, the overweight cook turned away in disgust. With hatred in his voice, he snarled, "Get outa my kitchen, and don't come back. I won't have some damned snot-nosed kid threatenin' me. Go on, get outta' here. I hope Slade rips ya to pieces if he catches ya without your bodyguard around."

Will pulled off the apron he was wearing and threw it at the cook,

"With pleasure." he said and headed out the door. He didn't know what that last comment was about, and he didn't care. He was free of the kitchen and free from that fat, lazy, no-account cook. He wondered what Tye would say when he told him about the incident. Would Tye agree with him, or would he would be upset? And what was he going to do for a job? Tye had never said anything about paying him. Would Charlie Hicks keep him on now that he no longer worked in the kitchen?

Chapter Three

Will found Tye in the barn repairing tack. When he told him about his argument with Cookie, he expected anything but what happened. Tye looked at him for a moment then asked, "What do ya want outa life, Will?"

Will looked at him in astonishment. Here he was without a job, and this man wanted to know what he wanted out of life. He stood there staring, the silence hanging heavy in the air.

"Do ya want to be a cowboy for the rest of yer life for forty a month and found, or do ya want more than that?" The seriousness in his voice made Will wonder even more at the reason behind Tye's question.

He didn't know what Tye was digging at. So taking a deep breath, he said, "Well, this mornin' I was a cook's helper wishin' I was a cowhand. Now tonight I've been fired as a cook's helper, and I don't have any idea what my future holds, and yer askin' me what I want outa life. Right now I'd settle for a steady job and a good night's sleep. I hurt in so many places, I got pains on top of pains. Does that answer yer question?"

Tye threw back his head and laughed. When his laughter finally subsided, he turned to Will and said, "Ya know, sometimes a fella can get so wrapped up in his own dreams he forgets about the things other folks is feelin'. Sorry. I forgot this was yer first day ridin' broncs. I got some liniment in the bunkhouse ya can use. It'll help keep some of the sore outa yer walk. As far as a steady job goes, ya got one. I'll pay ya two dollars for every horse we break. How's that?"

"That's great. Thanks, Tye," Will replied as the burden of being unemployed was lifted from his shoulders.

"Don't thank me yet. Ya'll earn every dollar, and ya may decide it ain't worth it," Tye answered, watching Will's face.

"I'll be there when the last horse is broke and yer lookin' for another," Will replied.

Tye smiled at him and went back to working on the saddle in front of him.

Will lost himself in his thoughts. What did he want out of life? Would he be satisfied with forty a month and found for the rest of his life? Is that why he'd left the farm in Kansas? It was true his mom and pop had six other children, and having one less mouth to feed was gonna make it easier on 'em, but what did he want? Something was driving him, and he didn't think he'd be content with working for wages the rest of his life. But things were moving too fast for him to know just what it was he wanted. But why had Tye asked the question?

"Why did ya ask me what I wanted outa life?" Will asked

Tye didn't look up from the lacing he was working with as he answered.

"No reason. Just was wonderin', that's all."

"Well, I don't know what I want outa life right now, but I don't think I wanna work for forty a month the rest of my life. Seems to me if a fella's got a little ambition and uses his head, he can make somethin' out of himself out here. I don't know what I want yet, but since ya've asked, when I find out ya'll be the first to know."

Tye smiled to himself but didn't reply. Will didn't expect one.

* * *

During the next two weeks Will worked with the broncs Tye had ridden. He managed to keep from getting himself thrown again and even received Tye's approval.

Several of the ranch hands who had stopped by to watch Tye ride had spoken to Will as if he was an equal instead of a cook's helper. Although they probably didn't even realize it, this affected Will like nothing else could. Being accepted by the other hands was important to him, and he was finally seeing that acceptance take place.

Slade made a point of avoiding him. When Will passed him, he would give him a baleful stare and turn away. His behavior puzzled Will. He still wasn't aware of the confrontation between Slade and Tye the morning Slade tripped him. Will expected him to say something about his change in status, but Slade avoided Will and walked away if he approached him.

Even though Slade's behavior puzzled Will, he was thankful for the reprieve he got from his abuse. But Slade hadn't forgotten Will or the fact that Tye had backed him down, and he swore to himself that one day both of them would pay. That day came a few weeks later, but with results Slade had not expected.

* * *

One warm day in May, Will was sitting on the corral fence watching Tye ride a big roan gelding. Will had just finished riding one of Tye's horses and had come back for another one. Little Joe McCutchen and Lanky Thompson were sitting beside Will, watching the ride.

The roan was one of the best horses Will had seen, and he knew it belonged to Tye. Standing just over sixteen hands tall and weighing fifteen hundred pounds, the roan was the biggest horse Tye owned. He'd traded for him a couple of weeks earlier with a rancher who'd bought three horses from him. The rancher had traded him because none of his hands had been able to stay aboard the animal.

Tye had been riding the roan for ten minutes and hadn't felt any give in him yet. He had known he would be in for a tough ride when he stepped on him, but he had no idea that the battle would be this rough. The muscles in his arms and legs were starting to ache, and he was tiring. At the moment he wasn't sure he was going to be able to outlast the bronc. The big horse was trying every trick he could think of to lose the demon on his back, and every time he hit the ground—legs stiff and back arched—Tye felt as if his back would break. Then Tye's whole body would be snapped like a whip as the horse instantly bunched itself and became airborne again, reversing direction in mid-air. When this failed to unseat the cowboy on his back, he would throw his head up, rear on his hind legs, and walk backward as if he could somehow force Tye to slide off. Just as it seemed he was going to fall over backward, he would throw his head forward and come down hard on his front legs, burying his head between them and bringing his hindquarters up into the air.

The fight had been going on longer than expected, and Tye knew he couldn't last much longer. He was considering bailing out of the saddle when he felt the roan give a little. It wasn't much, just a relaxing of the muscles and a slowing between jumps, but it was enough to tell him that the battle was almost over for the day. The roan made a few more attempts at unseating Tye, but those watching could see the fight had gone out of him. With a final twist and jump, the big horse stopped and lifted his head slightly, nostrils flaring as he fought for air. Tye let him stand for a full minute, stroking his neck and speaking softly to him. He touched him lightly with his spurs, but instead of stepping out, the roan lunged ahead, burying his head between his legs and bucking across the length of the corral. When he reached the corral fence on the opposite side, Tye pulled his head up, and the big horse came to a stop, eyes rolling, and nostrils flaring. This time Tye didn't let him rest. He pulled him around and touched the spurs to him. The roan started at a run around the corral, and Tye had to pull him down into a trot to prevent him from running into the corral fence. After trotting him twice around the corral, Tye pulled him to a stop in front of the three spectators sitting on the fence.

"I didn't think I was gonna outlast him," Tye gasped. "He is, without a doubt, the stoutest horse I've ever ridden."

"That was some ride Tye," Little Joe agreed. "I'd of paid money to see a ride like that, and here I got to see it fer free. Maybe ya ought to start chargin' people money to watch ya ride."

"Now there's an idea," Tye said. "Charge people money to watch some fool tangle with a bronc. I doubt ya'd get enough people willin' to pay hard-earned money to see somethin' like that."

"I don't know—" Little Joe began, but the piercing scream of a horse in pain snapped their attention to the horse corral where the horses Tye was breaking were kept. The first scream was followed closely by a second, and before the sound had died Tye was off the roan and over the fence. He was running in the direction of the horse corral before any of the other three could move.

When Tye turned the corner of the barn, the sight that met him made his blood run hot. Slade was mounted on Tye's big red sorrel and was using his spurs to rake the horse from shoulder to flank. Tye could see blood on the horse's side where the spurs had cut into flesh. The big red sorrel was bucking for all he was worth, trying to unseat this man that was causing him such pain. Slade was smiling as he continued to rake the horse. His pleasure at inflicting pain on the animal made the bile rise in Tye's throat.

Quickly apprising the situation and the line the horse would take as he worked to free himself from the lunatic on his back, Tye climbed the fence to the top rail. There he waited, crouched and ready. The direction the horse was bucking would bring him and his rider within three feet. The horse continued his frantic bucking, screaming with each rake of the spurs. As he neared the spot where Tye was waiting, Tye tensed, the muscles in his legs tightening as he prepared for his leap. Tye timed his leap to the precise moment when the horse's feet would hit the ground, then like a wolf attacking its prey he sprang from his perch, catching Slade around the neck in a choke hold as he went across the horse's back.

Intent on riding the red horse, Slade had not seen Tye perched on the top rail. He knew Tye would come running when he heard his horse cry out in pain, but he thought he would come into the corral on foot, where he planned to force the big horse to run him down, crushing him beneath those hooves. When he glanced up and saw Tye hurling through the air at him, the shock at seeing his plan fail slowed his thoughts and prevented him from bracing himself for the impact as Tye hit him.

The momentum of Tye's leap carried him over the horse's back as he hit Slade with his left shoulder and grabbed him around the neck. Both men hit the ground hard, breaking Tye's hold on Slade's neck and causing both men to roll under the horses milling about in the corral.

Tye rolled from beneath the horses, barely dodging hooves as he did. Coming to his feet a second before Slade, he stepped in quickly, swung hard from his knees, and caught Slade in the stomach, knocking the air out of his lungs. Tye stepped back, swinging a roundhouse right to Slade's face, connecting solidly and knocking him to the ground, splitting his lip and loosening teeth. Tye backed off, waiting for Slade to get to his feet. The blood was pounding in his head. Never had he wanted to kill someone as badly as he did now. He wanted to humiliate him. Destroy him.

Slade got his knees under him. Looking at Tye and wiping blood from his cut lip with the back of his sleeve, with a wicked smile on his lips he said, "Ya've been asking for it Garrett. Now yer gonna get a taste of what that horse got."

Tye's anger overrode any caution he might have had as he rushed in to smash Slade again. It was just what Slade wanted. Pushing himself off the ground, he drove his head into Tye's stomach, grabbing his legs as he did and pulling him off his feet. Tye hit the ground flat on his back, the air slammed out of him by the impact. Slade jumped back and brought the heel of his right boot down, trying to impale Tye with the spur. As he saw the intent of Slade's attack, Tye twisted to avoid the boot. He was almost fast enough, but the spur caught him on the outer thigh, tearing through his jeans and cutting a gash in the flesh of his leg. Tye rolled over and came to his feet as Slade regained his balance.

Tye knew he'd made a mistake by letting Slade taunt him into being careless. He would have to use his head, or Slade would cut him to ribbons with those spurs.

The two men circled each other in the dust of the corral, each looking for an opening in the other's defense. Slade feinted with his right hand, then looped a left to Tye's head. Tye slipped under the swing, bringing a right to Slade's midsection, then driving a left to his nose. Tye wasn't set when he swung, and neither blow was enough to bring Slade down, but both slowed him and he had the satisfaction of seeing blood come from Slade's nose.

Tye's leg was bleeding, and the pain was intense. He could feel the blood running into his boot, but the heat of battle made him ignore the pain and concentrate on the enemy before him.

Slade's eyes were narrow slits as he moved in on his opponent. Tye gave ground as Slade advanced, staying away from the bigger man's reach. He knew a blow from one of those large fists could finish him.

Slade mistook Tye's retreat for weakness and rushed in with both arms swinging, triumph in his eyes as he anticipated crushing his enemy. It was the move Tye had been waiting for. Sidestepping the rush and planting his feet, he delivered a sledgehammer blow to Slade's kidneys. As Slade straightened, his face a mask of pain, Tye pivoted on his feet and brought a punch over and down to Slade's jaw. Slade's eyes glazed as he went down in a heap, a groan escaping him as he hit the ground. He attempted to rise to his knees, and Tye stepped in, grabbing a handful of Slade's hair. Holding him upright, Tye swung his fist in a full arc, catching Slade at the point where his ear connected with his jaw. Slade hit the ground again, and Tye grabbed him by the front of his shirt. Dragging him to his knees, he hit him a smashing blow to the face. Slade went over on his back and lay there, not moving. Tye stepped back, his breath coming in gasps. Bending over to rest his hands on his knees, he tried to catch his wind. Finally, he walked over to Slade and grabbed him by the boot, unbuckling the spur, then doing the same with the other one. Removing the spurs, he walked over to the horse trough, picked up a wooden feed bucket, filled it with water, and walked back to where Slade lay.

The sounds of battle had brought all the hands to the horse corral. A fight was entertainment, and nobody wanted to miss any of the action. No one made a move to stop the fight, and no one would. It was between these two, and if one should kill the other, then it would be dealt with after the fight.

Tye took the pail of water and poured it over Slade. When he saw Slade was coming to, he dropped the bucket and, holding the spurs in one hand, grabbed Slade by the back of the shirt collar. Pulling him to his feet, he dragged him to the corral gate. One of the hands standing by the gate, opened it as he saw Tye's intent. Tye dragged the dazed man through the gate, then headed toward the blacksmith shop.

The blacksmith was a large German named Hans Stuber. Everyone called him Stub. He was a large man with arms as big as most men's legs, gained from long hours of swinging a forge hammer. He was the only other man on the ranch, besides the foreman, who had his own quarters. He lived in a small house behind the blacksmith shop with his wife and their three small children.

Stub had heard the commotion coming from the horse corral and had joined the other hands to watch the fight. Now as Tye dragged Slade toward his shop, he hurried to get there first to see what Tye's intentions were and to lend a hand, if needed.

Tye dragged Slade under the lean-to where Stub had his forge set up. Flinging Slade to the ground, he carried the spurs to the large anvil and, picking up the tongs used for holding hot shoes, he placed one spur in the grips of the tongs. Then, after placing the spur on the anvil, he took the large forge hammer in his right hand and, with a full swing, struck the rowels of the spur. The rowel shattered and flew off, sending pieces of metal flying in all directions. He did the same with the other spur. Slade watched as Tye hammered out the rowels and beat the shanks off the spur as well. Once he was finished, Tye walked over to Slade, who was still lying dazed in the dirt of the blacksmith shop. Dragging him up, he led him over to the anvil. Slade made one attempt to pull away from Tye's grasp, but a backhand slap to the face changed his mind. Tye placed one of his arms on the anvil. Then, taking one of the spurs, he fitted it to Slade's wrist. Positioning wrist and spur on the anvil, he grabbed the large hammer again.

"Ya move, and I might just miss and break yer arm," he said as he lifted the hammer to swing. Seeing Tye's intent, Stub stepped forward and held Slade's arm. Looking straight into Tye's eyes, he nodded. Tye held the hammer over his head, nodded to the big blacksmith, then swung the hammer, striking and bending the spur around Slade's wrist. Slade screamed as the metal bit into the flesh on his wrist.

Once Tye finished bending the spur around Slade's wrist, he did the same on the other wrist as Stub held Slade. Stepping back, he watched as Slade stared at his bracelets.

"Yer so fond of them spurs, ya can wear 'em where they can't hurt nothin' but ya." With that he handed the forge hammer to Stub, turned, and walked out of the lean-to, leaving Slade on his knees looking wretchedly at the bracelets he now wore.

Slade looked at the men gathered there, his eyes pleading. But all he saw as he looked from one face to another were contempt and disgust. One by one they turned and walked away. Stub strode past him and began building up the fire in his forge. Giving Slade another look of disgust, he turned and began hammering a horseshoe into shape.

Will had watched the fight. It reminded him of the Bible story his mother had read to him of David and

Goliath. He wondered what had possessed Slade to ride one of Tye's horses. It was evident that he had done it to provoke a fight with Tye. Well, he certainly got his wish, Will thought. He'd never seen a man beaten down as badly as Slade. He didn't feel sorry for what Tye had done to him, only surprised that he had done such a thorough job of beating the man.

Will looked around for Tye. Not seeing him among the other ranch hands, he went to the horse corral to care for the sorrel. There he saw Tye pulling the saddle off the big horse, talking to him and soothing him while he examined the wounds on his sides and shoulders.

Will saw the blood on Tye's pants and boot and noticed that Tye was favoring his leg when he walked.

"Here, let me take care of him while ya see about that leg," Will said, stepping into the corral.

"I'm all right. I've got to get something on these cuts before they get infected," Tye replied, stroking the horse's neck.

"If ya don't get somethin' on yer cuts, infection will set in on ya," Will stated. "Go wash the blood off, and get somethin' on that leg. I'll look after Red. I've had plenty of experience at this, and I can handle it."

Tye turned away from the horse, grimacing as he placed his weight on the leg. "Yeah, I guess ya have," he agreed. Then, looking back at the big horse, sadness washed over his face. "It's a shame some men have to hurt horses to feel like men."

"Yeah, it's a shame all right," Will agreed bitterly. "Now go on and get that leg tended to. I'll take care of Red."

Tye hobbled off to the bunkhouse as Will began putting salve on the big horse's bloodied sides. Each time the horse flinched from the pain, Will remembered Slade's face as he sat in the dust of the blacksmith shop, the spurs bent around his wrist. Slade's look of total defeat helped ease the pain he felt for the horse.

Later that day, Slade saddled a horse and rode out. He

wasn't missed, and the only time his name came up was when someone would start talking about the day Slade had his spurs made into bracelets. Tye was glad Slade was gone, but something told him it wasn't over between them, that their paths would cross again.

* * *

Two weeks had passed since the fight, and things had returned to normal. Will spent his days riding the horses Tye had broken. Although most of them still bucked when first mounted, his skills had improved so much he looked forward to it.

There were three horses Tye wouldn't let Will ride, even though he had begged for the chance: the big roan gelding, the bay mare, and a large, gray stud horse. All three horses had fought and bucked hard when Tye first rode them, but they now were gentled to some degree. Even though they bucked harder than the others when mounted, Will figured he'd acquired enough savvy to ride them. But Tye had said no without giving a reason, and Tye was the boss. Will knew he usually had a pretty good reason for the things he did, so he didn't push the issue.

As Will rode the black horse he'd been working in the horse trap back to the horse corral, Tye was putting one of the horses through his paces, working him along the fence in the corral to put a rein on him. When he looked up and saw Will, he rode over to the gate and, leaning down, unhooked the latch. He gently kneed the horse around and swung open the gate for Will to ride through. He then eased the horse around and closed the gate behind him.

"Ya've really got 'im workin'," Will said. "He's about ready for the ranch remuda."

"He is ready," Tye answered. "All of 'em are about ready. I figger about one more week of this, and I'll be out of a job."

"Out of a job?" Will asked incredulously, not believing he'd heard right.

"Yep, out of a job. All the horses are broke," Tye replied, not looking at Will.

"Yeah, but I thought you worked cattle 'till they had more horses for ya to break," Will replied, thinking about what this meant to him. If Tye was out of a job, more than likely that meant he was out of a job, too. He had no idea what he was going to do once the horses were broken, and he'd been too busy to talk to Tye about it. Now his future was looking even more bleak as Tye broke this bit of news to him.

"Usually I do, but not anymore. I told Charley I was pulling out when I finished these horses." Tye watched the expression on Will's face.

"What'cha gonna do?" Will asked, as his shoulders slumped. He was feeling about as low as a man could feel. Just when things were starting to work out for him, Tye was pulling up stakes and leaving.

"I thought I might head down to Wyoming and catch me some wild horses," Tye said, a smile coming to his face as he thought about it. "I talked to Charley about ya. He said if ya wanted to stay on, he'd put ya on as a horse wrangler. He figgers ya got the makin's of a good bronc rider."

"Thanks," Will said. Even though that answered the question of his employment, it didn't ease the pain he felt at the thought of Tye leaving.

"Course, I was kinda hopin' ya might want to ride along with me." Tye said it in such an offhanded way that a moment passed before it sank into Will's consciousness. When he looked up, Tye had a grin on his face.

Will's spirits rose immediately. But he maintained a straight face as he said, "I don't know. A horse wrangling job sounds pretty good. I wouldn't have to put up with a hardheaded, hot-tempered fella that tries to get me throwed every chance he gets."

Tye laughed as he watched the gleam in Will's eyes.

"Well, I was just invitin' ya along cause ya look so funny when ya hit the ground. I figgered ya'd be good entertainment. But since ya don't want to go, well, I'll just have to find someone else to go along for entertainment.

It's gonna be hard to find someone who can fall off a horse the way ya do."

Will grinned at Tye. "Nah, I guess I better go with ya. There ain't no one else who can put up with your cantankerous ways. Sides that, you'll need me along to ride the rough horses fer ya. You're gettin' on in years, and it won't be long 'till someone will have to help ya into the saddle."

"Yeah, well Junior, I'm not ready for the grave yet, but when I get too old to work my own broncs, it's reassuring to know that ya'll be there to take care of me. Now let's go get some chow so we can finish these cayuses up before winter gets here."

Every day of the following week the two of them worked from sunup to sundown. Both Will and Tye rode as many horses as they could, putting the finishing touches on them before turning them over to the horse wrangler to be included in the remuda of ranch horses.

Tye continued to educate Will in the proper techniques of horse training. He found Will to be a quick learner and was pleased with his results on each of the horses he rode.

Chapter Four

On Saturday evening, after a full day of riding, Tye took the last four horses in the string to the horse pen and turned them in with the ranch remuda. Will was in the tack room putting away his saddle when Tye walked in.

"We'll be riding out before daylight in the morning." Tye spoke as he hefted his saddle onto the wooden rack. "Charley said to tell ya you could keep the riggin' ya been usin', and he also said if ya ever needed a job, come see him. Said he'd put ya on as a cook's helper any day."

"That's mighty nice of him." Will replied. "If you get to actin' mean and nasty in yer old age, I'll have a place to come to."

Will put his saddle and roll on the rack, then with a thoughtful look at Tye asked, "Where we headed to in Wyoming, anyway? Here I am, leaving in the mornin', and I don't even know where we're goin' or what we're gonna be doin', except catchin' wild horses."

"That's what I like about ya, Will. Ya don't ask too many questions. We're goin' to a place in northwest Wyoming, around the Yellowstone River. I was through there a few years back, and I saw the wild herds runnin' in the mountains. I've had a hankerin' to go back there and catch me some of 'em ever since. I've got enough buyers now to sell all we can catch and break, if we can keep our hair long enough to get 'em out."

"Keep our hair!" Will fairly shouted. "Ya didn't say nothin' about keepin' our hair! I gather there's Injuns out there?"

"Ya gather right. Yer not gettin' cold feet on me now, are ya?" Tye asked, watching Will's face closely

"I ain't gettin' cold feet," Will replied, "but I don't want my head to get cold without any hair on it either. How do ya plan to get these horses out of there without losing both our scalps? And how do ya know there still are wild horses down there?"

"Will, I just got through sayin' one of the things I like about ya was that ya didn't ask a lot of foolish questions. Now, here ya go, askin' a whole passle of 'em. There's some horses there. I've checked with folks from time to time, and they tell me they're there. As for the Injuns, well, I've got me some ideas about them, too. Ya'll just have to trust me."

"I do trust ya," Will said, with a touch of sarcasm in his voice. "It's the Injuns I don't trust. But if ya say there's horses there, then they're there. And if ya say we can get 'em out without our heads hangin' in some Injun's teepee, then I guess we can. I just hope ya know what yer doin'." Will looked thoughtful for a second, then said, "I would like to have a gun though if we're goin' to be ridin' into Injun country."

"Ya know how to use a gun?" Tye asked.

"I used a rifle a bit on our farm back in Kansas. I got to be a pretty good shot."

"What were ya shootin' at?" Tye asked.

"Deer, rabbits, and other game," Will remarked innocently.

"Ya ever shoot at someone who's shootin' back at ya?" Tye asked, the question coming hard and forceful.

"Never had any reason to," Will remarked hotly. " Have ya?" He watched Tye closely.

"Yeah, I have, a time or two, and it ain't no fun," Tye replied, his voice softening as he continued.

"We'll pick ya up a rifle and a colt at Alder Gulch* as we pass through. We'd better pick up enough shells for ya to do some practicin' with, too."

Will and Tye left the ranch before dawn the next morning. They were several miles down the trail before the sun came up. Ten head of horses were strung out between them, with Tye leading the first and each of the others tied to the tail of the horse in front of him. Will brought up the rear. His job was to watch behind them and alert Tye should anyone or anything approach. Tye had warned him before they left that morning that they could encounter Indians or bandits along the way, so he'd better ride with his eyes and ears open. If he saw or heard anything, he was to sound a warning.

As Tye came out of the bunkhouse with his roll, Will noticed that he wore a Colt belted around his waist and tied to his leg. He also carried a rifle in the boot on his saddle. Even though Will had seen the other hands wear irons when they rode the range, this was the first time he'd seen Tye wearing one. Realizing they could be riding into danger had a quieting effect on him. There was always the threat of Indians, and they'd even had problems once or twice with them stealing horses when they were out in the large horse trap. But as far as Will was concerned, since he'd never seen any, he didn't feel threatened by them.

Now they were riding away from the safety of the ranch and into unknown dangers. Will searched his conscience and found that although he wasn't afraid, he sure would have felt better if he had a rifle.

There were only a couple of hours of sunlight left when Will and Tye topped the hill overlooking Alder Gulch.

"Before we get to town—not that ya can call that much of a town—there's some things ya need to know. Alder Gulch is what's left of a mining town. It's not much now, but there's still a lot of riffraff hanging around, preying on those that haven't given up on gold. All the big gold strikes

---

Gold was discovered in the 1860's in Alder Gulch (now Virginia City), as well as Grasshopper Creek, Confederate Gulch, and Last Chance Gulch (Helena). The gold rush brought a large influx of people into the area where several tribes of Indians and only a few ranchers had been.

played out several years ago, but there's still those that think there's gold to be found.

"There's still some traces found here and there, and that keeps these fools lookin', hopin' to strike it rich. We won't have any trouble out of the miners, unless there's one lookin' to steal a horse and hightail it outa here. But as for the others, there's those that would slit yer throat for the gold fillings in yer teeth.

"It's best not to say too much or ask too many questions. Let me do the talking, all right? If prices ain't too high, we'll buy supplies here to get us down the trail. I know of a trading post in Wyoming where we'll buy most of our supplies." Tye paused, looking at Will to make sure he was understanding what was being said. Satisfied that Will was paying attention, Tye went on.

"Once we're out of town, I'll fill ya in on the rest of my plans. If ya don't know anything about it, ya can't tell no one. It's not that I don't trust ya, it's just that sometimes not knowin' somethin' can keep ya outa trouble. Understand?"

"Yeah, I understand. Ya don't want me sayin' something that might make folks suspicious. Right?"

"Ya got it," Tye replied, a somber look on his face. "We'll be spending the night here and getting our supplies in the morning. I want to get as much information as I can about the country ahead of us."

Will looked around him. Then, as if he was afraid someone might hear, he grinned and whispered, "Don't forget to ask about Indians while yer at it."

Tye chuckled. "I promise ya, I won't let that slip my mind."

They rode into town and pulled up in front of the livery stable. Will swung down and opened the gate so Tye could lead the horses into the corral. After taking the halters off the horses, they unsaddled their mounts and rubbed them down with loose hay. Tye was glad to see that none of the locals paid any attention to them. They finished rubbing their horses down, then filled the hay manger with fresh hay. When finished, they carried their saddles and gear into the barn. Tye dropped his gear inside the door and made his way to a door that had a faded OFFICE sign above it. Will followed close behind. When Tye opened the door, Will could see a man sitting in a chair, his feet propped up on the desk and his head tilted forward.

Soft snores came from him, and Tye almost hated to wake him. But he needed to be about his business, so he knocked lightly on the door. When there was no response, he knocked louder, causing the glass pane in the door to rattle. The sleeping figure came awake with a start, feet banging loudly to the floor as they slid off the desk.

The man before them was in his sixties, with long gray hair and a mustache that drooped at the corners of his mouth. His hat had seen better days, and where it had once been a well-creased Stetson, it now flopped in all directions. It looked more like a bonnet than a hat.

When he saw Will and Tye standing there, he stood up and cleared his throat. "Hmmph, can I help you fellas?"

"Sorry to wake ya from your nap," Tye said, extending his hand. "I'm Tye Garrett, and this is Will Paxton. We've just put some horses in yer corral, and we need to store our gear."

"Wiley Topps," the man said, shaking hands with Tye and Will. "How many horses ya got?"

"Twelve head," Tye said. "We've already given them hay. They don't need nothin' else."

"Ya spendin' the night here?"

"We might," Tye replied as if the thought hadn't occurred to him until just now. "Are there any good sleepin' places in town?"

"Only one. That's the Ruby Inn. It's a one-story building and don't have no saloon with it. The other places in town have the sleepin' rooms above the saloon. Been more'n one feller gone to bed at night and woke up dead from someone shootin' through the saloon ceilin'. The Ruby's got good food, too. They hired 'em a chef what came out here from back east to look fer gold and didn't have any luck. Prices ain't bad, though, not like they was a while back when the gold strike was goin' on."

"We're gonna' be needin' some supplies," Tye said. "Is there a good mercantile in town where we can get some?"

"Yep, and prices ought to be pretty good on them, too." Wiley answered, pointing to a building. "Sooner's up the street on the right has a large stock and is tryin' to get shut of it. Seems old Clyde wants to sell everything and light a shuck outa here. Too bad, too. He's a decent sort of fella. Made himself some money during the strike, but now that that's over there ain't much here except leftovers and out-laws.

"We ain't got no sheriff, and the riffraff has just about run off all the decent folks. I liked things a whole lot bet-ter before they found gold. I've made myself a pretty good livin' out of it, but I ain't got no place to spend it and pret-ty soon I won't have no friends left here. So what good is money if ya ain't got no friends and no place to spend it?"

"Ya got a point," Tye agreed, not really having a response to the question. "I'd be obliged to ya if ya'd throw them broncs some hay in the mornin'. We may be pullin' out early, and I'd like to have 'em fed before we hit the trail."

"I'll feed 'em on my way to breakfast in the mornin'," the old man promised "Since the Ruby's got that new chef, I usually eat all my meals there. Not that I can't cook. It's just that a feller don't get a chance to taste that kinda cookin' very often, and I aim to take advantage of it while it lasts."

Tye and Will laughed at the old man's statement, and Tye asked, "It's about time for supper now, ain't it? I'll buy us some grub if yau don't mind sharin' some informa-tion with me."

"Don't know what kinda information you'd be awantin', but I never turned down a free meal in my life. I'll tell ya anything I know and make up a whole lot more fer a free meal. Let me lock up here, and I'll be ready to go."

When Wiley had the doors shut and locked, the three walked up the rutted street to the Ruby Inn. As they walked through the front door, the aroma hit them like a rainstorm, completely drenching them in the smell of cooking food. Both Tye and Will stopped, breathing in the delicious smells lingering in the lobby of the inn.

"If ya boys think it smells good, just wait till ya taste it," Wiley said, leading the way into the dining room.

There were few vacant tables in the room, and they had to settle for one in the back close to the kitchen.

"This place is always like this," Wiley declared. "Sometimes there's a waitin' line out into the street."

An exhausted waitress brought them menus and a promise to return shortly to take their orders. When she returned, all three ordered steak, potatoes, biscuits, and gravy. The smells coming from the kitchen were so over-whelming, Will thought he was going to pass out from hunger before she brought out their meal. Finally the wait-ress brought out three steaming plates of food and set them down on the table, then in a rush left to take another order. All three ate in silence, attacking the plates of food like this was the first meal they'd had in a week. There was nothing left on any of their plates when they finished. Even the gravy was soaked up by the last biscuit.

"I'm so full I hurt," Will moaned, "but if they brought out another plate, I'd have to eat all of it, too."

"I know what ya mean," Tye agreed. "I don't think I've ever eaten anything that tasted that good."

"I told ya boys ya'd like it. Didn't I? Course it wasn't always like this. When this here New York chef first start-ed cookin' here, he was always tryin' to fix some of them fancy dishes like they have back east. Nobody would order the durn stuff. Liked to 'ave closed the place down. Finally he gave up on all that and started cookin' real food like that we just ate. Business has been boomin' ever since."

Tye leaned back in his chair and crossed his legs in front of him. "How long you been around here, Wiley?"

"Since forty-eight. Been about twenty-four years. I come up from Texas with a trail herd and liked it so well I just stayed."

"What part of Texas?" Tye asked

"North of San Antonio," Wiley replied. "My family had a small farm down there. Ma and Pa tried hard to make a go of it, but they wasn't good at raisin' nothin' but young-uns. Pa finally gave up and became a clerk at a dry goods store. I hired on with one of the ranches down there. Stayed with 'em a couple a years till I got the wanderlust and hired on with a feller who wanted to come up here and start a ranch. He was bringin' a small herd with him, and I figgered I'd help 'im trail them critters up here. We fought Injuns and rustlers the whole way. Lost four men along the trail. By the time we got here, I'd had enough travelin' and decided to settle down. Married me a Swedish gal, big enough to eat hay and pull a wagon. She sure could cook. Got meaner'n a sore-toothed mule, though. I was doin' some horse tradin' and doin' all right, but it weren't good enough fer her. She'd gripe and complain every time I come home. Griped about everything, nothin' seemed to please her. One day while I was gone, a drummer come through sellin' his wares, and she ups and leaves with him. Folks around here figgered I'd be plum tore up over it, but to tell the truth, it was the happiest day of my life. I've been a bachelor ever since, and I aim to stay that way."

It was apparent to Will and Tye that Wiley liked to talk and didn't need much coaxing.

"I come from Texas, too," Tye said. "West of Austin, on the Colorado River."

Will, who'd been listening to Wiley talk, now looked at Tye. This was the first time he'd heard him speak about himself or where he'd come from.

"Well, I'll be! A fella Texan, and one close to home at that. I rode through that part of the country a couple a times. Sure was nice land."

"Sure is. I got a small piece of it still down there. Someday I plan to go back and build me a spread. I haven't been there since before the war, but there's some folks down there lookin' after it for me. I'm lookin' forward to the day when I can settle down there."

"Ya mentioned ya needed information, and since I done 'et the free meal ya promised, I reckon I owe ya whatever information I can give ya," Wiley said.

"I need information about the trails leadin' into Wyoming, especially the ones in the northwest part of the territory. There's a large lake that the Yellowstone River empties into. I'm interested in any information you might have on the country east of there. Especially about Indian activity."

"Wyomin', huh? Ya know, I wouldn't give ya a plug nickel fer Wyomin'," Wiley said with a sour look on his face. "Ya know they give women the right to vote in that state."*

"I didn't know that," Tye stated. "But I don't plan to be there long. I just got a little business to do there, then I'm headin' to Texas."

This last statement caused Will's eyebrows to raise. Tye hadn't mentioned anything to him about Texas. He didn't know if Tye really meant it or if this was just something to throw anyone who might be interested off the track.

"If ya was smart, ya'd bypass Wyomin' and go straight to Texas," Wiley said, shakin' his head. "Women votin'. What's this world comin' to anyway?"

Even though Will wanted to hear about the Indians and the land and was getting impatient with Wiley's ramblings, Tye seemed relaxed and willing to let him ramble.

"I don't know that it's all that bad," Tye said. "I've known some pretty smart women who could probably make better decisions than I could when it comes to politics. Sides that, look at the mess we men have made of things in the last few years. If women had been allowed to vote from the beginning, we probably wouldn't have gone to war with each other."

Wiley gave Tye a look of disbelief, then said, "Son, ya got a powerful lot of learnin' to do about women. We may

*In 1869 Wyoming became the first state in the Union to give women the right to vote, earning the title "The Equality State."

not 'ave done so good ourselves, but I guarantee ya if women had been runnin' the country we'd be in a whole lot worse shape than we're in right now. But arguin' about it ain't gonna get us nowhere. Ya wanted to know about the trails 'tween here and Yellowstone Lake. I can't tell ya a whole lot, 'cept what I've heard. They's pretty good most of the way, not a lot of people travel there, 'cept some trappers and some prospectors. The Injuns is the biggest problem. Captain Powell whupped the Sioux pretty good about five years ago and drove most of 'em back up here to Montana, but there's still raidin' parties and a few small villages around that part of the country. There's some Shoshoni Injuns around there, but so far they ain't caused much trouble. I've talked to some fellers who have traded with 'em on a regular basis, and they say they're friendly enough. Yer biggest problem will be with the young Sioux braves who are tryin' to prove themselves."

Wiley didn't ask why they were going to Wyoming or why they wanted this information. That was the way it was. A man's business was his own, and if he wanted you to know why he was doing something or going somewhere, he'd tell you. But you didn't ask.

Tye sat up in his chair and spoke. "Ya've been a lot of help, and I appreciate the information. Is there anything else we need to know?"

"Just this," Wiley replied. "Watch yer backside here in town. There's some mighty salty characters hangin' out. There's some who would stick a knife in your gizzard just for the boots yer wearin'. There's fewer of 'em now than there were. Maybe they'll all be gone soon, but while yer here, watch yerselves and don't hang around dark places."

"Thanks." Tye said. "We'll do that. I'm gonna get us a room and turn in early, so there ain't much chance we'll be gettin' into trouble."

Chapter Five

It was dark out when they left the dining hall, and after shaking hands and saying goodnight, Tye and Will crossed the lobby to the hotel desk. Neither noticed the man watching from the darkness outside as Tye got the room key and they started down the hallway.

The room wasn't fancy, but it would do, with a double bed and a washstand with a fresh pitcher of water and a chair by the foot of the bed. There was a small window about head high that could be opened to let in fresh air. Tye crossed the room and raised it an inch to let in a little air. Even though it was almost June, the nights were still cool.

Will lit the coal oil lamp on the washstand, not knowing as he did, that someone was watching from across the street for the glow coming from the window.

"This reminds me of back home." Will said. "It's been awhile since I shared a bed with anyone."

Tye closed the door and turned the key in the lock. Then he took the chair and wedged it under the doorknob.

"As long as ya don't snore or steal the cover, I'll let ya share this one. But ya do either one, and I'll kick your tail out and ya'll sleep on the floor," Tye stated as he sat on the bed and started pulling off his boots.

"Like I said, yer gettin' older and more cantankerous every day. It won't be long till I'll have to shoot ya just to put ya outa your misery," Will replied as he walked around the bed to the other side.

"Puttin' up with smart-mouthed babies makes a man

old and cantankerous, and I'd almost let ya shoot me just to keep from havin' to listen to all yer squawkin'," Tye complained as he pulled the cover over himself.

"Now turn out the light and come to bed."

"But the light's on yer side of the bed," Will cried indignantly. "Why don't ya turn it out?"

Tye covered his head.

"Cause," came the muffled reply, "I'm too old and decrepit to get back outa bed. And 'sides that, last one in always turns out the light."

"I'll remember that one, too," Will said as he made his way around the bed to turn out the light, stumping his toe on the bedpost on his way back.

The light fading in the window was observed by the man standing in the shadows across the street. He watched for a few more seconds, then made his way across the street.

Will came awake to the feel of someone's hand over his mouth. For a moment he fought the smothering effect until he heard Tye whispering, "Shhh." Then the hand was removed. The room was dark except for the small amount of light coming in the window.

When Will's sleep-filled eyes became accustomed to the dark, he saw Tye holding a pistol in his hand and his finger to his lips, telling Will not to make a sound. Then Will heard the footsteps outside the door. The steps were slow in approaching, not the rapid steps of someone just passing by. Will held his breath as the footsteps stopped by the door to their room. He heard the rattle of a key as it was inserted in the door lock and held his breath as the key was turned and the knob slowly rotated.

Tye was backed against the wall, gun in hand, waiting for the next move. There was a push against the door and when it resisted, there was another push, this time a little more forcibly. Only the chair, placed under the knob, prevented the door from being opened.

Will was sitting up in the bed, looking first to Tye then to the door, wondering what action to take. The next thing he knew, Tye was leaping across the room at him. Tye's leap caught Will in the chest, and both went tumbling off the bed to the floor. To Will it seemed as if Tye's body hit him at the same time as the loud noise. It took him several seconds to realize that someone had shot at them through the door.

As the echoes of gunfire died, Tye leaped up and, kicking the chair away, jerked open the door. He looked up and down the hallway before stepping out. Wearing nothing but his underwear, he raced to the back door of the inn, opened it, and stuck his head out, looking both left and right before stepping out into the alley. No one was around, and no sound came from either direction.

Upset that their would-be assassin had escaped, Tye returned to the room.

The sound of gunfire had roused the other two guests and brought the manager running. All were crowded into the small room as Will tried to explain what had happened.

When Tye pushed his way in, he noticed Will's ashen face. It wasn't hard to figure the cause, for there in the mattress where Will had been sleeping were three holes left by shots fired through the door. There was one hole in the mattress on Tye's side of the bed and one in the headboard, low enough to have taken its toll on a sleeping man.

"What's going on here?" the manager demanded. "I won't stand for gunplay in this establishment. I'm going to have ask ya to leave. Now!"

"Let me ask ya somethin'," Tye said casually, swinging the colt up until it was aimed at the manager's mid-section. "Does each room have its own key, or does one key unlock all the rooms?"

Everyone in the room turned to look at the manager.

"Each room has its own key, of course."

"Then do ya mind tellin' me why it is that someone was able to unlock this door when I had the key in here with me?"

"Well, uh ..." the manager started, but Tye ignored him and continued.

"I'm sure ya keep an extra key to each room in case one gets lost, don't ya?"

"Yes, of course we do," the manager answered, not near as sure of himself as he had been.

"Well, someone unlocked this door tonight from the outside. If I hadn't placed the chair under the doorknob, he'd of been in here with us and the outcome would've been a lot different. Now suppose ya tell me how it is that someone had a key to our room. Did ya let someone have it?"

All eyes in the room turned to look at the man. Sweat was starting to break out on his forehead as he looked at the Colt Tye was holding. His arrogance drained from him now as he thought about the dilemma he faced.

"I assure ya, Mr. Garrett, I didn't give yer room key to anyone other than yerself," he said, his voice almost whining.

"Where are the extra keys kept?"

"Behind the desk on a board."

"Well, let's just walk down there and see if there's a key missing." Tye motioned to the manager with the pistol barrel.

The manager led the way as they walked down the hall to the lobby. Will had slipped on his pants, but Tye was still dressed only in his underwear, a fact that did not seem to bother him at all. Of course the other two men, both who appeared to be salesmen of some sort, took no notice and seemed more interested in the key situation than anything else.

When they reached the lobby, the manager went directly to the desk and, walking behind it, looked at the board until he came to Tye and Will's room number. With an embarrassed look, he turned to Tye and said, "It's not here. I don't know what happened. It was here earlier this evening when I gave you your key, but now it's gone."

"Did ya leave for any length of time?" Tye asked.

"I left for just a few minutes to get some coffee. I couldn't have been gone more'n five minutes."

"How long do ya reckon it would take a man to cross the lobby, get the key, and slip down the hall unnoticed?" Tye asked.

After looking from the front door to the desk, then down the hallway, the manager looked at Tye and said, "About thirty seconds, I would guess."

"And where were ya when the shooting started?" Tye asked

"I was behind this desk."

"How long after gettin' yer coffee was it before ya heard the shots?"

"Maybe a minute."

"So what do you reckon happened?" Tye asked, staring intently at the man.

"I guess someone took the key while I was getting coffee, then slipped down the hall to your room," he answered.

"So whose fault is it that we almost got shot in our sleep?" Tye asked.

In a weak voice the manager replied, "Mine," then hurried on. "I'm sorry, Mr. Garrett. I never thought about anyone doing such a thing. How can I make it up to ya?"

"Ya can start by givin' us another room, and this time I'll take both keys with me, just to insure nothin' happens to one of 'em." Tye replied.

"Of course, Mr. Garrett." the manager said, handing Tye the keys to another room. The other two guests had never said a word, but when Tye asked for the extra key to his room they both asked for theirs as well, just in case this person was someone who liked to shoot people in their beds for the fun of it.

Tye and Will returned to their room to collect their belongings and move them to the new room. This time Tye left the window closed and didn't light the lamp. When he and Will were settled in bed, Will asked, "Who do ya reckon it was that shot at us?"

"I been ponderin' that ever since it happened." Tye responded. "It wasn't someone bent on robbin' us, or he wouldn't have shot through the door. Whoever fired those shots was out to kill one or both of us, and he came real close to doin' it."

"If it hadn't been for ya, I'd be full of holes right now and ya'd be lookin' fer someone else to entertain ya. Thanks fer savin' my bacon," Will said.

"Yeah, that could've been a mistake." Tye replied with no humor in his voice.

Will sat up in bed and, looking at Tye, asked, "Just how do ya figure it was a mistake saving my life?"

"Well think about it. If I hadn't jumped across and saved yer life, I could've shot him through the door, and then we wouldn't have to be worryin' about who it is that's tryin' to kill us. Don't ya agree?"

"I don't reckon I'm too crazy about yer thinking'," Will answered. "But I sure am glad ya decided to save me instead of killin' that skunk."

"Well, chalk it up to my old age." Tye said. "I just don't think as fast as I used to, or I might've done otherwise."

"Well, ya might be gettin' old, but I gotta tell ya, ya really made an impression on them ladies on the street tonight."

"What are you talkin' about?" Tye asked.

"Well, I noticed while ya was talkin' with the manager in the lobby, some ladies passed by the window and looked in. I don't know what they was sayin', but they sure was gigglin' a lot and pointin' at ya. It must've been them legs of yours, I reckon."

Tye pulled the covers over his head and mumbled, "Yep, I definitely made the wrong choice. Now go to sleep before I shoot ya myself."

Will grinned as he rolled over on his side facing away from Tye. One thing about it, life sure wasn't dull now.

In the alley across the street, a man watched the scene in the lobby of the Ruby Inn. He knew he'd failed when he saw Tye and Will standing there talking to the hotel manager. He cursed under his breath and continued watching until the group broke up and went back to their rooms. Then he headed for the Gold Nugget Saloon, where he proceeded to get stone drunk.

"Wake up, Slade!" the bartender said, "You wanna sleep, go on upstairs."

Slade couldn't remember what time he had passed out, only that he'd drunk so much whiskey trying to erase the picture of the beating he'd received from Garrett.

Slade never hated anyone as bad as he hated Tye Garrett. Because of him, none of the other outfits would hire him. The news of the fight had spread through the country like wildfire, branding him as a troublemaker. Now he was reduced to holding up miners for what little gold dust they carried, which was usually just enough to get him drunk at night so he could drown the memories that burned in his mind.

Yesterday when he'd seen Garrett and that snot-nosed kid ride in, he knew his chance had come. He'd waited outside the Ruby Inn until he'd seen Garrett pay for a room, then he'd waited until he saw the light come on, telling him which room they were in. All he had to do then was wait until the manager left his desk, ease across the lobby, grab the extra key, and wait in the darkness of the hallway until the manager was back at his desk. Everything had gone like clockwork until he'd tried to open the door. He knew when it wouldn't open that a chair had been placed under the knob, so pulling his Colt he stepped back and emptied his pistol, aiming where he judged the bed to be. Then he'd run out the back door of the inn into the alley and cut around to the front, waiting for the crowd to gather and view the bodies. Only there weren't any bodies—not dead ones anyway. And the only crowd that gathered was inside. When he saw Garrett and the kid come into the lobby with the manager and two other men who must have been guests, he had slunk back into the shadows. When he heard footsteps approaching, he had hidden in the darkness until two of the girls who worked for the Diamond Lil' saloon passed by. He silently cursed them as they stopped in front of the window of the inn to watch the scene taking place. He heard them giggle, then walk on. Only when he was sure they were gone did he come out of the shadows to watch from a distance, until Garrett and the kid went back down the hall. He thought about trying again, but no light appeared this time and he didn't think he could get past the manager again. As he stood there in the shadows, he vowed that one day Garrett would pay for the humiliation he'd caused him.

Slade fought his way up the stairs in a drunken stupor. Finding his room was difficult, but since he had lots of experience locating it while staggering drunk, he managed once again. He didn't bother undressing but slammed the door closed behind him and fell onto the bed. His last thoughts before passing out were of Tye Garrett and the revenge he would someday have.

* * *

Tye and Will were up before the sun. Both felt rested, even though their sleep had been disturbed.

After a breakfast of eggs, biscuits, bacon, and hot coffee shared with Wiley Topps, who offered Tye more information on the trails and the Wyoming Territory, they left the Ruby Inn and headed to Sooner's, telling Wiley they would be along soon to settle up with him and collect their horses and belongings.

Clyde Sooner was just opening the doors of his mercantile as Tye and Will stepped up on the sidewalk.

"Howdy," he said as they walked in the front door. "Can I help you gentlemen?"

"We're needin' some supplies," Tye replied. "I've made a list of things we need. If ya don't mind, we'll look around while ya fill this list."

"Look around all ya want," Sooner said, taking the list from Tye. "If ya need any help, just holler."

Will and Tye walked along the aisles between shelves of dry goods. Most of the items were for mining, and since they didn't plan on doing any mining, they just passed on by. But when they came to the counter where the pistols were displayed, Will stopped to look through the glass top.

"Which of these do ya think I should buy?" Will asked as Tye looked at the selection of handguns.

"Let's see what kind of rifles he's got," Tye said. "We might as well get a pistol that uses the same shells. That way ya only have to buy one kind."

They chose a rifle and pistol for Will, as well as a belt and holster for the pistol and a saddle boot for his rifle. Will also picked out a pair of boots, chaps, and a wide-brimmed Stetson. Will paid for them while Tye picked out a pack saddle and supply boxes to carry their purchases.

Tye paid for the supplies and asked if they could leave them there until they collected their horses from the livery stable. Mr. Sooner assured him it would be all right.

"Ya wouldn't happen to know if old Clement Stoner still has a tradin' post on the Yellowstone, would ya?" Tye asked.

"Clement Stoner, huh? You know him?" Sooner asked

"I met him a few years ago," Tye answered. "I had a couple a Sioux on my tail, and he persuaded 'em to leave me alone."

"Bet it wasn't through no sweet talk that he persuaded 'em, either." Sooner said.

"Nope. As a matter of fact, he talked to 'em with a Sharps rifle. One of them Injuns probably won't be doin' any more talkin'. I think he hit him pretty hard, and that discouraged the other one from any further thoughts he might've had about takin' my hair," Tye replied with the hint of a smile.

"As far as I know, he's still there. I reckon he's tradin' with the Shoshoni some and what few trappers there are in the region. He likes the wilderness area up there and says he won't leave. I reckon they'll bury him in them mountains.

"It's been about six months since I last saw him. He come in here to trade me some furs he had. He should still be there if someone or somethin' ain't killed him," Sooner said

"We may swing by that way and see him," Tye said. "I'll tell him ya said howdy."

"I'd appreciate that," Sooner replied. "Tell him I'll come down that way when I get shut of this stock, and we'll play some checkers. He does love to play checkers. Cheats though. Ya gotta watch 'im like a hawk."

"Yep, ya know Clement all right," Tye replied. "I stayed with him for two weeks and never did win a game."

Tye and Will left the mercantile and headed down the street to the livery stable. Tye hadn't forgotten the events of the night before and was watching closely for any sign of trouble. He noticed Will was also watching and was impressed by the awareness he exhibited. Even though Will was young, he had good instincts. With a little help he'd grow into a capable man.

Tye settled their account with Wiley Topps while Will started catching and haltering the horses. Before leaving, Tye picked the largest horse from the bunch for a pack horse. They led him to Sooner's, and after fitting the pack saddle to him, they loaded the supplies. Once they'd said good-bye to Charley, Tye led out, leading the string of horses. Will brought up the rear, leading the pack horse. The pistol was stored in his roll, but the rifle was in the boot, attached to his saddle. It gave him a secure feeling knowing that he carried it. He hoped he wouldn't need it for anything other than hunting game, but after last night he doubted that would be the case. Besides, they were heading into Indian country, and who knew what was going to happen there.

Chapter Six

They were riding south at an easy gait, Tye turning often to watch back along the trail. Twice he had called a halt and had sat listening to the sounds and watching the horses. Will knew the horses would alert them if another rider was around. The land in which they were traveling was rolling hills with little timber. Topping knolls, they could see a long way back down the trail from which they came. There was no sign of anyone following them.

After traveling south for about three hours, Tye turned and headed due east. Will noticed the mountain ranges ahead and wondered if they were heading into them.

Tye called a rest at noon, and they stopped by a small stream to eat some canned peaches they'd bought at Sooner's.

"We'll make camp before reaching those mountains ahead of us," Tye said, pointing to the mountain range directly ahead of them.

"I want to be out in the open. There'll be no fire after dark. After tonight we'll still be riding in open country, but there'll be mountains on both sides of us for a couple of days. Then we'll be in the mountains till we cross into Wyoming. We should be at Clement's tradin' post in about five days, providin' we don't have any trouble."

"Do you reckon whoever shot at us last night is followin' us?" Will asked.

"It's better to believe he is and be ready for him than to think he ain't and get careless. I figger anybody who'd go through the trouble he went through last night won't quit just because we left town."

They rode the rest of the day in silence and made camp two hours before dark. Will could see they were entering a valley between two mountain ranges. A man riding in between the mountains would be out of rifle range of anyone trying to dry gulch him from either side.

Tye made a small fire and soon had water boiling for coffee. Will and he fixed a small meal of biscuits, gravy, bacon, and beans. After eating, they let the fire burn down before covering it with dirt. There was a small stream about twenty yards from the camp, and after watering the horses they picketed them close to the camp, where the horses could still feed on the lush prairie grass.

"The horses will warn us if anyone's out there," Tye said as they came back into camp.

They rolled out their bedding, and Will took out his Colt, holding it in his hand to feel the balance.

Tye noticed Will looking at it and said, "Once we get to Clement's, I'll give ya some pointers and let ya practice. I don't think it would be safe to practice here."

"How far are the wild horses from Clement's tradin' post?" Will asked.

"About a day's ride east."

"How long ya reckon it'll take us to catch 'em?"

"I'm figgerin' about three weeks to trap 'em and rough-break 'em enough to get 'em out of there," Tye answered.

"How many head ya figgerin' on takin out?"

"I want at least two hundred. More if there's some good mares. We won't break the mares to ride though, just halter break 'em so we can lead 'em out," Tye explained.

Will was quiet after that, lost in his thoughts about how his life had changed. And where he was headed.

Tye broke the silence with a question.

"Ya said that night in the barn that ya didn't think you wanted to work the rest of yer life being a forty-dollar-a-month cowboy. How would ya feel about bein' a rancher in Texas?"

"I ain't never been to Texas, but it sounds like the kinda place I'd like to go. But bein' a rancher would require some money, and that's somethin' I just ain't got," Will answered.

"Not yet, ya don't, but as soon as we get these horses out, we'll have a good start. And I got some other things in mind that might just pan out to put some money in our pockets. We'll have to wait and see," Tye said.

"Wait a minute. You just said we. I thought I was just along workin' for ya," Will replied.

Tye looked at him, then in a voice that left little doubt as to his seriousness, said, "I could'a hired me a forty-dollar-a-month cowboy if I was lookin' to have someone workin' for me. I need a partner, someone who wants to make somethin' of himself. There's a lot of fellers who can work for someone else. There's mighty few who can step out on their own and make things happen. That's why I chose ya. Ya got good sense about ya, and ya don't make quick decisions. Ya keep your head about ya, too. Ya told me ya didn't want to be workin' for someone else the rest of yer life. Ya said ya thought a man could make big tracks in this country. Well, I think so, too. Especially if that man ain't afraid to gamble a little. If ya think yer up to it I want ya to ride with me till we make it big or go bust. What do ya say?"

Will was silent, letting Tye's words sink in. Tye wasn't just asking him to work for him. He wanted him to be a partner. Could he measure up? There was a lot he didn't know. Would Tye be willing to wet nurse him along until he was ready?

Tye sat watching Will's face, noting the changing expressions as he pondered the questions that had been raised. Finally Will looked at him and spoke.

"Ya haven't really known me very long. What makes ya think I'm the person you want to partner with? And how do you know I'll stand up to what ya got in mind?"

"I don't know fer sure. Nobody ever really knows how another person will act. The only thing I can trust is my instincts, and my instincts tell me ya'll do to ride the river with. Ya got some learnin' to do, but ya catch on fast, and with my help and guidance it won't be long till ya'll be a hand. Sides that, if ya don't work out I can always just shoot ya and hire me someone."

"So in other words, I either work out or ya kill me?" Will asked, a smile spreading across his face.

"I reckon that's about the size of it," Tye replied, grinning.

"Then let's go for it!" Will said. "I don't know of anyone I'd rather partner with. I just hope I can pull my weight."

"I do, too," Tye said, smiling as he lay down and pulled his hat over his eyes.

* * *

The next five days were uneventful as they traveled southeast into Wyoming. As they rode, Tye talked to Will about the country they were riding through and what it would be like where they were going. He showed him how to read tracks and how to identify animals by the tracks they made. He talked about the horses they were going to catch and what it would take to break them enough to move them out of the mountains. At night they talked about Texas, and Tye told Will about the ranch and his plans for expanding it. This included buying new land and stocking it with cattle and horses.

"Texas is still in bad shape from the war. If a fella's got some money and ain't scared of hard work, he can build himself an empire out there. I ain't lookin' to build an empire, but I think we can put us together a mighty fine spread."

Tye kept watching their back trail as they rode, and once when they topped a peak where he could see for several miles he called a halt and watched their back trail for nearly an hour, knowing that anyone following them would have to take the same trail. There was no sign, and Tye relaxed a little, hoping that their close call was just a case of mistaken identity. But he doubted that was the case.

It was early afternoon when they followed the Yellowstone River to Clement Stoner's trading post. Will was surprised to find it was little more than a shack with a lean-to attached to the front of it. The shack was butted up against a solid granite wall that towered a hundred feet above the basin they were in. An overhang jutting out from the wall served as protection from falling rocks. Will mentally noted the defensive position of the small cabin that allowed a view of the clearing in front of it. A man with enough water and food could hold off his attackers for days if necessary.

Smoke was coming from the chimney, but other than that there was no sign of life. When they were fifty yards from the shack, Tye pulled up and called out.

"Hello the camp." There was no response. Tye leaned over and spoke softly to Will.

"That old renegade should be here. There's smoke comin from the chimney, and there's fresh footprints leadin down to the river." Will's eyes went back to the door of the shack. Suddenly he was startled by a flurry of action as Tye's horse, suddenly riderless, shied into his own. Tye was on the ground, rolling as he landed. Will never saw him draw his gun; it just suddenly appeared in his hand. Tye came to a stop belly down, facing back the way they'd come, pistol aimed and looking for a target between the legs of the horses. Will felt rather than heard the presence of another person, and after bringing his startled horse under control, he swung from the saddle, drawing the rifle from its boot as he did. He went down on one knee, facing the woods behind him, keeping the horses between him and whoever was there.

Laughter broke the silence of the afternoon. "I mighta missed you, Garrett, but I shore would'a got the papoose. He's a little slow gettin' started. You and me's gonna have to work with him a might if'n he's gonna live long in this country."

Will watched as Tye came to his feet and holstered the pistol. Will stood up and walked around the horses, his face red, both from being called a papoose and knowing that what this man had said was true. Walking out of the woods was the largest man Will had ever seen. He stood well over six feet tall and could have easily weighed three hundred pounds. He wore a beard that was as black as coal and looked as if it hadn't been trimmed in years. He was smiling as he walked toward them, and the smile made his eyes sparkle.

Tye walked around the horses and faced the giant.

"Clement, yer too big and noisy to sneak up on anyone. Not only that ya smell like an old grizzly bear. I been smellin' ya for the last mile or so. Don't ya ever take a bath?"

Clement feigned a hurt look as he held up his arms, sniffing as he did.

"I just took one in March. Here it is just now the end of June, and yer wantin' me take another one? A man could wear out his skin bathin' that often." He let out a thunderous laugh at his own humor and grabbed Tye in a bear hug.

"Yer slowin' down some, Garrett. Last time ya was up here, I couldn't get nowhere near as close to ya as I did just now. Ya must'a been livin' the easy life lately."

Stepping back from the big mountain man, Tye replied, "I heard ya a long time ago. I just wanted to be sure it was ya and not the bushwhacker that tried to shoot us awhile back."

"Bushwhacker, huh? Come on up to the house and tell me about it over a cup of coffee," Clement said as he led the way down the trail.

They unsaddled their horses and turned them into a small pen that had been built by the river. Will and Tye followed Clement up the hill into the shack.

It took Will a minute after entering to let his eyes get accustomed to the dim light. When they had adjusted enough to see, he noticed the shack was bare except for a stove, table, chairs, and a wash basin. A blanket was stretched across the back wall. Will figured it was to cover the granite wall. As Will looked around, he wondered where Clement slept. There wasn't a bunk. As a matter of fact, there weren't any shelves either. How could a man have a trading post and not have any goods to trade? Hadn't Tye said they would pick up more supplies here? He was still looking around when he noticed that both Tye and Clement were watching him.

"What's the matter, boy? Don't ya like my home?" Clement asked, his eyes sparkling like the stars.

"It's all right, I reckon. It's just not what I expected for a tradin' post," Will responded.

"Well now, just what did ya expect it to look like?" Clement asked, the grin on his face was starting to irritate Will some.

"Well, if yer a trader where's the supplies ya trade with?" Will asked.

"Why they're right here in this house where they're supposed to be," Clement responded incredulously. "Where did ya expect them to be?"

Will looked around the small room trying to figure out if he was being made a fool of or if this was a test. Scrutinizing the structure from top to bottom and side to side, Will's eyes finally came to rest on the blanketed wall. Suddenly he realized that Clement had built this shack in front of a cave and the blanket covered the opening. Will walked to the blanket and gently ran his hands along the wall till he came to a place where the blanket gave under his hand. Reaching down and grabbing the blanket by the edge, he gave it a triumphant pull. As the blanket pulled away from the opening, Will got a brief glimpse of the contents before he heard a "click" that was followed by a loud boom and a blinding light pierced his eyes. Will jumped three feet back into the shack. Heart pounding and eyes blinded by the flash, he stumbled into the table, almost overturning it, then righted himself only to bump into Clement. Clement reached out a big hand and steadied him as he blinked his eyes and tried to clear his vision. Tye and Clement were laughing so hard that both spilled coffee from the cups they were holding.

When Will's eyes finally cleared enough that he could see the two men almost rolling on the floor, anger flooded through him. "Ya two planned that, didn't ya? If I had a gun, I'd shoot both of ya and leave ya here for the buzzards."

Tye finally got his laughter under control and slapped Will on the back.

"He got me the same way. Led me like a bear to honey. I almost shot him for it, too. So don't feel too bad about bein' took in. It happens to the best of us."

"What was that?" Will asked, his temper cooling as his heart slowed its pace.

"Just a little trap I rigged up to discourage curious folks from lookin' around while I'm gone. Don't go nosin' around in there by yerself. I got some traps set in there that'll do more'n just scare ya. Couple a years ago a feller come nosin' around here while I was gone to Jackson. I reckon he was gonna help hisself to some supplies, cause when I returned there was a pile of goods here in the floor and he was still back there. I reckon he'd been there a day or two judgin' by the smell. I buried him down by the river and put a marker on his grave: Caught Stealin'. Ain't had no trouble since. My powder flash has been set off once or twice, but I figgered it was just a Shoshoni lettin' his curiosity get the better of him. Come on, I'll give ya a guided tour of my warehouse."

Will followed Clement into the cave, wary of any more surprises that might be in store for him.

The cave ran back a good sixty feet. It was more than eight feet tall and about thirty feet wide in front, narrowing to about twenty feet at the rear.

"This old cave weren't near this big when I first come here," Clement explained as they entered. "I worked for more'n a year makin' it big enough to live in and store my wares, too."

Will could see that Clement was well stocked with items to trade. He had hardware for digging, climbing, chopping, or anything else you might want to do in the woods. He also had a large supply of pelts, which Will figured he must have traded for. Clement must have read his mind.

"I've got to take them pelts to Jackson soon and restock. The Shoshoni supply them for me, and I trade 'em tools for 'em. The Shoshoni are good farmers, which is real nice. I get all the fresh vegetables I need."

Will noticed bunks were built along the part of one wall, and upon further inspection he noticed a small stream in the back of the cave that came out of the rocks near the base of the cave. It ran along a shallow trough and disappeared under the rocks on the opposite wall, serving not only as a source for drinking and cooking water, but helping cool the cave as well. The coolness helped preserve the haunch of venison hanging over the small stream.

Clement finished up the tour and led Will back into the shack where Tye was enjoying his coffee. As Clement refilled his cup and handed one to Will, he looked at Tye and said, "Now what's all this about bushwhackers after ya?"

Tye filled him in on the details of their stay in Alder Gulch, leaving out the part where he pushed Will off the bed.

"Ya have any idea who it might be?"

"I've got my suspicions."

"How long ya plannin' on stayin'?" Clement asked.

"Long enough to get supplies and information," Tye said, looking at Will.

"Ya goin' after them wild horses?"

"If they're still there," Tye replied.

"Oh, they're still there, all right. I saw 'em couple weeks ago. There's even more of 'em now. I noticed some with brands on em. I reckon that wild bunch has taken to raidin' ranches now," Clement mused.

"Either that or they were stolen by the Sioux, and he got 'em from them," Tye replied. "Speakin' of Sioux, how many of 'em are still around?"

"There's a few still raidin'. They raid the ranches and settlements in the lowlands, then hightail it back up to the mountains. Can't nobody find 'em. Course ain't nobody asked me, either. I don't reckon I'd tell 'em if they did. So far the Sioux has left me alone. As long as they don't bother me, I won't bother them."

"How close are they to where we'll be?" Tye asked.

"A little over twenty miles. But that won't matter. They'll know yer there the day after ya arrive," Clement responded.

"How many of them are there?" Tye asked.

"Upwards of a hundred," Clement replied. "Course, that's countin' squaws and young-uns."

"Why haven't the Sioux captured these horses already?" Will asked.

"Cause they'd rather steal 'em from folks than catch 'em and break 'em themselves," Clement answered. "Once they know what y'all are doin', they probably won't bother ya until ya get 'em broke and ready to move."

"That's about the way I figgered it, too," Tye said. "All we got to do is figger a way to get those horses out of there without them Injuns stealin' 'em from us.

"I think I'll ride over that way tomorrow and do a little scoutin' around. Find us a place to set up camp. I remember seein' a box canyon with a stream comin' out of it. I want to scout it out and see if it'll hold horses. It's east of here about fifteen miles. Sits in between two big buttes, and there's a valley with good grazin' leadin' up to it. You know the place I'm talkin about?"

"Sure, I'll ride along and show ya," Clement volunteered.

"Thanks, but I'd rather go alone," Tye said. "I can travel faster, and maybe I won't attract as much attention goin' alone."

"Well," Clement said, feigning a hurt expression, "if ya don't want us along, then me and the papoose'll just take the day off and go huntin'. We could use some fresh venison."

Tye saw the pained expression in Will's eyes and knew he didn't like the idea of being left here with Clement, but he needed to scout the area and study the lay of the land. He could do that better without having to worry about Will.

"Ya still as sorry at checkers as you used to be?" Clement asked, breaking the tension that had suddenly filled the room.

"Ya still cheat?" Tye asked with a grin.

"Cheat!" Clement bellowed. "I don't need to cheat to beat the likes of ya. Let me get the board set up. I'll beat the both of ya."

Will lost count of the number of games that were played that night. The only time they took a break was to stop and eat a meal of venison steaks and potatoes, cooked by the odd man out, which was mostly Tye and Will, as Clement lost few games. It was late when Tye pushed away from the table after losing another game.

"It's gettin' late. I'm turnin' in for the night. I've got a lot of ridin' to do tomorrow."

"I reckon we better turn in, too." Clement said, looking at Will. "We want to get into the woods early if we wanna get there before the deer hibernate for the day."

Chapter Seven

When Will stepped out of the cabin the next morning, Tye was already saddled and ready to ride. He strode down to the makeshift corral as Tye led his horse through the gate.

"I sure wish I was ridin' with ya."

"I know, but like I said, I'll travel faster alone. And if I do happen to run into any hostile Injuns, all I'll have to worry about is gettin' my hide outa there. Ya listen to ol' Clement. He may sound kinda crazy, but he ain't. That ol' man's forgot more about these mountains and how to survive in em' than most folks will ever know. Listen to him and learn. What you learn could save yer life some day." Tye mounted his horse as Clement came out of the cabin. Looking at Will he said, "I should be back around dark if nothin' goes wrong. I expect a big venison steak when I get here, so don't disappoint me." He kneed his horse and headed off toward the east. The sun was not yet up as he headed into the woods.

* * *

Clement had been leading the way since they had left the trading post. Not a word had been spoken. They had been climbing steadily for the last mile. Will noted that the woods seemed to change as they continued their upward climb. The pines seemed to grow thicker, and the trail narrowed, allowing only single-file passage. The trail they were on wound its way up the mountain side, and though they weren't climbing straight up, the incline of their ascent had Will gasping for breath by the time Clement called a rest. Will noticed that Clement was breathing as if he were on a Sunday stroll in the park.

"It's the thin air that gets ya," Clement explained.

Will sat on the log next to Clement, trying to regain control of his breathing.

"A man has to take it easy till he gets used to it, or it can whup 'im," Clement continued. "Ya cain't hold a rifle steady if yer breathin' hard. And if ya cain't hold it steady, ya sure cain't hit what yer aimin' at. If ya got to walk very far, stop every so often and get your wind. Listen to the things around ya.

"Do ya hear that whippoorwill singin' or the sound of that stream runnin'?"

Will had to admit that he had heard neither of those things until Clement pointed them out.

"That's the things ya got to listen for," Clement explained. "Those things can make the difference between survivin' or dyin'. That stream means there's water. The whippoorwill will let ya know if someone's comin'. His tone will change if somethin' threatens him."

Will straightened himself, his breathing slowly returning too normal. He looked around at the majestic mountains surrounding them. The trees rustled as a light breeze caressed their branches and danced among their leaves. In the distance he heard the cry of a hawk, and he wondered if it called to a mate or talked of lost prey. A light rain had fallen during the night, leaving the air fresh and clean smelling.

The trail they traveled followed the rim of a canyon. Will had been too busy trying to catch his breath and keep up with Clement to take notice of what lay in this canyon, but now he walked to the edge to gaze at the canyon floor. What he saw was so majestic it nearly took his breath away. The canyon walls had begun to separate from each other about two hundred yards back down the trail, and they continued to separate until it formed a lush valley in its floor. The stream Will heard ran through the center of this valley, giving life to the wildflowers and grass growing along its banks. The effect was stunning in its beauty. The rainbow of colors that decorated the lush valley below looked as if a master painter had chosen each color with precision and care to blend with the others.

Will looked in wonder at the beauty before him, knowing there was no way man could ever create anything to compare with the picture he was seeing.

As if reading Will's thoughts, Clement spoke. "Beautiful, ain't it. But ya can't let the beauty fool ya. These mountains is like a woman. Ya treat 'em right, and ya can live in peace. Treat 'em wrong, and they'll fight ya every step of the way. Ya got to learn to live in harmony with nature if'n yer gonna survive. The freezing cold here can kill ya, but if yer wounded bad it can save yer life by slowing down the flow of blood and keep ya from bleedin' to death. There's plants here that can kill ya if ya eat 'em, but at the same time they can save yer life if prepared properly. The Shoshoni have taught me plenty about these here mountains. They say the gods dwell here. I ain't so sure they're not right. If I was a god, this is where I'd want to live."

"It's beautiful here," Will agreed. "I could stay right here lookin' at this forever."

"Ya'd get almighty tired of lookin' at it after a while. That's why there's so much land around here. It's so's a feller won't wear out one place lookin' at it too long."

"Tye says y'all are goin' to Texas," Clement said, looking quizzically at Will.

"That's what he says," Will responded. "I ain't never been to Texas. Does it have beauty like this?"

Clement scratched his beard in thought, then replied.

"I was down Texas way several times. It ain't got the same kinda beauty as these mountains, but it's got beauty, all right. The plains at sunset is as pretty as anything I ever seen. It's a place where a man can swing a wide loop, if he's man enough to haul in what he catches. Ya and Tye can make a place fer yerselves down there. Tye's a good one to ride the river with. Ya pay attention to him, and he'll learn ya things. He sets a great deal a store in ya. See to it that ya don't disappoint 'im."

"He thinks a lot of ya, too," Will said. Clement's face flushed with embarrassment, but Will could see he was pleased with the compliment.

"We better get a move on if we're gonna have venison fer supper," Clement said, rising to his feet and taking up his rifle.

* * *

Tye rode warily as he scouted the mountain region east of Clement's trading post. The only tracks he had seen were those of the wild horse herds. By his estimate, there were over four hundred head running in the valleys. He had found the place where he and Will would make their first camp. It was chosen not only for its location, but for defense as well. A small canyon branching off the larger one in which he was now riding, it provided the shelter he was looking for. There was a cave a hundred yards from the mouth that would allow protection from the weather, and the area around the cave was open and offered no cover for an approaching enemy. It could be guarded by one person, and it wasn't far from the box canyon he planned to use as a trap for the horses. Once they had the horses caught, they could move their camp to the mouth of the box canyon. Even though they would be more in the open, it still offered a good defensive position with little chance for someone to approach unnoticed.

Tye knew he ought to be heading back, but his urge to see the wild horse herd was stronger than the urgency to return. He knew he was getting closer to the Indian village Clement had told him about, but he rode on, following the tracks of the herd.

Tye remembered a small lake in a valley to the southeast. He suspected this was where the herd watered and bedded down at night. Turning his horse, he headed into the woods, climbing the ridge to approach the valley from the rim rock above them.

Only a couple hours of daylight remained when Tye

looked down at the small lake in the valley. He knew Will and Clement would be worried about him, but the view he looked upon now was worth the extra time he'd taken. There below him were no less than four hundred head of wild mustangs. Some were grazing, while others drank from the lake or lay upon the lush grass of the meadow. Colts ran and bucked, nipping each other in play as their mothers stood with watchful eyes, ready to sound a warning should danger approach.

Tye could not take his eyes from the scene before him. This was the beginning of his dream. If he and Will could pull this off without losing their hair to the Sioux or breaking their necks trying to break these brutes, they'd have their start. With great reluctance he turned his horse and headed back down the trail in the direction he had come. Glancing back over his shoulder, he saw a large stallion standing apart from the other horses. The big horse was looking in his direction, and Tye could see the nostrils flaring and the ears twitch back and forth.

"Soon, old son, soon," Tye promised as he turned in the saddle.

As if hearing Tye's words, the horse pawed the ground, shaking his head as if accepting the challenge.

It was ten o'clock when Tye rode up to the trading post. Both Clement and Will came out when they heard him call.

"We was beginnin' to wonder if ya'd gotten yourself scalped," Clement said as Tye swung down.

"I did," Tye said, "but I talked 'em into givin' it back to me."

"Well, it sure took ya long enough," Will said. The worry and disapproval in his voice wasn't lost on Tye.

"Sorry for causin' y'all to worry, but I wanted to see the horses."

"Did ya see 'em?" Will asked, his excitement overshadowing the worry he'd shown only moments earlier.

"Sure did," Tye said. "Good lookin' bunch of horses, too."

"How many are there?" Clement asked.

"I ain't tellin' ya'll another thing till I get me some venison steak," Tye said with a grin. "That is, if ya two got one. Knowin' ya two, ya probably couldn't even find one."

"Hmmph," Clement snorted indignantly. "I'll have ya know, Will here downed two big ol' bucks by hisself. The boy's a pretty good shot with that rifle. We done got 'em skint and quartered. Will and I 'et already, but if ya treat us nice we might just cook ya up a steak with some taters and corn."

"I'm so hungry I could eat this horse while he stands here," Tye said.

"Well, I'll get the fire stirred up while ya tend to 'im," Clement answered as he headed back to the cabin.

* * *

Over supper Tye related the details of his trip into the mountains. Clement and Will listened with rapt attention as he described the area he'd ridden over, the campsite he'd picked, the box canyon where they'd trap the horses, and finally the herd itself. Will's eyes brightened when he talked about the stallion he'd seen.

"Are we gonna break him, too?" he asked

"It depends," Tye said. "Some of these horses have been too long in the wild. They'll kill you and themselves before they'd allow ya to break 'em."

"When do ya plan on gettin' started?" Clement asked.

"In about a week. That'll give us enough time to get our supplies together and prepare the things we'll need, like halters, lead ropes, and lariats. Ya got enough hemp to make about sixty or seventy halters?"

"I think so," Clement said. "How come ya need so many halters? I thought ya was gonna break these horses to trail."

"I've changed my mind. I got to thinkin' on the way up there today. Rather than try to break all these horses up there in the box canyon, we're gonna halter break about sixty head and lead them out with the rest follerin'. That way we can leave quicker. We'll let the Sioux think we're gonna break all of 'em, then we'll sneak out in the middle of the night, leadin' as many as possible. We may lose a few, but that's better'n havin' to fight our way out."

"Did ya see any Injun sign?" Clement asked.

"Nope, but that don't mean they ain't there," Tye answered.

"That's fer sure," Clement agreed. "I'd rather see sign of 'em. That way ya knows to watch fer 'em. Kinda like a rattlesnake. Ya tend to watch a little more if ya know he's around."

"Well, we're gonna act like they're around all the time. But right now I'm gonna get some shut eye. It's been a long day, and we got lots to do to get ready."

The following week went by fast as the three worked, preparing halters and lead ropes for the horses and sharpening the axes needed for chopping trees. Clement cut rawhide strips from hides. These would be used to tie the poles for the gate and fence in place. In the evening Will practiced with the Colt.

"Don't worry about drawing so fast," Tye told him. "Just concentrate on gettin' it out and hittin' what yer aimin' at."

By the end of the week Will was not only clearing his holster with respectable speed, but hitting six out of six shots in the target Tye had nailed on a tree for him.

"Not bad for a papoose," Clement commented one evening as Will put six bullets in the circle of the target. He was thumbing the spent shells out of the cylinder as Clement spoke. Tye had been working on a pack saddle as Will practiced. All of a sudden the quiet was broken by a thunderous roll. Will whirled to see Tye standing with a smoking pistol in his hand. Looking from Tye to the target, Will could see six neatly spaced holes that he could cover with the palm of his hand. The shots had come so fast it had sounded like one shot rather than six.

"I do believe yer the fastest man I ever seen with a six-shooter," Clement said as Tye reloaded. "A man could end up gettin' hisself a bad reputation shootin' the way ya do."

"Only a fool would look for a reputation as a fast man with a gun," Tye replied.

"Sometimes ya don't have to look fer it. It just comes on ya cause of circumstances. I'm just tellin' ya to be careful, that's all," Clement warned.

"I know," Tye said. "I shouldn't be showin' off anyway. I just thought I'd give Will somethin' to try for."

Will laughed. "Maybe if I live to be as old as ya two, I might get to be that good, but hangin' around with you, I doubt I'll get a chance to find out."

"Ya might have a point there, Papoose," Clement agreed, turning to grin at Tye.

"Don't encourage 'im," Tye answered with a grimace. "I already have enough problems with this young upstart criticizin' my age and habits. Now he'll start thinkin' he's right all the time."

Clement winked and grinned at Will.

* * *

Two days later Will and Tye loaded up their supplies and prepared to leave for Horse Canyon, as they now called it. "We'll be back in about a month," Tye said to Clement as they mounted their horses. "I expect a good meal when we get here. I doubt this pup can cook anything but beans, and my cookin' ain't a whole lot better."

"I'll be waitin' fer ya," Clement promised. "I'll try to have some good elk or moose steaks by the time ya get back. Y'all watch your backsides, and keep yer hair on yer heads. And don't bring back no Injuns with ya neither. I ain't got enough room here fer no one else."

Tye and Will shook hands with Clement and rode away from the trading post. Will glanced back once to see Clement standing in the yard watching them depart. He raised a hand to bid them farewell. Will returned the gesture, wondering what would happen between now and when they next saw Clement. They were setting out on an adventure that was both exhilarating and frightening. Will knew this was the beginning of fulfilling Tye's dream. Was it going to be his dream as well? Was this the beginning of

Will Paxton's future, or was a road destined to take him in another direction? Many questions would be asked before the answers came. Tye knew where he was going and what he wanted to do. Will had never seen the wild horse herds. He'd never been to Texas. How could he say what his dream was? All he knew was that he trusted Tye Garrett and he'd never find a better partner.

They rode along in silence for the first few miles, leading the pack horses and allowing the others to move along ahead of them. The trail where they rode was in a wide canyon that eventually opened into the bigger Horse Canyon. The canyon they rode in was bordered by woods on both sides, sloping up to the rim rock that formed the upper edge and prevented all but the most agile animal from escaping.

"This is the route we'll be using to bring the horses out. We can keep 'em bunched here with little chance for escape. This canyon opens into the larger canyon. Our first campsite is about two miles east of there. The lake where the horses water is in another canyon about eight miles from the box canyon where we'll trap 'em. I'll be watchin' the herds for the first few days to learn their feedin' habits. Once we've established their range, then we can form a plan to drive 'em into the trap."

It was late afternoon when they arrived at the campsite Tye had chosen. Will gathered firewood while Tye unloaded the pack horses.

"We'll only unload what we need for the first week," Tye said as Will started the small fire they would use for cooking.

"How would ya like some fresh fish for supper? I saw some nice sized trout in the stream when I was here the other day."

"Sounds great. How we gonna catch 'em?" Will asked, looking about for some means of catching fish and not seeing any.

"We'll do it the Indian way. Come on. I'll show ya."

They walked down to the small stream running through

the canyon. Tye had cut a pine branch from a tree and was shaping it into a spear, sharpening the point with the hunting knife he now carried on his belt. Once the spear was sharpened, he pulled off his boots and rolled his pants legs above his knees, then slowly stepped into the stream. He moved about slowly watching the rippling water as it moved over the rocks. He worked his way slowly toward the shallow bank, then stopped, raising the spear in his right hand. He poised there for a brief moment, then with lightning speed brought the spear down, plunging it beneath the surface. He held tightly to the spear with both hands, then brought it splashing out of the water, a nice brown trout impaled upon the end. With a flip of his wrists he sent the fish flying through the air to land upon the grassy bank. Will, astonishment showing on his face, hurried to gather up the fish. Meanwhile, Tye had resumed his search in the swift water of the stream.

Will cleaned the fish as Tye threw them on the bank.

The coffee Will had started was smelling good as they carried their supper to the fire to be cooked. Tye cooked the fish while Will prepared potatoes in the hot coals. After cooking the fish, Tye prepared dough balls. Using some of the corn he had gotten from Clement, he wrapped the dough balls around it and dropped it into the hot grease.

The meal was one of the best Will could remember. As he lay back on his bedroll, his stomach stretching his belt tight, his eyes grew heavy.

"I'll take the first watch and let ya have the second one, seein' as how yer almost asleep anyway," Tye said.

"OK by me," Will replied with a yawn.

Chapter Eight

Will woke Tye an hour before sunup. The coffee was ready, and Will handed him a cup as he pulled on his boots, the only thing they took off at night. The horses were pulled in close to the cave at dusk to serve as watches, as well as a caution against being stolen by Indians.

Tye had seen several tracks around the mouth of the canyon, telling him Clement had been right in his prediction. The Sioux knew they were there, and even though they hadn't bothered them during this first week, with Indians you just didn't take any risks.

During the week, they had built the fence across the opening of the box canyon. Actually it was two large gates covered with brush to blend into the surroundings. Once the horses were herded inside, the gates could be swung closed to hold them. They also had built a fence across the large canyon consisting of two ropes, three hundred feet long, one on top of the other, with cedar stakes spaced along them and tied in place with rawhide strips. This fence would be used to turn the horses into the box canyon.

Tye had scouted the horses every morning for the past week, returning by noon to help Will build the fences. He had determined where the horses grazed during the day and the best route to stampede them to drive them into the trap.

Sitting by the fire the last night before the drive, Tye went over his plan one more time with Will. On the dirt floor of the cave, he outlined where the strategic points would be.

"The horses move away from the lake during the day, comin' down the valley to graze along the river. There are actually four different herds in this bunch, but they stay pretty well together. There are four canyons that offer escape routes for them between here and the lake. Three are on this side of the valley, and one is on the other side. The three on this side are the closest to the lake. Usually they graze past those three. If we start them after they've grazed past those three canyons, we only have one to worry about. This means in order to head them off one of us will have to be on the far side of the canyon when they start runnin'. That'll be your job. Once we're past that canyon, they'll run straight down this canyon, thinkin' their escape is in this direction. We won't push 'em hard until they get close. The fence across the valley should turn 'em into the box canyon. The smart leaders in the bunch'll know it's a box canyon, but we're relying on fear and timing to force 'em in. Once they go into the canyon we've got to be at the gates, swingin' 'em closed. More'n likely some of 'em will try the gate after it's closed. We'll have to stay by them until they settle down. Any questions?"

Will shook his head no.

"Well, let's put this fire out and get some sleep. We've got to be on the trail early in the mornin'."

As the sun rose in the eastern sky the next morning, Will and Tye sat on the rim rock above the horse lake. Will looked in awe at the horses gathered around the lake. He could not believe there were so many. Colts were running in the cool morning air, kicking and nipping each other as they ran. Mares were calling to their young from the grassy slopes surrounding the lake. The morning sun shining on the dew on the grass caused crystalline reflections, making the meadow come alive in a shimmering dance.

They had left their horses tied in the woods about a mile back down the trail so the wild herd would not catch their scent. They also wanted to be sure that their own horses could not send a warning call upon spotting the wild ones.

Keeping his voice low, Tye spoke to Will.

"They'll start moving out in a moment. They usually move down the valley about two miles before grazing. As soon as they've moved out of sight, we'll work our way down to the bottom and follow them at a safe distance. When they work their way past the three canyons I told you about, you'll move to the opposite side of the valley and be ready to block the fourth canyon." Will nodded but said nothing. This was it. There was nothing left to say.

After watching the herd move out of sight, they waited another thirty minutes before making their way back to their horses. Working their way to the valley below took another twenty minutes as they wound their way down the canyon walls, navigating boulders and trees.

Once they reached the bottom, Tye lead off at a ground-eating trot. It had taken them longer to reach the valley floor than he had anticipated.

He had explained to Will the night before how all the horses didn't always follow the valley, but sometimes one or more of the herds would break off from the others and follow one of the escape canyons to graze. There actually were four separate herds with four different leaders. Most of the leaders were wise, old mares who had been around for a spell. Tye had explained how horses established a hierarchy among themselves, much the same as humans would, with leadership going to the strongest and wisest and the others ranked according to strength and ability. He had told of one of the mares he'd watched. She was a large roan mare with several scars, no doubt the results of many battles to establish and hold her position as leader. Her leadership had been challenged by a young stallion, but she had quickly dispatched him with series of bites and a broadside kick that had lifted him off the ground and bowled him over. This, and a quick bite to the rump as he came to his feet, had dispelled any doubts he had about her leadership role.

The stallions with each herd were there for protection. Part of their role was to be guardian and watchdog for the herd, but few actually became leaders.

Tye had watched the herd for several days, determin-
ing which herds were led by which mares. He had graded
each herd by the number of colts over two years of age,
the number of mares compared to the number of stallions,
and the number of horses that bore saddle marks. He had
chosen the herd led by the roan mare as the best. It had
fewer colts under two years of age and more stud horses.
It was also the largest herd of the four, numbering two
hundred head. This would be the herd they would concentrate their efforts on, hoping to gather at least one of
the other herds with it. If this herd took one of the escape
canyons, they would postpone their drive until tomorrow.

They spotted the horses about an hour after making the
descent into the valley. The horses were moving at a
leisurely pace, grazing as they went. They had passed the
first two canyons and were approaching the third.

Will and Tye watched from a wooded area. Concealed
by the trees, they stroked their horses' necks and spoke in
whispering tones to soothe them. If one of the horses
called out, the herd would be gone before anything could
be done.

Tye and Will sat still on their horses until the herd
moved out of sight around a bend in the valley.

"They'll be up to the next canyon about ten minutes
from now, " Tye said. "We'll wait for a while, then ease up
and see if they kept going or turned into it."

As they approached the third canyon, Will could see
fresh tracks leading into it. Tye studied the ground and
looking at Will said.

"We're in luck. The smallest herd cut off here. Only
about fifty head. Now comes the hard part. Ya've got to
cross over to the other side of the canyon and stay under
cover until ya get past the herd. I'll give ya an hour to get
ahead of 'em, then I'll start 'em runnin'. Ya got to be at
the mouth of that canyon before they get there, or they'll
be gone and we might not get another chance."

"I'll be there," Will said with determination.

"I'll see ya at the box canyon. Keep 'em bunched, but don't push 'em hard until we get close," Tye warned.

Turning his horse, Will crossed the canyon, which was about a half-mile wide at this point. Trees grew along the canyon wall. These trees offered cover for the most part, but Will knew he would have to be wary once he was even with the horse herd. One slip and they'd be off like a shot, up the canyon and gone before he could get ahead of them.

Tye sat in the shade of a tree, watching the sun move across the sky. When he judged it to be an hour since Will had left, he stepped into the saddle and reined his horse in the direction of the herd.

It would take him half an hour to catch up with the herd, and that would give Will a little extra time to reach the mouth of the canyon.

Rounding a bend in the canyon wall a short time later, he could see the herd moving ahead of him. Estimating that there were more than three hundred head, he kicked his horse into a trot and moved toward the herd. He wouldn't have to worry about spooking the horses. Once they got wind of him, they'd be off and running.

* * *

Tye was riding his favorite bay mare. Normally he would not have ridden her on a chase, knowing the chance he would be taking with her. The chase would more than likely be a race over broken and unfamiliar ground, and there was a chance that a horse could step into a hole or stumble going down one of the many arroyos between here and the box canyon. But he also knew he would need her speed and endurance. She was tall, with long legs, a broad chest, and powerful hindquarters. Her speed could make the difference in capturing the wild herd. The risk was one Tye was willing to take.

He kicked the mare into a lope, watching the horses ahead. He knew they would spot him soon, and the chase would begin.

He had ridden two hundred yards when the shrill call from a stallion pierced the morning stillness. It was as if each horse in the herd had one mind as they bolted away, tails and manes flying in the breeze.

The old battle-scarred mare took the lead and headed for the escape canyon. Tye spurred his mare to keep up with the herd, flanking them on the right and hoping to push them away from the canyon. He wanted to be ready if they tried to force their way through.

He could see the bend in the canyon ahead and knew that the escape canyon was only yards away. He would be behind the slower horses and might not be able to push his way to the front if trouble started.

Even though the old mare was leading them from danger, she didn't outdistance the slower mares and colts. Tye knew that if she had wanted to escape, she could have easily pulled ahead of the stragglers and been gone.

Rounding the bend, Tye could see the canyon ahead. Was Will in place? Had he made it around the herd in time? Tye couldn't see him yet. The ground swelled ahead, making it impossible to see a rider from this distance. He remained behind the herd, matching his mare's pace to the herd's. He had to trust that Will was there to turn the herd down the valley.

As the lead mare topped the swell, Tye could sense the hesitation in the herd. Will must be there. The horses had hesitated as they approached the canyon. Tye put the spurs to the mare. The herd had to be kept moving, or it would double back. If that happened, he wouldn't be able to stop them. Yelling and swinging his rope, he pushed the stragglers faster. The lead horses veered away from the canyon. Tye had expected this and already was moving across the valley, urging the herd forward.

The old mare, head high, looked around at Tye. Seeing him coming from the rear, she turned and headed down the valley toward the box canyon.

As Tye topped the swell, he looked for Will and saw him move into the right flank position. From there he would prevent any of the horses from turning back to the canyon.

It was another three miles to the box canyon and the fence across the valley. Tye's horse was breathing hard, and sweat was pouring from both horse and rider. He eased the mare down to a slow lope, knowing he'd need her speed when they reached the fence. He kept the horses in sight, not allowing the mare to fall to far behind.

It was now two miles to the box canyon. Will was riding behind the herd, and Tye had fallen back to allow his horse to rest. The mare was loping smoothly, with no sign of tiring. He would rest her for the next mile, then catch up to the herd to race the last mile. They would push the herd fast for the last mile, then ease off before reaching the fence. If he drove them too fast they might try to go through it before Tye or Will could turn them.

With a mile left, Tye spurred his mount to overtake the herd. When he got even with Will, he nodded to him and both started shouting and swinging their ropes. The herd picked up the pace in response. The critical moment was fast approaching as the two watched the horses race toward the fence they had built.

When they had covered three-fourths of the mile, Will moved to the right and spurred his horse. The large roan gelding easily passed the stragglers. He pushed the roan until they had passed half the herd, keeping a distance of two hundred feet between them. His job was to turn the herd once they reached the box canyon.

Tye eased up on the mare, allowing the horses to slow a little. He could see the fence far up the valley. The lead mare, if she saw it, didn't slow her pace. Tye watched as they continued their run, following the stream as it wound its way through the valley.

Suddenly Tye felt the herd slow as the lead horses saw the fence. They were five hundred yards from it now. This was the critical point. If the horses cut back, there would be no way for Will and him to stop them. He doubted if twenty riders would be able to stop the herd if it took the notion to turn back up the valley. He could only hope that the lead horses would turn into the box canyon. Fear was their strongest ally now. He hoped the horses' fear would make them seek escape away from the two riders.

Will was still riding on the right side of the herd. Soon he would have to push his horse to the front in an attempt to turn the leaders. The roan was tiring now as they approached the fence, but when Will touched him with his spurs he felt a surge of power in the big horse. He waited until he was almost even with the lead horses, then changed direction. He set his course to meet with the leaders just before they reached the fence. Tye and he had rehearsed this maneuver time after time in the evenings around the fire. As he neared the lead horse closest to him, he could see it swing away, forcing the horse next to swing left. Soon the entire lead was moving away.

Riding in the rear, Tye watched through the dust as Will made the move they'd discussed. He watched the lead begin to change. If they continued to change course, they would be headed directly for the box canyon before they reached the fence. Tye swung his rope and shouted at the drag horses. Now was the time to push hard.

The old mare saw the fence. She slowed, her instincts telling her she was headed for a trap. With her head held high, she looked around for an avenue of escape. She saw the canyon on her left but knew it for what is was. She looked right and saw the man on horseback coming at them. Her only hope lay in front of her. She gathered herself for the leap that would carry her to safety. She didn't think of the herd now. It was to late for that. Her only thought was to save herself. She was now fifty yards from the fence. Laying back her ears and charging ahead, she was intent on reaching the obstacle in front of her. She was running tired now. The long run down the valley had taken its toll. Suddenly the horse to her right bumped her. She stumbled but managed to stay upright, but in doing so she was pushed even farther aside. She fought to regain her position, but to no avail. The lead horses were now forcing her toward the canyon.

Will continued pushing the horses to the canyon. They

were now running directly for the mouth. He could see the old mare being forced along as the rest of the herd closed around her.

Tye was riding hard now, bunching the herd as they neared the canyon. He saw Will turn them before they reached the fence and saw the lead mare pushed toward the canyon. He rode on the heels of the slower horses, yelling and swinging his rope. The panic he caused forced the horses to bunch with those ahead, allowing no room for the lead horses to turn.

Suddenly the horses were through the mouth and into the canyon. Tye and Will swung from their horses and rushed to the heavy gates, swinging them closed and placing the center pole in the hole they'd dug and covered with a large rock. Tying the gate closed with the braided rawhide ropes he'd made, Tye stepped back and wiped the sweat from his brow. Turning to Will, he grinned.

"Well, we got 'em in. Now all we got to do is hold 'em till we can get 'em broke."

Will took their saddle horses, loosened the cinches, and tied them under the shade of a large tree. He would water them later after they had had a chance to cool down. Tye stayed by the gate, waiting for the horses to come back down the canyon. He expected them to make a try at breaking it down.

The canyon they were in was a half-mile long. At the mouth it was probably two hundred feet across, and it narrowed to fifty feet at the other end.

They could hear the horses milling about. The mothers were neighing for their young as they became separated. Even though their fear was strong, the long run down the valley had taken the fight out of the herd. They soon stopped their milling and started to investigate their surroundings. Some walked to the small stream and began drinking, while others dropped their heads and began eating. Only the old mare and one or two stallions continued their search for escape, but when they ran down the canyon, the herd did not follow.

Tye and Will watched as the mare and stud horses came at the gate. Tye picked up his lariat and swung it over his head, yelling at them as he did. Will followed suit, and the mare stopped before the gate, rearing on hind legs and pawing the air. The stallions stood off to one side, necks bowed and nostrils flaring, but they ventured no closer. When the mare's front feet came back to earth, she whirled and charged back up the canyon. The stallions followed.

Tye and Will waited another hour before feeling it was safe to leave the gate.

"They'll all come down to check it out, but she's the only one, I think, who'd try to come across it. Tomorrow we'll start building our pens and sorting gates after we've roped some of these mares and put halters on 'em."

After watering the horses, Will stayed by the canyon while Tye rode back to the old camp to bring back their supplies and the other horses. They'd worked the night before loading everything for a quick move. Their new camp would be just outside the gates leading into the canyon. The overhang on the west side would provide shelter. Tye had scouted around and found a small cul-de-sac where they could put the saddle horses. The grass wouldn't last long, and they would have to be tethered out on the lush grass of the valley every day, but at least they could be guarded against Indians.

Tye hadn't forgotten the threat that lingered with them. The Sioux could decide to attack and steal their horses at their whim. He hoped that Clement and he were right, that they would wait until they had broken the wild herd before making their move. He knew they were gambling, not only for the herd but on their lives as well. He knew they were being watched. On the pretense of hunting, he had scouted the area for signs. He had seen the tracks of the Indians' ponies on the rim overlooking their camp. He also had seen a moccasin track in the box canyon. The track had been fresh. It had been made since the gates had been built. He found only one, but it was enough. He hadn't mentioned it to Will. No use in causing alarm at this point.

Chapter Nine

It was after dark when they finished caring for the horses and unloading the supplies. They had a cold camp that night, opting to turn in early after the hard day.

They were up early the next morning, cutting trees to be used for drags. These drags would be used for halter-breaking the horses. Each log would weigh approximately two hundred pounds. Each horse to be halter broke would be tied to one of the logs and left to drag the weight. Tye had explained to Will that after dragging one of these logs for three days, a horse could be led. It would also aid in gentling down the horses.

After cutting thirty logs, they set about sinking a snubbing post in the ground close to the end of the canyon. This would be used each time they roped a horse out of the herd. Several wraps around the post would help hold the fighting animal until it gave in to the rope.

It was late afternoon when they tamped the last of the dirt around the post. Tye stood back and surveyed the post with satisfaction.

"We'll get a few of these critters started on the halters tomorrow, and then we'll build a fence across this end of the canyon to use as our breaking pen. We should be breakin' horses by the day after tomorrow, but first we've got to cut out some of these mares and young colts that we ain't gonna keep. There's not enough grass in this canyon to run this many head as long as we need to hold 'em here."

"How many ya gonna cut out?" Will asked, as he looked over the herd.

"I've counted about fifty head of young colts. The ones that are too small to take a hard drive outa here. We'll cut them and their mamas out. That'll leave us about three hundred head. I figure there's about fifty head of mares that I'd like to keep and maybe four stallions. We'll sell some of the mares like they are, and maybe some of the others as well. I figure there'll still be about two hundred head of horses to rough-break."

"How many ya aimin' on breakin' before we drive 'em outa here?" Will asked.

"About fifteen or twenty," Tye replied. "That'll give us enough to hold them together."

"I'll be glad when that day comes," Will said, looking around himself. "This is pretty country, but knowin' them Injuns is around don't make me any too comfortable."

"I know what ya mean," Tye said. Then, picking up his rope, he motioned to Will. "You work the gate down there. I'll cut out the mares and colts and drive 'em out."

They worked the rest of the day, cutting out the horses they didn't want to keep. The next morning they began building the corral they would use to break the horses. Since they were using the narrow end of the canyon for the working pen, it required less work to build a fence across it than it did for the opening.

By late afternoon they had completed the makeshift corral and were ready to start working the wild bunch.

"Let's get a few of these mares haltered and tied to those logs we cut."

"Sounds good to me," Will agreed as he picked up his rope and started for the gate.

Tye, on horseback, cut out several mares and drove them into the corral. Will closed the gate and waited for Tye to dismount and join him before he entered.

"I'll rope the first one. Ya snub the rope to the post. Once ya've got her snubbed, yell and I'll move out of the way. Ya ready?"

"Yep," Will said as they opened the gate and entered the corral.

This was one of the dangerous tasks of working the wild horses. Once the mare was roped, she would fight for everything she was worth, attempting to crush anything or anyone in her path. It was up to the snubber to keep the rope tight at all times, preventing the mare from running him or anyone else down.

Will had helped Tye snub horses while working on the Triangle T. He had become quite adept at dallying the rope around the snubbing post and holding the fighting horses until, exhausted, they gave to the rope.

There were five mares in the corral, and Tye selected a large palomino as his first choice to halter. Tye used a technique called the wild horse loop, or hoolihan, to catch horses in a corral. This style of roping, a method used by the vaqueros in Mexico, required a backhand swing and throw. The advantage in using it was that it cut down on the swinging of the rope, which had a tendency to excite the horses.

Tye lined the horses out down the fence, allowing each to run by him until the palomino was singled out. Then with precise accuracy he threw his loop and braced himself as it settled over the mare's neck. Will moved in to grab the end of the rope and wrap it around the snubbing post.

Upon feeling the noose tighten around her neck, the mare went into an acrobatic dance, standing on her back feet and throwing her head high in the air. She fought against the rope, which was beginning to close off the air to her lungs. Stretched taut, the rope continued its restricting hold until the mare finally came down. This allowed her to suck air into her lungs, but immediately she pulled against the rope again, fighting the demon that held her tight.

Tye moved beyond the reach of the mare, allowing Will to keep the rope snug. The mare would fight the rope until she wore herself down, then he would ease up to her and put the halter on.

The fight continued for another ten minutes, the mare

pulling against the rope until she could no longer breathe. Then with reluctance she would move forward, easing the strangling effect of the noose that cut off her wind.

Finally, after one last desperate struggle to free herself, the palomino stepped forward and stood shaking as the rope slackened itself around her neck.

Tye stepped forward, placing one hand on the rope far enough from the mare to move away should she decide to attack. He worked his way down the rope, talking in soothing tones to the mare as she watched him with eyes rolling and flaring nostrils. He eased toward her, holding one hand outstretched before him, talking to her all the while. As his hand reached to touch the trembling horse, she exploded again, straining against the rope. Tye moved out of reach while Will held the rope tight, preventing the horse from pulling away. With her wind immediately cut off, the mare soon ceased her pulling and walked forward, the lesson of the rope quickly learned.

It took Tye two more tries before he could place his hand on her neck. When he did, she stood trembling as he gently stroked her and talked in low tones. He continued to rub her neck and head as he slowly slipped the halter over her head. Tightening it down, he stepped back and held the lead rope. Will loosened the rope from the snubbing post and opened the gate.

Tye herded the mare out the gate as Will held the rope, preventing her from bolting as she went through. Once outside, Tye rolled one of the logs cut earlier that day to a level area. Then he tied the end of the mare's lead rope to the log after slipping the rope from around her neck.

The palomino stood trembling, ready to bolt. Only the rope around her neck had prevented her from seeking escape, but now as the rope was removed, she rolled her eyes and snorted as Tye moved away. Feeling the absence of the rope from her neck she whirled and ran, only to be snapped around by the weight of the log, which was jerked along the ground for fifteen feet before the mare stopped. She stared at it in bewilderment before pulling back. The log skidded along the ground as the mare continued her backward trek. Finally, tired and frightened, she stopped her frantic pull and stood watching the log, confusion and fear showing in her eyes.

Tye and Will watched the mare for a moment longer. Then Tye turned to Will and said, "She'll be all right. Let's get some more staked out before it gets dark. Why don't ya work the next one?"

Will looked at the mares standing in the corral, then turned to Tye. "Maybe I should do the rest of 'em. Ya're lookin' a bit peaked. I wouldn't want you to wear yerself down. That could be dangerous for a person of yer age."

Tye looked at Will, hiding the grin that was coming to his face.

"Why don't ya do that, youngster. Since I've had to do all the work around here, it'll be nice to see ya carry yer weight for a change."

Will grinned at Tye, enjoying the easy banter they shared as they worked.

They roped and haltered ten head before the darkness closed in on them. They ate a cold supper that night and turned in early, worn out from the day's work.

* * *

The next morning they roped and haltered twenty more mares. The sight of thirty mares tied to the logs was something to behold. Tye looked on with pleasure as he noted the old roan mare tethered to one of them. She had fought the hardest of all and had come close to taking a bite out of Will's arm, ripping his shirt in the process. They had finally eared her down, twisting her ear and biting the tip to hold her still while they haltered her. Tye didn't intend to gentle the mare, but he wanted her as one of the lead horses when they took the other horses out.

They started breaking horses that afternoon, snubbing the broncs to the snubbing post and tying up a hind foot. Tye saddled the first horse. He placed the hackamore and blindfold on the horse's head then motioned Will to climb aboard. Will looked shocked as he saw Tye's intent.

"Ya want me to ride the first one?" he asked.

"Why not?" Tye asked, grinning at the shocked expression on Will's face.

"Ya wouldn't even let me ride the rough horses on the ranch. I figured ya'd never let me ride one of these till ya'd ridden it first."

"I had other reasons for ya not riding those horses. This is different. We're both gonna break these. We'll take turns ridin.' That way we can break more of 'em."

Will grinned as he pulled his hat tighter on his head. He untied the horse's foot while Tye eared the horse down and placed a blindfold over its eyes. Then, taking hold of the reins, he stepped into the saddle. When he was seated, he took a tight hold on the reins in each hand and said, "Let him go."

Tye removed the blindfold and let the horse have his head, moving swiftly out of the way as he did. By the time he turned to look back, the horse's head was between its legs and Will was seated firmly on his back.

Will allowed the horse to buck across the pen, getting the feel of him to find out what kind of tricks he would use. As he got in time with the horse, he began to use his spurs to get in rhythm with each jump. Each time the horse lunged into the air, Will would rake him with the spurs from the shoulder points to the flank. This kind of timing helped him keep his balance and let the horse know that with each jump it would feel the punishment of the spurs.

The horse was a black stud about three years old. Tye wanted to break the younger horses first, saving the older ones until they were away from the canyon. The black was a stout horse and was giving Will a good fight. He would jump straight into the air, coming to earth stiff-legged, then flex his knees and lunge forward. The combination of jarring and lunging made for a hard ride, but Will was making a good show of riding the animal. He kept his seat and followed the horse's head the way Tye had taught him. He had learned quickly that where the head went, the body was sure to follow.

Tye watched Will spur the horse around the corral. He was satisfied with the way Will rode. Only once or twice did he feel the need to yell advice or correction to the young man, and those were only minor matters. He smiled inwardly as he reflected on the progress that had been accomplished in only a few short months. As he had predicted, Will had a natural ability with horses and would soon be a better bronc rider than he himself. As the thought came to him, he was somewhat puzzled by the fact that this didn't bother him. He had always made it a point to be the best he could possibly be at whatever he undertook. To him that meant he had to be better than everyone else. Now here was someone who was going to be better than he was, and he was proud of the fact, rather than envious. He thought about this for a moment, then smiled as he turned his thoughts back to the corral to shout encouragement to Will as he continued to spur the black horse.

Will had been riding the black for ten minutes when he felt it start to tire. The leaps were coming slower, and each had less energy behind it than the previous one. Finally the horse stopped, front legs spread wide, head down, breathing hard. Will let it stand for thirty seconds, then touched him lightly with the spurs. The black lunged forward, and Will pulled him around hard, forcing the horse in a circle. Finally exhausted, the horse stepped out, walking in a tight circle as Will continued to pull him around. Will then pulled him around in the opposite direction, kicking him and making him respond to the reins as he guided him around the corral.

After a few minutes of working the colt around the corral, Will rode up to where Tye was standing. As he approached, Tye reached up, as if to scratch his head.

"Ya throw that hat at me, and I'm gonna run over it and stomp it flat," Will said as he watched Tye closely.

Tye chuckled and dropped his hand to his side. "I swear yer sure gettin' suspicious these days."

"I got good reason to be suspicious," Will replied, still not taking his eyes off Tye.

Only after he was sure Tye wasn't going to try anything did Will ease off the black colt.

"Let's unsaddle him and tie him to one of the logs for a while," Tye said. "Then we'll catch another, and I'll see if I can ride it, unless ya want to ride 'em all."

"Na, I reckon I'll let ya ride a few. Don't want ya gettin' outa practice. Ya'd start gettin' fat and lazy, and then I'd have to do everything for ya."

"I can see where that might be a problem for ya," Tye agreed, "seein' as how I do most of the work around here while ya lay around till noon takin' life easy."

Will grinned and started removing the saddle from the colt, talking over his shoulder as worked. "Sure is dark around here at noon. I guess bein' this far back in the mountains just takes the sun longer to get here, huh."

Tye didn't respond as he walked over to one of the logs and positioned it to tie the colt. Then, taking a halter, he held the black's head as Will placed the halter over his ears. Between the two they herded him out the gate and tied him to the log.

Will went to his horse and, tightening the cinch, said, "I'll pick ya out one and bring him in. Reckon you can handle the gate?"

"I think I can handle it all right," Tye replied. "Just don't take all day bringin' one up here. I want to ride at least one more before I'm too old and decrepit."

Will cut out a nice-looking four-year-old buckskin stallion. The horse was fifteen hands tall and well developed. He herded him into the corral and watched as he cantered around the enclosure, head and tail high, sniffing the air as he went.

Tye entered the corral, rope in hand, while Will brought in his saddle and hackamore. One throw was all it took to catch the horse around the neck. It was soon snubbed to the post, where Tye and Will went about blindfolding and saddling it.

Once Tye had the saddle cinched down, he nodded to Will and stepped into the saddle. He held the reins tightly in his hand as Will removed the blindfold and stepped out of the way.

The buckskin stood still for a moment, blinking as the sun hit his eyes. Then realizing there was something on his back, he reared on his hind legs, pawing the air with his forelegs as he lifted.

Tye leaned forward in the saddle, holding the reins and mane in his hands until the horse started his descent to earth. He let go of the mane and held tightly to the reins as the horse's feet hit the ground.

The buckskin was a smooth bucking horse, bucking in a straight line around the corral. Instead of trying tricks to loose the rider on his back, he relied on brute strength to batter down the resistance. His leaps were long, and the impact with the ground was bone-jarring.

Tye sat the saddle, keeping rhythm with the horse's jumps. He relaxed his muscles as the buckskin hit the ground to lessen the jarring on his body.

The horse bucked for another ten minutes, then leaped forward and ran around the corral. Tye pulled him around to prevent him from jumping the fence. Slowing the horse to a lope, he watched him warily, expecting him at any moment to duck his head and resume his bucking. But after loping twice around the corral, the buckskin allowed himself to be pulled to a stop. Pulling the horse's head around and holding him by the headstall, Tye stepped off.

"That was a nice one. If the rest of 'em were like him, we'd have 'em all broke before we left here," he said as he walked over to where Will was preparing another log.

"How many do ya reckon we can rough break before we pull outa here?" Will asked.

"If we can have around twenty head of these younger ones ready, I figger we'll have enough to lead the others out. With these and the mares we'll have halter broke, we should have enough to keep the herd together."

"We should be able to have twenty head ready in a week or so. Ya plan on leavin' that soon?" Will asked.

"I'm figgerin' on two more weeks at the most. Let's get

this one started on the log, then grab a quick bite. Maybe we can get a couple more ridden this afternoon. Then we'll ride these again in the mornin' and start some more tomorrow afternoon. That way we break in a few new ones each day and keep the ones we've already ridden from forgettin' what the saddle is all about."

"Sounds like a good plan to me. As long as I keep pickin' out the easy ones for ya to ride, things ought to go along smooth and easy."

Tye looked at Will through one eye, then shook his head and grinned at him as they headed down the canyon to their camp.

Chapter Ten

The next two weeks were grueling, bone-jarring, hard days, but even though Will felt as if every muscle and bone in his body was sore and bruised, he had to admit he'd never felt more alive in his life. Breaking the wild horses was like a tonic to his soul. He'd never in his life experienced anything close to the pleasure he got while aboard a bronc, matching his new-found skills against the wild animals trying with all their will and might to rid themselves of the man on their backs, but fighting more to hold to the freedom to which they had been born.

Will knew they would soon be moving the herd out of the canyon and making a run for Clement's trading post. They had broken twenty-four head of the wild mustangs and had forty mares halter broke. He hoped this would be enough to keep the herd together. It was going to be a risk moving the herd at night to keep the Sioux from stealing them.

Will had seen signs of the Indians twice while riding in the valley. Once while riding he had caught a glimpse of two Indians riding along the tree-lined wall of the valley. He had quickly hidden in a stand of cedar and had watched until they were well out of sight. After that he had kept a close watch around him, knowing they were probably being watched by the Sioux.

Will was finishing off one of the three-year-olds he had ridden. The horse was responding to his commands, and Will was pleased with the young horse. He thought he might keep this one for himself.

Tye was leading one of the mares they had halter broken back to the corral. It was a hot afternoon, and he had removed his shirt while he worked to drag a log up close to the corral where he could tie another horse to it.

Will rode up to where Tye was struggling to pull the log into place.

"We pullin' out tomorrow night?"

"What makes ya ask that?" Tye asked.

"Cause ya been busy as a beaver, gettin' all these horses up here close to the corral. I figger if yer gettin' em all together, then ya must be plannin' something. And the only thing that could be is leavin' here."

"I'm impressed, Papoose. Yer gettin' to be pretty smart for a pup still wet behind the ears."

The name Clement called him was not lost on Will as he grinned at Tye.

"I reckon we'll pull out tomorrow night if everything looks good. Ya ready?"

"Yep, my hair ain't felt safe since we got here. I'm ready to put some distance between me and them Injuns," Will answered, then went on. "What else we to do to get ready?"

"Nothin' today. We'll go about tomorrow just like it was any other day, just in case we're being watched."

"I guess I'll finish this one out then and get another one," Will said.

"Why don't we knock off early today and take us a swim in that deep pool down the valley. I been sweatin' so much, I'm startin' to smell like a wet saddle blanket, " Tye said as he reached for the shirt he had placed on the ground.

Will grinned. "So that's what that smell is. I been lookin' for somethin' dead all day long."

"Let me tell ya, Junior, ya don't smell none too sweet yerself. I durn near passed out a time or two, just bein' close to ya."

"I guess it is time to wash a few layers of dirt off," Will agreed, slapping his gloves against the legs of his jeans and watching the dust fly off.

The pool of water was at the base of a small waterfall.

Years of flash floods and running water had eroded the sandstone, forming a natural pool with a depth of ten to twelve feet in the middle.

Will was the first one in. Taking just enough time to unbuckle his holster and lay his Colt aside, he removed his boots and ran to the top of the falls. Giving a Comanche yell, he jumped in, clothes and all. Tye followed close behind.

Despite the warm days, the water was cold enough to take their breath away as they plunged beneath the surface, gulping for air as they came to the top.

Lying on the sandstone rocks afterward, the sun drying their clothes and warming their chilled bodies, Will watched a hawk circling overhead as it searched the valley for prey. The long, gliding pattern of the bird was hypnotizing, and Will was content to watch as it continued its search. Suddenly the hawk swerved upward and changed course, flying away from the valley wall.

Something had scared the hawk away, and Will suspected it wasn't an animal. He glanced over at Tye, but Tye was lying on one of the flat rocks facing the opposite side of the valley. His eyes were closed, and Will suspected he was dozing.

He cut his eyes back to the rim of the valley. Nothing moved, and the only sound coming to his ears was the sound of the stream as it continued its course down the valley. Will knew something was out there, but what was it? It was a sure bet that whatever it was, it wasn't friendly.

Their horses were tied in a stand of trees a hundred yards from the pool. Will could see them standing in the shade of the aspens. They were standing with their ears up, looking at the rim rock. Will knew they could not be seen by anyone up there, but at the same time he knew he and Tye were out in the open. He did not move but continued scanning the horizon.

* * *

Two Eagles led the remnants of his raiding party along the rim of the valley. He was not in a pleasant mood as he rode.

He was weary and wounded. The pain in his side where the bullet had struck him reminded him of his failure.

His raiding party had started out with fifteen. They had killed three white men, stolen their horse herd and two of their women. Now they had only one of the women, none of the horses, and only eight left in the party. Of those eight, four of them, including Two Eagles himself, were wounded, all the result of encountering an army patrol returning to Fort Bridger.

Two Eagles rode staring ahead, eyes looking neither right nor left. The pain in his side reminded him of his failure. The girl on the white pony sat staring at his back, wishing she could kick the wound in his side again as she had done while trying to escape when the soldiers had surprised them.

She had almost escaped, except she had no way of guiding the horse she was riding when it had pulled away from the Indian leading her. The Indian brave had suffered a wound to the shoulder, causing him to drop the lead rope.

Rebecca Kincaid rode staring at the back of the Indian in front of her. He was the one who had pulled her screaming and kicking out of the house after her father, brother, and uncle had been killed by these ambushing savages.

Hearing the gunfire shortly after her father, brother Tim, and uncle John had left the house, Rebecca had run to the window to see her uncle and Tim lying in the dust of the yard. Her father was bringing his rifle to his shoulder when his body was violently twisted around, his rifle discharging into the air. Only her mother holding her had prevented her from rushing from the house to aid her fallen family.

Mrs. Kincaid had dragged Rebecca, struggling and fighting, to the closet at the back of the house. As Rebecca stood there sobbing and shaking in fear and anger, she remembered her father building the closet for her mother, the pride he had taken in fitting the rough boards into place, the cedar shakes he had used to line it. The smell of the cedar reminded her of the times she had hidden from Tim in this closet while playing hide-and-seek.

Her father and Tim lay dead or dying in the front yard, and she and her mother cowed in the closet, waiting. The waiting had been the worst part. They heard the front door burst open, the sound of the savages overturning the kitchen table that her Uncle John had made, the crash of her mother's dishes as they were thrown to the floor. Rebecca hugged her mother tighter as a fresh sob escaped her. Those dishes had been her pride and joy. She had brought them west with her on her long trek from Virginia. They had belonged to her mother. Rebecca thought of the time she had broken one of the precious plates while washing dishes. Her mother hadn't scolded her, but the sadness in her eyes at seeing her precious plate lying in pieces on the floor had been punishment enough. Now they were all destroyed, but what did it really matter. In a few moments—if they were lucky—they would be dead.

But they hadn't been lucky. The Indians had discovered them shortly afterward.

Dragged from their hiding place, Rebecca knew what would take place. She had heard of other women taken by Indians, had heard the stories of the things done to them.

She and her mother were thrown to the kitchen floor. All the Indians circled around them. Rebecca looked up into the faces of her captors. She had steeled herself to show them no fear, though her heart was beating so fast it felt as though it would burst from her chest at any moment. She saw the lust in their eyes, both from the killing and in anticipation of what was to come. She forced herself to meet their eyes. She showed each of them the contempt she felt, but when her eyes passed the bloody scalp hanging from the belt of one of the savages, her resolve slipped, and her eyes blurred with tears. Her heart felt as if it would stop. Then slowly she felt a hatred such as she'd never experienced enter her conscience and burn into her soul.

Before they could react, she sprang from the floor. Like a cougar going for a kill, she leaped on her prey, a shrill scream escaping from her as she attacked the savage brandishing the fresh scalp. Before he could react, she had raked her nails the length of his face, feeling with satisfaction the skin and flesh embedding itself under them as she was suddenly grabbed by the hair from behind and slung to the floor, scraping her knees and elbows on the hardwood floor. She leaped to her feet, only to be slapped hard by one of the braves standing there. She landed again on the hard floor, her eyes clouding with pain as her head hit the hard surface. Raising herself on her elbows, she shook the cobwebs from her brain, her vision clearing in time to see the Indian whose face she'd clawed draw his knife and start for her. She knew this was the end, and she felt no regret at having hurried the process along. Her only regret was that she could do nothing for her mother.

As the brave advanced, Rebecca pushed herself up on her elbows, determined to make one more attack before the animal advancing on her took her life. But before she could rise, a voice from the front door of the house quieted the group and stopped the advance of her executioner.

All eyes turned to the large brave as he entered, surveying the scene before him, his eyes going from Rebecca to the face of the brave. Rebecca could have sworn she saw a flicker of a smile cross his face as he studied the long gashes on the face of the Indian before him. Then instantly his face clouded, and his tone turned harsh and commanding. The Indians turned from the women and started gathering things from the house. When one of the Indians reached for Rebecca, she kicked out at him, catching him on the shin and having the satisfaction of hearing his howl of pain. The next instant she saw flashes of light as she was slapped hard across the face, but the pain of being slapped was nothing compared to the humiliation as she was grabbed by her long blond hair and dragged staggering out the door into the bright sunlight of the day.

She was dragged to a horse being held by another Indian. Then her hands were bound, and she was lifted bodily, as if a child, and placed on the back of the horse.

She hurled insults at the back of the Indian as he walked away from her, vowing she would even the score.

Rebecca watched as they led her mother, wrists bound together, to another horse and lifted her to its back. Tears came to her now as she watched her mother turn to look at the bodies of her husband and son lying in the yard of their home. When she turned back, Rebecca was shocked to see the dullness in her eyes. It was if she was already dead.

Rebecca called to her. "Mama, we'll be all right. We'll escape somehow. Mama…"

But her mother said nothing. She just sat there staring straight ahead.

They were led from the yard at a full run, and all of Rebecca's concentration was centered on remaining aboard the running horse. She thought once about letting go, hoping the fall would kill her, but she couldn't bring herself to do it. As long as she lived, there was hope of escape.

When the cavalry come upon them, Rebecca's spirits soared. She had seen the Indian leading her mother's horse fall in the first volley. She had seen her mother's horse run away from the gunfire and had seen no one give pursuit. She knew her mother had escaped. Her chance came when the Indian leading her horse had been wounded. Although he had tried to hold onto the lead rope, Rebecca had dug her heels into the horse, sending it bolting ahead of her captor's horse and jerking the lead from his hand as he ran in fright.

Rebecca held to the horse's mane as he plunged into the thick undergrowth of the wooded area. Try as she might, she couldn't turn the horse as he ran on into the woods. If she had been able to turn the frightened animal, she might have been able to reach the soldiers, but with her hands bound by the rawhide strips, she couldn't reach the lead rope as it trailed the ground. She tried using her feet and knees to force the horse to turn, but, frightened as the animal was, it was all she could do to keep from being knocked from its back as it continued its frightened run through the trees, jumping fallen logs and crashing through thick undergrowth.

Rebecca was so intent upon remaining aboard the running animal, she didn't notice the Indian in pursuit until it was too late. Suddenly he was beside her, leaning over to catch the trailing lead rope.

Recognizing him as the one who had dragged her from the house by her hair, Rebecca's fury came to her stronger than before. She saw his bloody side, from the bullet wound, and grabbing a stronger hold on the horse's mane, she raised her foot and kicked out, feeling her foot connect solidly. She had the satisfaction of seeing the agony wash over him as he pulled away. For a brief moment she thought she might have succeeded in driving him away, as he pulled his horse up and bent over its neck. Then her spirits fell and her heart beat faster as he sat up and kicked his horse after hers.

This time, instead of coming beside her, he angled his horse to meet with hers where he would be at her horse's head, allowing him to grasp the lead where it was attached to the halter and preventing her from kicking him again.

Grabbing the lead, he headed deeper into the woods. As they pulled away, Rebecca glanced back over her shoulder. All she saw were trees as she was led away from the sounds of battle. At least Mama was safe, she thought as she glared at the back of the Indian in front of her.

Chapter Eleven

Will continued to watch the rim of the valley, some sixth sense warning him of danger. He was about to give up his vigil, figuring it was a bear or cougar, when he spotted a horse coming into view, an Indian mounted on its back. Will held his position, not daring to move. Even though the distance was great, he could still make out the Indian leading a horse behind him. His breath caught in his throat as the rider of the second horse came into view. The long, blond hair reflected the sunlight. Even though Will could not make out the features, he knew it was a woman.

Will glanced over at Tye, but Tye wasn't to be seen. Will did not move a muscle as he watched the rim of the valley. He knew any movement could be seen for miles, and if he moved the Indians might see him.

He continued to watch as seven more Indians followed the path taken by the first Indian and the woman. He continued to watch as they rode along the rim rock, then disappeared into the woods, apparently following a trail leading to their village.

After what seemed an eternity, Will heard Tye whisper, "I think it's safe now. Move down off the rock and get up under the bank."

Slowly Will moved off the rock, dropping to the sandy soil of the river bottom then easing up to the river bank. Here he was out of sight from the rim rock.

Tye crawled up to where Will was lying. "How many did ya count?" he asked.

"Eight, not counting the woman," Will replied, his voice weak.

"That's what I counted, too."

"Where do ya reckon the woman came from?" Will asked.

"No tellin'. That was a raidin' party, judgin' by its size."

"What are we gonna do?" Will asked, looking back over the bank of the river in the direction the Indians had gone.

"I don't know, Will. They're takin' her to the village. They might kill her once they reach there, or they might be plannin' on makin' her a squaw. One's not much better'n the other."

"We got to do somethin'," Will said, looking at Tye. "We can't just sit here and do nothin'. I couldn't live with myself."

"We're gonna do something," Tye said. "I just got to figger out what it is we're gonna do."

Tye looked up at the sun. It was sinking into the west, leaving only a couple of hours of daylight. Turning to Will, he asked, "Are ya up for a ride to that Indian village?"

After thinking for a moment, Will replied, "I'd rather fight a grizzly bear, but I don't see one around right now. So I guess I'm up to it."

"Let's ride up there and check things out. We'll decide what to do from there."

It took them three hours to reach the ridge that over-looked the Indian village.

The sun had set an hour earlier, and they looked down from darkness at the fires in the valley. Both carried rifles, as well as the pistols on their belts. Their horses were tied a mile back down the trail, hidden in a cedar stand off the trail.

As they watched the activity below, they could see the large fire in the center of the village. Several Indians were standing in front of the fire, addressing the rest of the tribe but speaking mostly to three men seated on the ground. Tye explained that the three men probably were the chiefs of the tribe, and the Indians were describing their raid.

Will was watching intently as the large Indian doing most of the talking waved his arms and made signs with his hands while he talked. Even though they were too far away to hear any of the talk and wouldn't have been able to understand it if they could hear, Will and Tye were mesmerized by the proceedings taking place before them.

Suddenly the large Indian doing the talking turned to two braves standing outside the ring of listeners and motioned to them with his arms, while at the same time shouting orders. Both braves turned and ran to a teepee that was facing the circle.

Will watched as the Indians entered the shelter, only to return shortly, dragging a kicking, screaming woman behind them.

The two braves dragged the woman to where the three chiefs sat. There they unceremoniously dumped her on the ground. Will could hear her screaming insults at the Indians as she tried to gather her torn skirt around her. Even from the far distance, Will could hear the words the woman was screaming at the Indians, and he felt his face turn red as he heard every word. He had never heard a woman speak such language. At first he was ashamed for the woman, then he considered the situation she was in and wondered if he himself might not react the same way.

The woman continued to rant and rave at the Indians until the large brave, who had been doing most of the talking, drew back his arm as if to strike her. She instantly hushed her rantings and held up her arms to protect herself. When the brave saw she wasn't going to say any more, he continued his talk, pointing to the woman occasionally during his oration.

Tye tapped Will on the shoulder and motioned him back. When they were away from the ledge, he whispered quietly, "I've got a plan, but it's a'might risky."

"I think anything to do with that bunch down there is goin' to be a'might risky. What is it?" Will asked, keeping his voice low.

"If I can work my way around to where their horses are and stampede 'em through the village, it may cause enough of a diversion where you can sneak in and get the woman."

"I thought ya said it was gonna be a might risky. Sounds more like it's gonna be suicide if ya ask me," Will said, not smiling.

"If ya got a better plan, let me hear it.".

"If I had one, you would've already heard it," Will replied, tight-lipped.

"Then I guess we go with mine, unless ya can talk me out of it." He smiled at Will, and Will grinned back.

"Ya just remember ya promised me we'd make it outa here with our hair still on our heads. I aim to hold ya to that promise."

"I'm gonna do my best to keep it," Tye declared.

They crawled up to the rim of the valley, and Tye pointed to a group of trees just outside the village.

"I want ya to work yer way down to those trees there and wait until ya hear the horses coming. As soon as their attention is drawn away from the woman, ya sneak in there and grab her, then head back here to the horses. Don't wait for me. Just get her on yer horse, and hightail it back to the canyon. I'll be right behind ya as soon as I know these devils aren't following us.

"We'll pull out as soon as I get there. So start getting our things together. Any questions?"

"Nope," Will said. "Ya be careful. I don't want to have to find another partner."

"Ya do the same. Good luck."

Tye moved off into the darkness. Will waited a few seconds, then moved away from the rim. He circled away from the valley and made his way down the mountainside, moving slowly and cautiously, stopping every few feet to listen to the sounds of the night.

As he moved closer, he could hear sounds coming from the Indian village. The talks were still going on, and Will was close enough now to make out the words, though he understood none of them. He steadily worked his way through the woods until he came to the clearing before the trees. He would have to cross twenty yards of clear open space before he would be hidden by the trees. He would be in the open and exposed to any eyes that may be looking in that direction. He couldn't circle around and come into the trees from any direction where he couldn't be seen. He had no choice but to cross where he was and hope none of the Indians would look his way.

Sweat broke out on his brow as he looked across the clearing. Twenty yards had never looked so far. He drew his pistol from its holster. If they saw him, he was going to take at least one or two before they got him.

Saying a silent prayer, he bent over and moved as close to the ground as he possibly could, watching the encampment as he moved. It took only a few seconds to cover the twenty yards, but to Will it seemed a lifetime. He expected a warning to come from the direction of the village at any moment. His heart stopped beating as he crossed the clearing and moved behind the trees, releasing his breath only as he reached the large cedar. The Indians were still arguing. One of the chiefs was talking now, and all eyes in the village were upon him.

Will waited, not daring to breath for fear the sound could be heard. His heart was racing so fast he feared it would burst from his chest at any moment. Watching the scene taking place before him, he tried to imagine what the chief was saying. From where he was, he could see the face of the large brave who had been doing most of the talking earlier. It was plain he was not pleased with the chief's words, for his face was downcast. Will could see pain in his eyes when he looked at the speaker,

The chief continued to speak for several minutes, then motioned toward the captive. Two braves stepped beside the woman and drew her to her feet. Seeing her up close for the first time, Will was shocked by the realization that this was no woman but a girl not much older than himself. He wondered where a girl of her age had learned the words he had heard earlier.

Suddenly the tall brave moved to the girl and, pushing the braves away, grabbed her by the arm and pulled her to him, yelling at the chief as he did so. This move seemed to excite the entire village, and they all started talking at the same time, some seeming to side with the chief, some with the brave holding the girl.

Will was caught up in the scene before him and was unaware of anything else. He had forgotten about Tye and the horses until suddenly the Indians stopped their heated discussion and looked in the direction of the herd, which was now thundering toward the village.

For an instant everyone seemed riveted to the ground. Then at once pandemonium broke loose, and Indians began running in all directions.

The tall Indian holding the girl shoved her to the ground and ran in the direction of the stampeding horses.

The girl, hands still bound together, was attempting to rise to her feet. Realizing this was the only opportunity he was likely to get, Will sprinted from the trees, closing the gap between them in a few seconds. The girl's back was to him as he approached her, and he yelled at her to run. At first she looked around, confused by the sound of his voice. Then as if coming out of a trance, she turned and ran toward him. He grabbed her arm as she came to him, then led her toward the woods, running for all he was worth.

Will's heart was pounding as he raced toward the wooded area, dragging the girl behind him. He was close now. Only a few more feet, and they would be hidden by the trees. If they managed to get away undetected, it would be hard for her captors to follow.

He was almost to the trees when he heard the sound of running feet behind him. Instinctively he knew it was one of the Indians. The moccasined feet made little noise as they moved across the ground. Will whirled to meet his pursuer, yelling at the girl as he did.

"Run for the woods!"

Will turned and saw the brave who had been holding

the girl running toward them. His long knife was in his hand, and his eyes blazed with the lust of battle.

Will held the pistol in his hand. For an instant he started to bring it to bear on the Indian, but his mind froze his hand. A shot would alert the rest of the tribe and bring them down on him and the girl. He couldn't risk losing the slight edge he had gained. He would have to meet his attacker hand to hand.

Will's mind raced as his opponent continued toward him. He had wrestled much with his brothers on the farm and the other boys at school. He was a good wrestler and a fair boxer, winning most of the rough-and-tumble fights he'd been in, but this was different. This was for his and the girl's life. Could he win against an opponent who outweighed him by at least forty pounds? This last question came to his mind as the Indian hurled himself through the air, knife drawn back and ready to be plunged into Will's heart.

Will watched as the Indian came diving toward him. He seemed to be riveted to the spot, unable to move, as the tall brave flew through the air, bent on destroying this white man who had dared come to his village and take his hostage.

Rebecca watched from the trees as Will stood his ground. She wanted to yell at him to run, but she knew it would be too late. The brave was almost on top of him. She covered her eyes with her bound hands, partly from not wanting to see her rescuer impaled upon the sharp knife, but also from the certain dread of knowing her escape was to be thwarted.

Will stood as the hurling figure came toward him, his heart pounding in his chest. He could see triumph in the red man's face as he started to bring his arm down for the death thrust. At this moment Will ducked and moved sideways, then came back to a standing position as the arm holding the knife missed his head by inches. Will was already swinging his arm, and the pistol caught the Indian's arm that held the knife just below the elbow. Will could hear the bones crack. The Indian let out a howl of pain and dropped the knife as he hit the ground.

Before the Indian could get to his feet, Will was on him, using his pistol as a club. He hit him twice, either blow enough to knock him senseless, but Will wasn't taking any chances.

Unable to stand it any longer, Rebecca removed her hands from her eyes. She expected to see her would-be rescuer lying dead on the ground, her hopes of escape dead with him, and her eyes widened with delight and her knees went weak with relief when she looked up and saw Will running toward her. The body of the Indian lay on the ground.

"Come on, we got to get outa here before some more of 'em see us," Will shouted, grabbing her by the arm.

"Is he dead?" Rebecca asked, looking at the brave lying on the ground.

"Nope, but he sure is gonna have one heck of a headache when he wakes up. I want us to be a long way gone by then." Will pulled her along behind himself.

"I wished ya'd killed him," Rebecca answered with such bitterness that Will stopped to look at her. Wondering for a brief second if maybe her captivity had caused her to go insane, he looked in her eyes. He could see the hate and anger there, but otherwise she seemed to be all right.

"Come on, we got to get outa here."

Will led her around through the woods and climbed to the ridge where Tye and he had watched the village. Looking down, he could see the Indians gathering the loose horses. He could still see the body of the large brave lying where he'd left him. If only he had thought to drag him into the bushes, it might have given them a little more time before they found the girl missing. Well, it was too late now. They had to reach the horses and make it to the canyon as fast as possible.

Will wondered about Tye. Where was he? Was he all right? He had to believe he was, but he couldn't stop now to worry about him. Grabbing the girl by the arm he started off down the trail, but she pulled back.

"Just a minute. Could ya possibly remove this rope from my wrists before we go any farther? It's cutting into my flesh, and besides it's hard to run with my hands tied together and ya pullin' me along."

Will felt his face burn hot with embarrassment. He should have thought about that, but in his haste to get away from the Indian village, he'd only thought about escape. He had paid little attention to the girl he had been dragging along behind him.

"Sure," Will said, fumbling for his pocketknife. "Sorry I didn't do it sooner. I was in such a hurry to get us outa there, I just didn't think about it."

"That's all right," Rebecca answered., "I'm beholdin' to ya for gettin' me outa there."

"If ya wanna stay outa there, we better get outa here in a hurry. They're likely to be coming for us pretty soon," Will said, returning his pocketknife to his pocket and coiling up the ropes he'd cut from the girl's wrist. He stuffed them into his pocket, then grabbed her hand and started down the slope to where the horses were tied.

Will moved cautiously through the woods, stopping to listen from time to time. The only thing he heard was the noises coming from the Indian village. He led Rebecca to the horses and was untying his mount when he heard a rustling in the bushes. It was coming from the direction they'd just come. Grabbing Rebecca by the hand, he pulled her behind a large oak tree, drawing his pistol as he did.

Rebecca had heard the noise and tensed at the sound. She moved behind Will and held her breath as he looked around the tree. She could almost feel herself shaking, and she felt herself jump when she heard a whispered voice call.

"Will. Over here."

Will pulled her from behind the tree and walked back to the horses.

"What took ya so long?" Tye asked, coming out of the brush.

"Had us a little trouble back there."

"Ya all right?" Tye asked, looking first at Will, then Rebecca.

"I'm fine."

"I'll be fine as soon as we're away from here," Rebecca answered, looking back in the direction of the Indian village.

"Let's get goin' then," Tye said. "We still got a long ride ahead of us before the sun comes up."

Will climbed into the saddle, then extended his hand to help Rebecca up. She grabbed his hand, then, pulling her dress up above her ankles, she raised her foot to the stirrup and swung up behind him.

Will felt himself blush as his eyes fell on the well-shaped calf. He averted his eyes to the ground as he pulled the girl up.

Rebecca caught Will's glance and smiled as she adjusted herself on the back of the horse.

"By the way, what's yer name?" Will asked.

"Rebecca. Rebecca Kincaid. What's yers?"

"Will Paxton. And that's my partner, Tye Garrett."

"Pleased to make your make yer acquaintance, Will, Tye."

"Enough of these pleasantries," Tye said, "We'll all get acquainted once we've got away from these red savages."

"Don't mind him," Will said as he kicked his horse into a fast trot. "He's just old and cantankerous, but he's harmless."

For the first time since she could remember, Rebecca giggled. Will liked the sound and grinned as he headed the horse down the trail leading to the box canyon.

Chapter Twelve

It was fifteen miles from the Indian village to the box canyon where the horses were held. The terrain over which they traveled was scattered with large rocks, and more than half of the trail was covered by forest. Ducking and dodging the low limbs and jumping many of the larger rocks as they rode, they raced away from the Indian village and covered the distance in little over an hour.

Tye was shouting instructions as they raced up the valley to the box canyon. "Catch ya up a fresh horse, and catch one for Rebecca. I'll gather up the herd and tie the horses together while ya load up the gear. Hurry, I figger them redskins will be after us at first light."

It took them just over an hour to have the pack horses loaded and Will and Rebecca mounted on fresh horses.

Rebecca had to ride bareback, since there were no spare saddles. She told Will not to worry. She'd ride totally nude if that's what it took to get her out of there.

Will blushed at the thought and hurried to help Tye get the horses ready to move. He wanted to put distance between himself and Rebecca before she could see his red face.

Tye was throwing his saddle on a fresh horse when Will rode up the canyon. Will could see the horses they had broken, as well as the halter broke mares tied together, head to tail.

"You ready to go?" Tye asked as Will rode up.

"We're ready. The pack horses are loaded. Rebecca's holdin' 'em down by the mouth of the canyon."

ride back up the valley and head off any of 'em that might try to go that way. I'm gonna stay in front of 'em. I think they'll follow these that I'm leadin'. But if they don't, ya'll have to ride ahead of 'em and push 'em away from the canyons till we get to the canyon leadin' to Clement's place."

"There's only two canyons between here and there, and both of 'em are on this side of the valley. I shouldn't have any trouble headin' 'em off," Will said.

"Once we get 'em headed down Clement's canyon, we're gonna pick up the pace. I'll try not to let 'em run full out. If they'll follow these horses, we'll keep to a fast lope. Don't push 'em, but don't let 'em slow down neither."

Will nodded and rode down to the mouth of the canyon to tell Rebecca their plan and instruct her on what to do. He rode up the valley and waited. Soon he saw Tye coming out of the canyon leading the line of horses. Some of the mares started a nervous dance as they realized they were being led out of the canyon that had served as their prison, but with their heads tied to the horses in front of them and their tails being held by the horses behind them, they were prevented from bolting and forced to follow.

Soon Will heard the other horses moving behind the ones Tye led. As the horses followed the lead horses out, they raised their heads and looked about, recognizing the freedom the valley offered. But as the caravan continued on down the valley, each of the horses turned and followed.

Will waited until Rebecca came out, then reined his horse beside her. "Can ya push 'em from behind all right?"

"Sure. If I have any problems, I'll call ya."

"Watch your backside. If ya see any sign of Indians, forget the horses and hightail it up to where we are."

"Ya can count on it," Rebecca promised.

Tye was leading the horses at a steady trot. Although most of them followed those Tye was leading, a few stopped to graze along the way. Will and Rebecca were kept busy pushing them back into the herd and keeping them moving.

They moved past the two canyons where the horses

could break away. Will had ridden out around the herd to block the openings of the canyons should any of the herd decide to make a break for it. After the last canyon was behind them, he rode up to where Tye was leading the string of horses.

"They seem to be moving along fine," Will said.

"Yep, I figger we've been on the trail for about two hours now, and I don't think we've lost any. As soon as we get around this bend in the river up here, I'm gonna open 'em up and see if we can't put some miles behind us. Ya let Rebecca know, then ride the perimeter to keep an eye on the herd. If ya have any problems, yell and I'll swing them into the wall of the valley and slow them down."

"How long do ya think it will take us to reach Clement's trading post?" Will asked.

"About another four hours if everything goes all right."

"You think those Indians will follow us tonight?"

"Normally Injuns don't like to attack at night. They think the spirits are against 'em in the dark. But since we've stolen their hostage, they might just decide to chance it. On the other hand, they might figger their medicine ain't too strong, seein' as how we went into their camp and stole her away from them. Either way, it's best to keep movin' and keep yer eyes and ears open. Ya can never predict what Injuns might do."

"I aim to," Will said. "I don't think I'll feel safe again until we're back in Montana."

"That's still a few weeks away, if everything goes as planned." As Tye turned to look back at the herd, he asked, "What are we gonna do with her?"

"Good question," Will responded. "Ya reckon she's got any family around here?"

"I don't know. Why don't ya ask her and see."

"I reckon I could do that," Will said, a hint of a smile on his face. "What do we do if she ain't got any?"

"Let's cross that river when we get to it. Now get on out there and do yer job, before we lose what we've worked so hard to get."

"Yes, sir," Will said grinning as he wheeled his horse and began to circle the herd.

Will circled the horses, checking for any stragglers that might be drifting away from the herd. When he rode up to Rebecca, he noticed her head was nodding as if she was dozing. The lead rope for the pack horse was tied to her wrist. He called softly to her.

"Rebecca."

She came awake with a start, looking around as if expecting someone. When she saw Will, her face dropped. Will noticed the look of disappointment and grief that touched her face.

"I'm sorry. I didn't mean to startle ya," he said as he rode up beside her.

"That's all right," she answered. "I shouldn't have been dozin'. It's just that I ain't had much sleep for the last three days, and I guess I was plumb tuckered out."

"I been meanin' to ask how it is that ya come to be a prisoner of the Sioux." Will watched her face closely. He saw tears come into her eyes and hurried on.

"Ya don't have to tell me if ya don't want to. It's just that Tye and me was wonderin' if ya have any kinfolk around here that we could take ya to?"

Rebecca wiped the tears from her eyes and sniffed at her running nose, then said, "It's all right. I guess I need to tell someone. Maybe it'll help ease the pain if I tell ya."

She told Will the whole story, leaving out none of the details of her ordeal with the Indians.

"I reckon that Injun was arguin' about me belongin' to him when ya'll come along and pulled me outa there. He don't know it, but it's a good thing you and Tye come along when ya did. Otherwise I was going to find some way to kill me one Sioux Indian."

Will smiled, believing she would have done just that.

"So ya figure yer mother got away?"

"I'm pretty sure she did. I saw her riding away from the Indians, and I don't think any of them were chasing her."

"Do ya reckon she would have gone back to the farm?"

"I don't know. Mama's not what ya'd call a strong woman. She may have gone on to the fort with the soldiers."

"Well, we'll find her wherever she is," Will said. "Ya reckon ya can stay awake for a spell? We've got to push these horses a might faster."

"I'll stay awake. If I don't, ya just pour water on me."

"I'll keep an eye on ya. If ya start noddin' off, I'll holler at ya," Will said with a grin.

"Thanks." Rebecca smiled at him. "And Will?"

"Yeah," Will replied, looking over at her.

"Thanks for savin' me from those Indians. I'm beholdin' to ya. Y'all risked yer lives for me, and I won't be forgettin' that."

"Ya don't need to thank us," Will said. "We didn't do any more than any God-fearin' man would have done."

"Well, thanks just the same. Like I said, I won't be forgettin' it."

"Ya hang on to that horse," Will said. "I'll be close by." With that he reined his horse away and moved to the edge of the herd, moving them to a faster pace. He stayed close enough to Rebecca to keep an eye on her. Her words of thanks had left him embarrassed and at a loss for words of his own. He thought about the feelings he was having and wondered why all of a sudden he felt as if he had a thousand butterflies in his stomach. It must have been from the excitement of the evening, he told himself, but he knew, even as he thought it, that wasn't the reason.

* * *

Tye led the horses down the canyon at a ground-eating lope, all the time keeping an eye on the herd to make sure they were all following. He kept up the pace until he estimated they'd traveled fifteen miles since leaving the box canyon, then slowed to a walk. He wanted to have the horses calm when he brought them into Clement's.

Two hours later they walked into the clearing of the trading post. Tye stopped the horses he was leading, and the rest of the herd moved up around them.

"Hello the camp!" he shouted.

Slowly the door of the shack opened slightly.

"That you Garrett?" came Clement's sleepy voice.

"No, it's the whole Sioux nation come to have breakfast with ya. Of course it's me. Who else ya expectin'?"

"Well, ya never know. Could be expectin' someone important," Clement grumbled as he came down the slope toward the corrals.

"How many head ya got there?" Clement asked.

"Somewhere around three hundred," Tye replied.

Clement let a low whistle escape. "I'd say ya had a pretty successful hunt."

"If we can just hang on to 'em now, it will have been a successful trip."

"Ya expectin' trouble?" Clement asked as he swung open the gate that led into a large trap.

"Could be," Tye replied. "We had a little run-in with the Sioux."

"They huntin' you?"

"Could be. Reckon ya can take a little trip and find out for us?"

"Soon's we have some breakfast, I'll head out."

Will and Rebecca herded the horses into the corral after Tye had ridden in, leading his band of halter-broke horses.

Clement studied Rebecca as she pulled up to the corral and dismounted.

"Hey, Garrett, ya picked up a stray along the way. Looks like a right purty stray, though. Where'd ya get 'er?" Clement asked as he swung the gate shut.

"Rebecca, meet Clement Stoner, the proprietor of this fine establishment and our host for the next few days. He may be ugly as sin, but he's really harmless, except for the smell. Ya'll get used to that after about a week." Tye turned to Clement, a twinkle in his eye and a smile on his lips.

"Clement, meet Miss Kincaid. She was a guest of the Sioux but got tired of the accommodations and decided to ride along with us for a spell."

Will was surprised to see Clement's face turn red as he took Rebecca's outstretched hand. What was it about women that made grown men act foolish when they were around?

"Pleased to meet ya, Miss Kincaid," Clement said, removing his hat and bowing slightly as he held Rebecca's hand.

"Please, call me Rebecca, Mr. Stoner. And it's a pleasure meeting ya."

"Rebecca, that's a purty name. But please call me Clement."

"Thank you, Clement." Will could see the flush on Rebecca's cheeks as she smiled at Clement. He was surprised by the touch of jealousy that he felt as she continued to smile at him.

"Would ya like to come up to the house and freshen up while I get us some breakfast rustled up, Rebecca?"

"Thank ya, Clement. That would be nice. But I reckon I better help Tye and Will with the horses."

Tye nodded toward the house and said, "Ya go on and wash up. Will and me will take care of the horses."

Will thought he saw a look of disappointment cross Rebecca's face as she nodded and turned, following Clement to the house. He watched her as she walked away. Secretly he wished she had stayed to help them. Why? He wondered. Then he put her out of his mind as he turned to help Tye remove the halters from the horses.

Tye had seen Will watch the girl leave, and he smiled to himself as he saw the look on his face. Will was growing into a man, and it was plain Rebecca was turning his head. Tye just hoped Will would take it slow and easy, but knowing his partner the way he did, he doubted that would be the case. Will didn't seem to take anything slow and easy.

They removed the halters and unsaddled their horses, then led the pack horse up to Clement's shack and removed their supplies and pack saddle.

"I'll take the horse back down to the corral," Tye said. "Ya go on in and get some breakfast."

Will glanced nervously at the house, then said, "I reckon I better help ya get that horse back down to the corral."

Tye grinned and picked up the lead rope. He started back toward the corral, Will falling in behind.

Tye led the animal into the corral and removed the halter. As he turned back to the gate, he noticed Will leaning on the fence, his face fixed with a look of worry.

"What's the problem, Will?"

"It's Rebecca," Will said. "Her mother escaped from the Sioux. Rebecca thinks she got back to the soldiers, but she doesn't know where she might be now. You reckon we can swing by their farm on the way back and see if she's been there?"

"Sure, and if she ain't there we'll swing by the fort and see if they know where she might be."

"Thanks, Tye. I know Rebecca will appreciate it."

"Well, I don't know about ya, but I could eat a bear right about now. How about we head on up to the house and see if Clement's got some food ready?" Tye asked. He was glad to see a smile come across Will's face.

"Now yer talkin'," Will said. "I been eatin' yer sorry cookin' for so long, I think I almost forgot what real cookin' tastes like."

"Yeah, I noticed yer havin' trouble eatin' the meals I fixed," Tye replied.

"I only pretended to like yer cookin' so's I wouldn't hurt yer feelin's. I know how cranky ya get," Will said with a laugh.

The smell of food cooking hit them as they opened the door of the shack. Clement was busy frying elk steaks, while Rebecca was flipping pancakes on the griddle.

"Y'all come on in and wash up," Clement said. "Breakfast is about ready. Course ya two probably ain't hungry for any real food, after eatin' each other's cookin' for so long."

Will and Tye grinned at each other as they headed back to the cave to wash up.

After everyone was seated around the table, plates piled high with pancakes and elk steaks, Clement asked, "What are yer plans now?"

"Once we know how the Sioux situation is, then we'll know more about our plans," Tye answered. "I reckon Rebecca would like to find her ma, and then we've got to get these horses up to Montana before the snow hits. I'd like to rest up here for a few days before moving out. Ya reckon you can put up with us for a spell?"

"I reckon I can manage to put up with ya fer a few days, long as ya don't get no ideas about makin' it permanent," Clement said as he stuck his fork into another flapjack.

"Don't worry," Tye said. "We'll be outa here just as soon as we know it's safe."

"As soon as I finish eating, I'll head back up the valley and see what I can find out," Clement told them as he put half a pancake in his mouth. "If ya two ain't got them Injuns too stirred up, I may be able to calm things down a mite. I done some tradin' with Two Wolves. He's the head chief at the village. Me and him hit it off pretty good. I reckon I can make up some story about the girl here bein' bad medicine, and it would be better for him to leave her alone."

"That would be some trick," Tye said. "I'd dance at your weddin' if ya could pull that off."

"And I'd almost get married, just to see ya do it, too," Clement laughed.

After all had eaten and the dishes were cleared from the table, Clement took up his Sharps rifle and his shoulder pack and walked outside. It was still dark, but the eastern sky was starting to pale a little. Tye walked alongside of Clement as he started down the trail leading into the valley.

"Ya be careful. There's no tellin' what kind of mood those Indians will be in when ya find 'em."

"Don't ya be aworryin' about me. I ain't lived this long without knowin' how to take care of myself." With that he raised his hand in a farewell salute and started down the trail.

Tye watched him until he disappeared into the woods. Then with a sigh he turned and went back to the cabin. Will was washing the dishes as Tye entered, and Rebecca was nowhere to be seen.

"She sleepin'?" Tye asked.

Will nodded.

"Why don't ya get some shut eye, too. I'll keep watch fer awhile, then wake ya."

"If ya see anything, ya better run up here and holler at me. I don't know if I can hear anything through these walls," Will said as Tye headed out the door with his rifle.

Tye woke Will later that day. The sun was already starting its western descent when Will walked outside.

Clement hadn't returned. Though they weren't expecting him back for several more hours, Tye and Will both looked toward the trail heading up the valley.

"I sure hope he's all right," Will said.

"He is," Tye replied. "He's a tough old coot, and he knows what he's doing. He'll be all right. I'm gonna get a couple hours sleep. Wake me when he comes back."

"Sure thing." Will said.

* * *

The sun was setting in the west when Will heard noise coming from the trail. At first he thought it was a wild animal making the sound, but as it grew louder he could make out the words to a song. Even though it was sung off key, he couldn't mistake the voice behind it.

Will let out a whoop and hurried along the trail.

"Clement, would ya quit that caterwauling before you scare the horses plumb to death!" Will warned. The grin on his face showed the relief he felt at seeing the mountain man safe.

"Caterwauling?" Clement asked indignantly. "Ya just don't know how to 'preciate fine music, boy."

"If that's fine music, then yer right. I don't know how to 'preciate it," Will replied. "Did you meet with the Sioux?"

"That's what I went up there for, isn't it?"

"Well, how did it go?" Will asked impatiently.

Clement eyeballed Will for a few seconds, not saying a word. Then with a shake of his head he said, "Yer really turning into something, aren't ya?"

"What do ya mean?" Will asked, confused by the old man's statement.

"Let's get up to the house. I don't want to have to tell this more'n once. Are the other two awake?"

"They're both asleep, but Tye said to wake him the moment ya came in."

"I guarantee ya, he'll want to be awake for this," Clement said, chuckling to himself.

Clement opened the door to the cabin and walked in, yelling a loud rebel yell as he did.

Tye came bursting into the room, throwing back the blanket covering the opening to the cave. He had his pistol in his hand, and he still wore his boots, ready for trouble should it come.

Rebecca was close behind. She stood there blinking as the light in the room fell on her sleep-filled eyes.

"I declare, I think ya'd sleep your life away if I give ya the chance," Clement said, grinning at Tye as he holstered the pistol.

"A man ought to be shot for yellin' like that. After what we been through the last couple of days, my nerves are almost shot. Then ya come in here yellin' like a wild Indian. It's a wonder I didn't shoot ya first and ask questions later."

"Well, if ya'd done that, ya sure would've missed one of the best tales ever."

"What tale is that?" Tye asked.

"The one about the evil spirits that visited the Sioux camp last night."

"What's that?" Tye asked, a perplexed look on his face.

Clement chuckled. "Yep, it seems an evil spirit paid a visit to the Sioux camp last night and played havoc with a young brave there."

"Clement, you're not makin' a bit of sense. Would ya get on with the story!" Tye said in exasperation.

"I've traveled all day long to find out what's goin' on with them Injuns. I put myself in danger goin' into their camp. Now I'm goin' to tell this story my way. So if ya want to hear it, ya just hush yer yap, or I'll hush my mouth and ya won't hear any more."

Tye grinned at Clement's outburst, but knew better than to say any more.

"Now, if everyone will just hush up," Clement began, casting a warning glance at Tye, who held up his hands in surrender, "I'll go on with the story."

Looking around at Will and Rebecca to make sure they weren't going to say anything, Clement proceeded with his story.

"I had no trouble gettin' into the village, which was surpisin', considerin' the raid you two pulled off. I asked to see Two Wolves and was led to his teepee. The old chief come out, and we talked for a spell about the old times and how things used to be before so many people started movin' in. Then he started talkin' about evil spirits comin' into his village and stealin' away a hostage they'd taken. I could tell by the way he talked that he didn't really believe it was evil spirits, but his son Two Eagles had been attacked by the demon and had suffered a broken arm and a couple of knots on his head. He said it must have been an evil spirit, else how could such a thing have happened to a brave warrior like Two Eagles. The old chief kinda smiled when he talked of this, but explained that they was goin' to be spendin' the next few days wardin' off evil spirits, lest they be plagued by the durn things for the rest of the summer. Things like that could mess up the huntin' for the whole village, and with winter comin' on, they couldn't afford that."

Tye was looking at Will as Clement finished up his story.

"Was that the little trouble ya had back there in that Indian village?"

"I didn't know who he was," Will replied with a smile. "There was this rather large Injun who didn't take kindly to me takin' his hostage. He had some idea about splittin' my gullet with a knife. I just convinced him it wasn't such a good idea."

"He laid him out cold," Rebecca injected. "I thought

that buck was going to cut him to pieces, but Will stood there cool as you please, then knocked him out with the barrel of his pistol."

Tye shook his head and smiled. "I knew ya were a scrapper, boy. But I didn't know ya were an Injun fighter."

"I hope that's the last one I have to fight," Will replied, still blushing from all the attention.

"I don't know," Clement said, smiling. " Anyone who can get the reputation of bein' an evil spirit after just one fight might have quite a future as an Injun fighter."

Tye, Will, and Rebecca stayed with Clement for four days, resting and restocking their supplies. On the fifth day they rode away from Clement's trading post, leading the halter-broke mares and horses. By now the rest were used to following and fell in behind, grazing along as they went.

Clement muttered around all morning, talking about how nice it was going to be to have some peace and quiet again. But when it came time to say good-bye, there were tears in his eyes as Rebecca hugged the big mountain man and thanked him for his hospitality.

"Ya take care of these two no-goods, ya hear. I don't want to have to come get 'em outa trouble."

"I will," Rebecca said with a laugh. "Ya take care now, ya hear?"

Will and Tye shook hands with the old man and thanked him for his help. They promised to stop by and see him again if they were ever around that way.

As Will fell in behind the horses, he turned and looked back to see Clement standing in the doorway of his cabin. He knew he probably would never see the old mountain man again, and it saddened him to know another chapter of his life was ending. But what lay over the horizon promised to be even more exciting, and with that thought he flipped the end of his rope against the rump of one of the horses and they moved up the river, heading back to Montana.

Chapter Thirteen

Three days after leaving Clement's trading post, they pulled up to the farm that had been Rebecca's home place. As they rode into the yard, Rebecca's' eyes clouded with tears as she remembered the events of the last days she had been there.

Seeing the tears, Will and Tye busied themselves with the horses. They knew there was nothing they could do to ease her pain. It was something she would have to deal with on her own.

They turned the horses into a trap by the barn, then unsaddled and rubbed down their saddle horses. They did not hurry to finish. Neither relished the thought of going to the house, but finally, with nothing left to do, they crossed the dusty yard and entered the front door.

Rebecca was busy preparing the evening meal. Her eyes were dry, but Will and Tye could see redness from tears she had shed.

"I'll have supper ready in a little while," Rebecca said. "Why don't ya two wash up? There's a well and pump out back."

"Sounds good to me," Will said with an enthusiasm that sounded hollow.

"Yeah, I could use a good washing," Tye agreed as they headed out the door. Both were thankful for the excuse to escape.

They located the pump in the backyard. Will grabbed the handle and started pumping, and Tye leaned down catching the water in his hands as it poured from the pipe.

Will was in midstroke on the pump handle when suddenly he stopped.

"What the blazes ..." Tye stammered, his cupped hands empty.

"Over there," Will nodded, motioning toward a large oak tree fifty yards from the back of the house.

Tye looked in the direction Will was motioning. When his eyes found the object of Will's stare, he stood upright, immediately grasping the impact of what he saw.

"Fresh graves," Tye stated. "I reckon that's where Rebecca's kin are buried. Soldiers from the fort probably came back and buried them."

"Tye, there's four graves there. Rebecca told us her father, brother, and uncle were killed. Who does the fourth grave belong to?"

"I don't know," Tye answered gravely. "And I hate to speculate."

"We got to tell Rebecca."

"I know, but I sure hate to be the one to tell her. She's already pretty upset just bein' here. Did you see the look on her face when we rode up and her mama wasn't here?"

"Yeah, I saw it. It durn near brought me to tears."

Will looked at the fresh graves again, then turning to Tye he said, "I'll tell Rebecca."

"All right," was all Tye could say as he stared out across the open prairie.

Will walked back to the house, dreading the task at hand. Rebecca was mixing dough for biscuits when he walked in the front door.

"Supper will be ready shortly," she said.

Will stood in the doorway, uncertain of what to say as he watched Rebecca knead the dough. He saw her back go straight and her hands stop their motion. Slowly she turned to face him. She could see the anguish on his face.

"What is it, Will?" she asked, her voice calm.

"I think ya better come outside with me," Will said, feeling sick to his stomach as he watched her face go white with fear.

"Why, what is it?" Rebecca asked, panic rising in her voice.

Will walked over and gently placed his hand on her arm, then slowly he led her out of the kitchen. He could feel her trembling as they descended the steps and walked to the backyard.

Tye was standing by the pump as Will and Rebecca came around the corner of the house.

"I'll finish fixin' supper," he said.

Will nodded, but Rebecca turned to him and with a weak smile said, "Thank you, Tye. The biscuits are about ready to go in the oven."

Tye nodded, his face clouded with concern. Then he turned away and walked to the front of the house.

Will reached for Rebecca's hand and gently led her toward the big oak tree. He felt her stumble as she saw the fresh mounds of earth. He took her elbow and supported her as they walked the last few feet to the graves.

Tears streamed down Rebecca's face. Will looked straight ahead, not daring to look at her for fear of losing control of his own emotions. Pictures of his own mother and father came to mind as he felt Rebecca's grief pour out.

There were no markers on the graves, only hastily made crosses constructed of old lumber at the head of each.

Rebecca's body shook as racking sobs escaped from her. Will held tightly to her hand, trying to will his strength into her. She turned from the sight before her and buried her head into his shoulder. He encircled her with his arms and held her while she poured out the grief he knew she was feeling.

When Rebecca finally pulled away from Will, her tear-filled eyes looked up into his. "There's four graves there, Will."

Will remained silent. There was nothing he could say.

"Will, who's in the other grave?"

The pleading in Rebecca's voice was clear to Will. Was it her mother? If so, how did she die? If it wasn't her mother, who was it?

"I don't know, Rebecca," Will replied softly.

Rebecca looked once more at the sight, then whispered softly, "Rest in peace. I love ya." Then she turned and placed her hand in Will's. Together they walked slowly back to the house.

Tye had supper on the table when they entered. Rebecca looked at the food on the table, then said quietly, "I'm tired. I think I'll lie down for a while."

Will and Tye watched her leave, neither saying anything. No words would ease her pain.

Will and Tye tried to eat, but the food had little taste. Both men sat in silence, each lost in his own troubled thoughts. Finally Tye broke the silence.

"I'm gonna ride over to the fort tomorrow and see how the Indian situation is. I might even be able to sell 'em some horses while I'm there."

Will looked at Tye but didn't say anything. He knew why Tye was really going to the fort. They had planned to stop there when they left Rebecca's place, but now he had another purpose for going. He wanted to find out who was in the fourth grave and what had happened.

"Would ye mail a letter for me while yer there?" Will asked quietly.

"Sure," Tye agreed, not needing to ask who the letter was for. He knew Will was thinking of his parents. He'd been thinking of his folks, who were long dead and buried in Texas.

Tye rode out early the next morning. Will saw him off, handing him the letter to be mailed.

Rebecca was still in her room sleeping, Will hoped. Rest and time would help cure her losses.

Will spent the day working some of the colts in the corral. He rode two of the new ones, allowing the feel of a bucking horse under him to take his mind off the gloom he felt.

He was just finishing the second one when he looked up and saw Rebecca standing by the gate watching him. He reined the horse over to where she stood and stepped down.

"How long ya been there?" he asked, smiling. He was relieved to see her return the smile.

"I was watchin' ya from the house when ya got on him. I wanted to get a closer look. Ya make it look so easy."

Will blushed at the compliment.

"Have you had any breakfast?" Will asked, changing the subject.

"I fried me up a couple of eggs and some bacon," Rebecca replied.

Will stood there, not knowing what else to say. It seemed to him it was getting harder and harder to talk to this girl. He'd never had any trouble with the girls back home. In fact, it seemed they enjoyed talking to him. Now he always seemed to be stumped for what to say next.

Rebecca smiled as she noticed Will's discomfort.

"Would ya like me to show you around the place?" she asked.

"Sure," Will replied. "If ya feel up to it."

"I think I feel up to it," Rebecca smiled again.

Will caught and saddled their horses while Rebecca went back into the house to fix them a lunch to carry.

They rode out of the yard, Will letting Rebecca choose the direction. She rode east, showing him the hay meadows her father had cleared. When she talked about the things her father and uncle had planned and had done, Will noticed there was no sadness in her voice, only pride at what had been accomplished.

They stopped by a stream to eat the lunch Rebecca had brought. As she talked about the land and the plans her father had, Will found it easier to talk with her. They talked about cattle and horses, and Will told her how he'd come to be in Wyoming capturing wild horses. Rebecca laughed out loud when Will told her about Tye throwing his hat under his horse. He watched her as her laughter subsided. Then the words came out of his mouth before he knew it.

"I don't think I've ever seen anything as pretty as when ya laugh like that."

Rebecca looked him in the eye, her face unreadable. For a second he thought maybe he'd said something wrong and silently cursed himself for the fool he was.

"I don't think anyone has ever said anything nicer to me in my life. Thank ya, Will Paxton."

Will blushed again, and Rebecca laughed.

"Will Paxton, yer goin' to have to stop blushin' all the time, or the blood's goin' to stay in yer head and make ya pass out."

They rode back to the farmhouse, riding slow and talking. Will couldn't remember when he'd enjoyed an afternoon as much as he had this one.

As they rode into view of the house, Will saw Rebecca stiffen. Looking up, he saw Tye's horse standing in the corral. As he reached over and touched Rebecca's arm, she looked at him. He saw the corners of her mouth try to smile, but the attempt failed miserably.

They rode up to the corral in silence. Will took the horses and unsaddled them while Rebecca waited. Then they walked up to the house.

As soon as they entered the front door, Will knew Tye's news was not good. He was sitting at the kitchen table, his hat hung on the back of one of the chairs, his face solemn.

Rebecca held her head up as Tye looked into her face. Then in a low voice he told her the story.

"The soldiers are the ones that buried yer family. They straightened up the house, too. They regretted that they couldn't free ya from the Sioux, but there was only six of 'em and they couldn't risk following ya in the woods."

Rebecca stood there, holding her breath and dreading what was coming. Tye took a deep breath, looked down at his hands, and in a strained voice said, "As God is my witness, I wish I weren't the one to have to tell ya this, but that fourth grave belongs to yer mama. She was shot by one of the Indians while escaping. She lived for a spell, but without any doctor or medicine, they couldn't save her. Her last words were, 'Tell Rebecca I love her.'" Tye's voice broke as he said, "I'm truly sorry, Rebecca."

There were tears in Rebecca's eyes, but she held her head high.

"Thank you, Tye. I guess I already knew mama was in that grave. I guess I was hopin' I was wrong. I cried my tears for her last night. I'll be all right. I need a few minutes by myself. Then I'll see about fixin' us some supper."

She turned and went outside. Will and Tye knew she was going out to the big oak tree in the back to say farewell to her mother.

Will sat down at the table across from Tye.

"Got to be hard on her, losin' all her kinfolk like that."

Tye looked out the window toward the barn. His eyes held a look that said he was seeing something far away.

"It's one of the hardest things there is, but that girl's got grit. It may take some time, but she'll be all right."

"What do you reckon she's gonna do now?" Will asked.

"I don't know," Tye responded. "I guess we'll have to ask her. She can't stay here. There's no cattle or horses, and I doubt she's got any money."

"Ya reckon she could go with us?" Will asked hesitantly.

Tye turned to look at him questioningly, and Will continued.

"It would be nice to have someone to cook for us, and she can ride real good. She'd be a help with the horses, and we could even pay her a little."

"I don't think the trail we'll be travelin' is a good place to be takin' a girl. Besides that, what makes ya think she'd want to go with us?" Tye asked

"Well, I don't know for sure, but I figured we could ask her. I don't see where she's had any better offers."

Tye looked thoughtful for a minute, then said, "What if she doesn't want to go with us? What do we do then?"

"I guess we mount that bronc when we get to it," Will answered with a shrug of his shoulders. "Look, Tye, she's not a fragile girl. She's been raised here where life is tough. They've scratched a living out of this place and worked hard to do it. I think she'd do all right traveling with us."

"Ya really like her, don't ya?" Tye asked.

Will looked at him, thinking he was making fun of him, but Tye's face was serious.

"Yeah, I really like her. She's got a toughness about her that makes me believe she can do anything, but she's also soft enough to be a female. Does that make any sense?"

"More than ya know," Tye said, "more than ya know."

Will raised an eyebrow to look at Tye, but he read nothing in his expression.

"Why don't you ask her if she wants to come with us?" Tye said.

"Don't ya think it would be better if we both asked her?" Will asked.

Tye grinned at him and said, "No, I don't think it would. I think she'd rather have ya ask her."

Will smiled shyly. "You really think so?"

"Yeah, I think so. Go on and ask her."

Will hesitantly stood up. He pushed the chair back under the table, then stood there leaning, both hands on its back. He started to turn away, then turned back to look at Tye.

Tye nodded as if to say, "Go ahead," but didn't say a word.

Finally Will turned and walked out the front door. He stood on the porch, surveying the grounds in front of the house. Rebecca wasn't in sight, and he knew she was still around back saying her good-byes to her mother.

* * *

Rebecca wiped the tears from her eyes as she stood over the graves. She had promised herself she wouldn't cry anymore. She just wanted to say good-bye to her family. She didn't know what she was going to do now, but she knew she couldn't stay here. She would ask Will and Tye to take her with them until they got to a town where she could find a job. She didn't know what kind of job, but she was sure she could find something. She was going to miss Will and Tye. They had come to mean so much to her in the few short days she had known them.

Another tear ran down her cheek as she thought about how her life had changed so fast. Only a few days ago she had been happy living here with her family. Now her family was gone, and her future was uncertain. She dried her eyes and wiped the tear off her cheek with the back of her hand. Feeling sorry for herself wouldn't get her anywhere. She'd make it. She knew she would.

Turning away from the graves, she started back toward the house. It was time to get supper started for Will and Tye.

Rounding the corner of the house, she saw Will sitting on the top step of the porch. She wiped her eyes dry one more time, to make sure all the tears were gone. With a cheery note in her voice she asked, "Ya gettin' hungry?"

"I'm always hungry." Will smiled at her resolve.

"I'll get us some supper started," she said, starting up the steps.

"Rebecca, I need to talk to ya," Will said. He had been sitting there wondering how to approach her with his idea, but now that she was standing here, he'd suddenly become tongue-tied.

"Uh, what do ya plan on doin'? I mean, uh, what are yer plans now that … What I mean is, how are ya gonna make it alone?" Watching her as he fumbled with the words, he saw her lips turn up as she fought to keep from smiling. As he finished, she turned and looked out over the land that had been her home place for the last six years.

She turned back to him and with a sigh said, "I don't know. I've been thinking about that very thing. I can't stay here. There's nothing left for me. I was hoping ya and Tye would give me a ride to Cody or Cheyenne if yer headed that way. I'm sure I could find me a job somewhere."

Will came excitedly to his feet.

"That's what I wanted to talk to ya about," he said. "Tye and I talked it over, and we want ya to go with us. We'll pay ya to cook for us and help us out. It won't be easy. We'll be travelin' some rough trails, but I figure ya won't have any trouble. So what do ya say? Wanna go with us?" He rushed it so fast, it took Rebecca totally by surprise.

She stood still for a second, then flung her arms around Will's neck, squeezing him tight. Tears of joy ran down her cheeks as she laughed. "Of course I want to go with ya," she said, hugging him even tighter.

Will stood there, his arms reaching around her. Then he stepped back and, looking serious, said, "It might not look too good for a single woman to be travelin' with two men, you know."

Rebecca smiled at the look on his face. Fighting to put on a straight face, she asked, "Well, what are we gonna do about it?"

"Uh ... well, I don't know," Will stammered.

"Ya could always marry me. That would solve the problem, wouldn't it?" Rebecca asked.

Will looked at her, expecting to see her smiling at him in her mischievous way, but she wasn't smiling, and that threw him. He was surprised at how the idea appealed to him. He hadn't thought about it before now. He knew he liked Rebecca. But marriage—that hadn't crossed his mind. But why not? She was pretty and smart, and he cared for her.

"All right," Will said matter-of-factly. "I'll marry ya."

Rebecca was taken back. The shocked expression on her face surprised Will.

"I was only kidding," she said, laughing at his response. "Will, I wouldn't expect ya to marry me just because of what people might think."

He stood there studying her for a moment, feeling foolish for saying it the way he did.

"I wouldn't marry ya just for that reason neither," he said, looking at his boots.

Rebecca caught the meaning of his words. Her heart beat fast as she stood there looking at the young man in front of her. As she saw the pained look on his face, her heart went out to him.

"Will, are ya saying ya want to marry me?" she asked.

Will looked into her eyes, and she barely heard him as he said, "Yes, Rebecca, I do."

"Will, this is a serious matter, not to be taken lightly.

We've only known each other a couple of weeks. How can ya be sure ya want to marry me?" Rebecca asked, feeling the heat rise to her face.

"I'm sure," Will said. "Now that I think back on it, I reckon I knew that first night we rode out of the valley. If ya don't want to marry me, I'll understand. I don't want ya feelin' yer obligated or anything."

Rebecca smiled at his words, then said, "Will, I reckon I could look for the rest of my life and not find a better person. If ya want me to be yer wife, it would be my honor, but only if we wait until October. That's when my parents got married, and I want to get married on their wedding date."

Will looked at Rebecca, shocked by the answer she had given. When he finally found his voice, he replied weakly, "Sure, that's fine, Rebecca."

"And one more thing," Rebecca said, a smile on her lips. "Now that we're properly engaged, would you please call me Becky?"

Will grinned and nodded. "It would be my pleasure. Becky Paxton—it has a nice sound to it."

"Yes it does," Rebecca agreed. Then she surprised both herself and Will by standing on her toes and kissing him.

Will was so shocked it was a second before he could react, and by then she was pulling away. But he put his arms around her and drew her back to him, hugging her tightly. He moved away from her slightly and looked into her eyes, still holding her in his arms. Then he bent and kissed her, his lips seeking hers. This time the kiss was more passionate, and both of them felt their hearts pounding as they embraced. They were lost in each other, forgetting the world about them when they heard, "Hmmph." They broke apart instantly, Becky almost falling as she stepped off the front step. Only Will holding her arm prevented her from falling down the steps.

Tye was standing in the doorway watching the two of them, a large grin spread over his face.

"Have ya talked her into comin' with us, or are ya just

now workin' up to that point?" Tye asked. Will and Becky stood there, both red-faced.

"Cause if yer just now workin' up to it, I'm gonna go ahead and start supper. I'm gettin' hungry, and it looks like ya two may be out here a spell," Tye added, watching both of them turn redder and redder.

"I don't see how ya can talk, though, bein' that close together. Must be some sort of Indian sign language I reckon."

Will looked up, grinning at Tye like a little boy who had been caught with his hand in the cookie jar.

"She's goin' with us," he said. "We was just puttin' the finishin' touches on the deal."

Becky laughed and said, "Will and I are engaged to be married."

Tye looked from one to the other, surprise showing on his face. Then he smiled and said to Will, "Boy, ya are full of surprises. Still wet behind the ears, and here ya've gone and caught yerself the prettiest filly this side of the Mississippi. Allow me to be the first to kiss the bride."

Will stepped in between Becky and Tye.

"Oh no, you don't. Ya can kiss her at the weddin'. I ain't takin' no chances on you bein' a better kisser than I am until I got her hog-tied and married."

Becky laughed and pushed Will out of the way. Then, placing her arms around Tye's neck, she hugged him and kissed him lightly on the lips. Then she stepped back and looped her arm through Will's.

"I may marry ya, Will Paxton, but ya'll never hog-tie me."

"I reckon I won't," Will said smiling. "I don't reckon I'd really want to."

Chapter Fourteen

Tye, Will, and Rebecca rode out before sunrise the following morning. She looked back once before the house was out of sight feeling the loss she'd experienced and the pain of leaving behind all that was familiar. Then Will was beside her, reaching for her hand in the darkness. She held his hand and looked ahead, head held high and a smile on her lips.

They drove the herd to Fort Bridger. Tye had made a deal with the commander of the fort to buy fifty of the horses for forty dollars a head. The cavalry was short on horses, having lost some to Sioux raiding parties, and needed replacements.

Tye had not sold any of the horses Will and he had broken. The commander figured that if his men had to break their own horses, they would be a little more careful to hang on to them.

When they came in sight of the fort, Tye rode on ahead, leaving Will and Rebecca to hold the horses. He came back shortly, followed by six mounted soldiers. As they drew up, Tye introduced the man beside him as Captain Harper.

The captain touched his hat when introduced to Rebecca.

"Sorry about your folks, Miss Kincaid. I wish there was more we could have done."

"Thank you, Captain. I appreciate what ya did."

The captain looked embarrassed, then turned to Tye and said, "Let's take a look at these horses."

The soldiers went to work. Riding among the herd, they

selected their horses and cut them out until they had sixty or seventy head separated from the rest of the herd. Then they went to work selecting the ones they wanted. The captain looked on, talking to Tye about each of the horses, discussing their strong points, and pointing out the weak ones. It was clear to Will that the captain knew horses.

It was late in the day when the soldiers drove the fifty head back to the fort.

"You are welcome to spend the night at the fort," Captain Harper said as he paid Tye for the horses.

"Thanks," Tye said as he put the money in his saddle-bag, "but we've got a long ways to go, and I think it best if we get started."

They all shook hands, and Captain Harper tipped his hat to Rebecca. "You should have a safe journey to Montana. I haven't heard of any problems with Indians along the route you will be taking."

"Thank you, Captain," Tye said.

They circled the herd, and Tye led out with his string, the rest falling in behind.

Keeping the horses bunched and moving the next two weeks was hard work. Will rode the sides to keep the horses from straying. He had to change horses three times a day, as the grueling work quickly tired the horses he was riding. Rebecca tried to help as much as possible, but leading the pack horse prevented her from being much help. Since Tye knew the trails they were to follow, he had to remain in the lead.

By the time they reached Montana, Will was worn to a frazzle. Between riding hard all day and keeping watch at night, he had worn himself out. Rebecca worried about him but knew there was nothing she could do to help him.

"We'll be at a resting place tomorrow," Tye announced as they ate the supper Becky had cooked for them.

Will was leaning against his saddle, almost too tired to eat. "Where's that?" he asked.

"Ya remember me tellin' ya about some mares I had?" Tye asked.

"Yeah. If I remember right, ya said ya had some folks lookin' after 'em for ya," Will remarked.

"That's right," Tye said. "We'll be at their place tomorrow. That's where we'll keep the horses. We'll ride out to the ranches from there. That way we can find out what they want, then deliver only the horses they need. We won't have to drive the whole herd with us."

"Sounds good to me," Will agreed. "Wake me when we get there."

The next afternoon they drove the horse herd into the ranch headquarters of the Flying W Ranch.

Jim Lansing was in the corral doctoring some calves when the caravan came into sight. He shaded his eyes as he watched Tye lead his string down the road. Jim walked over to the gate leading to the horse trap and opened it, then stood back and waited as they herded the horses into the trap.

Jim Lansing was in his early thirties, but the hard lines around his eyes and the weathered skin made him look much older. He had started the Flying W ten years earlier and had fought Indians, drought, and hard winters to make a go of it. Now he had a nice spread and was starting to see some of his hard work pay off.

"Hello, Tye," he said as Tye stepped down from his horse to shake hands with him.

"Looks like ya got yourself some fine horses. Who'd ya steal 'em from?"

"I guess ya could say we stole 'em from the Sioux," Tye replied as he turned to Will and Rebecca. "Jim, I'd like you to meet my partner, Will Paxton. And this young lady is Rebecca Kincaid, soon to be Mrs. Will Paxton.

Jim shook hands with Will, noting the redness of his face at the introduction.

Rebecca dismounted from her horse and walked over to Jim. "I'm pleased to meet ya, Mr. Lansing."

"Jim will do fine. My father was Mr. Lansing."

Rebecca smiled, liking him immediately.

"Where's Judith?" Tye asked.

"I reckon she's up to the house startin' supper. That woman loves to cook more than anyone I ever met. She'll be tickled to death knowin' y'all are here. It'll give her an excuse to show off her cookin'. Hope ya brought an appetite with you."

"Cullen around?" Tye asked, looking around as if hoping to see someone.

Cullen was Jim and Judith's thirteen-year-old son. Tye was his idol, and he worshiped the ground he walked on. Tye looked at Cullen as a younger brother and enjoyed the youngster's company.

"He's over on the west range checking on the cattle we have over there. He's sure gonna be happy to see ya. Let's get yer horses cared for. Then we'll go up to the house where y'all can clean up."

Judith Lansing was a short, plump woman with exuberant energy. She hugged Tye as he came in the door, then hugged both Will and Rebecca as her husband introduced them.

"Tye Garrett, I swear you're as thin as a rail! You haven't been eating right, have you?" Then she looked at Will, shaking her head and clucking her tongue.

"There's only one side to ya, ain't there. Ya ain't got enough meat on yer bones to throw a shadow." She turned to Rebecca, taking her affectionately by the arm and ushering her into the house.

"Ya come with me, dear. I've got water heating, and we'll soon have ya a nice hot bath. Ya look like ya could use one." Then turning to the men, she said, "Y'all go on out to the pump and clean up. I'll have supper ready in a little while."

Rebecca turned and looked questioningly at Will. He smiled and shrugged as if to say he was no longer in control. Rebecca smiled at him and let herself be led into the house. Soon she was soaking in the large bathtub, filled with hot water and perfume soap. She regretted that she did not have a clean dress to put on. It seemed a shame to put on her dirty dress after taking such a luxurious bath. She felt

guilty soaking in the tub while Will and Tye washed up outside, but she wasn't about to argue with Judith Lansing. It
wouldn't do any good anyway, she thought, then smiled to
herself as she slid further down in the tub.

She soaked for the better part of an hour, then got out
and toweled herself dry. She didn't see her dress anywhere
in the room and was wondering what she was going to do
when Rosa knocked on the door.

Rosa was married to Ramon, who worked as a cowhand
for the Lansings. She helped Judith Lansing around the
house, doing the laundry and the cleaning, but Judith
Lansing did all the cooking. Rosa had told her all this
when she'd brought the hot water for her bath.

When Rebecca opened the door, there stood Rosa holding a beautiful dress adorned with pink roses. There was a
petticoat and undergarments as well. Rebecca stood there
looking at the assortment of clothes, feeling embarrassed
for not having any of her own.

"The Señora wants you to have these," Rosa said. "She
says these were perfect for you. I think she right. They
belonged to her sister." She pronounced it "seester," in her
heavy Mexican accent.

"Her sister?" Rebecca asked, looking questioningly at
Rosa.

"Sí, her sister. She died four years ago. She used to live
with the Señor and Señora. She got the fever and died.
Poor Mrs. Lansing, she was very sad for a long time."

"But I can't wear her dress. Won't it make her sad to
see someone else wearing it?"

"No, not anymore," Rosa said. "You put on the dress, it
make the Señora very happy."

Rebecca quickly dressed, then looked at herself in the
mirror. She was surprised by the reflection looking back at
her. The dress was made of light material, and it swirled
around her as she moved. The neckline dipped down in
front, revealing just enough to be decent. Rebecca was
surprised at how well the dress fit her and how well she
filled it out. She was curious to see what Will's reaction

would be, then blushed as she realized how important it was for her to have his acceptance. Rosa helped brush her hair, then pulled it back into a loose fall behind her, fastening it with an oyster shell hair clamp.

Will was sitting in the large living room listening to Jim and Tye talk about cattle and horses when Rebecca walked in. It took him a moment to realize that it was Becky standing there, and when it did dawn on him, he jumped to his feet, his eyes opening wide.

"Well, what do ya think?" Rebecca asked, turning around to give a full view.

Will stood there, wide-eyed, his mouth hanging open.

Jim and Tye were on their feet staring at Rebecca. Neither could believe the change that had transpired.

"Yer beautiful," came the throaty whisper from Will.

Rebecca's face reddened as she heard Will's comment and noticed the way he looked at her.

Tye grinned as he watched the scene before him. Then finding his voice, he said, "I was wondering what was under all that dirt. It's nice to know there was a pretty young lady hiding under there, but how on earth are ya gonna wrangle horses in that dress?"

Rebecca laughed and was about to respond in kind when Judith Lansing came bustling in to the room. She put both hands to her cheeks, pressing them together, which made her lips pucker and made her look like she had just eaten a sour lemon.

"Oh, my goodness!" she exclaimed. "Ya look like an angel!" Then grabbing Rebecca by the arm, she hustled her out of the room, saying, "Let's leave the men to their talk. I've got some ribbon that would make a beautiful bow for yer waist, and since yer so thin, ya need something. Ya poor dear, we have to get some meat on yer bones." Rebecca cast a glance at Will as she was being led from the room. He was still standing in the same spot, staring at her as she left.

"Boy, if ya know what's good for ya, ya'll saddle ya and that young lady a horse and hightail it outa here as fast as ya can. Ya stay around here for very long, and the Mrs. will have that girl turned into a proper lady and ya won't stand a chance. That or she'll have her weighing two hundred pounds and nagging you about bein' skinny."

Will hardly heard Jim Lansing's caution as he continued to look down the hall where Rebecca had been led. Right now he was wishing he could be alone with her, so he could look at her and tell her how beautiful she was. The sound of laughter coming from Tye and Jim made him turn. Then he blushed again as he realized they were laughing at him. He joined them as they went outside to look at Tye's horses Jim had, but his thoughts remained in the house. He kept glancing that way as Tye and Jim talked about each of the horses.

They had looked at the horses and were walking through the barn when they heard the ringing of a bell.

"That'll be the Mrs. calling us to eat," Jim said. "Reckon we better get on up to the house before she raises a ruckus."

Will had never seen a spread of food to equal what was served at the Lansings. There was a roast and a ham, and vegetables fresh from the garden.

Mrs. Lansing was bustling around getting everyone seated and making sure things were properly placed. Will and Rebecca were seated side by side, and Will felt a nervousness in his stomach each time he glanced at her.

Jim Lansing asked the Lord's blessing, and Will said a silent prayer himself. "Lord, let October hurry and get here." He hardly tasted the food as he kept casting nervous glances toward Becky.

Cullen Lansing came in before the meal was finished, and Will noticed how he looked at Tye as the two shook hands.

Tye introduced him to Will and Becky. Cullen shyly said hello to Rebecca, ducking his head instead of looking her in the eyes. He shook hands with Will, and Will noticed he had a firm handshake and looked him in the eye while introductions were being made.

"Did ya find those heifers?" Jim Lansing asked.

"Yes, sir, they were over by the sulfur springs."

"Any of 'em have calves yet?"

"No, sir, but there's a couple of 'em due any day now. I think that brindle heifer is gonna be the first one to pop."

"That'll be enough talk about cows and such at the table," Judith Lansing admonished her husband and son. "Ya men can talk about that when you're alone."

Jim Lansing chuckled, and Cullen attacked the plate of food his mother had fixed for him. When their eyes met, both smiled as if sharing a secret.

The evening was spent with the men talking in the large living room and the women talking around the kitchen table. As darkness settled over them, Judith lit the coal lamps in the house. The glow from the lamps cast warm shadows and created a comfortable atmosphere.

The comfort of the house, along with the meal and the talk afterward, gave Will a warm, pleasant feeling. As he watched Rebecca through the open doorway talk to Mrs. Lansing and Rosa, he hoped that someday together they would have a home such as this. It felt good to sit here and dream, far away from the dangers of the Sioux Indians and the rigors of the trail.

It was late when Judith Lansing showed Tye and Will to the bedroom they would share.

"At least there are two beds in here. I don't relish sleeping in the same bed with ya again," Will said as they entered the bedroom.

"That's news that don't make me feel too bad. Seems the last time I shared a bed with ya, I almost got killed."

Will sobered at the thought of their stay in Alder Gulch and how close he'd come to getting killed. If it hadn't been for Tye's quick reactions, he would be dead and buried now.

"Let's just hope nothin' like that happens while we're here," Will said.

"I think we're safe," Tye said. "Better get some sleep. Tomorrow's goin' to be a rough day for ya."

"How's that?" Will asked

"Yer goin' to start ridin' some of those stallions we brought with us."

Will blinked at Tye's words. "I'm goin' to do what?" he asked incredulously.

"Ya heard me. Yer goin' to start ridin' the stallions we brought."

"I thought that's what ya said. Why the stallions, and why now?" Will asked, watching his partner and wondering what he was up to now.

Tye sat on the opposite bed and began pulling off his boots. "Ya remember, when we started into Wyoming I told ya I had some other plans to make us some money besides just catchin' wild horses."

"Yeah, I remember," Will said, still looking at Tye suspiciously.

"Well, those plans include ya being able to ride those stallions."

"Do you mind tellin' me how riding those stallions is going to make us money?"

"I'll tell ya when the time's right. Right now, I just want ya to concentrate on yer ridin' skills."

Will shook his head as he pulled off his boots. "Ya sure do like to keep things a mystery, don't ya'?"

"I just figger a young whelp like ya can't handle all the grown-up things in life, so I take care of 'em for ya."

Will smiled as he pulled the covers over him. "That makes me feel real good, knowin' an old-timer like ya is takin' care of me."

"We'll see who feels like an old-timer tomorrow after ya've ridden some of those stallions," Tye said with smug satisfaction.

Will grimaced at the thought but said nothing as he rolled on his side and thought about Becky in the other bedroom. He fell asleep thinking about their future, a large smile on his face.

Chapter Fifteen

The men headed to the corrals the next morning after breakfast. Tye had enlisted Jim and Cullen to help cut out and drive five of the stallions into the small holding corral by the barn.

Once the horses were in the corral, Tye cut one out and moved him into the larger corral. Picking up his lariat, he shook out a loop as he approached the young horse.

The horse Tye had chosen was a large black with a streak of white running down his face and three white stockings. The horse had the powerful look of a stallion about him, and Will looked on with a dry mouth as Tye moved to corner the animal.

The black had moved away from the man approaching him and snorted through his nostrils as he felt the danger about to entrap him. He moved himself into the corner and sought escape, but rather than turning and bolting as most horses would, he turned and faced his enemy, neck bowed, ears laid back, and teeth bared.

Tye approached the animal cautiously, knowing the large horse would attack if he closed in too quickly. When he felt he was at a safe distance, he brought his loop across his body, never taking his eyes from the horse. Suddenly he brought the loop back across his body and over his head, letting it go at precisely the right time. It opened and settled around the horse's head, and Tye pulled the slack in the rope.

The loop tightening around the big stallion's neck had

an immediate effect on him. He reared to his hind feet, shaking his head and pulling against the tightening of the rope.

Tye, expecting the black to react this way, wrapped the rope around one hip and set his feet to hold fast to the end of the rope, not allowing himself to be pulled close to the pawing hooves.

The black fought on his back feet for a few seconds more, then coming to the ground he charged his assailant. Tye moved away at the last moment, letting the large horse rush past him. He held the rope and braced himself for the impact of the jerk he knew he would take when the horse hit the end of the rope.

When it came, it pulled Tye fifteen yards along the dirt of the corral before he managed to turn the animal.

The black was now near the center of the corral where the snubbing post could be used, and Tye stepped forward and wrapped the rope end around the post. The horse was secured with two quick wraps. Tye quickly tied off the rope end, then moved back out of the way to watch the black horse as he fought the rope.

The stallion fought the rope as it continued to shut off his wind. Pulling back with the full force of his weight, he struggled to shake off the villain that had closed around him. It was a battle that could only have one ending. As the rope continued its constricting hold, the horse's air was cut off. Soon the big black was wheezing as he tried to draw air into his lungs. Eventually he gave to the rope, then fought valiantly again, only to have his air closed off again. It was a lesson hard learned, but a necessary one if the horses were to be broken to ride.

With a final struggle against the rope, the stallion walked forward and stood. Tye eased up to the snubbing post and slowly inched his way down the rope toward the big horse. He had taken only a few steps when the black charged him, ears back and teeth bared. Tye moved swiftly out of the way, and the horse went by him, only to be brought up by the rope again.

Tye moved back to the snubbing post and untied the knot in the rope. Then, holding the end of the rope, he eased toward the black horse once again. This time when the horse ran at him, Tye pulled hard on the rope, pulling the horse's head to the post. The black fought for a few seconds, then stood still, trembling, sweat forming on his body.

With the stallion's head held firmly to the post, it was only a matter of minutes until Tye had his back foot tied to a loop around his neck and pulled off the ground.

Tye motioned to Will, and Will picked up his saddle and carried it to the snubbing post. Easing up to the black, he placed the saddle on its back. The horse trembled again but didn't fight as Will cinched the saddle tightly.

"This is going to be the toughest horse ya've ridden. It's going to take yer total concentration and strength to ride him."

Will said nothing. His mouth had gone dry. The thought of mounting this magnificent animal thrilled him as nothing ever had.

Tye blindfolded the black horse, and Will untied the back foot. As Tye eared the horse down, Will stepped easily into the saddle.

"Ready!" he shouted. Tye removed the blindfold and moved away.

The explosion beneath him was like sitting on a keg of dynamite as Will fought to gain control of the black horse. The first lunge snapped him back, causing him to lose his right stirrup and setting him up on the cantle of the saddle. It only took two more powerful jumps before Will was flying through the air. He landed on his feet as he came off and managed to remain upright.

"Ya underestimated him," Tye said as he moved to catch the black.

"I've never felt such strength," Will marveled as he moved in to help Tye corner the horse.

Tye roped the black and was in the process of moving him to the snubbing post when Jim Lansing spoke from the corral fence.

"I've got an easier way to do that if yer interested. I've got a special pen for bucking out horses. It's the one we use to break our colts in."

"Why didn't ya tell us this earlier?" Tye asked, cocking one eye at the man.

"I wanted to watch ya do it your way and see how good ya were." Jim said with laughter in his voice. "Besides that, I wanted Cullen to see what it was like before we got civilized."

Tye shook his head and grinned. "I hope ya got yer money's worth."

"I guess we did. Ya put on quite a show. Now open that gate over there, and we'll run that horse down the alley.

Tye looked around and saw a gate leading into a small pen. Off the pen was an alley that led up to another gate. He could see that when that gate was opened, the horse would be in an enclosure just large enough for him. Another gate came off this enclosure and opened into another corral. A rider could mount his horse in the small pen, then be turned out into the larger corral to ride.

"Where did ya get an idea like that?" Tye asked, studying the construction of the bucking chute.

"I saw one on a big ranch in Colorado. It sure saves a lot of time and hard work."

"I can see where it would," Tye said. "Let's get that horse in there and see if Will can stay on this time."

They worked the horse into the chute and closed the gate behind him. Will climbed the fence behind the horse, then eased himself down into the saddle. He felt the horse quiver as he found his stirrups and took hold of the reins.

"Just nod when yer ready, and we'll open the gate for ya," Jim said.

"Pull yerself down into the saddle, keep your knees into the swells, think about ridin' this bronc. It takes a lot of concentration to keep in the middle of him," Tye warned as he stood by the gate waiting for Will to nod.

Will grabbed the reins tighter in his hands, pressed his knees harder into the swells of the saddle, and nodded his head.

The gate swung open, and the black stood there for the count of three before realizing he'd been freed from the chute. Then he exploded like a charge of dynamite, lunging out and coming down hard on his front feet.

The impact jarred Will's back. As the big horse came to the ground, Will fought to maintain his seat as the horse lifted high into the air, kicking his back legs hard as he did. The impact of coming back to earth was like being hit by a runaway train, Will thought as he watched the horse's head.

Will made a better showing this time, but he lost his seat when the black started a fast turn to the right, then instantly switched directions to the left. Will flew through the air and landed solidly on the ground, feeling the air leave his lungs as he hit.

"Ya were anticipating his moves rather than watching his head. He caught ya with yer guard down. Come on, let's try it again," Tye explained as he reached a hand down to help him up. Will slowly accepted the out-stretched hand and came to his feet.

"How many times I got to ride that devil?" he asked as he dusted his jeans with his hat.

"Till ya do it right, and then till ya do it better."

"Better'n what?" Will asked.

"Better'n anyone else," Tye replied, opening the gate to run the horse back into the chute.

Will rode the black horse two more times before he brought him to a standstill. He had been bucked off into the fence the third time and had bruised his ribs. They hurt now as he rode the black up to the chute. Will let Tye hold the horse's head as he dismounted.

"I'll get ya another one, and we'll see if ya learned anything with this one," Tye said, leading the black away.

Will sank to the ground, leaning against the chute fence.

"I don't know what he has in mind, but if killing me is part of the plan, he's doing a pretty good job of it."

Jim and Cullen laughed at Will's misery.

"I'll tell ya one thing," Jim said to Will. "Yer learning to ride broncs from the best there is. I don't know of anyone who can ride horses the way Tye Garrett does. If he thinks yer worth teachin', then ya must have somethin' workin' for ya. I know a lot of fellas who'd like to have Tye teachin' 'em to ride broncs."

"Yeah," Will grinned, "right now I'm feelin' real lucky."

Tye kept Will working steadily for the next ten days. Each day he would bring in four or five of the stallions they had captured and coach Will on the fine points of riding each horse.

Rebecca slipped away from the house whenever she could to watch Will ride. She loved watching him ride the rough, bucking animals. Her heart seemed to stop each time he came out of the chute and didn't start again until he was safely on the ground. She was proud that he rode so well, and she noticed the improvement as Tye worked with him each day. She was disappointed that they never got to spend any time together alone, but she knew it was impossible to sneak away from Judith Lansing's watchful eye. Besides, Will was so tired by evening he usually ate supper and went directly to bed, leaving no time for them to talk in the evenings. Even though she was frustrated by the lack of time to spend with Will, she loved the Lansings and enjoyed being there. She wondered if she would hate leaving when they left. Thinking about it, she knew she would, but in her heart she knew she would rather be with Will, wherever that might be. She was surprised at her feelings. She had known him only a short time, but her feelings for him had grown stronger and stronger until he occupied her every thought, her every purpose. *This must be love*, she thought, then smiled as she thought about her discovery. *Yes, it is love.*

Will had just finished riding a large gray stallion to a complete standstill. This was the horse that Tye had kept till last. He was the one that would test Will's skill to the ultimate.

The gray stallion was six or seven years old, fully

developed and strong. He stood close to sixteen hands tall and weighed about thirteen hundred pounds.

Will had ridden the last twelve horses without once being thrown. Tye's instructions, coupled with Will's ability, had improved his riding skills to near perfection. He loved the feel of the horses beneath him and loved the rhythm as they tried to free themselves from him. Most of all, he loved the triumph of a successful ride, the surge of adrenaline as he conquered the animal beneath him.

The large gray was standing in the chute, Will's saddle cinched down on his back. Will climbed the fence and eased down on his back, the same as he'd done countless others the last ten days. He pulled his hat down on his head and gripped the reins tightly as he moved his spurs over the points of the horse's shoulders. Then he nodded to Jim to open the gate.

The ride that followed was nothing less than spectacular, as the gray came out of the chute rearing on his back legs. Will held tightly to the reins to hold himself in the saddle. With a mighty lunge, the horse shot high into the air, clearing the top of the chute gate with all four feet. As he crashed back to earth, Will relaxed his body to absorb the impact, but he still felt as if his body were hit by a train as the horse's hooves crashed into the hard, packed earth of the corral. He tensed as he felt the horse bunch for another leap into the air, watching his head all the while. The gray crashed to earth, then bunched himself for another leap, this time turning his feet to the sky and attempting to throw Will off balance. But Will leaned to his left, digging his spur into the horse's side to hold himself in the saddle.

As the gray came to ground again, he went into a swirling spin to the left, then straightened out and jumped right. Will remained in the saddle as if glued there.

The entire household had turned out to watch this ride. Rebecca stood on the fence shouting encouragement to Will as he rode the gray stallion.

Judith Lansing watched between the fence railings, a

handkerchief covering her mouth and nose. She had twice tried to pull Rebecca from the fence, fearing the girl would come to harm should the horse come her way, but Rebecca ignored her pleas and continued to stand on the railing cheering Will.

Jim and Cullen Lansing yelled encouragement to Will as the horse bucked across the corral.

Tye stood smiling as he watched Will ride. He shouted no words of encouragement, for none were needed. Will was making a picture-perfect ride. Tye reflected briefly on the horse Will was riding. It was without a doubt the roughest of the lot. He wondered if he himself would have been able to ride the animal, but it didn't matter. If Will could ride the horse, he could ride about anything with hair on it, and that meant he'd accomplished what he had set out to do.

Will watched the gray's head as it lined out to buck in a straight line across the corral. Then instantly his head came around, and he switched ends in mid-jump. But Will was ready and braced himself for the switch, digging his knees into the swells and leaning with the horse.

The battle had been going on for fifteen minutes, and Will felt very little give in the big horse as he continued to watch its head. He wondered how long his strength would last. He didn't feel tired, but neither did the horse. Which one would give out first? Right now he felt the adrenaline flowing through his body, and the excitement of the ride was still with him. Then a funny thought came to him: what if the horse never did stop bucking? What if they just kept on going till the sun went down and were going at it when the sun came up? A smile came to his lips as he thought about it, and he raked the gray once more with his spurs.

Another ten minutes went by before Will felt the gray slacken a little. He spurred the horse harder, making him expend his energy.

The gray reacted to the spurs and jumped into the air, letting out a squall and rolling his eyes. As he came to earth, Will jabbed him again, causing the horse to jump forward in a lunge. This time when he came to earth, Will held his spurs, and the big gray stopped, head up and breathing hard. Will touched him lightly with his spurs, and the big horse leaped forward, bucking twice, then loped around the corral. Will pulled him to a stop, then plow-reined him around to the right, touching him lightly with his right spur. The big horse jumped, coming around, but not bucking. Will eased up on the rein, then pulled him around to the left. The big horse responded to Will's guidance, and he rode him around the corral twice, reining him first to the right, then to the left. Finally he rode him up to Rebecca and sat smiling at her.

"What do ya think about him?" he asked her, excitement in his voice.

"He's beautiful!" she exclaimed, reaching up to stroke his nose. The large horse snorted as she reached up, but he didn't move as she touched his velvety nose.

"He's going to be my wedding present to ya," Will said, watching Rebecca's face.

She looked up at him, astonishment written on her face. She opened her mouth to speak, but nothing came out as she continued to look from the horse to Will.

Will smiled down at her, loving the surprised look on her face. He smiled at her once more, then turned the gray and rode over to where Tye was standing.

"How'd I do, partner?"

"I once told ya ya'd be better'n me when I got through with ya, and by golly you are, boy," Tye said smiling up at him. Will grinned down at Tye, feeling like he'd just won the grand prize at the county fair.

"Now we're gonna put that skill to work," Tye said, looking up into Will's face. "Day after tomorrow, ya and me are gonna start sellin' horses."

"Why do I need to ride these broncs to sell horses? We gonna break everything we sell?"

"Nope, not all of 'em, only those they pay us to break," Tye said.

"I reckon ya're still not going to tell me what you have

in mind," Will said, grinning at Tye.

"Ya'll more'n likely find out day after tomorrow. We're heading over to the Double A Ranch. Lon Taylor was one of my regular customers. I told him I would see him when we got back with the horses. We'll take some of the horses with us when we go, just to show him what we got."

Chapter Sixteen

Will sat in the easy chair listening to the idle conversations between Tye, Jim, and Cullen. His mind was wandering as he gazed out the large window of the Lansing's living room at the Montana countryside. Since his ride this morning, the entire family and crew had taken the day off and made it a day of rest.

Will was thankful for the respite. The last few weeks had been grueling, but he felt good in spite of it all.

As he gazed out the window, Becky caught his attention. She was walking by the row of trees at the side of the house. He looked closely, expecting to see Mrs. Lansing or Rosa close by, but a quick glance into the kitchen showed both women busy preparing the noon meal.

Will casually stood up and, without seeming to be in a hurry, walked to the door leading outside.

"Where ya headed, Will?" Cullen asked.

"Nowhere in particular," Will replied. "Just thought I might take me a little walk and stretch my legs."

"Sounds like a good idea. I think I'll take a little walk, too," Cullen said, rising to his feet.

"Uh, I'd really like to be alone if it's all right with ya," Will said, trying to sound casual about it.

"Ya sit down here with us, Cullen," Jim Lansing said. "Will don't need ya along right now." He smiled at Cullen, and Will saw Cullen return the smile. He turned and went out the door, his face red as he realized what Cullen had been up to.

Will walked down to the row of trees where he'd last

seen Rebecca. She wasn't by the trees, and he had to look for several seconds before he located her. She had continued walking past the row of trees and was following a small trail that led into the woods. Will figured it was a game trail.

He started to call her but realized that if he did, they would hear him at the house, and Judith Lansing might come out to investigate. So he followed her path, walking hurriedly to catch her.

Rebecca had just entered the tree-covered area when she heard footsteps behind her. She wheeled, fear showing on her face as the thought of her capture by the Sioux Indians came back to her. She clenched her fist and swung instinctively as she came around.

Will ducked the lethal swing and grabbed Rebecca as she fell forward from the force of the swing.

"Does this mean the engagement's off?" he asked as she looked up, a startled expression on her face.

"Will!" she said, relief flooding through her as she slumped against him. "Why did ya sneak up on me like that? I thought ya were an Indian or somethin'."

"Sorry. I didn't want to call out to ya. I was afraid Mrs. Lansing would hear and come tearing out of the house to save ya."

Rebecca laughed. "She's not an ogre, Will. As a matter of fact, she sent me out here."

"She did?" Will asked, not believing he'd heard right.

Rebecca laughed again. "Yes, she did. She knew ya'd come out after me."

"She was right. I was beginning to wonder if I'd ever get to spend any time alone with ya."

"Well, we're alone now. Would you like to walk with me?" Rebecca asked, smiling at him.

"Yes. I'd like that very much, but first there's something else I want to do," Will said, looking into her eyes.

"What's that?" she asked, smiling coyly.

"This," he said, taking her in his arms and kissing her deeply.

Rebecca melted against him. She had longed for this every day since he'd first kissed her on the porch of her parents' house. She felt her heart race as he pulled her closer to him and his mouth covered hers. He kissed her longingly, and she felt the passion of his kiss as it carried her along on a tide of emotions she'd never felt before.

Will forced himself to push away from her. His emotions raced as he looked at her, yearning for her, yet not totally comfortable with his feelings.

Rebecca's breathing was starting to slow as she stood there watching Will. "Let's take that walk now," she said, taking his hand and leading him along the path.

"I think that's a good idea," Will said, trying to bring his emotions under control.

They walked along the wooded trail, talking of the many events that had taken place and the things that were yet to come. They returned to the trail leading to the house. Walking hand in hand, they strolled along lost in each other's company for the moment.

"I know ya want to wait until October, but it's only July and I'm not sure I can wait that long," Will said as they approached the house.

"I'm not sure I can either," Rebecca confessed. "When I said I wanted to wait for October, it was really an excuse to give us more time, to make sure we were doing the right thing. But I don't need that excuse any more. If ya want to get married sooner, I'm ready."

Will looked at Rebecca, a slow smile spreading over his face.

"I'm ready right now. I was ready the night we helped ya escape from the Sioux, but I want you to be sure. Are ya?"

Rebecca looked into his eyes, her arms going around his waist.

"I've never been as sure of anything as I am of this. I can't wait to be Mrs. Will Paxton."

"As soon as I find out where a preacher is, we'll be married," Will declared, holding her tight.

"Make it soon. I don't want to have to wait too long," Rebecca said, smiling up into his face.

"I will. I promise!"

* * *

Two days later Will and Tye rode out of the Lansing place before daylight. They led six of the young horses they'd broken to saddle. Their destination was the Double A Ranch ten miles to the north. As they rode, Tye talked of his plans for their ranch in Texas.

"I want to head down that way before winter sets in. I figger that gives us about two months to sell these horses and prepare for the trip."

"Is that going to be a problem?" Will asked.

"No, it shouldn't be," Tye responded, "but we're still going to need more money than these horses will bring if we're going to get started right."

"How much do ya reckon we're gonna need?" Will asked.

"I'd like to have about twenty thousand. But if we can put together fifteen, I figger we can pull it off."

"I hear there are wild cattle in Texas," Will said. "Are ya plannin' on catchin' some of 'em?"

"Those are my plans. The demand for beef since the war has provided an opportunity for men who are willing to take a risk. Some of 'em built empires by rounding up wild cattle from the breaks and trailing them to the Kansas railheads. There aren't as many cattle still roaming free, but there are plenty if a man is willing to work hard rounding up enough for a herd. We can round up some cows and heifers and use them to start a herd. We can sell any bulls we find and use the money to buy more cows."

"What about the mares we're keeping?" Will asked.

"I figger where there's cattle, there's always going to be a need for horses. I want us to be the ones to supply those horses."

"How much land do ya plan on acquiring?" Will asked.

"I already have fifteen sections of land that belonged to my family. They were part of a land grant given to my grandfather by the government of Mexico. I want at least that many more. Land in Texas isn't like this land. It takes more acres to run cows down there than it does up here."

"That's a lot of land," Will said. "How do ya plan on the two of us taking care of that much land?"

"I reckon we'll just have to hire us some help," Tye said with a grin. "That's one of the reasons we need money."

They rode into the Double A headquarters leading the six horses. Will was still thinking about what Tye had said and the plans that were being laid.

Tye pulled up in front of the large barn where the blacksmith was in the process of shoeing one of the ranch horses.

"Is Lon Taylor around?" Tye asked, stepping down from his horse.

"He's around here someplace. Try the corral around back. They're workin' some horses back there."

They tied their horses to the hitching post in front of the barn and walked around back. They found three men working a horse on the ground. The horse had been roped and thrown and his legs tied to keep him from kicking the men as they worked to doctor a large gash on his neck.

Tye and Will stood back and waited until the men were through with the horse and turned him loose. One of them looked up and saw Will and Tye standing there. He turned and said something to one of the other men, who looked up and started toward them with a grin on his face. Will took this to be Lon Taylor.

Lon Taylor walked up to Tye, the grin still on his face. "Well, I'll be! I figgered the Indians would have yer scalp hanging in some teepee by now."

"I can't believe yer lack of faith, Lon. I told ya I'd be back with some horses to sell. Lon, I'd like ya to meet Will Paxton. He's helping with the horses."

Will shook hands with the man, noting that Tye didn't introduce him as his partner.

"Ya still in the market for those horses I promised ya?" Tye asked.

Lon looked back at the men and the horses, then motioning with his thumb, said, "If we don't get these mountain lions under control, I'm not goin' to have any horses or cattle left. I've lost six horses and twenty head of calves in the last two months."

"That's tough," Tye said. "Have ya thought about hiring professional hunters to get rid of 'em?"

"Yeah, as a matter of fact, me and some of the other ranchers hired three just the other day. They've killed two already, but that's only the beginning. By my calculations, there's probably between twenty to thirty of the large cats roaming the mountain areas around here. I hope those three hurry and kill 'em. I'm not sure which I distrust most, mountain lions or those hunters. They're a bad lot, I'm here to tell ya."

"Most of 'em I've seen are. Ya wanna look at some of the horses we brought back with us?" Tye asked, changing the subject.

"Ya bring some with ya?" Lon asked, surprised.

"Brought six with us so's you could get a flavor of the type horses they are," Tye said.

"Let's look at 'em. I want to see what kind of horses they got down there in Wyomin'."

They walked back to the front of the barn where the horses were tied. Lon walked around them, looking them over with a keen eye.

"These the best of the lot?" he asked.

"Nope, the others are just as good, some are even better. These are just a few that's been broke," Tye said.

"What ya askin' for 'em?

"Forty if they ain't broke, fifty-five if they are," Tye said.

"That your bottom dollar, or is there room to do some horse tradin'?" Lon asked, smiling at Tye.

"Ya know me Lon, I always quote you my best offer. Saves both of us time, and nobody feels like they got out-traded."

"How many ya got broke?"

"About twenty head," Tye replied.

"I'll take all twenty, and I'll take twenty of 'em that ain't broke if they're as good as these."

"They are," Tye said. "When do ya want 'em?"

"Can you have 'em to me day after tomorrow? I want to have 'em ready by fall gatherin'."

"We'll deliver 'em," Tye said. Then with a thoughtful look, he asked, "Ya got any bad ones that cain't be ridden?"

"Boy howdy, do I!" Lon said, chuckling. "I got one that's a real humdinger. He's managed to buck off every one of my hands so far. I got him in with a bunch of horses I bought a couple of months ago. Ya wouldn't want to do a little horse tradin' would you?"

"I'm afraid I'm not in the market for that kind of horse right now, but I might try to ride him for ya when I bring yer other horses over."

"I'm not even sure ya could ride this one, Tye." Lon said, his face serious.

"Ya want to put a little wager on that?" Tye asked.

"I might," Lon said, smiling at Tye.

"Well, if you do, I'll have a go at him," Tye said, matching the smile.

"We'll see day after tomorrow when ya bring the other horses."

"Why don't you have yer hands hang around that day. Maybe they'd like to see the fun. We might even have ourselves a little bucking contest," Tye said with the hint of a smile.

"Ya gone to showboatin'?" Lon asked.

"Na, nothin' like that. It's just that I enjoy a good contest, that's all." Tye's face was blank and innocent.

Lon Taylor looked suspiciously at Tye, then shrugged his shoulders. "We'll see," was all he would say.

Once they were away from the ranch and out of distance where they couldn't be heard, Will pulled his horse up beside Tye's. "Ya gonna ride that horse?" he asked.

"Nope. Ya are," Tye replied with a grin.

"That's what I suspected," Will said smiling. "Ya sure

set the bait back there. Ya reckon they'll bite?"

"Ya can count on it. If there's two things I know about cowhands, they love a chance to compete, and they love a chance to bet."

* * *

Will and Tye spent the rest of the afternoon and the next day riding to some of the small ranches in the area. They sold another sixty head of unbroken horses at forty dollars a head, with a promise they would deliver them in the next few days.

The day they were to take the horses to the Double A they were on the trail before daylight. It turned out to be a family event with Jim and Cullen helping with the horses and Ramón driving the team and wagon. Rebecca, Rosa, and Judith Lansing all rode in the wagon. Although Rebecca had argued that she wanted to ride horseback, Judith Lansing had finally convinced her it was proper for her to ride with Judith in the wagon.

They had packed a large lunch in the basket, and Judith had worked all day the day before baking pies and such to take to Lon's wife, Meredith.

The caravan reached the Double A shortly after sunrise. Tye had purposely planned it that way so the hands would still be around the headquarters when they arrived.

Tye had let Jim and Cullen in on his plan, but had purposely excluded Judith and Rebecca, stating that once women started talking there was no telling what they might say to one another. Will, though, had managed to sneak away with Rebecca on one of their walks and had told her of their plans, vowing her to silence. Her excitement at what was taking place came close to equaling Will's, and she smiled knowingly at him each time their eyes met.

Once the horses were corralled and the Taylors and Lansings had greeted one another, Lon had Ramón drive the women to the house.

The men watched as the wagon rolled away, Lon Taylor smiling as it went. "I reckon there'll be more gigglin' and cacklin' goin' on up there than there's been in a coon's age. I'm glad ya brought them gals along. Ma's been hankerin' fer some women to talk to."

They walked back to the corral where the horses had been put, and Lon walked in, surveying each animal, never commenting but studying each one carefully. He finished his inspection, then walked up to where Tye was standing. "I reckon ya was right. These are as good as the others ya brought. We'll go up to the house in a spell, and I'll get ya yer money."

They moved away from the corral and were walking around the barn when one of the hands came from the bunkhouse toward them. Tye stopped and waited for the man to come up to him.

"Howdy, Tye," the man said as he extended his hand.

"Johnny," Tye said in greeting, shaking his hand. "I thought ya was workin' for the Bar OM Ranch."

"I was until a couple of months ago. I got the itch to travel a little, so I packed up and headed west till I run outa money. Then I come back here and hired on with Mr. Taylor. I think this time I'll stay put."

Lon Taylor smiled and said, "Yeah, until he gets a little money set aside. Then he'll be gone again."

Johnny Day smiled and looked down, kicking the ground with the toe of his boot. Looking up at Tye he asked, "Ya gonna try to ride ol' Widow Maker?"

Tye looked sharply at Lon Taylor. "Widow Maker?" he asked, suddenly suspicious.

Lon chuckled and said, "That's the name they gave that horse when they found out ya was gonna attempt to ride it. As far as I know, he ain't killed no one that was married."

Tye looked at Lon and saw the grin on his face. Then he looked at Will and saw the color was slowly coming back. He started talking to keep eyes away from Will.

"Where is this horse that's got y'all so buffaloed?"

Johnny pointed in the direction of the barn. "We got him in the corral by hisself. He's so mean we can't put no other horses in there with him. He durn near killed four or five of 'em so far. We been kept busy tryin' to keep the poor devils alive."

Will smiled at that, remembering the horses that were being doctored the day he and Tye were here. Clearly Johnny was trying to build the horse's reputation to hedge any bet he might be making.

As they walked to the corral, cowboys started ambling over. It looked to Will as if all the hands had stayed at the headquarters. He counted fifteen cowboys, not including the blacksmith and Lon Taylor.

Tye climbed the corral fence and looked at the lone horse standing there. Will looked through the railings at a dark brown horse with black mane and tail. The horse stood looking at the people on the fence, his eyes rolling. He was broad across the chest. with powerful withers. He had a thickly muscled neck and strong, powerful hindquarters. Will thought he was the kind of horse any cowhand would like to have in his string.

"He don't look like much of a horse to me," Tye said.

Lon Taylor cast a sideways glance at him and said, "I thought ya was a good judge of horseflesh, Garrett."

"I don't mean he ain't a good-lookin' animal. I just don't think he looks like much of a bucker."

Several cowhands started laughing at the statement.

"He can buck all right," one of the cowboys said. "Ain't nobody been able to ride him yet, and there's been some pretty good bronc riders try."

"I still say he don't look that bad," Tye said, looking back at the horse.

"Well, why don't ya try him and see," another hand shouted.

"I don't know," Tye said thoughtfully. "I thought you had a real bad one here. I bet this young-un here could ride that horse," he said pointing to Will.

This brought a round of laughter from all the hands. Even Lon Taylor chuckled. "I'll bet ya twenty dollars ya can't ride that bronc," said a cowboy standing by the fence.

"I'll bet ya thirty," another cowboy shouted.

"Wait a minute," Tye said holding up his hands. "Y'all want to wager, then I'll make it interesting. I've got five hundred dollars here that says this youngster here can ride that horse."

The silence that followed was intense as all the hands looked at Tye as if he'd lost his mind. Then at once they began talking, each one pulling money out of his pockets, pooling their dollars.

"We've only got two hundred ninety five. Will you cover that, Mr. Taylor?"

"I'll cover the other two hundred and five," he said.

Tye looked at the rancher in surprise, but said nothing.

Will's mouth had gone dry. He looked again at the horse, then at the hands.

"If I ride him," he said to Lon Taylor. "I get to keep him." It was a statement, rather than a question.

"That's fair," Lon agreed. "I don't reckon yer gonna ride him though, so I ain't riskin' nothin'."

Will smiled to himself. He went to get his saddle while one of the Double A hands walked into the corral with a rope.

Chapter Seventeen

The Double A cowboy had the bay horse snubbed and a hackamore on his head when Will returned with his saddle. Tye walked into the corral with him.

"Remember what ya learned. This is a stout horse, but he ain't nothin' compared to the gray ya rode the other day. Don't let him pull ya down over the front of the saddle. I figure that's what makes him hard to ride. He has so much strength he pulls a fella out of the saddle. Give him his head enough to keep him from jerkin' ya, but not enough so's ya don't have a good hold. Ya'll have to learn him quick."

Tye was talking in a low voice as they walked through the corral. He stopped as soon as they were in hearing range of the cowhand.

Will eased up to the horse and set the saddle on his back. The big horse remained calm as Will reached beneath him and pulled his cinch, evidence of the number of times the horse had been tried. The cowhand holding him grinned and said, "He's gentle as a baby while you're saddlin' him, but once ya get aboard he's like a keg o' dynamite. Who's yer next of kin so's we can notify 'em?" He chuckled at his own humor.

Will just glanced at him and said, "I'll sell him to ya when I get through with him." Then grabbing the hackamore rein and saddle horn, he stepped up on the horse.

The cowboy, stepped back and ran to the corral fence, climbing to the top to get a good view.

For a brief moment the big bay stood there, not moving

a muscle. Then Will felt him bunch and tightened his legs against the swells of the saddle. The next instant it was as if the world had exploded beneath him. The bay lunged forward, springing into the air and driving his head between his legs. The force of the big horse almost pulled the reins from Will's hands. Only his quick reflexes prevented him from being pulled over the front of the saddle. He grasped the reins tightly and held to the horse's head, remembering the advice Tye had given him.

As the bay's big hooves met with the hard-packed dirt of the corral, Will relaxed his body but instantly tensed as he watched the horse's head come around to the right. Knowing the horse was going to reverse himself in a twisting motion, he dug his right heel into the horse's side and tightened his knee against the swell of the saddle.

When the reverse came, the speed with which the large horse moved surprised Will. He knew he was going to have to use all his skills to stay astride the horse until he could wear him down.

Rebecca had heard the shouts and yells coming from the corral and rushed outside, not hearing Judith Lansing call to her as she went. She hurried to the corral and climbed to the top rail, heedless of the dress she was wearing. The cowboys sitting on the fence looked with shocked expressions, but she paid no attention as she shouted words of encouragement to Will.

Will rode hard for the next fifteen minutes, learning the horse's maneuvers and adjusting to each. The big horse was using all his tricks to loose the rider on his back, but Will stuck to him, raking him each time he jumped.

Will knew the horse was tiring. He'd known for the last few minutes that he was going to ride it to the finish and that he wouldn't buck much longer. He had been hard to ride at first, but once Will had learned how to use the horse's own power against him, the rest had been an easy ride.

With nothing left, the bay stopped, sweat dripping from his flanks, his breath coming in large wheezes. Will touched his spurs to him, and he balked. Will dug in a little harder, and the bay stepped forward two steps and halted again. This time Will dug his spurs in hard, and the horse lunged into a running lope.

Will pulled up at the corral gate and stepped off the tired horse. Pulling his saddle from its back, he laid it on the ground, then turned to Lon Taylor and asked, "Have ya got a halter I can use? I'll return it in a few days."

Lon stared at Will. "Son, ya just cost me two hundred and five dollars and a horse, and now ya want to borrow a halter?"

Will looked at the rancher and saw a smile slowly spread across his face. "After the ride ya just made, I'll give ya a halter. I've never seen anything like it. Where did ya learn to ride like that?" Then looking at Tye his grinned widened. "No need to answer that. I reckon we been set up."

Tye protested, "I never claimed the boy couldn't ride. Ya boys just took it for granted that he couldn't."

Johnny Day came up to Tye, holding out the money from the other hands. Then turning to Will he said, "That was some kind of ride you put on there. Ya earned your money."

Turning to Tye, he said, "Yer a cool operator. There wasn't a one of us thought ya could ride that horse, much less the youngster. Ya reeled us in like suckers."

"I just gave ya enough rope to hang yerselves," Tye said, smiling at Johnny.

"One thing's for sure," Johnny said. "We'll be talkin' about this for months to come. It don't make it so hard to lose when you see someone as good as Will here make a ride like that."

"I'm glad there's no hard feelings," Tye said. He shook hands with Johnny, and the rest of the hands came by shaking Will's hand, slapping him on the back and telling him what a great ride he'd made. All the attention had Will blushing, but at the same time it was a great feeling to be accepted by men such as these. It hadn't been that long since he was just a cook's helper longing to be like them.

He looked at Tye and shook his head as he thought again about how this man had changed his life.

The ride back to the Lansing's ranch was a joyous one as Cullen recounted Will's ride time and again. The bay was tied to the back of the wagon while Will rode alongside. He and Rebecca smiled at each other each time one would catch the other glancing their way. Tye smiled all the way home, basking in the glory of his successful planning.

The next two weeks kept Will and Tye busy, delivering horses and riding to other ranches to sell more.

When they had sold and delivered to all the ranches in the area, Tye announced it was time to move out. They still had a hundred and fifty horses left. Tye reserved seventy-five of these to build their herd when they reached Texas, leaving seventy-five horses to sell along the way.

Judith Lansing cried the night before they left, promising she'd have Jim ride to the small town of Three Forks and bring back a preacher so they could have the wedding there. Will and Rebecca expressed their gratitude, saying how they'd like nothing better than to have their wedding at her home, but if they waited any longer they might not make it over the mountains before snowfall. They were cutting it close as it was.

It was still dark the next morning as they saddled their horses and prepared to leave. Judith Lansing cried as she hugged each of them. Tye and Will shook hands with Jim and Cullen, thanking them for their help and hospitality and promising them the same if they ever got down Texas way.

Rebecca hugged Jim and Cullen. Cullen blushed red, then blushed even more as Will, Tye, and Jim laughed at his discomfort. Rebecca scolded each of them, but the laughter in her eyes softened the chastening.

With shouts of good-bye and tears flowing from the women, they started the herd of horses moving. Rebecca smiled through her tears, thankful to be on the trail again but unaware of what lay ahead.

* * *

They had been on the trail for a day and a half, following the Yellowstone River. They would follow the Yellowstone until they came to the Powder River. Then they would turn south to Wyoming.

Tye was riding point, leading the pack horse and two other horses, one being the old, scarred mare, since most of the herd still looked to her as the leader. Free from the pack horse, Rebecca was able to help hold the horses in a herd. Tye was keeping them mainly to open country, avoiding wooded areas when possible and making it easier to keep the herd bunched. Will had put Rebecca on the river side because it was easier to keep the horses from wandering away on that side. If one did wander, it couldn't go far. Locating it and bringing it back to the herd was the hardest part. Will, on the other hand, was working the side away from the river, keeping the horses out of the wooded areas.

By now the horses were fairly well trail-broken, and, except for the occasional one that wandered away to find grazing, the herd stayed bunched, following closely behind the old mare.

By noon of the second day, they were riding through a thickly wooded area. Will and Rebecca were working hard to keep the herd bunched, preventing any from straying. Will was working his way around a dapple-gray mare that had left the herd to find better grazing. Working his way among the trees and undergrowth had moved him out of sight of the herd before he managed to get around the mare and turn her back in the direction of the other horses. He turned the mare back and headed her toward the herd, knowing her instincts would take her back to them.

Will was watching the rump of the mare moving before him, but his mind was on other things. The leisurely pace they were taking and the moving of the herd, already well trail-broke, gave him time for thinking and planning. He was thinking of Rebecca when he looked up and noticed the herd had stopped. He pulled his horse up and listened. He thought he had heard voices. He sat still, the gray mare moving back to the herd. He was in the dense woods, covered by thick trees. Before him was a small clearing through which the mare had just passed. He could see the horse herd about a hundred yards past the clearing. All the horses were stopped, heads up and ears forward.

Will looked around for Rebecca but saw no sign of her. His view was limited by the dense growth around him. He couldn't see Tye or the horses he was leading.

Suddenly Will's body went stiff as he heard Tye's voice raised to a near shout. "I suggest ya let her go and move away."

Will heard a reply, but he couldn't make out the words.

Slipping quietly from his horse, Will knelt, pulling off his boots and spurs, knowing he would have to move quietly.

Moving slowly, careful not to step on any branch or twig, Will slipped through the wooded area using the trees for cover. He moved parallel to the herd, circling around to come up behind whoever was there.

Will kept his pistol holstered, wanting his hands free for the moment. He'd left his rifle in his saddle boot, knowing there would be no chance to use it in the dense woods. His only chance was to come up from behind and surprise whoever was there, but what about Rebecca? He knew they had her. Tye's warning had been clear. He couldn't shoot if they were holding her.

He moved cautiously now, the voices growing louder. He could make out some of the words now.

"Nice herd ya got there, but not near as nice as this here filly." Will heard Rebecca's muffled cry and felt his blood chill.

"Where's yer dish boy? Don't tell me you got tired of baby sittin' and got rid of him." Will tensed as he heard the voice and the words spoken. It was Slade. How had he found them? He couldn't have been trailing them, or he'd know Will was here. He must have come upon them by accident, but how did he get the drop on Tye? The answer came to him as soon as the question formed in his mind: Rebecca. They had somehow gotten Rebecca, then used her to get Tye.

"Yer making a big mistake, Slade. Ya know what will happen to ya if ya harm that girl?"

Slade laughed, and Will felt himself shiver as he heard the sound. Old memories flooded back to him.

"Ain't nobody gonna do nothin', 'cause nobody's gonna know. By the time they discover yer bodies, there won't be nothin' left but a few bones. But first we're gonna have us some fun. I've waited a long time to get even with ya, and now I'm gonna make up for the waitin'. Yer gonna die real slow, Garrett. But first yer gonna get to watch what happens to yer woman here." Slade laughed again, and Will heard Rebecca scream.

It was all Will could do to keep himself from drawing his pistol and charging into the clearing. He willed himself to think. He had to get behind them. He started working his way through the trees, stepping carefully, making himself concentrate on the ground before him. He heard the voices but ignored the words. He was now even with them and, peering out from the brush, took in the scene before him.

Slade was holding Rebecca by the hair, twisting her golden tresses in his large, dirty hand. Will had never before felt such an urge to kill, not only kill, but inflict pain, such pain that the man before him would beg him to kill him.

Will noticed Slade had grown a beard. It was matted and dirty, as were his clothes, giving him an even more sinister look than Will remembered.

Tye was on his knees, blood dripping from his nose and a cut on his lip. Two other men stood beside him, and as Will watched they dragged him to his feet. As they held Tye between them, Slade hit him, first in the stomach, then catching him on the chin with an uppercut and snapping his head back. Slade had held on to Rebecca's hair, using his free hand to beat Tye and making Rebecca scream each time he jerked her hair.

Will turned his face from the scene, feeling sick to his stomach. He had to move. He had to do something before they killed Tye. He turned and started working his way through the woods. He had picked a spot where he would be behind them. His brain worked frantically for a plan, something that would move Rebecca away from Slade. He needed a diversion, but what? He could think of nothing that would reduce the risk to all their lives.

Will moved stealthily through the trees to the point he had chosen. He had chosen this particular place because it was directly behind the group and above them. It had taken half an hour since he'd seen Slade beating Tye to reach this spot. He was well-hidden by the dense trees, but he could still look down on them without being seen himself.

As he peered through the trees, he saw Tye sitting on the ground, his back against a tree, his face bloody and swollen. He at first appeared to be unconscious, but as Will watched, he saw him open one eye and look about. The three men, who were standing several feet away from him, seemed to be arguing about something. Rebecca was still being held by Slade, only now he had her in front of him, holding her with his arm across her throat. Will trembled with rage as he saw the fear in her eyes, but he quickly brought it under control. Now was not the time to lose his head. He had to think, had to wait for his chance. If only Rebecca were out of the way. He could move in on the three and have them covered, but as long as she was held by Slade, he could do nothing.

Will's hiding spot was thirty feet away from the group of people. He knew he would have to move closer. If a chance came to catch Slade off balance, he had to be close enough to take advantage of it.

He moved forward, his pistol still in its holster. He needed his hands free to move closer, sometimes crawling on the ground to maneuver around a low-hanging branch or undergrowth. Keeping himself close to the ground, he moved to within fifteen feet of the three men. He could hear their voices clearly now, but he couldn't see them because of the knoll in front of him. From his position he could see Tye leaning against the tree.

"I say we kill 'im now, take the horses and the girl, and

get outa here," one of the men was saying.

"Yeah, I agree with Hank," the other man said. "If we hang around here, someone's liable to come along."

"There ain't nobody comin' this way," Slade shouted. "And we ain't killin' Garrett till I'm good and ready. He ain't come close to bein' paid for what he done to me. As fer the little lady here, well, we may just have ourselves a little party and let the mighty Tye Garrett watch."

Slade's laughter sent chills through Will, and he glanced over to where Tye was leaning against the tree. Will went rigid as he looked at Tye's face. Tye was looking directly at him. As Will looked at him, Tye shifted his eyes to the ground ten feet away, Will followed Tye's line of vision and saw what he was looking at. There in the dirt lay Tye's pistol. They must have had him toss it away and forgotten about it. As Will looked back to Tye, he saw a barely perceptible nod. What did it mean? Could Tye get to the pistol if a fight started. Will nodded back, then moved back where he could watch the three men.

Slade was holding Rebecca by the arm now and was giving orders to the other two. Will moved to position himself where he could be in the clearing in two steps. Still hidden by the trees, he watched as the two men with Slade moved to Tye's horse. He watched as they removed the saddlebags tied to Tye's saddle and brought them back to the spot where Slade and Rebecca stood. As the man holding the saddlebags untied the leather straps binding the flap, Will saw Slade relax his grip on Rebecca's wrist. She looked at the hand holding her, then looked around. Was she looking for him, or was she looking for a place to run? Then her eyes stopped. She was looking in his direction. Did she see him? Then the thought came to him. Somehow Tye had let her know.

Will watched as her eyes searched the woods where he was standing. The men were concentrating on the saddlebags, their attention momentarily drawn from Rebecca. Will held his breath, then moved his head. Rebecca's eyes widened slightly as he looked into them, knowing she had seen him. If only she could do something to distract them. The thought had hardly entered his head when Rebecca turned back to look at the men holding her hostage. It was at this moment that Slade reached into the bag and pulled out the money Will and Tye had earned from selling the horses.

With a shout, he pulled the money from the bag, staring at it with a triumphant look in his eyes.

Seeing his attention diverted from her, Rebecca wrenched her arm free with such force it pulled Slade off balance, almost causing him to lose his footing and making him drop the money.

Free from Slade's grip, Rebecca ran toward the horse herd, drawing the men's attention away from Will's position.

Slade regained his footing, cursing as he did. His eyes burned with anger as he came around. He was reaching for the pistol at his side when Will's voice stopped him. "Don't do it, Slade."

Will had stepped from the woods and now stood directly behind Slade. His pistol was still holstered. He knew he could have opened fire and killed all three as they stood with their backs to him, but he couldn't do it. He knew he would be no better than they were if he allowed himself to bushwhack them.

Slade stopped in midstride, his hand poised over the butt of his pistol. Then slowly he turned, his lips curling into the sneering grin Will had seen so many times.

"Well, well, what have we here? A dish boy that thinks he's a man now. Looks like I'm goin' to get to kill two birds with one stone."

Will stood facing Slade, his feet spread slightly apart. He felt his heart beating, the steady rhythm pulsing in his ears. He watched Slade's eyes, knowing any move he made would show there first. He felt calm, his arms tingling slightly as he relaxed his muscles. He was going to kill Slade. It didn't matter if Slade got a slug into him first, he was going to kill him. It was the only way he could save

Rebecca and Tye. With Slade dead, the other two would cut and run. If he got Slade without going down, he would go for the man on his right next. He didn't have time to think about Tye. He knew he was hurt, probably hurt bad. Rebecca was out of harm's way, and all he had to do was kill Slade.

Slade's smile disappeared from his face, replaced by a sneer that made him look even more evil. His feet were spread slightly, his right hand relaxed at his side. "I'm gonna enjoy killin' ya, boy. Then I'm gonna kill yer guardian angel over there. I missed ya both in that hotel, but I won't miss this time."

Will saw the slightest twitch in Slade's eye, and then he heard the crashing sound of gunfire. He saw the surprised look on Slade's face and the red stain spreading over the front of his shirt. Then gunfire sounded again, and Slade jerked, straightened on his toes, and fell backward, his gun barrel still in his holster. Two more shots rang out, and Will whirled about. The two men with Slade were on the ground, one clutching his shoulder, the other shot through the head. He looked at the gun in his hand, the barrel still smoking. He didn't remember drawing, or pulling the trigger.

He looked around. Tye lay on the ground, a pistol clutched in his hand. He heard the sound of running feet and swung around in time to catch Rebecca as she dropped a rifle and threw herself into his arms, crying and laughing at the same time. Will held her close for a few moments, then gently pushed her away. He walked over to where Slade lay, still alive, but barely. He looked up at Will, his face a mask of confusion.

"Ya beat me. A stinkin' cook's helper beat me. How'd ya do it?"

Will looked down at the dying man. He felt no sorrow for what he had done. "Ya made a mistake by thinking I was just a cook's helper. I've been over the mountain and done some growin' since we last saw each other."

Slade looked into Will's face. He fought to say something, but his eyes closed as the last breath from his body mixed with the mountain air.

Will took a last look at Slade, then reached down and picked up the dead man's gun. He looked around, found the pistols belonging to the other two, tucked them into his waist band, and then he walked over to the wounded man, sitting on the ground.

The man groaned and looked up as Will approached.

"My arm's busted. Ya got to help me."

Will looked down at the man in disgust.

"Mister, ya were going to kill us. Ya beat my partner, and ya were plannin' to harm the woman I'm gonna marry. So what makes ya think ya got any help comin' from me? Tell me why I shouldn't shoot ya and leave ya for the buzzards."

The man looked into Will's eyes, then turned away as he saw the anger burning in them.

"Where are yer horses?" Will asked.

"Down by the river, about a hundred yards. They're tied in a clearing over there," he said, motioning with his good hand.

"Ya sit real still while I check on my partner. Ya make one move, and ya'll be joining the other two."

Will walked over to where Rebecca had Tye leaning against a tree. His face was swollen and battered, his breathing labored.

"Ya look terrible," Will said, trying to smile.

"Ya ought to see me from this side. It looks a whole lot worse," Tye answered. "But I feel a lot better'n those two gents over there."

"How bad ya hurt?" Will asked.

"Not as bad as it looks. I've got a couple of busted ribs, but I don't think they did any damage. My face feels like a bronc stepped on it with all four feet, but other than that I feel fine."

"Let me take care of these fellas, and I'll come back and start a fire to heat some water."

He located the horses without trouble. There were three

saddle horses, a pack horse for their supplies, and a horse carrying pelts, cougar pelts. These must be the hunters Lon Taylor hired, Will thought as he led the horses back to the clearing.

He loaded the two dead men on their horses, tying their hands and feet together underneath. Then he hefted the wounded man to his feet and helped him mount his horse, feeling no sympathy for him as he groaned with pain. When Will had all the horses tied together, he said to the injured man, "Ya head on outa here. If I ever see ya again, I'll kill ya on sight."

"What about them?" The man asked, looking at the bodies.

"They're beyond caring," Will answered. "Ya can either bury them or take them with ya. I don't care one way or the other." He slapped the horse on the rump and stood back as the caravan moved down the trail. Will watched it until it was out of sight, then turned back to Tye. Suddenly he felt very tired.

Chapter Eighteen

Will built a fire and started the water heating. He had found the pack horse and Tye's horse still ground-hitched where they'd been left. The other horses had run off at the sound of gunfire, and he knew he would have to find them before dark if he were to have any chance of finding them at all.

He rummaged through the pack and found some liniment and salve Clement had given them. The medicine was made by the Shoshoni Indians, and Clement had sworn it could cure whatever ailed a man.

Will gave them to Rebecca and told her how to apply each one.

"I've got to go get my horse and boots," he said, looking at his stocking feet.

Rebecca smiled, and Tye squinted at him through swollen eyes, "I don't know what to think about a cowboy who loses his boots and goes traipsin' about in the woods barefooted."

"Yeah, well it seems that's the only way I can keep this here hard-headed, bad-tempered fella outa trouble," Will grinned.

Tye turned his head to get a better look at Will. Looking him in the eye, he tried to smile, his face twisting with the effort.

"Ya sure pulled our bacon outa the fire." He paused, watching Will. "Ya ain't a boy no more. Ya've more than proved yerself a man, and I want ya to know I couldn't be prouder than to have ya as a partner."

Will's eyes misted as he heard Tye's words, a large lump came into his throat and he couldn't speak. He could not find words to respond to what Tye had said. He looked to the ground, trying to swallow. Finally he looked up, the hint of a smile touching his lips. He reached out a hand and laid it on Tye's shoulder,

"Thanks partner. Ya get some rest. I'll look after the horses and be back as soon as I can."

After retrieving his horse and boots, Will set about finding the horse herd. He followed their tracks through the woods. The horses were following the same trail, and Will rode another half mile down the trail before finding them.

Topping a rise, he saw the horses grazing alongside the trail. The scarred mare was standing next to the trail, the end of her lead rope lodged between two rocks. The others stood near her. The herd must have been following her lead, and now it waited for her.

Will untangled the mare's lead from the rocks, and with her behind him, he circled the others, starting them on the trail toward camp. Then he moved to the front. The horses followed the scarred mare as Will led off. He had seen a small canyon close to the camp. Hopefully he could enclose it to keep the horses in, at least for the night. He was tired and felt the need to rest. Tomorrow he would find a better place if one were needed.

It was growing dark when Will returned to Rebecca and Tye.

Rebecca had bathed Tye's wounds and treated them with the ointment and salve, and he seemed to be resting easy. His breathing seemed to be coming easier, if still somewhat labored. She had managed to get Tye's roll off his saddle, and he lay on it now, sleeping.

Rebecca had a stew simmering over the fire, and she handed Will a bowl as he sat by the fire. "Did you find the horses?" she asked.

"Yeah. I've got 'em in a canyon a little ways up the trail. How's Tye doin'?"

"He's resting quietly. I gave him some of Clement's

elixir. I think it's some sort of whiskey. It seemed to help his breathing."

Rebecca watched Will closely. His mind seemed to be elsewhere, and he only half-listened to her as she talked, nodding from time to time.

"Will, are you O.K.?" Rebecca asked tentatively.

"I've never killed anybody before," Will answered, his voice filled with remorse.

Rebecca moved around the fire until she was sitting at Will's side.

"I'd never even shot at anyone until today either. I was aiming to kill that man, and I'm thankful I only wounded him. I think I know how ya feel. I don't think I would care as much for you if ya felt any other way. Taking another man's life is nothing to feel good about, but if ya hadn't killed him, he would have killed all of us. I shudder to think what he and the other two would have done to me first." She paused to look at him. He was looking into the fire, and she gently placed her hands on both sides of his face and turned his head until he was looking into her eyes. "Ya did the only thing you could do, Will Paxton. Ya saved our lives. It's all right to feel bad about killin' a man, but don't ya for one second blame yourself for what happened. Those men brought about their own destiny, and nobody could have prevented what took place here today."

Will looked into Rebecca's eyes, her words soothing the anguish of torment he felt. He wrapped his arms around her and pulled her close to him, burying his head into the soft hair on her shoulder.

"Thank you, Rebecca. I guess I knew that all along. I just needed to hear it. I needed ya to tell me ya understood." Then softly he whispered, "I love ya, Rebecca Kincaid."

Rebecca smiled as tears ran down her cheeks. The tension of the day eased out of her as she held tightly to Will.

It was five days before Rebecca pronounced Tye fit enough to ride. During those five days, Will moved their camp down by the river where it would be more convenient to water. He spent his days looking after the horses and providing wood and water for the camp. He was restless and wanted to be on the trail, away from this place that had brought so much misery to them. But he held himself in check, knowing Tye needed the rest and could not ride until he was well.

Tye was a terrible patient. He would have mounted a horse and ridden out the next day had it not been for Rebecca putting her foot down and threatening to take his boots and saddle away if he even attempted to mount a horse until he had time to heal.

Tye pleaded with Will to intercede for him, but Will held up his hands and told Tye he was on his own. He was not about to take sides in a fight he knew he couldn't win.

Tye finally relented, but only because he feared Rebecca would carry out her threat. He remained sullen and complained daily about losing time and having to get out of the mountains before snow fell, if they were to reach Texas before next spring.

Rebecca ignored his complaints and continued to nurse his wounds. She bandaged his broken ribs with strips torn from her dress, binding them tightly to hold them in place until they could heal.

On the morning of the fifth day, they broke camp before daylight. Tye led the way with the pack horse and the old mare. His face was almost back to normal, and most of the swelling had gone down. His ribs were bandaged, and they didn't hurt with every breath drawn. But he winced every time his horse stumbled or jumped over obstacles along the trail.

* * *

Three days later they rode into Bozeman. The town was a hub of activity. After finding a small ranch on the outskirts of town where they could leave the horses, the three rode into town. They pulled up in front of a brick building bearing the sign of the Bozeman Emporium.

"Let's get some rooms. Then we'll find a livery stable for the horses. I want to find out if the army at Fort Ellis needs any horses," Tye said.

Tye asked for and got the keys for three rooms, asking for a bath to be delivered to Rebecca's room as soon as possible. He and Will would find a bathhouse after taking care of the horses.

The three rooms were side by side on the second floor. Tye took the first one and Rebecca the second, leaving the last for Will. After dropping his roll in his room, Will locked the door behind him, then knocked on Rebecca's door.

"Who's there?" she asked.

"It's me, Rebecca. Open the door."

Rebecca opened the door an inch, looking into Will's face.

"It's not proper for a young lady to allow a man into her room."

"Rebecca, would ya quit foolin' around," Will answered impatiently. "I've got something to give ya. Will ya open the dadburn door."

Laughing, Rebecca stepped back and opened the door for Will to enter. As Will stepped in, she closed the door behind him, wrapping her arms around his neck as he turned to face her. "I've got something to give ya, too," she said as she pulled his head down and kissed him.

Will pulled her close to him and kissed her hungrily. Then remembering his reason for being there, he pushed her away and stood holding her at arm's length.

"I swear I could forget my name when I'm in yer arms, but I've got to meet Tye in the lobby. I wanted to give ya this," he said, pulling a pistol from his belt. "I don't think there'll be any need for it. But just in case, I wanted you to have it."

Rebecca smiled and took the pistol from him. "Will Paxton, you really know how to sweep a girl off her feet. Why, I bet you give one of these to every girl you meet."

Will smiled back, "Nah, just the ones I want to keep around for a while. I've got to go. We should be back in a couple of hours. Ya keep yer door locked." He kissed her quickly and went out the door. Rebecca smiled as she put the pistol in the dresser drawer.

Tye was waiting in the lobby as Will came down the stairs. He gave Will an impatient look as he approached.

"I thought maybe ya was takin' a nap or something," Tye said.

"I had to give something to Rebecca," Will replied, in the way of explanation.

"There's a stable down the other end of town," Tye said, as they walked through the front door and into the street.

They led their horses down the street, watching the activity taking place. The livery was marked with a hanging sign and they walked up to the front of the large barn. The big man standing there watched them as they came up.

"Howdy," Tye said. "Ya got room for our horses?"

"Sure do," the man said. "Fifty cents a day per horse, and I give 'em grain and hay twice a day."

"That sounds reasonable," Tye said. "We'll probably be in town a couple of days. My name's Tye Garrett. This here is Will Paxton."

Tye held out his hand, and the big man took it, saying, "I'm Hal Bonner, owner and operator of this here fine establishment."

"Pleasure to meet ya," Will answered, shaking his hand.

"How's the horse market around here?" Tye asked.

"Depends on whether you're buyin' or sellin'."

"Sellin'," Tye responded.

"Well, yer on the right side then, especially if ya got any plow horses."

"Nope, we ain't got any of those," Tye remarked, "but we got the makin's of some good saddle horses."

"Young stuff?" Hal asked.

"Some of it is," Tye said. "Some of 'em are upwards of seven years."

"How many head ya got?"

"About a hundred and fifty head."

Bonner let out a whistle. "Where'd ya get that many horses?"

"We captured 'em," Tye said.

"Wild horses, huh?"

"Yep, but they're the best of the herd. We cut out the culls. Everything left is top grade."

"I might be interested in a few of 'em. Are any of 'em broke?"

"We've already sold all the ones we had broke," Will said.

"How much you wantin' for 'em?"

"Forty a head, and that's the bottom dollar," Tye answered. He liked the looks of this man and felt an instant trust. He knew it was just instinct, but his instincts were seldom wrong.

"If they're good solid horses, I might take ten or fifteen head. I'm always gettin' folks in here lookin' for a horse. I know a man I can get to break 'em for me. Unless you fellas want to break 'em. I'll pay ya ten dollars a head extra."

"Thanks, but we won't be here long enough," Tye said. "How about the army at Fort Ellis? Reckon they might be in need of some horses?"

"If I was guessin', I'd say they needed some. The way they have to ride over the territory lookin' after these nesters comin' in here, I'd say they probably need a whole bunch of horses. Ever since John Bozeman blazed that trail from Wyomin' up here, we've had more nesters comin' in here than you can shake a stick at. I think most of 'em hope to find gold, but some of 'em are settlin' in and farmin' this country, doin' real good at it, too. That's why I was wonderin' if ya had any plow horses."

"I heard about Bozeman. He brought some settlers up through the Sioux territory, didn't he?"

"Yep, and others followed. That trail is marked with graves all the way. They've closed the trail now, but there's still those who try to make it. Nelson Story brought a herd of longhorns up that way a few years ago. I wouldn't try it. Those Sioux are mighty protective of their huntin' grounds, and they don't like folks traipsin' through there."

"Thanks for the information. I think we'll ride out to the fort in the mornin' and see if they're in need of some horses. We'll pick ya out fifteen or twenty of the best ones and bring 'em in to ya."

"I appreciate that," Hal said. "I'll take care of yer horses for ya and stow yer gear in the tack room."

"Thanks," Tye said. "By the way, is there a bank in town with a safe? I've got some papers I'd like to store until we leave town."

"Yeah, sure. The Bozeman bank down the street has a safe."

Will and Tye headed down the street. Tye carried his saddle bags over his shoulder.

The Bozeman bank was in one of the older buildings in town. Tye asked to see their safe and was pleasantly surprised to find a large safe, just recently installed.

"We had it brought in from St. Louis," the bank teller explained as Will and Tye looked at the large vault with a door two feet thick.

Tye took six envelopes out of his saddle bags. All six were tied together with a piece of string.

"I've got some important papers I'd like to put in your safe until we leave," he said, handing the bundle of envelopes over to the clerk.

"Yessir, the charge is twenty-five cents a week or seventy-five for a month."

"I'll only be leaving 'em here for a couple of days, but here's twenty-five cents. I'd like a receipt for the envelopes, please, and a wax seal put on the string."

Tye got what he asked for, and they left the bank to find a bathhouse.

An hour later they emerged from the bathhouse and started toward the Bozeman Emporium. Will stopped, looking up and down the street.

"What ya lookin' for?" Tye asked.

"Nothin' in particular. Ya go on back to the hotel. I'll be along in a minute. There's something I need to do."

"All right, but don't be too long. I'm gettin' real hungry."

"I won't be long. If ya see Rebecca, tell her I'll be along directly."

Tye turned and made his way to the hotel, while Will started down Main Street looking at the businesses on the way. He went into the Main Street Dry Goods Store and came out a few minutes later. Crossing the street, he entered a small shop with a sign out front saying, Miss Lettie's Alterations and Sewing. He emerged from there twenty minutes later, a big smile on his face. He whistled as he made his way back to the Bozeman Emporium.

Chapter Nineteen

As they ate supper in the hotel diner that evening, Tye talked of their plans for the next day. "We'll ride out to Fort Ellis and see if they need some horses. We may also see if they got any rank ones." He smiled as he said this, looking at Will to see what his reaction would be.

Will grinned and said, "Ya reckon those soldiers are as eager to wager on the outcome of a bronc ride as those cowboys were?"

"I figger they like a little excitement every now and again," Tye said.

Rebecca had been sitting quietly, listening to the two men. She smiled as she saw the light in Will's eyes sparkle at the thought of riding rough horses.

"I don't know what it is that makes a man want to climb on one of those brutes and risk breaking his fool neck," she said, rolling her eyes in mock disbelief.

"I wish I could tell ya what it was," Tye responded, "but to tell the truth, I don't know myself."

"Well, while ya two are out at the fort tomorrow, I think I'll do a little shopping. If you'll give me a list of the supplies we need, I'll go ahead and have the mercantile get them ready."

"That sounds like a good plan to me," Will agreed. "And while yer at it, stop by Miss Lettie's. It's a dress shop across from the dry goods store. I stopped in today to see if they could make ya a couple of dresses. They need your measurements," Will reddened slightly, "and I didn't know what they were. I told the lady I'd have ya stop by."

Rebecca's face lit up, and the smile she gave Will was one of pure joy.

"Why, Will Paxton, yer full of surprises. Can I pick out the material?"

"Sure ya can. I asked the lady if she could have 'em ready in two days, and she assured me she could if ya came by early in the morning."

Rebecca leaned over and kissed Will on the cheek. "I think being captured by the Sioux was the best thing that ever happened to me."

Will blushed again and looked around to see if anyone in the room had witnessed the scene. An older couple sitting at the table next to them smiled as Will glanced their way, and his face burned even hotter as he quickly turned away.

Tye had been quietly observing Will and Rebecca. A smile played on his lips at Will's embarrassment.

* * *

Will and Tye left early the next morning for the fort. Before leaving, Will had given Rebecca some money and told her to buy anything she might need for the trip to Texas.

Fort Ellis was about a mile north of Bozeman. Will and Tye arrived late in the morning, and the sentry at the gate let them pass after directing them to the post commander.

Entering the commander's office, they were introduced to Captain Terry, a tall, thin man with locks of blond hair and a blond mustache that curled up at the ends. His blue eyes sparkled as Tye introduced Will and himself and explained the reason for their visit.

"You've come at a most opportune time, Mr. Garrett. We are indeed in need of horses. The only problem is that at the moment I don't have the funds to pay for them. The supply train from Fort Laramie was attacked by Indians four days ago. Our payroll and operating funds were on that train. The Indians didn't get the money, but the supply train had to turn back, and I'm afraid it will be another three to four days before a dispatch will reach us with the money. The local banks have been good enough to lend us money to meet payroll, and the local stores have supplied us with enough staples to keep the men and horses fed. But there is no money for purchasing such things as additional horses, as much as we need them. It's very hard to find horses right now, with the gold strikes and the rush of people coming in. If you're willing to wait a few days, I'll have the money."

Tye looked thoughtful for a moment, then spoke, "Well, Captain, I wish I could wait, but we've got a long way to go and not much time to get there. But I think there may be a way around your problem. We're going to be traveling south through Wyoming on our way to Texas. We'll be passing close to Fort Laramie. If ya'd give us a voucher for the sale of the horses, we could pick up our money there."

"That would work fine," Captain Terry said. "Where are the horses now?"

"We've got them held on a small spread west of town," Will replied. "How many would ya be in need of, Captain?"

"How many have you got?"

"I think we got about fifty-five or sixty head, dependin' on how many Mr. Bonner wants."

"I'll take all of them," Terry replied, "if the price is right."

"Fifty dollars a head," Will replied.

Tye looked up, surprise showing briefly on his face. Then he turned to look at the captain.

"How many of them are broke to ride?" Terry asked.

"None of them," Will replied. "They're all green, but they're tough stock and they'll make good mounts for yer men."

"If they're all sound horses, you have a deal," Captain Terry agreed. "How soon can you deliver them?"

"We can have them here tomorrow if that'll suit ya," Will said.

"Tomorrow will be fine."

They started for the door, but before they reached it,

Tye turned back. "Captain, ya wouldn't happen to have any horses too rough to ride, would ya?"

"Rough stock, huh? We don't have any what you call rough stock, but we do have one that's bucked off every new recruit we bring in. The men love it when a new recruit comes to the fort. It makes for a little sport when they put him on ol' Brownie."

"Ol' Brownie, huh. Sounds like a ringer name for sure."

Captain Terry chuckled. "Yep, it's a ringer, all right. He's bucked off lots of good riders."

"Do you think the men would be up for a little sport with a wager tied to it?" Tye asked.

"You mean, in other words, you would like to attempt to ride ol' Brownie and would like to put some money on it?"

"That's about the gist of it," Tye said, "only it'll be the kid here ridin', not me."

Captain Terry lifted an eyebrow as he looked at Will, "He doesn't look old enough to be riding rough stock, but then again half the kids that join up aren't old enough to be fighting Indians either. If you want a shot at riding our ringer, I'll set it up for you. How about tomorrow when you bring the horses?"

"That'll be fine," Tye said. "We'll see ya tomorrow."

When they had ridden away from the fort, Tye turned to Will. "Fifty dollars a head? What made ya think he would pay that much for horses?"

"He did," Will replied, smiling.

Tye looked at him questioningly.

"He said he wasn't able to buy horses because of the gold strike and immigrants. That meant that horses must be going for a premium. I figgered if I said fifty and he thought it was too high, he would have haggled over the price. If we'd had to come down to forty, we still wouldn't have lost anything."

"How about the horses we sold to Hal Bonner? We sold those for forty dollars a head. What if the captain finds out we sold them to Hal cheaper than we sold them to him?"

"I don't reckon Hal's going too be to eager to tell anyone what he gave for those horses. After all, he's in the business of sellin' 'em, too."

"Yer right 'bout that. Well, partner, ya just made us ten dollars more a head than we hoped for. I'd say that calls for a special celebration. I think a steak supper would be in order for tonight."

"Don't forget Rebecca's been shopping all day. It may take the extra money we made today to pay for everything she bought."

They both laughed as they kicked their horses into a lope and headed back to town.

* * *

The evening was a festive event as they enjoyed a steak dinner at the finest restaurant in town. Tye bought a bottle of wine, and the three toasted the success of the sale. They had sold all the horses they had, with the exception of those they were keeping to start their herd in Texas. Rebecca had made arrangements for all their supplies to be ready in two days and had been fitted for two dresses.

"I bought each of ya a present as well," she said, smiling in anticipation.

"What did ya get us?" Will asked

Rebecca reached into her handbag and pulled out two small packages wrapped in colored paper. She handed one to each of them.

Tye looked embarrassed as he took his package. He looked it over as if expecting something to jump out at him.

"Go ahead. Open them," Rebecca ordered.

Will tore the paper away to reveal a small box. Cautiously he opened the box to reveal its hidden secret. As he peered at the contents, a smile slowly spread across his face. Reaching into the box, he pulled out a silver belt buckle with a bronc rider etched in the center. Turning it over he saw something inscribed on the back. Looking closely, he saw the words, "To Will Paxton With All My Love, Rebecca. 1872."

Tye's present was a gold watch attached to a chain. It

played the "Lovers' Waltz" when the cover was opened. Inside the cover was the inscription, "To Tye Garrett. May all your days be blessed with happiness. Rebecca 1872."

Tye stared at his watch, listening to the melody that played. "Thank you, Rebecca. It's beautiful. I'll cherish it always."

Will thanked Rebecca for his buckle and promised to wear it always.

They finished the evening by attending a performance of *The Taming of the Shrew* by a traveling company of Shakespearean actors that had arrived in town. Both Will and Tye fell asleep before the last act began, but Rebecca sat enthralled by the actors' costumes.

* * *

The following morning all three rode out early to the ranch where the horses were being kept. Tye had sold Hal fifteen head of horses, leaving them with sixty head to sell to the army. They cut out the ones they wanted to keep, plus the fifteen to be delivered to Hal, then started the others on the road to the fort.

Will waited until the horses were strung out. Leaving Rebecca to bring up the rear, he rode up to the front where Tye was leading the scarred mare.

As he rode along side of Tye, he said, "I know ya wanted to leave tomorrow, but I really need for us to stay one more day."

Tye looked at him questioningly. "Ya got a good reason?" he asked.

"Yep, I've set up Rebecca's and my wedding for tomorrow. The wedding dress I'm having made for her won't be ready until this afternoon."

Tye smiled. "I reckon a man's wedding is a good enough reason to wait around an extra day."

Will returned the smile. "Thanks, Tye. By the way, I'd like for you to be my best man. Will you?"

"Sure," Tye said, as if there shouldn't have been any doubt.

"Are ya ready for the ride today?" Tye asked, changing

the subject.

"The way I feel, I'm ready for anything," Will responded.

"Well, don't get too cocky. I got a feeling there's something about this horse that's different from the ones ya've ridden before."

"What would that be?" Will asked, sobering at the Tye's warning.

"I don't know," Tye responded, "but the army doesn't keep bad horses around very long. They don't have time to mess with 'em. If they get a bad one, they usually get rid of him real quick. This horse has been around for a while, if what the captain told us is true."

Will thought about this as he made his way to the back of the herd where Rebecca was keeping the herd moving. Riding up beside her, he smiled and asked, "How would ya feel about getting married tomorrow?"

Rebecca looked at him in astonishment. "Do ya mean it? Do ya really mean it?"

"Nope I just wanted to see yer reaction when I asked ya," Will said, smiling at her.

"Well, in that case, the answer is no," Rebecca said, matching his smile.

"I talked Tye into sticking around for another day. I've already made arrangements with a pastor to marry us in a church. I thought ya might like to have a church wedding, since I don't think there'll be many churches around where we're headed to."

Rebecca reached over and laid her hand on top of Will's, their horses moving closer together as she squeezed his hand gently. "Thank you, Will. I've always wanted a church wedding, but I wouldn't care if it was out on the open plains as long as yer the man I'm marrying."

"Well, if I'd known that, I could have saved myself two dollars and had that minister meet us out on the plains." His mischievous smile caused Rebecca to laugh.

Chapter Twenty

They entered the fort and turned the horses into a large round pen used to hold horses. As they pushed the last horse in and closed the gate, Captain Terry was walking across the parade ground toward them. Tye and Will turned to greet the captain as he walked up to the corral.

"We got 'em here. There's sixty head of tough mustangs. They'll make yer men some good mounts once they're broke," Tye said, motioning to the horses in the corral.

"They look to be top grade," Captain Terry said, looking over the rail at the horses milling around in the corral.

"You wouldn't be interested in working a deal to break them for me, would you?"

"I surely wish we could," Tye said, "but we've got to get on down to Texas before it gets too cold."

Terry nodded. "I remember you telling me that. I just thought I'd give it a shot. Let's get a closer look at these wild horses you brought me."

The captain walked around the corral, looking at each horse and commenting on each one's conformation.

"They're everything you said they were, gentlemen. Come on up to my office, and I'll give you a voucher for them."

Rebecca, who had remained mounted during the inspection of the horses, now dismounted and joined Will as they started for the main building. Captain Terry removed his hat as Rebecca came up.

"Ma'am," he said, nodding at her.

Will suddenly remembered his manners and stammered, "Uh, Captain Terry, I'd like to introduce you to my fiancée, Rebecca Kincaid."

"Pleased to meet you, Miss Kincaid." The captain took her hand and brought it to his lips. Standing beside Rebecca, Will felt a stab of jealousy as Rebecca flushed and giggled nervously.

"It's not very often that we have someone as beautiful as yourself grace our post. If there is anything you need while you're here, please do not hesitate to ask."

Rebecca removed her hand from the captain's grasp. "Thank you, Captain. That's very kind of ya."

Captain Terry led them to his office, stepping aside to allow Rebecca to enter. Will followed, scowling at Terry's back as the officer went to his desk and pulled out one of the drawers. He pulled a sheet of paper out and, after filling in the proper spaces, signed his name and handed the paper to Tye.

"I believe you will find everything in order, Mr. Garrett. Just present this draft to the commanding officer at Fort Laramie, and you'll be given your money."

Tye took the draft and, after looking it over carefully, folded it and put it in his shirt pocket. Then, extending his hand to the captain, he said, "Thank ya, Captain Terry. We appreciate doing business with the army. Did ya set up our little wager with the men?"

"They are anxiously awaiting you now at the north corral. I believe they have ol' Brownie ready."

"Well, we shouldn't keep the men waiting, should we?" Tye asked, smiling.

As they left the office, Will took Rebecca's hand in his and guided her through the front door. Rebecca smiled to herself and squeezed Will's hand.

Captain Terry led them to the corral at the north end of the post. As they approached, they could see about thirty men gathered around. Some were already seated on the top rail of the fence in order to have a good view when the show began.

In the center of the corral stood a soldier holding a large brown horse. Will noted that the horse was really unimpressive, standing about fifteen hands tall, with too broad a chest and hindquarters and large hooves. His body was short and powerfully built, but he looked as if he would fit more into a harness than a saddle.

Will and Tye walked to the horse, looking him over from all angles.

The soldier holding the animal didn't say a word until they had finished their inspection, then remarked, "Ol' Brownie's really a sweetheart."

The brown horse stood stone still as Will and Tye walked around him. As the soldier scratched and petted him, the horse's eyes began to close with pleasure.

"Let's go get yer saddle, Will," Tye said as he looked suspiciously at the animal before him.

They walked down to the corral where Will had left his horse tied. Once out of hearing range of the crowd, Tye spoke in a low voice.

"Somethin's not right about this. That horse is like a big ol' puppy. Did you see the saddle marks on him?"

"Yeah, I noticed 'em. Somebody's been riding that horse on a regular basis. He's been well-cared-for, too. Did ya notice how good his coat looked, like it's been brushed regularly?"

"Uh-huh," Tye responded, "but I'll bet ya my bottom dollar that horse can buck a blue streak."

"I reckon we're about to find out," Will replied with a smile

They walked back to the corral where the soldiers were waiting. The captain came forward as they approached and said, "The men have put together a sizable pot to wager against young Will here. They're willing to give you two-to-one odds that he can't ride ol' Brownie to a standstill."

"How much have they got?" Will asked

"Two thousand dollars," Captain Terry said, showing a roll of bills.

"Two thousand?" Tye asked, astonished at the amount.

"Where in the world did soldiers get that much money?"

Captain Terry chuckled. "It seems they got some of their friends in town to invest a little of their money as well. And I don't mind telling you I put a few dollars into the pot myself."

"I sure hope we don't get run out of town on a rail after I ride that horse of yers," Will commented, looking around at the soldiers lining the fence.

Captain Terry chuckled again. "I doubt you'll ride ol' Brownie, but if you do succeed, I give you my word there will be no reprisals against you."

"What are the rules here?" Tye asked as they made their way to the corral.

"Very simple," Captain Terry responded. "You are allowed one buck-off. After that, if you fail to ride ol' Brownie to a standstill, you lose."

"That's fair enough," Will responded. "Let's do it."

Will removed the saddle from his horse and carried it into the corral where the brown horse stood, looking as docile as a pet dog. Will placed his blanket and saddle on the horse's back, noticing that he stood as if it were an everyday experience to him. Once Will had the saddle on, the soldier handed him the reins and started walking away. Will stopped him.

"Just a minute."

The soldier stopped and turned back to Will.

"Will ya hold him for me for a minute?"

Looking uncertain, the soldier walked back to the horse and took the reins from Will.

Will walked out of the corral to where his horse stood tied to the hitching post. Taking his lariat from the saddle, he slipped the hackamore from the horse's head, fashioned a halter from his lariat, and tied the horse back to the hitching rail. Taking the hackamore back to the corral, he slipped the bridle from ol' Brownie's head and handed it to the soldier. Then he slipped his hackamore over Brownie's ears.

"I like to ride with my own rig," Will commented as the

soldier looked at him. "Leather reins ain't much account on a bucking horse. Ya going to hold him for me while I get on?" Will asked.

"He don't need to be held," the soldier said with a grin that said he knew something Will didn't.

Will was about to step into the saddle when he heard a commotion coming from the front gate of the fort. Stepping away from the horse, he watched as a procession of wagons and riders came through the gate.

"What's this?" Tye asked as he looked up and saw the assemblage entering the gate.

There were three wagons, loaded with men, women, and boys. Riding alongside were no less than twenty men mounted on horses.

"These are the people from town coming to watch. I guess they want to check on their investment," Captain Terry said with a smile.

Will waited in the center of the corral until all the people found themselves a viewing area and the grounds grew quiet. "I feel like a rooster on parade," he mumbled to himself as he took the reins in his hand and mounted.

He fully expected the brown horse to explode beneath him when he settled in the saddle, but to his surprise nothing happened. The horse stood there, quiet as could be.

The crowd began to laugh at the sight of Will sitting there, his muscles tight, looking expectantly at Brownie's ears, with his feet extended and ready for the first lunge. But Brownie just stood there, looking around as if this were an everyday occurrence, and nothing more was expected of him.

Feeling like a fool, Will relaxed his seat, allowing his feet to hang at Brownie's sides.

Brownie still stood, totally unconcerned at the events taking place.

Tye and Rebecca exchanged glances, and Tye shrugged his shoulders.

Sitting in the center of the corral, hearing the laughter coming from the spectators, Will clicked his tongue, hoping to draw a response from the horse beneath him, but Brownie just stood, totally unconcerned.

Feeling the humiliation of the laughter, Will dug his spurs into Brownie's sides. The next thing he knew, he was flying off Brownie's rump, landing hard on his back in the packed dirt of the corral, the air knocked out of him.

The crowd was roaring with laughter as Will lay in the corral, trying to breathe. Catcalls and whistles reached his ears as he slowly breathed in precious air.

A soldier led the brown horse up to him as he slowly came to his feet. His back felt as if it had been broken, and his head hurt where it had hit the ground.

Will looked up to see the soldier smiling at him and holding out the reins. "Ya got one more chance, cowboy. Better make it a good one. These people came to see a show, and they're going to be mighty disappointed if that's the best they get to see."

Will wanted say he didn't give a hoot about what they wanted to see. All he wanted was to sit down until the pain in his head subsided, but instead he just nodded and took the reins from the soldier. He looked at the brown horse in front of him.

Brownie stood there as calm as ever. No malice showed in his eyes as Will looked at him. Will had expected to see the horse wild-eyed and nervous, but there was none of that in the animal.

Will gathered up the reins and mounted the brown horse once again.

Tye stood watching through the corral fence. He was nervous as he thought about the wager they'd made. Will had already been thrown once. If it happened again, they would lose a thousand hard-earned dollars. He didn't blame Will. He doubted anyone could have stayed aboard ol' Brownie in that situation. The horse had literally blown Will out of the saddle. Of course, Will had been relaxed, a mistake he wouldn't make again, but the power and quickness of the horse was amazing.

Will sat in the saddle, adjusting his mind and body to

ride the horse. He knew when he touched the horse's sides, he was going to have to be ready, both mentally and physically.

Taking the reins in both hands and pulling Brownie's head up as far as he could, Will touched his spurs to the horse's sides. Instantly Brownie snorted and leaped forward, his front feet coming off the ground, his back feet propelling him forward. The saddle horn was the only thing that kept Will from having a repeat of the previous ride. It was what cowboys call grabbing leather, and Will grabbed for everything he was worth.

Brownie's front feet came to the ground, and Will felt himself being pushed forward by the power of the horse's hindquarters coming up into the air. Will fought to regain control and get in rhythm with the horse, but he was finding it difficult to do. The left rein had slack, and while his right hand held the rein, it also was holding the saddle horn in a desperate attempt to stay aboard.

He forced his mind to concentrate on the task before him. He willed himself to look at Brownie's ears and follow his direction. Then, glancing down, he worked the left rein through his fingers, taking the slack out of it. It took him three more jumps and a lot of punishment, before he managed to get the rein tight in his hand. Using his left hand to pull himself into the saddle, he began working the right rein through his fingers, forcing himself to let go of the saddle horn. This maneuver forced Brownie's head to the left and pulled him in a bucking circle, which was Will's intent. By keeping the horse turning left, it took the pressure off his right side, allowing him to work the rein up faster.

Brownie bellowed each time his front feet hit the ground. Will had his left spur dug into his side and was holding on for everything he was worth. Finally he worked the slack out of the right rein and pulled himself down into the saddle. He released the pressure on the left rein, allowing Brownie to pull his head around and straighten out.

For the first time since mounting the horse, Will felt that he had control of the situation. Both reins were now held tightly in his hands, and he was seated firmly in the saddle. Even though he'd taken some punishment during the early part of the ride, he now felt he could finish it.

Brownie leaped high in the air, twisting his body as he did. Since the horse was so short, the quick turns were more like a series of jerks, rather than a smooth turn, causing Will to move in the saddle more than he would have liked.

Each time the brown horse hit the ground, Will would dig in with his spurs. Brownie would then bellow and sky-rocket forward, snapping Will's neck.

The crowd was shouting and yelling, cheering for the horse. Will heard their shouts through the din of sound about him, but he paid no attention to it. It was taking all his concentration to stay aboard the horse.

Rebecca watched from the top rail as Will fought to stay on ol' Brownie. She could see that it was a punishing ride, and it was beginning to take its toll on him. There was blood coming from his nose, no doubt a result of the stiff-legged jolts to the ground. She had never seen a horse leap so high in the air, nor come down so stiff-legged when it hit. There was no give in the horse's legs when he hit the ground in the corral. His legs were so large and muscular, he could take the punishment without injuring himself, but how long could Will take that kind of punish-ment? She held her fist to her mouth as Will rode, biting into her hand each time the horse came down. She would gladly have paid the thousand dollars, if she'd had it, to end this ride now before Will took any more punishment.

Twenty minutes into the ride, Will still felt no give in the brown horse. He was not riding well, for the horse had no rhythm. One time he would jump straight up, coming down hard. The next he would spin, then lunge forward without warning, only to come to earth and jump either left or right. Each time the horse's feet hit the ground, Will would dig in his spurs, preparing for the next leap. Will knew he couldn't last much longer. His body was aching all over, and the blood from his nose was getting into his eyes, making it difficult to watch the horse's head. He was going to lose, he knew that. No one could ride a horse such as this, but someone did ride him. Why then did he buck the way he did?

Will's mind was churning. What made ol' Brownie buck? Why could he be mounted and ridden? What made him change? Will was thinking fast, remembering the horse when he first mounted him and watching his head at the same time to be ready for the next jump.

"Spurs" that's what it was. Brownie bucked when touched with spurs. The question now was would he quit if Will quit using his spurs?

As the horse lunged again, Will held his feet away from his sides, not touching him as he hit the ground. This time Brownie didn't bellow, and Will thought he felt a slight difference in the horse's power.

It was all Will could do to keep his spurs away from the horse's side. It meant he had to change his entire riding style in midride. This threw him out of rhythm with the horse and made it even more difficult to remain aboard, but Will knew it was the only way to win.

Will was riding with pure strength now, using the power in his arms to hold himself in the saddle since he couldn't squeeze with his legs for fear of digging his spurs into the horse's side.

Brownie had taken four more leaps without the feel of the spurs, and Will could definitely feel a difference in the horse's leaps. The anger was gone. There were no more angry bellows as the horse's feet hit the ground. His bucks weren't as strong as they had been.

Will started talking to the horse as he fought his own awkwardness to remain in the saddle.

"Easy Brownie, easy boy. Hold up now, steady, whoa. That's it, easy now."

The brown horse slowed his leaps, blowing through his nostrils, releasing his rage. After three more half-hearted bucks, he brought up his head and stopped. Will groaned, then sat there, feet well away from the horse's side. After he was sure the horse wasn't going to buck anymore, he looked at Captain Terry and saw the captain nod. The ride was over.

Will tried to swing his leg over the horse's hips, and found he didn't have the strength to lift it. Rebecca opened the gate and ran to his side, Tye right behind her.

"I can't lift my leg over," Will said, trying to smile.

"We'll give you a hand. Just slide off. I'll catch ya," Tye replied.

"Not until ya take my spurs off," Will said. "I don't want any more of what I just had."

"Spurs, huh?" Tye smiled. " So that's what made a gentle saddle horse turn into a mad bronc. I was wondering what ya were doing there at the end."

Rebecca unbuckled Will's spurs, then helped Tye hold him upright as he slid off Brownie's back. Will's knees wouldn't support him as he tried to stand. Rebecca held him on one side and Tye on the other until he could manage to stand on his own.

"I'm walkin' outa of here on my own," Will said. " Just give me a moment to catch my wind and still the shaking in my legs."

Rebecca and Tye continued to hold Will until the shaking left his body. Rebecca took her kerchief and wiped the blood from his face, spitting on the cloth to wash where it already had dried.

Finally Will stood and walked over to where the brown horse stood. He was obediently ground-hitched and stood waiting patiently. Other than the sweat dripping from his coat, there was no sign there had ever been a battle. He allowed Will to remove his saddle and hackamore, never giving the slightest sign that he distrusted the man who had ridden him.

Will removed his gear and, setting it aside, rubbed the horses' neck, talking in low tones to him as he did. Then, turning away, he picked up his gear and made his way to the gate, swaying slightly as he went.

Chapter Twenty-One

The crowd was silent as Will walked through the gate, which was held open by one of the soldiers. Rebecca and Tye followed him out. "Captain," Will spoke as he walked toward him, "I believe yer holding our money."

Captain Terry unbuttoned the breast pocket on his tunic and took out the roll of bills. He handed it to Will.

"You earned every penny of that money, young man. You're the only man to ride ol' Brownie while wearing spurs. I didn't think you were going to catch on, but you fooled me, me and a lot of other folks as well. You rode one heck of a ride though before you figured it out. There's some folks here that were making side bets you wouldn't last the first five minutes."

"I almost didn't. I can easily say that is the toughest horse I've ever been on."

Captain Terry glanced at the people standing around the corral. No one had made a move to leave, and concern clouded his eyes as he watched the crowd.

"You've created a small part of history for yourself here today," the captain continued. "Ol' Brownie has bucked off more than three hundred riders. Of course, not all of them were seasoned riders, but plenty of them were. I don't know how people are going to react to you now that you've ridden him. Seems people around here put a lot of stock in having a legend in their midst. They might resent you for it."

Tye stepped in between Will and the captain. Staring into the commander's eyes, he spoke quietly. "Captain, ya told us before this began that we had yer word there'd be no trouble over this. Are ya backing out of that promise now?"

"No, no, of course not. You have my word as an officer and a gentleman. No one will make a move against you. I was merely informing you that you may not be the most popular people around Bozeman."

Will looked around at the people still gathered around the corral. Most of them were talking in low tones and watching him. He picked up his rig and walked over to where his horse was tied. Removing the lariat, he put the hackamore over the horse's head and began saddling him. His back was to the crowd, and he didn't notice the three men who came up behind him until he heard one of them clear his throat.

"Hmmph."

Will turned around cautiously, wondering what to expect. The three men standing there didn't look menacing. Instead, they looked friendly.

"What can I do for ya, gentlemen?" Will asked hesitantly.

"I think the question is more what can we do for ya?" the tall man in the middle asked.

"What do ya mean?" Will asked, confusion clouding his face.

"Son, ya put on quite a show out there today, and even though most of us lost money on ya, it was worth it to see ya ride ol' Brownie. Now we want to show you our hospitality. We hear yer plannin' on gettin' married tomorrow, and we'd sure be happy if ya'd allow us to give you and yer bride a wedding reception after the ceremony."

Will stood staring at the three men, hardly believing his ears.

"Uh, that would be great," Will responded, " but let's not tell my fiancée about it. We'll let it be a surprise."

The three men smiled at Will's request, then one by one they held out their hands and introduced themselves. "I'm John Oates," the spokesman of the group said. "This here is Oatum Grant. Claims to be related to Ulysses S. Grant, but he cain't prove it. This other gent is Hiram Walker. He owns the Bozeman Emporium where yer staying."

Mr. Walker extended his hand and gripped Will's in a firm handshake.

"Anything ya need while staying with us, just be sure to ask."

Will nodded, hardly believing his ears.

"By the way," Walker continued, "I'm taking the liberty of having yer things moved to the presidential suite while yer at the church tomorrow. Consider it a wedding present, and don't worry. I won't say anything to yer fiancée. We'll let that be a surprise as well."

"Thank ya, Mr. Walker. That's mighty nice of ya."

"Why don't ya come on over and let us introduce ya to the rest of the townsfolk."

Will followed the three men to the wagons where the rest of the people from town were gathered. He met each of them, and each in turn expressed his appreciation at the ride he'd made.

Rebecca and Tye stood with Captain Terry and watched as Will went among the townsfolk shaking hands with them. The fort commander shook his head and laughed.

"It looks as if we were worried for nothing. Seems young Will has won the hearts of the townspeople. I must say I am relieved to see they bear him no ill will. Why don't you come up to my office, and we'll have some refreshments?" Even though the captain's invitation was extended to both Rebecca and Tye, he was looking at Rebecca when he spoke.

Rebecca smiled. Looking into the captain's eyes, she replied, "Thank ya very much, Captain. But I'm afraid we must be getting back to town. Tomorrow is my wedding day, and I have preparations to make. Ya are, of course, invited to the wedding. I do hope ya'll come."

Captain Terry had the decency to redden at Rebecca's mention of her wedding. "I would be most delighted to attend. I was wondering. Is there anyone to give the bride away?"

Rebecca stopped short, her heart catching as she thought about her parents. She recovered quickly, determined not to let anything spoil the occasion.

"No there isn't, Captain. My parents are both dead."

"I am sorry, Miss Kincaid. I did not mean to bring up unpleasant memories, but I was wondering if you would allow me the honor of giving you away."

Rebecca smiled. "I would be grateful, Captain Terry. Thank ya for yer kindness and yer hospitality. I think we should be going, if we can pull Will away from his new friends."

The ride back to town was an agonizing one for Will. It seemed as if every bone in his body was bruised, but what hurt the most was his tailbone where he'd slammed the saddle trying to get seated on ol' Brownie. It was only later, after soaking in the hotel's bathtub, compliments of Hiram Walker, that the soreness began to leave his body. He fell asleep while soaking and woke only after Rebecca banged on his door so loudly the other guests came into the hall to see what the racket was about.

They ate an early supper in the hotel dining room, but the conversation was mainly between Rebecca and Tye as Will's eyelids grew heavy. Rebecca laughed as Will fought to stay awake during dessert. Finally she took Will by the hand and said, "Come on, cowboy. We'd better get ya to bed. I don't want you falling asleep during the ceremony tomorrow."

"I've got to stop by the desk first," Will answered, letting go of Rebecca's hand.

He caught up with Rebecca and Tye at the head of the stairs, walking beside them he smiled to himself.

"What are ya so happy about?" Rebecca asked.

"It's just great to be alive. I rode the toughest horse of my life today. We made two thousand dollars, and tomorrow I'm marryin' the most beautiful girl in the world. What more could a man ask for?"

Rebecca kissed his cheek as they walked down the hallway to their rooms.

"How about a good night's sleep?" Tye asked.

"That would be good," Will agreed, stopping in front of Rebecca's door.

"Ya did real good today, Will," Tye said. "I thought there for a while we'd lost a thousand dollars, but ya came through and won. Ya know how much money we got now?"

"I figger somewhere around twelve thousand, but I haven't really been keeping up with it. Yer the banker. I thought I'd let ya handle that end of it. At least until ya start getting too old and feeble to count. I reckon that'll be at least another year or two." Will grinned and Rebecca hid her mouth to suppress a giggle.

"We now have just over fifteen thousand dollars, the minimum we need to start our operation. If we can set up another two or three rides between here and Texas, we'll be in great shape. That is, if I can keep ya two kids outa trouble long enough to make it outa here." He smiled as he unlocked the door to his room.

"Ya'll get a good night's sleep. Tomorrow's yer big day, and I want it to be the best possible."

"Thanks, Tye," Will and Rebecca said simultaneously.

"Good night ya two," Tye said as he entered his room, chuckling to himself.

Will took the key from Rebecca and opened her door. Then, leaning down, he kissed her longingly before pulling away and whispering goodnight. He left her and opened the door to his room. He lay on his bed thinking about what had happened that day and what lay ahead of him. He fell asleep with his clothes on and was still dressed the next morning at six o'clock when the desk clerk knocked on his door.

Will opened his eyes and tried to block out the pounding noise vibrating in his head. It took him several seconds to realize that the pounding was coming from the door. He rolled off the bed, groaning as the soreness in his body reminded him of his ride the previous day. He opened the door to see the clerk standing in the hallway.

"It's six o'clock, sir."

"Thank ya," Will replied, fishing in his pocket for a tip. "Will ya have the cook fix me steak and eggs for breakfast? I'll be down in about fifteen minutes."

"Yes, sir, Mister Paxton. I'll see that it's taken care of."

Will closed the door, then turned to the task of shaving and packing his clothes in his travel bag. After he had finished, he took a piece of hotel stationary and wrote a brief note to Rebecca. He slipped it under her door as he walked by on his way to the dining room.

He was just finishing his breakfast when Tye entered the dining room.

"Yer up awful early. What's the matter? Ya got the jitters or something?" Tye asked, grinning at Will.

"Nope, just got some things I got to take care of before the weddin'."

"Need me to do anything for ya?" Tye asked.

"Just be there when the music starts playin'," Will said, smiling back.

"I'll be there. Are you sure yer goin' to be there?"

"Wild horses couldn't keep me away. I've got to run. Got a lot to do. I'll see ya in about three hours. If ya see Rebecca, tell her I've gone to take care of some business, will ya?"

"I'll tell her ya chickened out and ran away with one of the local dance hall girls. That'll fix ya up real good," Tye's said, grinning at the thought.

"Thanks partner," Will said. "I hope I can return the favor someday."

Will left the diner whistling a tune as he stepped through the front door. His first stop was the livery stable. He had a lot to do before one o'clock, and it was going to be rushing things to get them all done.

* * *

At eleven-thirty Rebecca was pacing the floor in her room. She hadn't seen Will all morning and was beginning to wonder if perhaps he had decided to run away. She was considering asking Tye to go look for him when someone

knocked on her door. She opened the door expecting to
find Will standing there. Instead it was a delivery boy carrying a package.

"Miss Kincaid?"

"Yes," Rebecca replied.

"I was told to deliver this to ya," he said, handing
Rebecca the package.

"What is it?" Rebecca asked, her brow wrinkling in a
questioning look.

"I have no idea, Ma'am, I was just told to bring it to
ya."

Rebecca took the package, thanking the boy as she
closed the door. She set it on the bed and looked for a card.
There was nothing to show where it had come from. She
pulled the wrapping paper from the package to discover a
long, slender box beneath. Untying the string from around
the box, she slowly lifted the lid to peer at its contents. As
realization of what was in the box struck her, tears
streamed down her cheeks. She was trying to stop the flow
of tears when a knock on her door drew her attention away
from the package. Walking to the door, still dabbing at the
tears, she opened it to find Will standing there, a grin on
his face from ear to ear. Without saying a word, she threw
herself into his arms, burying her face into his shirt.

Will stood there holding her, wondering what had
brought this about. He was wondering if she thought he
might have changed his mind when he spotted the package
on the bed.

"Do ya like it?" he asked.

"I love it," she said softly.

"Does it fit?"

Rebecca laughed. "I haven't tried it on yet. I haven't
even taken it out of the box." She took him by the hand
and led him into the room. Walking over to the package,
she pulled out the contents.

"How did ya do it?" she asked.

"A man's got to have some secrets, or else it takes away
the appeal."

"Ya just better not have too many secrets," Rebecca said, laughing as she took the white wedding dress and held it front of her.

"How does it look?"

"Ya look beautiful," Will replied, staring as she held the dress in front of her. "I've never seen anything more beautiful in my life." He pulled her to him, kissing her passionately. Rebecca responded, wrapping her arms around his neck and clinging to him as their lips met. The dress crushed between them as they clung to each other.

A sharp intake of breath from the door took them by surprise, and they broke apart as they realized the door had been left open. Standing in the hallway was an elderly couple. The woman, a look of shock on her face, was holding a handkerchief to her mouth. The man was openly gaping, apparently enjoying the scene before him.

Rebecca turned, holding the dress before her. "It's our wedding day," she said laughing.

Relief flooded through the elderly lady's face. "Oh," she exclaimed. Then almost timidly she spoke to Will. "Young man, don't you know it's bad luck to see the bride before the wedding?"

Grinning, Will walked out the door, addressing the woman as he went.

"No, Ma'am, I sure didn't. But as ya can see, a man would be hard-pressed to stay away from something that beautiful. I'm sorry if we embarrassed ya. Please accept my apology."

The grin remained on his face as the elderly couple smiled and nodded. Will watched them as they walked away. The man turned and smiled, giving Will a wink as he did.

Chapter Twenty-Two

If Will was surprised at the number of people who attended the wedding in the small Methodist church, then shock could be the only word to describe what Rebecca felt as she entered the front door and saw the packed pews and people standing in the aisles.

"Where did all these people come from?" she asked Tye as they waited for the ceremony to begin.

"I told them Will was a famous evangelist. They've come to hear him preach," Tye said, keeping a straight face.

Rebecca covered her mouth to smother the laughter that threatened to bubble out.

"I'd like to see that myself," she said.

When the time came to walk down the aisle, she smiled proudly as Will took his place at the front of the church. He was wearing a new black suit, with a new white shirt and string tie. His boots were polished, and his hair was slicked down. She could see that he'd gotten a haircut. Then she was standing beside him, and the minister was speaking to the crowd.

Rebecca tried to follow the ceremony, but the butterflies in her stomach prevented her from concentrating as she leaned on Will for support. She remembered Captain Terry giving her away and remembered answering the preacher as he asked her questions. Then Will slipped a beautiful gold band on her finger. She stared at the ring, as it reflected the light from the candles on the altar. Then Will was taking her in his arms and kissing her, and then they were walking down the isle to the bright sunshine outside.

The reception, planned and held by the townspeople, was held in the theater where only a few nights ago Rebecca, Will, and Tye had watched a play.

The women had gone all out in their planning and preparation. There was food of every kind, presents for the bride, most of them handmade by the women themselves, and even a wedding cake that was large enough for everyone to have a piece.

Someone had brought a guitar. Another had brought a banjo. A fiddle was pulled from its case, and soon there was music. The floor was quickly cleared for dancing.

Will stood beside Rebecca as she opened each of her gifts, tears of joy filling her eyes as she smiled and laughed. Will felt as if he were going to choke to death in the stiff collar and felt relief when his new bride, noticing his discomfort by the redness of his face, stood up and loosened the button on the starched collar.

Will took a deep breath, rubbing his neck where the collar had dug into it. "Now I know how it feels to be hanged."

The party was still going strong when Will, after dancing another waltz with Mrs. Walker, spotted Rebecca alone at the punch bowl and made his way to her. He had sought out a young boy earlier and had whispered something in his ear, then handed him a quarter. The boy shoved the coin in his pocket and made his way through the crowd to the front door. Will waited until he saw the boy return and give him a nod before turning to Rebecca and saying, "I still haven't given ya yer wedding present."

Rebecca looked at him, searching his face to see if he was joking.

"Ya have given me the greatest gift I could ever hope to have," she said with such emotion Will had to swallow before he could speak.

"Well, I have another one for ya."

"What is it, Will?" Rebecca asked excitedly.

"Are ya ready to leave?" Will asked.

"Heavens, yes. I've been ready to leave for the last hour. My feet are killing me, tops and bottoms. I've had my toes stepped on so many times today it may be a week before I can put on a pair of boots."

"Let's find Mister Oates and thank him before we leave," Will said, looking around the room and spotting him.

Will almost regretted his decision to thank John Oates. As soon as he announced their intentions, Mister Oates quieted the crowd to announce their intentions. This caused a pandemonium of shouts, cheers, and a few comments that caused both Will and Rebecca to blush.

"Now, now," Mister Oates said, smiling. "Let's wish this young couple a prosperous and healthy life." With that he lifted his glass in a toast, smiling at Will and Rebecca.

They had to shake hands with everyone as they left, and Will didn't think they were ever going to make it out the front door. Finally they were through the crowd and outside.

The sun was starting to sink low in the west when they stepped through the doors, waving to the last of the well-wishers. Will took hold of Rebecca's hand and led her down the steps of the theater.

Standing at the hitching rail was the gray stallion Will had ridden at the Lansings. "I promised ya I would give him to ya as a wedding present. Remember?"

"I thought ya'd forgotten," Rebecca replied, smiling in delight as she walked up to the horse.

"Nope. I've just been breaking him in for ya. He's still got a ways to go, but I figure ya can handle him."

Rebecca looked at the beautiful animal standing tied to the hitching rail. As her eyes took in the saddle on its back, she turned to Will, a questioning look on her face.

"I didn't reckon ya'd want to ride a western saddle with a weddin' gown on, so I had the livery stable put a side saddle on for ya."

"Ya mean I can ride him now?" Rebecca asked excitedly.

"That's what I planned on," Will said, untying the reins

and handing them to her. Rebecca didn't hesitate but took the reins from his hand. With Will lending a hand, she was soon seated on the stallion's back. Will stepped to the next hitching rail and untied the large bay he always rode. It was the first time Rebecca had noticed the horse standing there, and it brought a smile to her lips as she realized the plans Will had made.

People on the dusty street turned to stare as Rebecca in her long wedding dress and Will in his black suit rode side by side, oblivious to those around them. Many smiles followed them as they rode down the street toward the open range, then turned and rode back to the hotel.

*   *   *

Will and Rebecca spent most of the next day riding the countryside around Bozeman. The hotel had packed them a lunch and included a bottle of wine. They found a cottonwood grove at noon and stopped to eat the lunch and drink the wine. It was a relaxed time as they planned their future, talked of things they both wanted, and reveled in each other's company.

Meanwhile Tye was busy preparing for their departure the next day. He loaded up the supplies Rebecca had ordered at the local mercantile, went to the bank and withdrew the funds they had deposited in the safe, and placed them in the hotel safe for the night, making arrangements to remove them early the next morning. He then rode out to the ranch where the remaining horses were being held. After paying the rancher for caring for them, he drove them back to the livery stable where he'd made arrangements to keep them for the night.

Completing all the preparations for the trip, he decided to do a little shopping for himself, buying new shirts, new jeans, a new pair of boots, and a new hat.

It was late afternoon when he paid for his purchases and stepped through the door and onto the wooden walkway. Shading his eyes against the setting sun, he glanced up and down the street, then started walking toward the hotel. He didn't notice the two men dressed in blue uniforms following him. As he stepped down from the walk to cross an alley, the men closed the distance between them. One of them walked up on Tye's left side, and as they came to the alley, he turned and pushed Tye into the area between the buildings. The other glanced quickly around, making sure no one saw, then turned into the alley.

Tye cursed himself as he staggered into the alley. He should have seen the men. He had dropped the packages as he stumbled. Regaining his balance, he wheeled to meet his attackers, but the soldier had stepped close and swung as Tye came around. The blow crashed into the side of his head. It was short and without full power, but lights exploded in Tye's head, and he staggered backward, flailing his arms to balance himself. But the man didn't give him a chance. He came in swinging a roundhouse blow aimed at Tye's head. Tye saw the blow coming and, even though he was off balance, managed to bring his arm up and deflect the hit. Even so, the large fist glanced off the top of his head, sending pain shooting through him. Tye planted his feet and shook his head. The other soldier was running into the alley now. It was going to take all his skill and wits to come out of this alive.

"Come on, Clyde," the soldier who had hit Tye yelled.

"I'm coming. I just wanted to make sure no one saw us come in here."

Tye looked around the alley. It was a dead end, with buildings on three sides. There were no windows in any of the buildings that he could use for escape. The only way out was through the two soldiers standing before him. He glanced around for a weapon to use. His pistol was back in the hotel room, and he cursed himself for leaving it there. The two soldiers before him both carried side arms, but he felt they would not use them for fear of drawing attention.

They had drawn back from him a little in order to set themselves before beginning their attack.

"Why are ya doing this?" Tye asked, knowing the reason but trying to buy some time.

"Ya took our money the other day. We don't like losing. Now we want it back," the soldier who had hit Tye said.

"I don't have it with me. It's at the hotel. Let me go get it, and I'll give it back to ya," Tye said, knowing they wouldn't let him do it. He was buying time, his mind working all the while.

The soldier doing the talking threw back his head and laughed, but there was no humor in it. "Sure, we're just goin' to let ya walk outa here and go get our money for us. Ya must think we're stupid, mister."

A smile came across Tye's lips, and his eyes closed slightly. "Well, now that ya mention it, I guess I do think yer stupid."

Both men stiffened at Tye's words. The one named Clyde spoke first.

"Lyle, I think this gent needs to be taught a lesson." He started forward, but the one named Lyle put out an arm and restrained him.

"He's mine."

Lyle stood two inches taller than Tye and outweighed him by at least thirty pounds, but Tye could see the paunch around his middle and knew that he was soft from lack of work.

Tye stood relaxed, his arms hanging loose at his sides, the smile still on his face.

Lyle moved toward Tye, drawing his arms up as he moved. Tye could see he was confident in his size and power as he moved closer.

Lyle moved to within four feet of Tye. Then, lunging, he swung a large fist at Tye's head. Tye saw the move coming and ducked under the blow. He had set his feet as he ducked, and as the punch sailed harmlessly over his head, he brought his fist from the ground into Lyle's stomach. He heard the air whoosh from the soldier's lungs as he set himself and threw a short punch to the jaw. Lyle went down, but rolled and came to his feet. Tye had turned to watch Clyde, to be sure the other soldier was not coming in. Clyde had started forward upon seeing his companion hit the ground, but had backed off as Tye turned toward him.

Lyle came off the ground in a lunge, driving his head into Tye's stomach and knocking the air from him. Forced into the building behind himself, Tye felt a stab of pain as the impact with the building jarred his backbone.

Lyle stepped back to set himself. Tye had just an instant to raise his arm and block the roundhouse blow that came at his head. The raised arm partially deflected the blow, but the main force caught Tye above the ear, making his head ring and knocking him to his knees.

Lyle smiled wickedly. Seeing his opponent on the ground, he raised his foot to aim a kick at Tye's midsection.

The haze cleared from Tye's vision as Lyle brought his foot back. Tye saw his opportunity and swung a right to Lyle's midsection. The blow was timed perfectly. As Lyle's foot came off the ground, Tye's fist connected above his buckle. Lyle's face lost its color as he bent over, gagging for air.

Tye wasted no time. Swinging an uppercut to Lyle's nose, he felt the bones crush under the force.

Lyle's head was snapped back, his eyes starting to glaze. Tye didn't wait but stepped in and threw two wicked blows to the smashed nose, feeling bones crunch with each blow that connected. He swung another fist to Lyle's stomach, then pivoted on his heel and drove a wicked punch to his kidneys. The large man groaned and tried to straighten, but Tye had already moved to his left and timed a swinging blow to Lyle's jaw. Tye swung around to face Clyde as he saw the light go out in Lyle's eyes.

Clyde was standing there, his mouth hanging open, his face registering disbelief at what he had just witnessed. As Tye turned toward him, realization struck him, and he started clawing for the revolver at his side. Tye reached him as he was drawing the pistol from its holster. Tye's hand clamped on his wrist, preventing him from bringing the pistol up. He grabbed the pistol with his free hand and twisted it from Clyde's grip. Throwing the pistol aside, he swung a short jab to Clyde's mouth, feeling a small amount of satisfaction as he saw blood gush from the cut lips. Clyde fell instantly to the ground, holding his arms in front of his face, cowering away.

"Don't hit me. It was his idea," he said, pointing to Lyle's prone figure.

Tye retrieved the pistol from where he'd thrown it and turned back to Clyde, leveling the barrel at him. Clyde threw up his arms, closing his eyes and turning his head away from Tye. He began to whimper as he begged, "Please don't shoot me. I didn't want to do it. He made me come along. I promise."

Tye looked at the cowering figure in disgust. "Get up. I'm not going to shoot ya."

Clyde opened one eye and looked cautiously at Tye. Seeing the pistol was not aimed at him, but held loosely at his side, he lowered his arms and tried to regain a little of his dignity.

"What are ya gonna do?" he asked, his voice sounding more forceful.

"I'm turning ya over to the local authorities. They can hold ya until Captain Terry comes for ya. I reckon he'll deal with ya properly, especially since he gave his word there would be no action taken against us. Now get to yer feet."

Clyde pushed himself to his feet, staggering slightly as he stood.

"Pick up yer friend over there and let's go," Tye said, motioning with the barrel of the pistol.

Clyde walked over to where Lyle lay on the ground, looking warily at the pistol in Tye's hand.

"Pick him up, and let's go," Tye repeated.

Clyde pulled Lyle's inert form to a standing position, then bent slightly, allowing him to fall over his shoulder. It was all he could do to straighten under the load. He staggered under the weight, looking pitifully at Tye, but the motion of the pistol told him there was nothing to do but start walking.

Tye fell in behind Clyde as he started out of the alley.

Bending to retrieve his fallen packages, he kept the pistol leveled at Clyde's back.

It was this strange procession that people watched as Tye marched his prisoners down the street to the sheriff's office. People stopped to stare at the spectacle as Clyde staggered under his load, while Tye walked behind carrying his packages, with the pistol aimed at Clyde's back.

The door to the sheriff's office was open as they came to the jail. As Clyde maneuvered his load through the opening, a man wearing a tin star on his vest and a surprised look on his face, came swiftly to his feet.

"What the ...?" he exclaimed, coming around his desk and facing the three.

"It seems a couple of soldiers decided they didn't like the way things came out at the fort the other day, so they decided they'd rearrange my face and body a little to make up for it," Tye said, still holding the gun on Clyde. "I thought I'd bring 'em to ya and let ya hold 'em 'till Captain Terry could collect 'em."

"Ya pressing charges, Mister?" the sheriff asked.

"I am," Tye responded. "If ya'll send someone to the fort with a message to Captain Terry, we can probably get this taken care of right now."

The sheriff looked thoughtfully at Tye, then, walking to the open door, looked around until he spotted the person he was looking for.

"Sam. Sam, come here. I got an errand for ya."

A boy of about thirteen came running at the sheriff's call. A few minutes later he was mounted on a horse, galloping out of town toward the fort.

Clyde was still standing in the center of the office, Lyle's limp form still on his shoulder.

"What do I do with him?" he asked pleadingly.

"I ought to make ya hold him 'till the captain arrives," the sheriff said. "Because of ya I'm gonna be late for supper. My wife's gonna be madder'n a wet hen." Then noticing the strain Clyde was under, he said, "Put him in the cell over there."

When the sheriff had both prisoners locked up, he turned to Tye.

"Looks like they got a few blows in on ya. Ya might ought to have the Doc look at that cut on yer head."

Tye reached up and felt his scalp where Lyle's big fist had connected. He felt the blood that had started to dry, matting his hair. His fingers came away red, and he rubbed them on his pant leg.

"I'll be all right. I'm going to my room at the hotel and clean up a little. I'll be back before the captain arrives."

The sheriff just nodded as he threw the keys to the cell on the desk.

Captain Terry arrived an hour later with a two-man escort. He listened to Tye tell of the events that had occurred and then asked the two men in the cell for their version. Lyle attempted to lie his way through it and might have been convincing had it not been for Clyde breaking down and telling the truth.

The prisoners were led handcuffed from the jail. As they were placed on their mounts, Captain Terry turned to Tye. "Please accept my apology for this incident and rest assured, these two will be dealt with in the strictest manner possible."

Tye smiled at the captain, "I just hope there aren't any more of yer men who are upset over losing. I don't think I could take another battle like this one."

"After what happens to these two, I don't think you'll have to worry," the captain said, looking after the departing soldiers. He held out his hand and Tye shook it. He stood watching as the captain rode out of town, then he made his way to the hotel. He felt in need of a hot bath and a soft bed.

Chapter Twenty-Three

Rebecca stretched and yawned as Will tickled her nose with the feather he'd pulled from the pillow. The sun was still two hours from rising, and the moonlight reflected through the window, casting a warm glow across the bed.

Will smiled as Rebecca wriggled her nose, fighting consciousness. He couldn't blame her. It had been late when they had finally drifted off to sleep. His smile deepened as he thought about their second night together. The nervousness they had felt on the first night was gone, replaced by a new closeness.

"Wake up, sleepy head," Will said, shaking Rebecca slightly. "We've got to meet Tye in a half-hour, and ya haven't packed yet."

Rebecca opened her eyes, smiling up into Will's face. "I don't ever want to leave this wonderful bed."

"I'm afraid it would be hard to carry ya and the bed all the way to Texas."

Rebecca laughed and, wrapping her arms around Will, pulled him down and kissed him longingly.

* * *

Tye was waiting in the dining room when Will and Rebecca descended the stairs. "I thought I was going to have to come up and get ya two. I waited to order breakfast. Are ya two hungry, or are ya still living on love?"

"Ya sure know how to ask a loaded question, don't ya?" Will said, smiling.

"Well, I'm still in love, but I'm starving to death,"

Rebecca replied. Then, looking at Tye closely she asked, "What happened to your head?"

Tye reached a hand up to touch his scalp, "Oh, nothing much. Just a couple of soldiers who were a little upset over Will riding their horse. Seems they didn't care too much for us walking away with their money, and they decided to take it back. I convinced them it wasn't a smart thing to do."

Will looked questioningly at Tye, but he had already turned to his menu and was studying it. The subject was closed.

Will picked up his menu and asked, "How long do ya reckon it'll take us to reach yer place in Texas?"

Tye looked up from his menu. "I figger it'll take us about five weeks. That'll put us there about the middle of September. We won't have much time to prepare for winter, but the winters aren't that bad there. And it's not my ranch. It's our ranch. We're partners now."

Will and Rebecca looked at each other, surprise showing on both their faces. Will was the first to speak. "I knew we were partners in the horses, but that land belongs to you."

"It belongs to us. We're partners. Ya two own forty-nine percent of everything. I've written it all down, and I plan to file it as soon as I get to Texas," Tye said.

"I don't know what to say," Will said.

"There's nothing to say," Tye responded. "We're partners. We work together and split everything. Now let's order breakfast and get on down the trail."

* * *

They left Bozeman as the sun was coming up. Tye led the pack horse and the scarred mare. Will and Rebecca brought up the rear.

They traveled south into Wyoming, keeping to the flatlands as much as possible. The only Indians they saw was a small band moving east. They held up until they were out of sight, then Tye altered their course to skirt widely around them.

They rode into Fort Laramie twelve days after leaving Bozeman. Tye presented his voucher for the horses sold at Fort Ellis, and the quartermaster paid them without question.

They stopped in Cheyenne for two days, spending two nights in a hotel. All three enjoyed the layover but were ready to take to the trail on the third day.

They crossed into Colorado north of Fort Collins and stopped to gather information about the southern trails and Indians in the area.

Fifty miles north of Denver they stopped at a ranch owned by Sam Starr. He had settled in the area ten years earlier and was building himself a nice spread.

Sam's wife, Katie, took Rebecca under her wing, and the two of them spent the evening looking over the gifts Rebbeca had received in Bozeman and talking of the wedding.

The next day Will rode a bronc that had bucked off several good riders. The ride added another two hundred dollars to their roll, and all the hands talked Will into riding another horse, exhibition only.

They left at noon, Rebecca promising to write once they reached Texas.

They spent one night in Denver, enjoying the excitement of the booming city. But they were eager to be on their way.

Tye headed southeast out of Denver. There were fewer towns this way, but the plains were rolling, the route missed the mountains, and there was less chance of running into Cheyenne Indians. William Bent's half-breed sons were still leading their band of renegades against the white settlers, making travel hazardous in the mountainous regions of Colorado.

They passed through Las Animas, spending two nights in town. While they were there, Tye had the blacksmith shoe several head of their saddle horses. This task would fall to Will and Tye once they reached Texas, but for now they did not have the time or the tools.

They crossed the Oklahoma panhandle, breathing the

dust as the wind blew the dry, arid earth across the plains coating everything in its path and blinding those who rode against it.

They arrived in Texas three weeks after leaving Bozeman. The wind and dust still blew as they continued their southward journey toward Austin.

They camped on the south bank of the Canadian River. There was a makeshift holding pen used by ranchers in the area to hold their cattle before swimming the river. After grazing the horses for a while, they herded them into the pen for the night.

Rebecca cooked up a stew with some potatoes, jerked beef, and wild onions. The night breeze blew the long prairie grass, making the plains come alive as if in a slow, willowy dance.

Will walked to the river and washed the evening dishes as Tye took one last look at the horses.

As they all settled down to enjoy the warmth of the fire, Rebecca looked to Tye and asked, "How much longer till we reach Austin?"

Tye studied the grass stem he was chewing on before answering. "It'll probably take us another two-and-a-half to three weeks if everything goes right."

Rebecca's face registered disbelief, and Will looked up in surprise.

"But I thought ya said we were in Texas," Rebecca said.

Tye chuckled. "We are, but Texas is a big state, and we're at the very top of it. We have a long ways to go to reach Austin."

Rebecca looked crestfallen as she heard the news.

Noting her look of disappointment, Tye asked, "You're not gettin' tired of travelin' are ya?"

"Yes, I am," Rebecca stated boldly. "I'm ready to get someplace and start buildin' a home. I want to sit on something that's not moving for a change."

Will and Tye both laughed at her outburst, and Rebecca couldn't help but grin, even though her words were spoken in earnest.

Tye looked at her thoughtfully for a moment, then said, "It's going to take a while to build a home. The houses out here are built out of adobe bricks. That's a mud and straw that's mixed together and formed into a brick, then dried in the sun. We'll have to find us some Mexicans who can make 'em. That may be the hardest part."

Rebecca looked surprised once again. "Ya mean there's no house on the land now? I thought this was yer family's place."

She has spoken the last softly, almost reverently, understanding the need to tread softly on the subject. Tye had never spoken of his family or his past, and Rebecca saw pain in his eyes whenever she broached the subject.

Tye stared into the fire, not answering Rebecca's question. She felt pangs of guilt for bringing the matter up and was trying to think of a way to change the subject when Tye spoke.

"My father was one of the first settlers to come into Texas with Stephen Austin. He came first, leaving my mother, sister, brother, and one slave in Louisiana until he had established a homestead. I wasn't born at the time.

"He received fourteen hundred and fifty acres under the grant laws of the colony. That was six hundred and forty for him, three hundred and twenty for my mother, one hundred and forty for my sister, and the same for my brother, plus eighty acres for each slave. He had three slaves at the time.

"My father was a visionary. He established his claim in 1823. With the help of two slaves, he built a cabin for the family, a barn for the livestock, and slave quarters. Leaving the two slaves to tend to the place, he returned to Louisiana and brought his family back, but before he left for Texas he traded the one slave in Louisiana for sixty-five head of cattle. He somehow managed to trade for another fifty head. When they left Louisiana, my mother drove the wagon, while my brother, sister, and father drove the cattle to Texas.

"Cattle were scarce in Texas in those days. There were plenty of wild horses roaming the ranges. These horses were descendants of horses brought to Mexico by Cortez in the early fifteen hundreds. During the first years, as many as one hundred horses were eaten by the early settlers, and of course every one owned several head. The land cost each settler twelve-and-a-half cents per acre, but most of the settlers couldn't even afford that much.

"My father was selling beef to the Mexicans in San Antonio at twenty-five to thirty dollars a head, delivered. It was a dangerous journey between Austin and San Antonio in those days. Several tribes of hostile Indians roamed the plains, and there was no protection in the beginning. My brother was killed by Caranchahua Indians during one of the drives. I never met him, but my mother had a lithograph she kept on the mantle.

"My father claimed more land under the Mexican Colonization Law of 1823. This allowed him forty-four hundred more acres, since he was running cattle. He was one of the few who could afford to pay the twelve-and-a-half cents per acre. The rest bartered with corn, cattle, swine, or just failed to pay. It made things very difficult for Stephen Austin, who was responsible for payments to Mexico.

"There was continuing strife between Texas and Mexico as Mexico changed leaders and leaders changed the laws governing Texas. My father was caught in the middle many times because he traded with the Mexicans, but his loyalties were always with the Texans. He fought for Texas Independence and was with Houston at the San Jacinto River where Santa Anna was defeated.

"After Texas won her independence from Mexico in 1836, my father came home to tend to his land. He had spent much of his money helping finance the Texas army, but he had managed to hold on to some of it. My mother and sister had managed to keep things going with the help of the two slaves. They had planted corn, potatoes and cotton in my father's absence and had managed to take care of things properly. My father freed the two slaves, keeping them with him and paying them wages. He continued to raise beef and eventually was able to ship them to New York from Galveston.

"Ten years after Texas won her independence, I came along. I was a total surprise to both my father and mother. My father was in his fifties by this time, and my mother was in her late thirties, but my younger brother coming three years later was even more of a surprise. My older sister had married by the time I came along. She and her family had built a house on my father's land, and her husband was helping him with his business. By now my father had acquired over nine thousand acres, some of it farm land. But most of it was used for grazing cattle."

Tye quit talking and stared into the flames. Will and Rebecca remained quiet, each wondering if Tye would resume his oration or if there were memories too painful to talk about.

Without looking up Tye continued.

"I met Robin Lisa on a trip to San Antonio. She was the daughter of a shop owner where we bought supplies. We fell instantly in love and married three months later. I had just turned seventeen, and she was sixteen. The War Between the States had been going on for two years, but we had taken no part in it. It seemed so remote to us. My father didn't agree with seccession, but he wouldn't fight against Texas.

"I was restless at that age. I loved my wife and wanted to be with her, but I had to have excitement as well. By now my father's operation had grown quite large, and even with the war on he was managing to ship beef to New York. He was using contacts on both sides to get the beef through, and sometimes he would receive payments in Confederate currency and sometimes in Union dollars. He was playing a dangerous game, but I think that's the reason he did it.

"I began trailing the cattle to Galveston. I was the ramrod, and the excitement of being on the trail provided me with the outlet I needed. We fought Comanches, rustlers, and Confederate deserters, but we always got the herd through."

Tye's voice broke as he continued.

"I was away on one of the drives when our place was hit by Comanches. They came early one morning as the sun was coming up. We hadn't had any trouble with them for quite some time, which should have been warning enough, but the defenses were slack and they hit unexpectedly. My father was killed in the first rush, along with my older sister and her husband. They killed four of the six hired hands in that rush. They burned the house where my wife, mother, and younger brother were holed up, then stood back and shot arrows into them as they ran out of the burning house. My wife and mother weren't dead when the Comanches found them. Lisa was three months pregnant with our first baby. It was a boy, I know, because they had cut her open and taken the baby out."

Rebecca gasped as Tye related the events of his wife and unborn son's death.

"There were four survivors of that raid: the two Negroes that had been slaves and two hired hands. The Indians had burned all the buildings and run off most of the stock.

"When I returned and saw what had happened, I tried to go on, but I had no heart to rebuild. I blamed myself for Lisa's death. If I hadn't been gone, maybe I could have made a difference. At least if I'd been there, I could've died with her, which would have been better than living without her.

"I left the place in care of some long-time family friends, who promised to look after it until I returned, if I ever did. I joined the Texas Rangers to help fight the Indians, until I could quench my desire for vengeance. Then I traveled north, riding for various ranches, breaking the rough string. The horses are really what saved me. They brought back to life something that had died. Anyway I wound up in Montana, and when Will here showed up, he reminded me of myself. I started getting homesick for Texas, and the rest you know."

Will and Rebecca glanced at each another. There were

tears in Rebecca's eyes and a lump in each of their throats.

"It must have been awful for ya," Rebecca said.

"It was, but ya two have made it easier. I've never told anyone about my past before this. It feels good to get it out. I think it means I'm about over it."

Tye still stared into the fire. Memories of the past still flooded his thoughts, but at least they didn't torment him as they once had. They didn't enter his dreams and cause him to wake in a cold sweat, yelling Lisa's name.

Will watched Tye, noting the look on his face. He had seen the anguish there as Tye had told of his family, but now that anguish was gone, replaced with a look that was sad but at the same time peaceful.

"What kind of shape do ya think the place is in?" Will asked.

"I don't know for sure, but I'd say it was going to need a lot of work. The Burkes have been keeping an eye on it for me, but no one has worked the place since I left. I don't know what became of the two Negroes. I reckon they drifted off once I left."

"Well," Will said with a grin, "I reckon we'll find out in a couple more weeks if we can keep Rebecca in the saddle."

Rebecca gave Will a look of indignation. "I've managed to stay in the saddle this far. I figure I can make it the rest of the way without any problems."

"Well, we better turn in for the night," Tye said, "or none of us will be able to stay in the saddle tomorrow."

Chapter Twenty-Four

As they continued their southward journey, Rebecca and Will noticed how the country around them changed daily. Leaving the flat prairie land of the Texas panhandle behind them, they moved into rolling plains sparsely covered with mesquite bushes. The nights had been cool when they had crossed the Canadian River, but as they traveled southward, the nights and days had become warmer.

They had been following the Chisholm trail since crossing into the panhandle, so it was no surprise when they encountered a large herd of cattle being brought up from San Antonio. It gave them a chance to catch up on the news from Austin and surrounding areas. Tye was pleased to find the Texas Pacific Railroad had laid track to Austin the previous year. It meant Austin would grow. Already there was a large migration of people from the southern states.

Texas had been under Reconstruction since the war was officially over. Texas wasn't as devastated by the fighting as most of the other southern states since no major battles had been fought within her boundaries.

No one with the herd had any news about the area around Tye's ranch. There was talk of outlaws roaming the area. Confederate outcasts with no homes to return to had taken to rustling and looting to survive.

Rebecca sat by the fire listening to the men talk of the changes taking place. An excitement filled her as she thought of the challenges facing them in this vast land with opportunity for the bold.

Will listened with half an ear as he watched the glances from the cowhands being directed toward his new wife. He was only half listening to the conversation when he heard the ramrod mention a bad horse they had acquired.

"I got him with a bunch I bought back down the trail. I've been tempted to shoot him on several occasions. He stampeded the herd once when he bucked into the middle of 'em. He broke the leg of one of the best hands I had. I had to leave him back down the trail, which has left me short-handed."

"Sounds like a bad 'un." Tye agreed.

"He's as bad as I've seen," the ramrod said.

"I'll bet ya five hundred dollars Will over there can ride him."

Will looked up in total surprise. He hadn't expected to find a ride out here in the middle of the plains.

"If I had five hundred dollars, I'd take that bet," the ramrod said.

Tye shrugged his shoulders. "Too bad. I think it would have been an interesting match. I don't suppose yer hands would want to wager anything."

The ramrod threw back his head and laughed. "I doubt ya could find two dollars between the lot of 'em. I gave 'em a two-day layover in Austin, and they spent their last dollar doin' the town."

Tye glanced in the direction of the herd as an idea came to him. "Ya own any of these cattle you're pushing?"

Tye saw a veiled look come over the man's eyes. Then with a grin he said, "Yeah, I own about four hundred head."

"What are they worth?" Tye asked.

"About thirty dollars a head delivered to the railhead in Kansas."

"Ya got any cows in the herd, or are they all steers and bulls?"

"There's probably a hundred cows."

"How about yau put up forty head of cows against our five hundred dollars?" Tye asked, watching the man closely.

He could see his mind working as he thought about the wager.

"Those cows would be worth twelve hundred dollars in Abilene," the ramrod said.

"But yer not in Kansas yet, and ya've got a long ways to go. Besides, if that horse is as bad as ya say, then ya'll be five hundred dollars ahead."

The cowman was mulling it over when one of the hands sitting by the fire said, "Come on, Lou. I want to see ol' Strawberry throw this feller here."

"All right, ya got yourself a bet, mister. We'll hold up long enough in the morning for this young feller to give it a try."

* * *

Tye, Will, and Rebecca left the herd shortly after dawn the next morning, driving forty head of cattle behind the horse herd. Tye wasn't sure they were going to leave without a fight. Lou had ranted and raved about being taken advantage of. Tye wasn't sure he was going to cut out the forty cows, until three of the hands rode in and started cutting the herd, in spite of Lou's scowling face.

When they had driven the cattle and horses four miles, Tye pulled up and rode back to where Will and Rebecca were pushing the stragglers.

"That was a good ride ya put on back there. How do ya feel?"

"Fine," Will said. "That horse couldn't hold a candle to Ol' Brownie."

"Nope. But he was still a rank horse, and ya rode him to a standstill," Tye said. The pride he felt reflected in his voice.

"Ya reckon we'll be able to find horses like that to ride when we reach Austin?" Will asked. "Cause I sure wouldn't want to sit around and get fat and lazy."

"I reckon we can find us some broncs to play with, but ya sure won't have time to get fat and lazy. We're goin' to be busy for a long time just gettin' things in order and turnin' this place back into a workin' ranch."

* * *

Two weeks later they came in sight of Austin.

Rebecca couldn't contain her excitement as she looked at the town before her.

"It's just as I imagined it would be," she said.

Tye let his eyes roam over the city. "It's grown quite a bit since I was last here. It's bound to grow even bigger over the next few years with the railroad being here and the number of Southerners looking for a better place to live."

"How far is our place from here?" Will asked.

"About twelve miles west," Tye answered, noting Will's use of the word *our*. It gave him a good feeling to know Will now accepted the fact that they were partners. "I want to see a few people in town. We'll spend the night and head out to the ranch tomorrow."

Tye rode on ahead to find a suitable place to hold the stock, while Rebecca and Will stayed with the herd. While they were waiting for Tye to return, they let the horses and cattle graze on the lush prairie grass and rode out a short distance to inspect the surrounding land.

"It is beautiful," Rebecca commented.

"I remember Clement tellin' me how Texas didn't have the mountains, but it still had beauty of its own. I see what he meant now. Looking at all this makes me feel as if I could do anything."

"I think ya could do anything," Rebecca said. "Providing ya have the right woman with ya to make sure ya do it right." She laughed at her words.

Will grinned and said, "Well, it looks as if nothing can stop me then, cause I sure picked the right woman."

Tye returned in less than an hour, having found a place to hold the cattle and horses for the night.

Tye led them into Austin. Riding up to a livery stable, he stepped down and hailed the proprietor. A man walked slowly out of the barn, looking them over slowly as he came.

"What can I do for ya?"

Tye looked at the man for a moment, then said, "I heard some horse thief named Orrin Taggert owned this livery stable. We were thinking about boarding our horses here for the night, but I'm not sure they'd be here in the morning when we came to get them."

The man looked Tye up and down. "I know you, don't I?" he said.

Tye grinned at him. "Yeah, you know me. It's been a while, but I didn't think you'd forget the man that rode your red stallion for you."

Recognition lit up the man's face. "Tye Garrett, well I'll be!" He grabbed Tye in a bear hug, and the two men laughed as they slapped each other on the back and shook hands.

"I never would have known ya, Tye," Orrin said as he stepped back and looked at him. "Ya've aged some, but it looks good on ya."

"Well, you're still as ugly as ever," Tye said, grinning. "Orrin, I'd like to introduce ya to my partners. These are the Paxtons, Will and Rebecca."

Orrin shook hands with Will and took Rebecca's hand in his, holding it gently. "I'm pleased to meet ya, but if ya two are partnered up with this sidewinder, ya better hang onto your purse."

Tye was standing to one side, a grin on his face. "Orrin, are ya still upset over losing that money to me?"

"Nope. I'm not upset, but I'll tell ya one thing. I'll never make another bet with ya as long as I live. I still don't see how ya rode that bronc, but by golly you did, and it cost me a thousand dollars to see it."

Will looked at Tye. "A thousand dollars?"

"Yeah, that's what he bet. I'll tell ya about it sometime. Right now ya two need to find us a room while I talk to Orrin here a little while."

Sitting in Orrin's office after Will and Rebecca had left to get rooms for the three of them at a hotel Orrin had recommended, Tye looked at Orrin and asked, "So how are things around here these days?"

"Business is great. I can't keep enough horses on hand to meet the demand. "

"How is all this new growth affecting the oldtimers around here?"

"Some like it, some don't," Orrin answered, "but the growth is good for Austin. There are some problems though. I guess ys got to take the good with the bad."

"What kind of problems?" Tye asked, raising an eyebrow.

"Well …" Orrin hesitated, "it seems there's a band of outlaws operating somewhere around here. They're led by a Confederate deserter named Lomas Cantrell. They've hit ranches for a hundred miles in every direction, stealing cattle and horses, then taken them into Mexico and sold 'em. There's even rumors that they steal from the Mexican side and sell over here as well. They've hit a few stagecoaches, and there's even been a couple of train robberies credited to them."

"Doesn't the law do anything about them?" Tye asked.

"They try, but by the time the law gets a posse together and heads off after 'em, they've done crossed the border."

"Do they hit ranches around here?" Tye asked.

"Here most often. That's why some folks think their headquarters must be around here somewhere."

"What about the Cattlemen's Association? Have they been able to do any good?"

"Oh, they put up a big reward, but that ain't done nothing to stop the stealin'. When Cantrell heard about it, he sent a message to every town. He'd kill anyone trying to collect the reward and burn the ranch of anyone trying to stop him. That pretty well quenched any desires to go after them. A couple of bounty hunters tried. Their horses came back to town with them strapped belly down to 'em."

"Sounds like a tough customer," Tye said. "Have ya been out to my place lately?"

"It's been over a year since I been out that way. John Burke's still looking after it for ya. Not that there's that much to look after any more. Ya plannin' on stayin' or just passin' through?"

"We're gonna stay. We've got us some horses and cattle bein' held on the Thomas ranch north of town. We're
gonna move 'em out to the home place tomorrow and start
rebuildin'."

"I'm glad to hear it," Orrin said. "I know how hard it
was on ya, losin' all your family that way. And I know ya
had to get it outa yer system, but that's a mighty fine
spread out there and it needs someone to care for it."

"Yer right," Tye said, "and that's just what I intend to
do. I'm gonna need some more cattle. Do ya know where
I can get some?"

"If you're smart, you'll register yourself a brand and
head into the breaks and find yerself some of them strays.
There's men who are gettin' rich drivin' cattle out of the
wilds, brandin' 'em and drivin' 'em to market. I know
someone who'd be willin' to hire on with an outfit. He
knows more about chasin' them ol' mossy-horned cattle
than anyone around."

"I'm lookin' to hire some good hands. Can he meet me
here in the mornin'?"

Orrin grinned. "I'll have him here first thing."

"Thanks, Orrin. It's good to be back. One more thing.
Is Henry Lawrence still practicin' law?"

"Yep, he's got him his shingle hangin' in an office just
west of the courthouse."

"Thanks again, Orrin. I'll see ya in the mornin'." Tye
walked up the street until he saw a sign hanging outside an
office. "Henry Lawrence Attorney at Law." He opened the
door and went in.

*   *   *

Over dinner that evening, Tye told Will and Rebecca about
the hiring of help and going after the longhorns.

"If we're going to build a ranch, we might as well get
started right away. I plan to take three men and head south-
west about fifty miles. I hear there's still a fair amount of
cattle in the breaks down there. Orrin knows a man that's
willin' to show me where they are. Ya two can start the

buildings while I'm gone."

"How long will ya be gone?" Will asked.

"I'm not sure, but probably about two months."

"We should be able to get quite a bit done in two months," Rebecca said.

"If ya can find some help, ya should," Tye said.

They talked late into the evening, making plans and talking about things they would need for the ranch.

"I'll talk to Orrin tomorrow about buying a wagon. We'll need one if we're goin' to be haulin' supplies out to the ranch. We'll have to break about six horses to harness, but that shouldn't be too difficult," Tye said, smiling at Will's dubious look.

* * *

The next morning Tye and Will met at the livery stable with Orrin and the man he'd recommended. Rebecca took the list of supplies they would need to the local mercantile.

Orrin was waiting for them in his office. With him was a man wearing a large black hat. The brim was flat and the crown tall, but what caught Tye and Will's eyes was how thin and tall the man was. He topped six feet by at least four inches and looked like a fence post with a hat on top.

Orrin stood up and introduced the men.

"Tye, Will, I'd like ya to meet Rowdy. He's lookin' for a job wranglin' cattle. He's been roamin' around the country for the last few months tryin' other things. Now he's come back lookin' for a job."

Tye shook hands with him. Looking up into the grinning face, he asked, "Ya know how to gather longhorns out of the brush?"

Rowdy smiled, showing a row of white teeth. "I choused a few of those critters out before I started roamin' around."

"Good," Tye said. "I'm lookin' for some hands to gather about a thousand head. Ya know where we can round up that many."

"Yeah, I know a spot where there's that many and more. It's rough country, but if a man has enough horses to ride, he can get 'em."

"We've got the horses. Do ya know anyone else worth their salt who might be lookin' for a job?"

"I know three or four fellas who're lookin'. I might be able to find a couple more. How many you want?"

"We'll hire five, including you."

"When do you want 'em?" Rowdy asked.

"Day after tomorrow," Tye said. "Do you know where the Garrett ranch is?"

"Are ya kin to the Garretts that had a place northwest of here?"

"I'm Abel Garrett's son."

"I remember ya now. Ya joined up with the Rangers after that Comanche raid, then ya just kinda disappeared. Folks around here wondered what happened to you. It was too bad about yer family. They was good folks."

"Thanks," Tye said. "Why don't ya meet me back here in about two hours. I'll lay out our plans then."

"All right. Ya want me to bring the other hands around so you can meet 'em?"

"If you can round 'em up."

"I'll round 'em up," Rowdy said with a grin as he left .

Will and Tye talked with Orrin for another hour. They traded for a wagon and a team of horses, but only after Will persuaded Tye that they would need a team immediately and he wouldn't have time to break one in.

They walked to the mercantile where Rebecca was still ordering supplies.

"They've got almost everything we need," she said as Will and Tye came in. "They've got to order some of the things, but they promised they would be here within a week."

"Fine," Tye said. "We'll have Rowdy bring the things out day after tomorrow when he comes."

"He's the guy we just hired," Will said at Rebecca's questioning look.

Oh, is he good looking?" Rebecca asked, her eyes twinkling with merriment.

"He's real handsome," Tye said, "if ya like 'em short and broad."

"He's almost as wide as he is tall," Will said, picking up on the mood.

"I want to leave town in about an hour. Can ya two be ready?" Tye asked.

"We'll be ready," Rebecca said.

* * *

Tye and Will met Rowdy at Orrin's livery stable two hours later. He had four other men with him.

"Will, Tye, I'd like you to meet Shorty, Wayne, Curly, and Bo. They're all top hands, and they're lookin' for work."

Will and Tye shook hands with each of the hands. Shorty fit his name. He was short, but broad across the shoulders and lean in the waist. There was a strength about him that could be felt in his handshake. Wayne was of average height and build, while Curly, not as tall as Rowdy, stood just at six feet, without a hair on his head. Bo was the youngest of the four. Maybe seventeen or eighteen, he still had the look of youth about his face, but his eyes told a different story. He had seen plenty and had ridden the trails.

Tye hired all four men, then laid out his plans, telling them to drive the wagon and supplies out to the home place the day after tomorrow. They would leave from there in a week.

Chapter Twenty-Five

Tye, Will, and Rebecca gathered the horses and cattle from the ranch where they'd been left, and with Tye leading the pack horse and the scarred mare, they began the last leg of the trip. Pushing the horses and cattle, it took them two hours to reach the canyon overlooking the Garrett homestead.

Rebecca caught her breath as she looked into the valley at the charred remains of what had once been a house and barn. Even the ruins and the story behind them could not diminish the beauty of the valley and its surroundings.

Tye pulled up and sat on his horse, looking at what had once been his home. He had wondered how he would feel when he saw his place again. Would he still be haunted by those who had died here while he was away? He sat waiting for the emotions to envelop him, but they didn't come. Gone was the guilt, most of it anyway. Gone was the feeling of hopelessness. He found he could look at the burned house and see the future, not the past.

Will and Rebecca remained behind the herd, understanding Tye's need to face this alone.

Tye touched his spurs to the horse's side and started down the road. He was home, and he was starting over. It was a good feeling.

Tye led them up to what had been the house. All that was left to identify it as such were the two rock-formed chimneys that stood among the charred ruins.

"Orrin is sending out two Mexicans tomorrow. They know how to make and lay adobe bricks. I figger if we clean up this mess, we can build upon the foundation of the original house. We'll build two living quarters with the kitchen being the center for both. That way we can each have our private quarters. How does that sound to ya two?"

Will looked at Rebecca, and she nodded agreement. "That's fine with us," he said. "As soon as Rowdy gets here with the wagon, I think I'll get a load of lumber and start building us some corrals. We're going to need some to break the rest of these horses."

"That sounds like a good idea," Tye said. "Why don't we set us up a camp over by the river, and tomorrow I'll show ya two around the place. We can let the horses and cattle graze here in the valley for a while. I don't think they'll wander off too far."

After building a lean-to and setting up camp, Will and Tye helped Rebecca prepare supper. They were sitting around the fire, having finished eating and washing the dishes, when Tye cleared his throat.

"I registered us two brands while I was in Austin. One I figure we'll need for a trail brand. The other will be for the ranch stock. I registered a turkey track for the trail brand, and for a ranch brand I registered a rafter TP, the T for my first name and a P for Paxton. The P will connect to the leg of the T like this." He drew the brand in the dirt to show them what he meant.

"I told Orrin to start making our irons. We'll need them for the herd we're going after. What do ya think?"

Will looked at the drawing on the ground. Then looking at Tye, he said, "Well, I think it should have been the PT since I have to do most of the work around here, but since ya already ordered the irons, I guess we'll stay with the brand the way it is."

"I appreciate that, Will," Tye said with mock sincerity, "and since ya do most of the work around here, why don't ya go get us some more firewood for the night. It feels like it may be getting colder, and my old bones can't take the cold the way they used to."

Rebecca smiled as Will went in search of more firewood.

"Ya two are just alike, ya know it? Ya'd rather dig a spur into each other than eat."

"I know," Tye said, returning her smile. "It's what makes it possible for us to be close. Ya married yourself a good man there. He's gonna make a name for himself out here."

"I know he is," Rebecca said, looking in the direction Will had gone. "So are ya, Tye Garrett. That's what I meant when I said ya two were just alike."

* * *

The next day was spent riding as much of the property as possible. Tye outlined the boundaries and pointed out where the best grazing and watering places were. The traps that had been fenced would need some work to hold stock, and Will made a list of the things he would need before he could do the repairs.

When they returned late in the afternoon, they were surprised to find two Mexicans cleaning up the charred timbers and removing the debris from the old home site.

"Señor Taggert tell us you want to build a new house here," the older of the two men said as they rode up. "We start cleaning this up. You tell us what you want us to build, and we build it for you."

Tye outlined the house plans for the Mexican, whose name was Pedro. Rebecca made some minor modifications.

Pedro and Felipe made their camp by the river, sleeping under the wagon they had brought. The wagon contained the tools they would use to build the adobe bricks for the house.

Shortly after sunrise the next morning they heard the rattle of the wagon making its way down the canyon road. Shading their eyes against the sun, they saw Rowdy sitting in the wagon seat, foot pushed hard against the brake. Shorty, Wayne, Curly, and Bo rode beside the wagon, which made them wonder who sat on the seat beside Rowdy. As they forded the river and came up the bank, Will got his first look at the man sitting there. At first glance Will thought the man old enough to be his grandfather. His hair and mustache were shocking white, but as they drew up to the camp and stepped down, Will could see he wasn't as old as he'd first suspected.

"Howdy," Tye said as the group pulled up.

"Hey, boss," Rowdy said, stepping down off the wagon. "I brought along another hand. I figured if we was goin' to be out in the breaks for a spell, it might be nice to have a cook along with us. This here is Ringo. He was captured by the Comanche when he was a youngster. When the cavalry raided the village he was in, they found him there, his hair as white as snow. No one knows what made it turn white as he won't talk about what took place. He can out ride, out shoot, and out fight any two hands, but his specialty is cookin'. He can cook some of the tastiest meals you ever put in your mouth."

Tye and Will each shook hands with the newcomer, noting that he had yet to speak a word.

"I'm pleased to have ya," Tye said. "I hadn't thought about a cook, but I know I don't want to chase longhorns all day, then come in at night and eat my own cookin'."

Rebecca had been standing by the lean-to, looking at the new arrivals, but now she stepped forward. "Ya must be Rowdy. Ya don't look anything like what I was expecting." She looked at Will and Tye, and they both cast their eyes to the ground to cover their smiles.

"Yes ma'am, that's me," Rowdy said, taking off his hat.

"I'm Rebecca Paxton. We're glad to have ya here," she said, offering her hand.

"Pleased to meet ya, Mrs. Paxton." He introduced her to the other five men. She shook hands with each of them, welcoming each to the Rafter TP. Ringo took her hand but looked shyly at the ground as she smiled and shook his hand.

"Let's get this wagon unloaded and start getting ready," Tye said. "Ringo, tell Rebecca what you'll need in the way of groceries, and she and Will will pick them up when they go to town. Let's go pick out the horses we'll be taking with us."

Will and Rebecca took the wagon to town the next day to pick up a load of lumber for the corrals, as well as the list of supplies Ringo needed.

*   *   *

Tye stayed at the ranch with the new hands and started preparation for the trip to the breaks. The horses they had chosen needed to be shod. This job fell to Wayne, who had worked as a blacksmith for a spell.

Each of the horses chosen was ridden to determine how well it would handle in the rough, brushy area. It was going to be grueling work, and it would take a horse with a lot of stamina to maintain the pace required to chase the longhorn cattle out of the dense brush. The horses had to be strong enough to hold the cattle once they were roped. The cowboys would use one of two methods for roping and holding the rangy cattle once they were out of the brush. A single rider would rope a steer or cow around the horns, then spurring his horse he would ride by, flipping the rope around the animals rear as he went by. When the horse hit the end of the rope it would jerk the back legs from under the cow, thus sending it crashing to the ground in a pile of thrashing horns and feet. The rider would then jump from his horse's back, run to the downed bovine, and tie its front and back legs with strips of leather or rope. The beast would then be left to thrash and bellow on the ground until it wore itself down, enabling the cowboys to drive it to a holding pen.

The other method was to double up, one roping the horns and turning the cow back, while the other rode in and threw a heel loop, snagging the two back feet and stretching the animal out. The header would then dismount and tie the legs in like fashion, achieving the same results. Although this method required teams and sometimes slowed the gathering process, it took a lot of the danger out of subduing the cattle. Tye decided this would be the option they would use. He wanted to reduce the risk of injury as much as possible. The trip would have enough dangers with the threat of Indians and rustlers. He didn't want to add to it by having them all riding single. This way there would always be two riders together, leaving one man to watch the herd.

And of course Ringo would be alone in camp. Tye doubted that would bother the man. He seemed to enjoy his solitude, talking very little to those around him and staying mostly to himself. The only person he had talked to at any length was Will. Will had mentioned he was building corrals for breaking the remaining horses. Ringo asked about the corral and the horses, making suggestions that would make them more versatile. Will had told him about the chute he was going to build, modeled after Jim Lansing's in Montana. Ringo's interest was peaked by the bucking chute, as Will called it, asking questions and making suggestions. Tye made a mental note of Ringo's interest in the horses. It might come in useful at some time.

A week later the six men rode out, Rowdy leading the way, with Curly and Wayne bringing the remuda of horses. They had chosen twenty head of young, strong stock to take with them. Some of the horses had only been ridden once or twice, but they would be seasoned ranch horses by the time they returned. Ringo led two pack horses loaded with supplies to carry them through for the three months they would be gone.

* * *

Bo stayed behind to help Will with the cattle they had acquired by trading. Tye had spotted cattle on his rides out to inspect the ranch, and he hadn't seen any brands on them. He imagined they might have been some strays lost by the cattle drives or left from earlier gathers. Bo and Will would spend part of their time gathering any unbranded cattle.

Will just about had the corrals finished and was working on the bucking chute. Once he had finished the chute, he would begin breaking the remaining horses, but first he had to repair the fences in each of the traps in order to hold any cattle rounded up.

Pedro and Felipe were making good progress with the

adobe bricks. Several hundred were drying in the sun.

"We will start building the house in a few days," Pedro said to Rebecca one afternoon. "As soon as we have enough bricks dried, I will bring out my two sons and two nephews from town. They will continue making the bricks and mix the mud for the bonding, while Felipe and I lay the bricks. We will have you a fine home in about one month."

Meanwhile Rebecca had set up housekeeping in the canvas-covered lean-to Will and Tye had built for her. The thought of having a house made Rebecca smile with pleasure.

A week later Pedro came to tell her he was going to town to pick up his sons and nephews. "If it's all right with the Señora, I would like to bring my family back with me. My Juanita does not like it being alone without me. She could help the Señora with the cooking and the washing of clothes."

Rebecca was taken back by Pedro's request. The surprise showed on her face. Seeing the look, Pedro was immediately embarrassed.

"I am sorry, Señora, I should not have made such a request. She will have to wait until I am finished with the work here."

"No, no," Rebecca exclaimed, hurrying to explain her thoughts. "I would love to have yer wife come out here with ya. I am just surprised is all. I wouldn't have thought she would want to come out here. She is welcome to come with ya. I would love to have her."

Pedro's pleasure showed in the broad smile on his face. "Gracias, Señora. Juanita will be so happy. I will bring her back with me two days from now. Gracias, Señora."

Rebecca laughed at Pedro's pleasure, thankful she would have another woman to talk to.

Will and Bo completed the corrals and chute and were repairing the traps. They spent each day riding to the various locations, stringing new wire or repairing broken ones. Rebecca packed them food to take with them, knowing they would not be back until the sun was setting.

She enjoyed the evenings with Will and Bo as they talked of the work they had done that day and their plans for the next day's work, but she felt the loneliness of the days. She had ridden out with them on two occasions, but found she was of little help. She opted to stay at the lean-to in order to have their supper ready when they returned.

Will had told her that most of the repairs had been made, and soon Bo and he would start gathering strays. When she asked to go along with them when they started the gather, Will eventually relented, but good sense told her that the best thing she could do was to have a hot supper ready for them when they came home, although she did want to ride out at least once or twice. Maybe she could make arrangements to have Pedro's wife cook for them. She smiled at the thought of spending her days with Will, even if they would be hard, grueling days with little time for conversation. At least she would be with him, and that was what mattered.

Pedro arrived at the ranch with his two sons, two nephews, and wife, Juanita. Rebecca went out to greet the newcomers, smiling as Pedro introduced each of them. There was nothing shy about his wife. She immediately wrapped her arms around Rebecca, giving her a hug and thanking her for letting her come to be with Pedro.

"You know how these men are, they don't like to be away from us for very long." She smiled as she stepped back, looking Rebecca over from head to foot. With a smile on her face, she said, "If I had known you were so beautiful, I would have been jealous of my Pedro being out here." Pedro smiled and shook his head at Rebecca, who smiled back at him. She took an immediate likening to Juanita.

"Would ya like to sit down for a spell?" Rebecca asked, pointing to the lean-to.

"Eeee, I don't know if I will be able to sit again for a whole week," Juanita said, rubbing her backside. "That wagon seat ees as hard as a beeg rock, and I think Pedro heet every hole een the road." Rebecca laughed, taking her by the arm and leading her to the lean-to.

"At least ya can enjoy a cup of coffee. I just put on a fresh pot."

"Sí, that would be very nice." She turned and called to one of the boys standing by the wagon. "Manuel, bring me the basket I feexed for Señora Paxton."

"Yes, mama," the young boy said, hurrying to follow his mother's orders.

When Will and Bo returned that evening, they were pleasantly surprised to find a meal of homemade tamales, venison burritos wrapped in flour tortillas, and stuffed chile rellenos. Both Will and Bo sweated from the hot peppers, but they continued to eat them, fanning their mouths and drinking water by the glassful.

"I've asked Juanita to help me with the cooking so I can ride out with you," Rebecca said.

Will looked up from his plate not sure how to respond. He spoke hesitantly. "That's great."

Rebecca picked up on the hesitancy in his voice. "Don't you want me ride with you?" she asked.

"Of course, I'd love for you to ride along. It's just that I figgered ya'd be tired of riding after the trip here from Montana. And with Juanita here now, I guess I figgered ya'd want to stay around."

Rebecca looked at her husband, wondering if that was all that was behind his hesitating. "I don't want to ride every day, but I would like to ride out sometimes. With Juanita here, I won't have to worry about the meals, but if ya don't want me along, I'll stay here."

"No, no. I want you along," Will hurried to say. "I think it's great that ya want to go along. Tomorrow we're going to start gathering cattle. Ya can be a big help to us."

Smiling, Rebecca put her arm through Will's. "I'll be the best help ya ever had," she laughed as Will blushed and Bo turned to look out the opening of the lean-to.

Chapter Twenty-Six

Tye spurred his horse after the rangy longhorn Rowdy had flushed out of the dense thicket. His loop built and swinging over his head, he pursued the thousand-pound animal at breakneck speed. He had to rope it before it reached the thicket on the far side of the opening. His horse, a stout quarterhorse with abundant speed, closed the gap between them in a short distance. Tye threw his loop with well-practiced accuracy, watching with satisfaction as it settled over the expansive horn spread. Jerking his slack, he reined the horse around and waited for the inevitable jolt that came an instant later.

Days of roping wild cattle had trained the horse to brace for the impact. He lowered his body and leaned forward as the big steer hit the end of the rope. The steer was pulled around as the horse dug his feet into the ground and kept the rope taut.

Rowdy was riding closely behind Tye, and as the steer was pulled around, he swung in behind it swinging his rope as the animal was forced forward. He threw his loop at the back feet, watching as it encircled both hocks.

Tye forced his horse forward until the longhorn was stretched between the two horses. Stepping to the ground, his horse keeping the rope tight, he raced to the animal's tail and pulled hard, forcing the animal to its side. Taking two lengths of rawhide from his belt, he first tied the back legs, then the front, securing the steer until they came to retrieve him.

They had been working the dense thickets for the past

four weeks, gathering over five hundred head of long-horns. It was grueling work, fighting the thickets to force the rangy cattle out into the openings where they could be roped and tied. After a day of fighting the rawhide bind-ings, the cattle were more subdued and could be driven to the waiting herd.

Ringo was cooking meals and, true to Rowdy's compli-ments, everything was delicious. Each of the other five men traded days watching the herd or roping cattle. The day spent watching the herd was considered the day of rest.

Curly and Wayne both proved to be top hands, roping and tying as many longhorns as Rowdy and Tye. It was a contest to see which team could bring in the most cattle every day. Each time it was close, with one team having more one day and the other team having more the next.

Driving the longhorns from the dense thickets of mesquite and yucca cactus was hard on both horse and rider. It was becoming routine to pick thorns out of both after each chase.

One of the biggest dangers came from the longhorns. Releasing one after a day of being tied required skill, agility, and a good horse. A loop was placed around the back legs of the animal and held tight by one man on horseback, while the other removed the rawhide bindings. The man on the ground then had to make it back to his horse while the other held the longhorn at bay.

Wayne was knocked from his horse and received a blow to the head when one of the steers managed to get free before he could get fully mounted. Reacting in terror, the horse reared as the steer came at him. With one foot in the stirrup and hanging on to a handful of mane and the sad-dle horn, Wayne was helpless and could only hold on and pray for the best. Luckily the horn spread on the thousand-pound animal was so wide, the horse missed being gored as the horns passed on both sides of him. But the impact of the collision toppled him over backward. Wayne was thrown into the air and brought up short by a mesquite tree, banging his head and bruising his body. Curly managed to get a rope around the steer before he could do any more damage, but Wayne nursed a headache the rest of the day.

There were no signs of Indians, but each man rode with his Colt at his side. They were constantly watching for signs. The only tracks seen so far had been those of shod horses. This in itself worried Tye, for he remembered Orrin's warning about Lomas Cantrell. He could be in the area. No one knew where he was holed up, and Tye warned all the other riders to keep their eyes open for tracks.

Even though it was November, the days were warm. The grass was still green and plentiful along the Llano River where they were holding the herd.

Tye was pleased with the gather so far. They were ahead of schedule, and if things continued to go as well as they had, they should finish the gather with more cattle than they had anticipated.

* * *

Meanwhile, Will and Bo were working from sunup to sundown gathering strays on the Rafter TP and driving them into the trap close to headquarters. The work was much like that of the men gathering in the breaks. Will and Bo would double-team a rangy longhorn, heading and heeling it, then tying its legs until later in the afternoon when they would release it and drive it with the others to the trap.

The most difficult part of the job was locating each of the strays. This job fell to Rebecca. Finding a high point where she could see the land as well as Will and Bo, she would spot one of the longhorns standing in the thick brush, attempting to blend with the foliage. She would direct the two men to it with a series of hand and arm signals, waiting with breath held as the two men roped and tied it securely. Then she would resume her search for another. The system had worked well, saving Will and Bo countless hours of riding the thickets in search of the elusive long-horned cattle.

It was an overcast day as Rebecca watched from her vantage point as Will and Bo closed in on a large bull. They had tried once before to capture this animal, but he had managed to escape by doubling back on them and lying down in the brush. Rebecca had not been able to see where he had gone. It was only by luck that they had come across him again, and Will was determined not to let him escape again. He and Bo were closing the space between them, working their way through the thick mesquite and pushing the bull toward a clearing twenty feet away.

Rebecca's full attention was on the scene before her, and she didn't notice the man who had ridden up beside her until he spoke. "If they get a rope on that one, they better have a good horse under 'em."

Rebecca let out a startled gasp as she whirled in the saddle to stare at him. He wasn't a large man, but for some reason he seemed big. He was dressed in a black shirt and wore a black vest and hat. His black mustache was neatly trimmed, but his eyes were what held Rebecca's attention. The light gray eyes held her mesmerized as she continued to stare. He allowed her to sit there like that for several moments, returning her stare until he spoke again.

"I didn't mean to startle ya. I was just riding through when I saw ya sitting here. I thought ya might be in trouble or something, so I rode over to check on ya. My name is Lomas Cantrell."

There was no way he could miss the sharp intake of breath at the mention of his name. Tye had told Will and her about this man, and now here he sat. For an instant she considered screaming, then she thought about the results and willed herself to become calm.

Lomas chuckled. "I see ya've heard of me. Well, have no fear. I don't have the reputation of harming beautiful women. Ya are quite safe, I assure ya." He smiled as he sat there looking at her, and her fears calmed as she watched him. He had done nothing to threaten her so far, and with Will and Bo close by she doubted he would try anything.

"They've got him in the opening," he motioned toward

the thicket where Will and Bo were. She had momentarily forgotten the bull and was surprised when he turned to watch episode below.

Will was closing the space between himself and the bull, swinging his loop as his horse pounded across the open ground, ears back, intent on the running animal before him. As the gap narrowed to fifteen feet Will threw his loop and pulled the slack as it settled neatly over the wide horns.

Will was riding the large bay he'd won at the Double A ranch in Montana. The horse had a lot of cow smarts and could handle the toughest longhorns. He turned and braced himself as the big bull hit the end of the forty-foot lariat. The large bull was jerked around as Bo moved in to throw the heel loop, but instead of resisting the pull of the rope as most did, the large bull charged straight ahead, running at Will, intent upon using his horns to impale horse and rider. Will felt slack in the rope and turned in time to see the bull close the distance behind them. The bay sensed rather than saw the bull advancing and immediately swung to the right. This move saved Will and the horse, as the big bull brushed past them, brought up short again as he hit the end of the rope. This time Bo was in position and threw a perfect heel loop that caught the bull's back legs. He held the slack until the animal was stretched between the two horses. Will wasted no time in tying the bull's front and back legs, taking caution to tie them extra tight.

Lomas smiled as Will finished the job of securing the big bull. "That's some horse he's riding. If he hadn't moved when he did, that cowboy would be hurting mighty bad right about now."

Rebecca looked over at the outlaw and was surprised to see admiration on his face.

"That's my husband, Will Paxton. He and his partner Tye Garrett own this ranch."

Lomas Cantrell looked surprised. "Own this place? I thought this was open range."

"No, it belonged to Tye Garrett's folks. They're dead,

and he's been away for a while, but he's back now." She
noticed his eyes take on a troubled look, but he instantly
smiled.

"Sure is a nice place. I'm glad to see someone's going
to be making good use of it."

Rebecca didn't respond but continued to watch him.
She wondered what his purpose was in being there.

"Well, I better be going. It was a pleasure meeting ya,
Mrs. Paxton. Perhaps we'll see each other again sometime," Cantrell said, touching his hat and smiling at her.

"Perhaps we will," she responded coolly.

She watched him as he turned his horse and rode away,
noticing how he rode in a direction that prevented Will and
Bo from seeing him. She didn't suspect it was from fear,
for she doubted the man she just met feared any man.

* * *

Later that afternoon she told Will about her meeting with
Lomas Cantrell. He was shocked that the man would so
boldly ride in the open.

"I don't like the thought of him comin' up on ya like
that," Will said to Rebecca as they were pushing the cattle
toward home.

"I don't either," Rebecca said, "but something tells me
he wouldn't have harmed me. He might be an outlaw, but
I think he has morals about him. I don't think he would
harm any woman."

"Well, just the same, I'd feel a whole lot better if ya'd
stay at the camp," Will said.

"And what if he comes there?" Rebecca asked. "Pedro
and Felipe aren't any hands with a gun. I doubt they would
be able to do anything should this man decide to harm
me."

"I guess yer right," Will conceded. "I just wish I knew
why he was riding out here."

"I don't know, but he seemed surprised that someone
had moved in and was running the place now," Rebecca
replied.

"We'll just have to keep our eyes open and be on the

watch. I don't like the feel of this. Tye should be back with the rest of the group in about a week. Maybe we can do a little scouting around and find out if there's anything going on around here. I'm sure there's nothing around. He was probably passing through and heard us thrashing in the brush. I doubt we'll ever see or hear from him again."

Rebecca nodded at Will's reassurance, but she had the feeling they had not heard the last of Lomas Cantrell.

* * *

Five days later Will and Bo rode out to look for strays. Pedro and Felipe were finishing the roof on the house that day, and Rebecca was intending to start moving things into the house.

They had rounded up three hundred head in the last few weeks, but they had found only three head in the last three days.

"I think we've gathered about all we're going to get," Bo said as they watched for fresh tracks along the stream they were traveling.

"I think yer right," Will agreed, "unless there's some further west. We haven't tried that part of the range yet."

"I thought Tye said to stay within the bounds of this here creek," Bo said.

"He did," Will said, "and I reckon we better listen to him. Let's ride over to that draw south of here and see if we can pick up any sign."

"I don't think we'll find any," Bo said, "but at least we can get a good view of things from the top of that peak."

They rode along watching for sign as they went, but they saw no new tracks. As they approached the peak, Will noticed a dust cloud to the west of them. "I wonder what's raising so much dust over that way?"

"Could be a duster blowing in," Bo commented, speaking about the hard blows that sometimes come upon the prairie, covering everything with dust and drying up water holes.

"I don't think so," Will said. "It's too even and seems to be following a path."

"How far off do you reckon it is?" Bo asked.

"Ten, maybe twelve miles."

"Why don't we ride over and find out?"

Will looked at the sun. It was still early in the day, and it wouldn't take that long to find out the cause of the dust. They could be back home before dark.

"All right, let's ride over and check it out. If it's what I think it is, we may be needed anyway."

They set out at a ground-eating trot, saving their horses but covering the miles.

Will watched the dust as he rode. It was moving south at a crawling pace. His first thought had been that the herd was being driven in by Tye and Rowdy, but the more he thought about it the more he was sure it wasn't them. They wouldn't have been this far south.

As the distance between them and the dust cloud narrowed, both Will and Bo could hear the bawling of cattle and shouts coming from the men as they drove them. They seemed to moving at a brisk pace. But why south, Will wondered.

"Something doesn't feel right about this," Will said as they drew near. "See that rise over there. Let's see if we can work our way around there where we can't be seen."

Will turned his horse and headed for the rise, which was nothing more than a drift that had built over the years until it rose out of the prairie to stand twenty feet above the land. A washout draw followed along the base of the rise, offering Will and Bo natural cover.

The herd had not yet reached the point where Will and Bo waited, hidden by the mesquite shrubs growing sparsely along the rim of the rise. Their horses had been tied in the draw several yards back.

Lying on their stomachs, they could see the cattle being driven hard by twelve men, their faces covered with bandannas to keep out the dust.

Will watched as the lead cattle approached the spot directly beneath him, the dust boiling up as their hooves tore into the ground beneath them. Will peered through the dust as the first of the cattle came even with him. He guessed there to be somewhere between a thousand and twelve hundred head. As his eyes searched the cattle moving before him, his breath caught. There on the left hip was a turkey track brand, the brand Tye had registered for their trail brand. He looked to the horse remuda that was moving on the other side of the herd. It was hard to see through the dust, but, watching closely, he saw several head of horses that he could identify as being from their stock. The large gray mare that Tye favored was there, along with a stocky black that Rowdy had chosen to be part of his string.

Pulling back from the edge of the rise, Will motioned for Bo to follow him. Easing along the draw, cautious not to be seen, Will waited until they were well away from the herd before he spoke. "Where does this trail lead to?"

"I don't know for sure, but I imagine it leads to Mexico," Bo answered.

"How long would it take this herd to reach Mexico?" Will asked, looking around nervously.

"Three days if they were pushed hard," Bo replied. "Why're ya asking?"

"Because that's our herd," Will responded with anger. "Someone's stole the herd from Tye and the boys. I don't know how, but they've got it, and that means something has happened to keep Tye and the others from pursuing."

Bo looked toward the herd as the impact of Will's words sunk in.

"What are we going to do?" he asked.

"I'm thinking," Will answered. "Can you draw me a map to get to where Tye and the rest of them went?"

"Yeah, it's pretty easy. But why do ya need a map?"

"Cause one of us has to go find out what happened to the others, and one of us has to stay with the herd."

"I guess I'm elected to stay with the herd," Bo said, trying to grin but not carrying it off very well.

"I have to find Tye," Will said. "Where can we meet three days from now?"

"There's an inn at Uvalde that would be about three-days ride from here. I imagine the herd will pass close to there."

"Good. I'll meet ya there in three days if I can find the others. If I'm not there, ya hightail it back to the ranch. Don't take any chances. Stay away from the herd. Ride just close enough to make sure it's still heading south."

"Don't worry. I ain't about to tackle twelve men by myself," Bo said, handing Will a map he had drawn on a tally sheet.

"All right, here's my canteen and the lunch Rebecca packed for me. I wish I had more. Maybe ya can find a village along the way to buy some supplies. Here's twenty dollars in case you need it." Will looked over at Bo, then held out his hand. "Good luck."

Bo took Will's hand in a firm grip. "I'll see ya in Uvalde. We'll show these thieves it ain't a good thing to mess with the Rafter TP."

"Ya bet we will," Will said with more confidence than he felt.

Chapter Twenty-Seven

Will slowed his horse to a trot, giving it a chance to regain its breath. He estimated he had come over half-way since leaving Bo at the draw. He was headed to the ranch first. There he would get extra horses and weapons, and then he would set out to find the others. He had been running his horse as much as he dared, but he couldn't afford to break him down at this point. Too many lives possibly relied on him.

Riding gave him time to think. How did the thieves manage to steal the herd? Had they killed Tye and the others? Were they now lying in the hot sun, dead or dying? How much time had passed since the herd had been stolen? Estimating the distance the herd was from where Tye and the others had started, Will figured they had been on the trail at least two days, possibly three. If he rode hard, he could be at the breaks in a day and a half. Would he arrive in time? He would have to try.

After another two hours of hard riding, he came in sight of the house. Pedro and Felipe were on the roof putting the last of the tin in place as he galloped into the yard, yelling for Rebecca.

Rebecca had just finished placing her mother's tablecloth on the kitchen table when she heard the pounding hooves and Will calling her name. She hurried outside, clutching her apron in her hands and knowing that for Will to be riding like he was, something was wrong.

Will dismounted from the weary horse before it came to a complete stop. Rebecca was standing in the doorway of the house, clenching her apron.

"We've got to gather the horses. The cattle have been stolen, and we have to find Tye."

All this came out in a rush as Will hurried past Rebecca. She didn't waste time with foolish questions but hurried into the house to change into a pair of riding pants, giving instructions to Juanita to pack some food, water, and bandages.

Pedro and Felipe came down from the roof, hurrying to assist Will in gathering the horses from the trap.

By the time Rebecca emerged from the house, Will had the horses in the corral. With Pedro and Felipe's help, he was frantically saddling five good mounts.

Rebecca hurriedly saddled her gray horse, then helped Will tie the horses head to tail. Juanita brought out the food and several canteens of water, as well as medicine and bandages. She and Rebecca distributed the supplies in the saddlebags of each horse.

Will worked in a frenzy, knowing that each moment lost could mean the difference between life and death.

"Pedro, I want ya and Felipe to go to town and buy as many rifles and pistols as ya can. Also buy ammunition for each. If ya have any problems, tell Orrin Talbert our herd has been stolen and Tye and the boys are missing. He'll help. Take the wagon and team, and when ya leave town, head toward Llano." Will showed him the map Bo had drawn. "Meet us here. If Tye and the boys are all right and headed this way, we should run into them before they reach this point. If not, I'll send Rebecca back to get ya, but ya wait here. Comprende?"

"Sí, Señor, we will be there. It will take us one day to reach this spot. We will wait for you there."

"I will be there also," Juanita said.

"Gracias, Juanita. We may need your help," Will said. Then handing Pedro a handful of coins, he said, "If this isn't enough, tell them to put it on our bill."

"Si Senor. Vaya con Dios."

Turning to Rebecca, Will asked, "Are ya ready?"

"Let's go," she said. "Tye's waiting for us."

Will smiled as he gathered the reins of his horse. Climbing into the saddle, he turned to Pedro. "We'll see ya tomorrow," he said. Then, spurring his horse, he led the horses out of the corral. Rebecca followed, yelling at the horses as they broke into a lope.

* * *

As the sun sank slowly behind the Texas hills, Will and Rebecca were twenty miles away from the ranch, alternating between a slow lope and a trot to conserve the horses. Will knew he should not wear down the horses. If they found Tye, they would have to go after the herd. He had to believe that Tye was all right.

Will pulled up as the darkness settled around them. "There'll be a full moon tonight. It'll help, but we won't be able to travel as fast. How are ya holding up?"

Rebecca was tired and sore, but she smiled. "I'm fine. Ya just set the pace, and I'll keep up with ya."

Will took her hand in his. "I don't know what we'll find up ahead, but I'm glad yer here with me. If ya get tired, let me know and we'll rest."

Rebecca squeezed his hand. "We'll have plenty of time to rest after we find Tye and the others. Let's keep moving. I'll keep up."

Will followed the Colorado River, keeping it to his right as they rode. The moon cast its glow on the trail, providing enough light to follow the trail Bo had laid out for them.

They had been traveling northwest. Upon reaching the Pedernales River, Will turned due west. The Johnson ranch lay on this path, and he planned to stop there. Tye might have made it this far.

The Johnson ranch was the gathering point for seven counties for driving cattle to the railheads in Kansas. If Tye had been able to make it this far, Will was sure he would have received help and may now be on his way after the herd.

It was after midnight when Will and Rebecca pulled up

to the gates leading up to the Johnson ranch headquarters.

"Hello the house," Will shouted. He knew it could be unhealthy to ride straight up to the house.

Several moments later a light appeared in the bunkhouse, then a voice called out, "Who's there?"

"Will and Rebecca Paxton. We have a spread over on the Colorado north of Austin. We're hunting our partner. We believe he was ambushed by rustlers and could be in danger."

"Hold on a minute," the man in the bunkhouse called down.

Shortly a man came down to the gate carrying a lantern. He held it up to get a better view of Will and Rebecca.

"You say your partner was ambushed by rustlers?"

"We believe so. I saw a herd wearing our brand being driven toward the border. Our partner, Tye Garrett, was gathering cattle in the breaks west of here, and some of our horses were with the herd. I believe rustlers stole the herd. I don't know what has happened, but I'm trying to find out. Have ya seen anyone come by this way?"

"Nope, but one of the hands saw a group of about twelve or thirteen men riding west four days ago."

"That sounds like the men we saw with the herd," Will said.

"Sounds like Lomas Cantrell's bunch. If it was, ya'll be lucky if yer bunch is still alive."

"How far is it over to the breaks?" Will asked.

"A day's ride from here."

"If I miss them on the trail, they'll probably try to get to this ranch. If they do, tell them to head to Llano. I'll meet them there tomorrow," Will said.

"If they make it here, we'll take care of them. If ya need any help going after yer herd, send word to us. We'll ride with ya."

"Much obliged," Will replied as he reined his horse around. "Sorry to have to wake ya."

They rode through the night, watching the trail as best they could for signs of cattle or men. An hour before dawn

Will veered off to the north, heading for a hill half a mile away.

"I want to be on high ground come daylight," Will told Rebecca. "Maybe we can spot 'em."

They were resting on the hilltop as the sun rose. Will had unsaddled both his and Rebecca's horses and built a small fire for warmth. Rebecca dug in her saddlebags and brought out some biscuits and cold steak.

"It ain't much, but right now it tastes like a restaurant dinner," Rebecca said as she bit into one of the biscuits.

"It does taste good," Will agreed.

They sat by the fire watching the lower regions for a sign of life. Will watched deer move about in the early morning, feeding on the lush prairie grass but never far from the thickets. He was watching three does and a buck as they grazed in a clearing not far from a washout that led into a draw. Suddenly one of the does lifted her head, looking in the direction of the draw. Will followed her line of vision, but he could see nothing to cause alarm. Suddenly all four deer bolted across the clearing and disappeared into the thicket. Will continued to watch the draw, but nothing moved. Something was in that draw, though.

Walking to his horse, Will lifted his saddle to its back, then saddled Rebecca's horse, too.

"There's something down there. I'm going to go down and check it out. I want ya to stay here with the horses. I'll wave to ya if it's clear."

"Will, ya be careful. If there is something down there, it might not be friendly. There still are Indians around here, and I don't want ya losing yer scalp to one of 'em. I never did cotton to a bald-headed husband." She smiled as she said it, but the concern in her eyes was easy to read as Will took her in his arms and kissed her.

"I'm glad yer here with me," he said. "I better go before I forget what I came here for."

Will mounted his horse and started off down the hill. He planned to circle around and come up from the northwest side. This would put him below whatever it was the deer had seen.

He rode cautiously, watching the surrounding area for signs of anything out of the ordinary. When he was within two hundred yards of the draw, he stopped and tied his horse to a mesquite tree, keeping him out of sight of the draw. Proceeding on foot, he worked his way to within a few yards of the edge of the draw. Getting down on his hands and knees, he crawled to the edge and peered over.

The draw was about ten feet deep and three feet wide. Will could see only part way up toward the mouth. A curve in the bank blocked his view.

Crouching down, he worked his way along the edge, watching the bottom as he moved. Working his way around the bend, he stopped short. There under a washout in the bank he saw a boot sticking out, but shadows from the bank prevented him from seeing any further. He eased along the bank, drawing his pistol as he moved and hoping to work his way around the bend to get a view of the area where the boot lay.

The bend in the draw was caused by a large bolder that blocked the rushing waters during the spring and fall rains. As Will worked his way around the bend, he kept his eyes on the floor of the draw. Crouched over, he eased up to the lip once again, peering over to the washout where the boot had been. It wasn't there any more. Moving closer to the edge, he looked at the sandy bottom where waters had eroded the soil over the years and saw footprints made by boots. Apparently more than one person had been there, for there were several prints. Peering into the washout where the water had eroded the sides and left a natural cave, he could see where the dirt had been packed down as if one or more persons had bedded down there.

Will was looking up the draw, trying to follow the footprints in the sand when suddenly he spun around and pointed his gun into the surprised face of Curly, who was holding a large mesquite branch over his head. Apparently he was intent on denting Will's hat.

Both men stood there, each shocked by the other's presence. Curly was hatless. His shirt was torn and dried blood showed on several scratches, but otherwise he looked unharmed. As they stood there looking at each other, both of them began to smile. Curly was relieved that it was Will, and Will was relieved that he had found at least one of his men alive.

Lowering his pistol, Will asked, "Where are the others?"

Curly lowered his club, leaning on it as if in need of the support. "They're down in the draw. Wayne took a slug in the shoulder, and Ringo's got a sprained ankle. Tye's behind ya."

Will whirled around to see Tye standing behind him, his hunting knife held lightly in his hand. Will grinned at the sight of him. His shirt was in shreds, his hat was missing, and his jeans looked as if he'd been drug in them.

"Ya all right?" Will asked.

"I've been better, but I sure am glad to see ya. How did ya know we were in trouble?"

"Bo and I saw the herd with our trail brand. It was heading south toward Mexico. I also saw several of our horses in the remuda, so I figured something must have happened. What did happen?"

Tye shook his head. "It all happened so fast I'm still not sure. We had finished gathering and branding the cattle. We had about thirteen hundred head, and we were starting them on the trail. It was hard work getting them broken to the trail. We were in the saddle sixteen to eighteen hours a day. On the third day we were breaking camp when ten men on horses rode into our camp and got the drop on us. Wayne and Ringo were on night watch. They shot Wayne in the arm. Ringo got off a couple of shots, but a bullet nicked his horse and he was thrown into some rocks. He's bruised up some and has a sprained ankle, but other than that he's all right. We've all got bruised feet and scratches from working our way through the thickets, but Wayne's the only one in bad shape."

"I've got horses for ya," Will said. "Pedro will meet us

this afternoon at Llano with the wagon. Bo's following the herd."

"I always knew picking ya for a partner was a smart thing to do," Tye said. "Where are the horses?"

"Rebecca's got 'em up on the hill over there. I guess I better let her know everything's all right."

"I think you're a little late," Curly said, pointing in the direction of the hill.

Will looked up to see Rebecca leading the horses down the hill toward them.

"That girl can't follow directions any better than ya can," Will said, looking at Tye. Tye grinned at him.

It was two hours before they got Wayne bandaged up and able to ride. The food Rebecca had brought disappeared soon after it was brought out.

Will looked at the sun. "We're going to have to push it if we're going to get to Llano before dark."

"We'll make it," Tye said. "Then we'll go get our herd back."

Chapter Twenty-Eight

The seven riders made it to Llano in the late afternoon. The ride had been hard on Wayne, and his face was drawn and haggard. Each time Tye had suggested a rest, however, he had protested, "Keep going, we got to get the herd back. I worked too hard to see those thieving skunks get away with our cattle."

Pedro was waiting on the outskirts of town. Beside him on the wagon seat was Juanita, the worry and anxiety draining from her face as she spotted the riders. Seeing Wayne, she immediately began giving instructions to Pedro and Felipe. A bed was made in the wagon from blankets she had brought, and Wayne was laid upon them. From a large bag she brought forth medicine and began cleansing his wound as the others were handed food.

Tye looked at the group of riders. The events of the last few days had taken their toll. Each face was haggard and weary from lack of rest.

"We've got to rest before we go after the herd. Pedro, is there an inn in Llano?"

"Sí, señor, there is such a place, but it is a bad place. There is a lot of shooting at the inn. My cousin and his family live close by señor. It would be better if we went there."

"Are ya sure they would welcome this many?" Tye asked.

"Sí, señor. My cousin is a good man, and he has a good wife. They will put us all up for the night."

"We won't be there all night, just long enough to get a little rest. Then we'll be on our way. I see ya brought the rifles and pistols. That's good. We need to go into town and buy supplies and some hats. The sun has already burned our heads enough. Is there a doctor in town?"

Juanita who had been listening to the exchange between Tye and her husband spoke up at the mention of a doctor.

"What for you want a doctor? I can take care of thees one. No doctor can fix him better than Juanita."

Tye looked questioningly at Pedro, who nodded vigorously.

"Sí, Patrón, she is a medicine woman. She knows the herbs with healing power. She will have Mister Wayne fixed up in no time."

Tye smiled. "Sorry, Juanita, I did not mean to offend ya. Of course ya are the one to care for him."

Juanita returned Tye's smile, then went back to caring for her patient.

Night had fallen by the time the group had bought supplies and ridden to Pedro's cousin's house. Pedro's cousin, Miguel, welcomed them to his humble house, assuring them that they would be of no inconvenience to him or his family.

Rebecca brought in some food she had bought in town, and soon Juanita and Miguel's wife, Maria, had the delicious smells of cooking filling the house. It was a small house with one large room that served as the living room and kitchen and one room that served as the bedroom. Miguel's three small children slept on pallets in the large room, close to the fireplace. Wayne was now laid on a pallet there, enjoying the warmth as Juanita's herbs worked their power on his wounds.

After a quick meal of flour tortillas filled with steak cuts and spices, washed down with cold milk, all of them lay down in the large room on pallets made from the blankets Juanita had brought and straw ticking Maria provided.

Will and Rebecca lay next to each other, exhausted but happy. They had found Tye and the others, and all were alive. Ringo and Curly had spoken little since this morning, and Will knew they were thinking about the men who had stolen the cattle and the revenge they wished to extract.

Tye had left instructions to be awakened in four hours. Then they would leave, heading south to find Bo and retake the herd. It would take them at least a day and a half to reach Uvalde, only if they rested little and rode hard.

Pedro woke them four hours later. Will felt as if he had just closed his eyes. Rebecca stirred and sat up.

"Are we leaving?"

Will looked at her, knowing he was going to be in for a battle.

"Rebecca, I want ya to stay with Pedro and Juanita."

"Well, ya can want all you care to, but I'm going with ya. I'm not about to sit at the ranch and wonder what in the world is going on while ya fight it out with those thieves. I promise ya I will stay behind when the fighting begins, but I'm going with ya. Besides, I can help bring the herd back."

Will looked at her in exasperation. He knew there was no use arguing with her, but he had hoped she would be reasonable about it.

"All right," he said, "ya can come. But ya'll stay behind when we get to the herd. Ya have to promise me that, or I'll hog-tie you and send you back right now with Juanita."

Rebecca looked at him and smiled. "I promise, as long as ya promise not to get yerself killed."

Will couldn't help the smile that came to his face. "I promise ya I will do my best to honor your wish."

An hour later they rode south out from Miguel's house at a brisk lope. They rode for six hours before stopping to rest the horses and eat. The country they traveled was rolling hills covered with mesquite brush and Yucca cactus.

They passed by Kerrville, the frontier post started by the Frenchman Charles A. Schreiner, now a cattleman who was reported to own over six hundred thousand acres. Tye had served with Schreiner in the Texas Rangers and had considered enlisting his help, but he decided against it. This was his and Will's fight, theirs and the men that rode with them. There was no use involving outsiders.

They rode late into the night, pacing the horses. At midnight Tye called a halt. They built a small fire and heated tortillas and beans for supper, then rolled out their blankets. They were asleep instantly. No watch was posted. They trusted the horses to wake them should anyone approach their camp.

Three hours later Tye woke them, and everyone rolled out. Nobody complained or spoke as they saddled the horses. Each of them drank hot, black coffee and ate the remaining flour tortillas. Then they mounted and rode out.

It was a weary group that rode down the streets of Uvalde that afternoon. Pulling up in front of the inn, they dismounted, knocking the dust from their clothes. Heads turned to look at the group of strangers that had ridden in.

Will entered the inn, looking around the lobby. As his eyes adjusted to the darkness of the room, he found what he was looking for. Bo was sitting in one of the two chairs against the wall, a paper in front of him. Will walked over and stood over him, waiting for him to look up.

It took Bo a moment to realize someone was standing before him. He lowered the paper to looked at the man, who was covered with dust and looked bone weary. It took Bo a second or two to recognize Will. When he did, he instantly came to his feet.

"Did you find the others?" he asked excitedly.

"They're waiting outside," Will answered. "Where's the herd?"

"South of town about five miles. They've got 'em held on the Nueces River. They got there yesterday afternoon. Three gents left the herd and rode south. I figure they've gone to contact the buyer. I think they're going to move the herd in the morning, I heard two of 'em talkin' about it."

They walked outside to where Tye and the others were waiting. Will told him what Bo had said.

"Let's get us some rooms and get some rest. We'll meet in the lobby at eight o'clock tonight and plan what we're going to do. Bo, you take our horses down to the livery stable and grain 'em down good. Did you get a good night's sleep?"

"Yeah, I spent the night here waiting for y'all to show up."

"Good. I want ya to stay awake in case any of those men show up. Wake us up at seven thirty."

* * *

Will woke feeling better, but still tired. He left Rebecca sleeping and slipped quietly out of the room. Tye was sitting in the lobby, looking rested and fit. Will almost resented him.

"Ya feelin' better?" Tye asked as Will poured himself a cup of coffee from the pot on the stove.

"Definitely better," Will said. Tye grinned at him but said nothing.

Curly and Ringo walked into the lobby a few minutes later, both looking better for the rest.

"Where's Bo?" Will asked.

"He's getting our horses ready. We're riding out in an hour."

Will sipped his coffee and waited for Curly and Ringo to join them.

Bo came in shortly afterward.

After everyone was seated around the table in the lobby of the inn, Tye looked at each one of them. "If we do this right, we can take the herd back the same way they took it from us."

"Bo, how many men do they have with the herd?"

"Nine, with the other three gone."

"How many guard the herd at night?"

"They usually have four out nighthawking."

"That leaves five sleeping. We're going to take those five first. Then we'll get the four nighthawks."

"How long are their shifts?" Tye asked.

"Four hours."

"That'll give us enough time to put our plan into place. Drink yer coffee. We ride in fifteen minutes."

Will went back to the room he shared with Rebecca.

She was sleeping but woke as he came into the room.

"Are ya leaving now?" she asked.

"Yeah, we got to move while it's dark. We've got a good plan, and if all goes well we should have the herd back by morning."

Rebecca looked into his eyes. "Come daylight I'm riding south to the herd. Don't make me ride too far, all right?" Tears threatened as she hugged him to her.

"I'll have them right outside of town for ya." He hugged her once more, then pushing her away, he turned and went out the door.

The moon was low in the eastern sky as they rode out of town. It provided enough light to show them the way. Bo led, taking them around the herd. Tye wanted to come upon them from the south. If guards were posted, they would be expecting trouble from the north, not the south.

They could hear the cattle lowing long before they sighted them. Bo led them across the river and followed the low-lying hills until they were close to the herd.

"Their camp is east of the herd," Bo said. "It's about three hundred yards away from the cattle. They don't have a wagon, just pack horses. Ya can see their campfire from the hill over there."

Tye looked around, locating a place where he could watch the camp.

"All right, Ringo. I want ya to take the first watch. The rest of us will catch some sleep while we can. Wake me in two hours if they haven't changed night riders. We'll make our move after the next change. Whoever is on watch, wake me when the change is made."

They picketed their horses well away from the herd, not wanting them to pick up the scent of the remuda. Ringo made his way to the top of the hill, which was well covered with mesquite trees. He could watch the camp below without being seen. The others rolled into their blankets, gaining whatever rest they could before the action started.

* * *

A hand shook Tye's shoulder. He was awake instantly, pulling on his hat.

"They changed riders fifteen minutes ago," Ringo said. "Four rode out, and four rode in. They have no guard posted. They must not be expecting any trouble."

"Let's go look at the camp," Tye said, pulling his blanket about his shoulders.

Will was sleeping fitfully when Tye shook him awake.

"It's time to ride, partner."

No one spoke as they started toward the camp on foot, moving slowly, careful not to make even the slightest noise.

Tye had worked out their approach from the hill overlooking the camp. Now he led the way, using the soft sand of the river bed as much as possible. Leaving the river bed, he led them around mesquite trees and yuccas until they were within thirty feet of the camp. Then with hand signals he directed them to the sleeping forms on the ground.

The fire had died down to coals. That would prevent any of them from being seen by those riding herd.

Each man moved cautiously, expecting at any moment a challenge or warning to be sounded. But none came as they moved into the camp.

Will moved toward one of the men sleeping on the ground. The man's pistol was in its holster, looped around his saddle horn. Will moved quietly, lifting the gun and holster and looping them over his shoulder. He didn't see any rifles but knew they were around somewhere. After he had taken the pistol, he moved back into the shadows. He was soon joined by the others. Each, except Tye who had stood guard, had a pistol and belt with him.

They unloaded their burdens, then turned back to the sleeping men, drawing their pistols as they moved back into the camp. Each chose a man and moved in, kicking them with the toes of their boots. One man started to protest, but a pistol barrel to his head quieted him instantly. The others moved as directed. Tye moved into the darkness and returned shortly with five ropes. Each man was tied to a tree and gagged, some with their own socks, which was Ringo's idea.

Tye, Will, Ringo, and Curly went to the picketed horses, each carrying one of the outlaws' saddles. They led their horses back into the circle where Bo was watching their captives.

"We should be back shortly. If anyone rides in alone, it's probably one of them, so be careful," Tye said to Bo. With that they mounted their horses and rode out, each knowing what to do.

When the four riders reached the cattle, they split up. Tye and Curly went in one direction, Will and Ringo went the other. If all went well, they would meet back here in less than thirty minutes.

Will and Ringo rode side by side, their hats pulled down low over their eyes. They had ridden a short distance when they heard singing. Many cowhands sang while on night watch. It helped to calm both cattle and rider, as well as letting other riders know your whereabouts. Will looked at Ringo, who was grinning. This rider was more likely to spook the cattle with his singing than calm them.

Will and Ringo saw the rider as he came toward them. He stopped his singing when he saw them, pulling his horse up and taking out the makings for a cigarette.

"I'm sure glad ya came along. I've run out of matches and haven't had a smoke in two hours."

The man was busy pouring tobacco into the paper when Will rode up beside him. He was carrying his pistol across his lap, and as the man looked up he brought it down across his head. The outlaw let out a moan and slid from the saddle. Ringo was on the ground, tying the man with his rope and gagging him with a rag. Ringo dragged him into the brush as Will led his horse into a clump of trees and tied him.

Will rode on alone, Ringo following at a distance. The next rider was whistling a tune as Will came upon him.

"What took ya so long?" the man asked as he saw Will.

Will grunted as he came up beside him.

The man peered through the darkness trying to see Will's face. He couldn't see the pistol in Will's right hand.

"Hey, yer not Lon!" the man exclaimed, reaching for the pistol at his side as Will brought the gun in his hand up to within inches of the man's nose.

The ominous click of the cocking hammer stilled the man's motions. He went stiff as Will softly said, "Mister, if ya want to live to see daylight, let that pistol drop to the dirt."

Will heard the pistol hit the ground.

"Now ride toward the camp, and don't make a sound. If ya do, it'll be the last sound you ever make."

Ringo came out of the darkness. "I'll go get the one we left under the tree."

"We'll meet ya there," Will said, riding behind his captive.

Ringo and Will arrived at the point where the four of them had split up. Tye and Curly weren't there, but they showed a few minutes later, with two riders in front of them. One was bleeding from a gash on his jaw, and Curly was rubbing a bruised knuckle and smiling.

They took their prisoners back to the camp. Tye threw wood on the fire, building it up until they had good light to see all their captives.

"Well, boys, it looks like we're going to have a good night for a necktie party," Tye said, taking a rope from his saddle. Curly grinned, and Ringo grabbed one man by the arm, leading him over to the center of the camp.

"This one goes first. He's the one that shot Wayne."

The outlaw's eyes seemed to grow to twice their normal size as Ringo threw the rope over a branch and brought the loop down to his neck. He looked around at the five men standing there. There was no mercy in any face, only hard lines.

Bo led a saddled horse up to where Ringo held the prisoner. Together they lifted the outlaw to the horse's back. His hands were now tied behind him.

Tye threw another loop over the branch of the mesquite

tree, and another man was brought forward, his hands bound behind him. He was lifted onto the back of his horse. When they had four of them lined up, each with a rope around his neck, Tye spoke.

"Do any of you have anything to say before you go to meet your maker?"

One of the men, the one Will had hit with his pistol, spoke up. "Yer gonna regret this when Lomas Cantrell catches up with you."

"We might," Tye said, "but mister, ya won't be around to see it." He slapped the horse with his hat, and the rider was pulled from the saddle. As if on cue, each of the other three horses bolted, leaving their burdens swinging from the mesquite branch.

The other five were dealt with in the same manner, quickly and with no regrets.

"Let's get this herd moving north," Tye said as the last outlaw was hanged.

Bo brought up the horses they had left tied by the river. He turned them loose with the rest of the remuda, and each man chose a fresh mount.

The sun was still two hours from rising when they started the herd moving north. Most of the cattle were trail-broke now, and with a full day's grazing and plenty of water, they were easily managed by the five riders. With the herd moving easily along, it still took them three hours to reach the outskirts of Uvalde. Rebecca had caught up with them as the sun cleared the horizon. But she had said nothing after seeing the expressions on their faces.

Chapter Twenty-Nine

Will found a place to hold the cattle outside of Uvalde. After they had bedded the herd down, Tye left them to go into Uvalde to find extra men. Everyone needed rest, and he needed at least six men to hold the herd at night.

Tye found eight men who would hold the herd and help take them to the Rafter TP. He told them to be at the herd at six that evening and rode back to help set up camp.

The lack of sleep and the ordeal of the last three days, left them all with little reserve. Will was dozing in the saddle when Tye rode up.

"Hang in there, partner. I've got help coming. We'll rest here for two days, then move the herd. I want to ride out tomorrow and look for water and a place to bed down the herd. We'll have to scout for places each day. I figger it'll take us four days to drive them to the ranch. I don't want to push them any harder than we have to. Why don't ya go on in and get some rest? I'll ride herd for a while. Curly and Ringo are already sacked out. Rowdy, Bo, and I will ride for a couple of hours."

Will grinned. "I'd argue with ya, but I'm too tired." He started to ride away but pulled up. "Do you think Cantrell will try something?"

Tye shook his head. "I don't think he will. We eliminated his gang of thieves, and I don't think he'll be able to get another one together. Thieves are superstitious. They don't like to follow someone who got all his men hung. He might try to get revenge, but I don't look for it."

"Well, I don't know about ya, but I'm going to watch my backside for a while. Something tells me Cantrell won't like us taking back the herd and hanging his men," Will said.

The men Tye hired showed up at six that evening. They rode night herd while Tye, Will, Rowdy, Ringo, and Bo slept the first full night in three days.

The next morning Tye and Will rode out to scout the trail leading back to Austin. Fifteen miles from Uvalde they found water and grazing for the longhorns. Returning to the herd, they made plans for the drive.

After checking the supplies, Rebecca informed them, "We'll need more since ya've hired extra men."

"We'll ride into town this afternoon and get what we need. How many of the new hands have rifles?" Tye asked.

"Six," Rowdy said.

"We'll pick up two more. I want everyone to have a rifle. I hope we don't need 'em, but ya never know."

The sun was high as Will, Rebecca, and Tye rode into town, their horses kicking up dust as they walked down the only street in Uvalde. Pulling up in front of the general store, they dismounted and walked up the wooden steps that elevated the sidewalk above the street.

"While ya two are getting supplies, I'm going over to that little shop over there and see if I can get some material for curtains," Rebecca said, pointing across the street.

"All right," Will said, "just make sure ya get some material with horses on it."

Rebecca looked at him in astonishment. "Horses? Are ya crazy? If ya want horses, ya can sleep in the corral. I'm not about to have anything with horses hanging in my house."

Will feigned a hurt expression as Tye walked into the store, hiding his smile as he went.

"I think horses would be nice hanging over the kitchen window. That way when yer washing dishes ya would be able to see them," Will said.

Rebecca shook her head. "Will Paxton, ya've lost yer

mind if ya think I'm hanging curtains with horses on them over my kitchen window."

Will grinned at her as she stood there, hands on her hips and a look of determination in her eyes. "Well, if ya don't want horses, how about somethin' with a cow on it?"

"A cow? Why I never …" She stopped in midsentence, seeing the grin on Will's face. "Will Paxton, I ought to shoot ya right here and now. Ya've been pullin' my leg all along, haven't ya?"

Will's face showed mock surprise. "Why, Becky, how can ya say such a thing?" He smiled and pulled her to him, but she pulled back away.

With a serious look in her eye, she looked up at him. "Just for that I'm buying pink material to put on every window in the house." She turned and started across the street. Will stood there, a truly shocked expression on his face. Shaking his head, he turned and walked into the store, wondering if she'd really do it.

Rebecca hid the smile on her face as she walked across the street. That would teach him to fool around with her.

Tye was looking over the shelves of stocked goods when Will walked through the door. Neither man saw the three men turn the corner at the edge of town.

* * *

Lomas Cantrell was filled with cold fury. The picture of the nine men hanging from the mesquite tree was still fresh in his mind. He had ruled these parts for three years now, no one daring to challenge him. He had made his threats and backed them up. He had reaped the rewards of being an outlaw, but he knew it wasn't luck. His success required careful planning and forethought. He knew whom to steal from and whom to leave alone. He never stole from the large spreads but hit the small ones instead, holding the stolen cattle and horses until he had enough to drive to Mexico. He had a buyer who enjoyed receiving cattle from those "Stupid Norteamericanos," no questions asked. Of course, stealing cattle from the small Mexican spreads and selling them on this side of the border was just as lucrative.

The two men riding beside him were Jake Black and Bart Tombs, both hardened gunmen who had been useful in keeping order among the men and insuring his safe passage into and out of Mexico. They had been very helpful in obtaining information from the cowboy at the herd. Hiding in the brush, they had grabbed the cowhand as he passed by. It took them only a matter of moments to know who was responsible for the hangings and where they were. They had left the cowboy unconscious, hidden in the brush, his horse tied to a mesquite, out of sight of any one passing by.

Now they were looking for two men, Tye Garrett and Will Paxton. Cantrell wondered why the name Paxton sounded familiar to him, but dismissed it. It didn't matter. He would be a dead man soon.

Rebecca was looking at a bolt of cloth on a stand by the window when she looked up and saw the three men ride up to the general store. Her heart froze as she recognized the man in the middle. Though she had seen him only once, his face was imprinted on her mind, and now he was here.

Dismounting in front of the store, Cantrell looked around, making sure no one was on the street. He motioned to the other two, and they started up the steps ahead of him.

Will heard the footsteps as the two men walked through the door. As he turned from the counter where he had been looking at the rifles, a sixth sense sent a warning to his brain. The men had automatically separated when they entered the store.

Tye was behind a shelf looking at the rolls of hemp. The owner was in the back getting the hundred pounds of flour Rebecca needed.

Will watched as one man stopped three feet inside the door while the other moved to his right. Will noticed that the move put him in a position where he couldn't see both men at once.

His mind racing, Will turned back to the counter as if the men held no interest for him. Picking up a box of shells and lifting the top, he took out a handful, pretending to inspect them as he mentally took stock of the situation. The counter where he stood was at the back of the store at the end of the wide aisle leading from the door. The shelves of goods began slightly to his left and about four feet behind him. The next aisle was a good ten feet away. He knew he could not make it to the shelf for cover before one or both of the gunmen nailed him. If he could distract the one closest to him, he might have a chance to make it around the shelves before the one standing in the aisle could get him.

Will heard the wooden floor squeak as the man standing closest to him shifted his weight. Glancing in that direction, Will saw him standing there, his feet slightly spread, his hand inches away from the pistol at his side. Will turned to look at the open doorway, his eyes widening as he looked. It had the desired effect as both men turned slightly to follow his gaze.

Will reacted instantly, throwing the box of shells in his hand at the gunman closest to him. The gunman, who had turned back as Will threw the shells, instinctively ducked as they flew in his direction, providing Will with the time he needed to draw and fire. Moving toward the row of shelves as he fired, he felt the force of a bullet as it hit him in the upper part of his leg. Throwing himself sideways, he landed on the floor behind the shelf.

Tye rounded the corner of the aisle in time to see Will fall between the shelves. He saw a second man down on one knee, blood covering the front of his shirt. At that instant another man came around the end shelf, apparently so intent on shooting Will that he didn't see Tye standing there, gun drawn, feet spread. When he realized the situation he was in, his face flushed in shock. Quickly shifting his feet, he brought his gun hand around, but he never made it. Tye's gun belched flame, once, twice, three times, and the man was hurled backward into the aisle, where he lay. His only movements were the jerking spasms of death.

Tye looked at the remaining gunman. Still on one knee, he was struggling to rise, a look of disbelief on his face as he stared at Tye. Then slowly he fell to his side, his pistol still in its holster.

Tye walked over to where Will was trying to rise, blood running down his pant leg.

"Here let me help ya." Tye took him by the arm and pulled him to a standing position. "Looks like Juanita will have another patient for a while."

Will grimaced at the thought, "I don't mind being laid up, but who's going to look after ya and keep ya outa trouble. I hate to think of all the trouble ya'll be getting into without me there to watch out for ya."

Tye bent and put Will's arm around his shoulder, and with his other arm around his waist he let Will lean against him as they headed for the door.

Lomas Cantrell watched as Jake took Will's bullet. He saw Bart get off a shot as Will jumped behind the shelves and figured Will for dead as Bart ran around the shelves to finish him. The sight of Bart dead in the middle of the floor stunned him. He was standing there in shock when Will and Tye came around the corner of the shelves, but instantly he came to life, drawing his pistol and stepping into the doorway. He brought the pistol to bear as the large man looked up and saw him. He stopped in his tracks and the other man, who looked familiar to Lomas, looked up at the gun pointing in his direction.

"Gentlemen, ya have cost me dearly, but ya shall pay for it with yer lives. I guess that will be compensation enough," Lomas Cantrell said as he pulled back the hammer on the pistol.

Never in his life had Tye heard anything as loud as the cocking of that pistol, but the absolute feeling of helplessness, knowing there was nothing he could do, was the worst part, he thought, as he looked into the cold, gray eyes of his executioner.

Cantrell smiled as if reading Tye's mind. He was enjoying the moment. First he would shoot the wounded man, and as he was falling he would kill the other one. He tried to shift the gun to the right, but his vision blurred and his arm suddenly felt heavy. There was a pain in his back that seemed to spread to his chest, and the gun in his hand slipped from his fingers and fell heavily to the floor. He stood there looking down at it. All he had to do was reach down and get it, then kill the two men standing there. Hearing footsteps on the walk behind him, he slowly turned, staggering as he did. A woman was standing there, a rifle in her hand. He knew this woman, but who was she? Where had he seen her before? Then it came to him—Mrs. Paxton. He'd met her out on the range just before they had stolen the herd. Why was she holding that rifle, and why did she have it pointed at him? Then the realization struck him as he sank slowly to his knees.

"Ya shot me, Mrs. Paxton. Why?" he asked, his face a cloud of confusion.

"Because ya were going to shoot my husband, Mr. Cantrell, and I couldn't let ya do that."

He eased himself down to the floor, as if lying down would ease the pain spreading through his body.

"I knew I'd seen him somewhere before. It was out on the range that day. He rode the big bay horse. I sure wish I owned that horse," he smiled. "Yer husband is a lucky man. He owns a fine horse and has a beautiful wife. A man can't ask for more than that, can he?" His face contorted in pain and his body arched, then he lay motionless, his eyes staring at the ceiling.

Rebecca stood there for a moment, too stunned to move. Then, dropping the rifle, she stepped around the prone body of Lomas Cantrell and walked to Will's side.

"Can we go home now?" she asked.

"Yeah, I think it's time to go."

"Me too," said Tye.

Chapter Thirty

July 4, 1873

All hands of the Rafter TP, as well as several from neighboring ranches, were gathered around the corral, waiting for the Fourth of July festivities to begin. A large steer had been cooking in a pit for a full day, and mouth-watering aromas filled the air. The women had prepared their favorite recipes and were in the house putting the finishing touches on them.

The men stood around in groups talking about horses, cattle, and the lack of rain. Some talked about the depression that had gripped the country and what it was doing to the cattle market. As usual, when cowmen gathered in Texas, the talk turned to those blankety-blank sheep that had invaded the ranges. Cattlemen as a rule hated the woollies and were convinced in their minds that sheep would overgraze the grasslands, starving out the cattle.

Rebecca knew she was the topic of many conversations when these cattlemen gathered. This neither bothered nor deterred her from her plans.

When Tye had driven the herd of longhorns to the Kansas railhead at Abilene, leaving Will at home nursing the wound in his leg, he never imagined what Rebecca would do with part of the proceeds from the herd, although he doubted he would have done anything different had he known.

Rebecca had taken a part of the money—after convincing Will that sheep would be more profitable than cattle one day—and bought one thousand head of sheep. She had hired two Mexican herders to look after the sheep for her and chose the roughest part of the Rafter TP range to run her flock.

Will and Tye, meanwhile, had bought more land and cattle. They now ran just over five thousand head of cattle on forty thousand acres.

Tye had ridden a train east after selling the herd in Kansas. There he had bought five hundred head of Hereford cattle to crossbreed to the Texas longhorns. They were waiting for the first calves with much anticipation.

They had made two more gathers in the breaks, gathering over twenty-five hundred head of longhorns. They already had bought some from small ranches around the area.

Both Will and Tye managed the horse operation, breeding the best mares to the best studs and keeping detailed records. They had contracts with several ranches to supply both green and broken horses. Tye worked with some contacts he had made in the East to supply trained horses to eastern buyers.

More and more people were moving into Texas, looking for work. Since Texas was growing and felt the depression very little, word got out through eastern papers that it was the land of opportunity and wealth. Those who came quickly discovered that the wealth was only there for those who were willing to work for it.

The Texas legislature had opened up more government land to homesteaders, but most of the land was in the dry, arid climate of West Texas where cattle had been king for some time. The land didn't take well to the plow, but eventually the people learned which crops would do well in the dry soil. Cotton proved to be the best crop for the Texas soil. Since there was a high demand for the crop, it didn't take long for cotton to replace cattle as king.

Will had been one of the first to recognize the value of cotton, and he had set aside three hundred acres of river land to be cultivated for it. He hired two families from Mississippi to oversee the production and harvest.

Overall, the operation of the Rafter TP flowed smoothly. Rebecca's sheep proved to be more profitable than the cattle, and the first cotton would be ready for picking in the fall. Will felt it would be a good cash crop if prices held.

Cattle prices were still low, but Will and Tye knew they could hold their cattle until prices came back up. They even planned to buy more while prices were low. It would be a good investment. They now had six full-time hands and a full-time cook working for them.

Not only had the house been completed, but also a bunkhouse, two barns, and a house for Pedro and Juanita. Rebecca had talked Tye and Will into hiring Pedro to help with the horses. He had proved to be a good blacksmith as well as an able hand at handling the mares and colts.

While Rebecca was the center of conversation in many circles because of her sheep. Men spoke of her with respect. It never failed, when her name was brought up, that someone told how she had been the one to put an end to the notorious outlaw, Lomas Cantrell.

Rebecca's fame had spread over Texas like wildfire. Several of the small ranchers who had been hit by Cantrell's band of thieves stopped by the Rafter TP to see her. They thanked her and told her they were beholdin' to her for ridding the range of such a scourge. Of course, Will and Tye received praises too, but most spoke of Rebecca when Cantrell's name was mentioned.

Rebecca wished people would forget about the incident. She never regretted her actions, or the results. But she did not want the notoriety that followed her. She hated the stares that followed her each time she went to Austin, as well as the questions by inquisitive people who wanted to meet the beautiful Mrs. Paxton.

As Rebecca worked in the kitchen, assisting the ladies in preparing the food and directing the setup of the tables, she thought about the day and what it would bring. Will and Tye had brought in several head of young horses that were due to be broken in the next few weeks. There would be contests between the hands to see who could ride the best, as well as roping contests in the large corral and races. All of this would be followed by a large feast and a dance later in the day. Since these kind of events were held only once or twice a year, the festivities would go on well into the night. Some of the folks would spend the night in wagons or in the barns and would return home tomorrow.

Rebecca smiled as she thought about the day and the impact it would have on Will and her. This was indeed a happy day, and she was anxious to finish up here and join Will at the corral. Spying Juanita bustling about the kitchen, she made her way to her and whispered something in her ear. Juanita smiled and nodded vigorously. Slipping out the back door, Rebbeca walked down to the corral. Looking around for Will, she spotted him sitting on the top rail of the corral watching a young cowhand attempt to ride a rather mean-tempered grulla horse. She made her way through the crowd, smiling and returning greetings as she went. Watching through the poles of the corral, Rebecca stood on the ground, waiting for the ride to end before getting Will's attention.

The ride ended shortly, with the young man flying off over the horse's head when the horse did a sudden cutback, planting his front feet, ducking his head, and sliding backward. The young man got to his feet and was rewarded with applause, whistles, and good-natured gibes from the crowd.

Will looked down and saw Rebecca standing beneath him.

"Did ya come to wish me luck on my ride?" he asked, jumping down beside her.

"Not exactly, but since I'm here I guess I might as well," she said, smiling at him.

"You better not be wishin' anybody else good luck," he said, returning the smile.

She smiled coyly. "Oh I don't know. There's a lot of handsome cowboys here today. I might just find me one to root for."

Will grinned at her. Then with mock seriousness on his face, he said, "Yeah, but none of 'em will give ya half the excitement as I do. So ya might as well stick with me."

Laughing, Rebecca said, "Yer right. Life would be plumb boring without ya around. Ya better go on and ride yer horse. I see Tye waving to ya."

He bent down and kissed her lightly on the lips, then hurried off to the bucking chute to mount his horse.

Will had drawn a large strawberry roan with four white stockings. It was one of his favorites among the young horses on the ranch. Rebecca watched as Will rode the horse to a standstill, dismounting to the cheers of the crowd.

Tye rode next, drawing a smaller but stout black filly. She reared as she came out of the chute, then lunged forward, giving Tye a good ride as she tried to throw him, but he rode her to a standstill as well. The crowd cheered as loudly for Tye as he dismounted as they had for Will.

The final contest came down to four riders: Will, Tye, a cowboy from the Circle C, and another cowboy from the Two Deuces. The horses were chosen by the judging committee, and each rider drew a horse's number from a hat, making the competition fair. The final rides would be judged on style and toughness by two judges picked from the local ranch owners. Each judge would score the horse and rider, scoring each ride between one and fifty. The two scores would be added, and the rider with the highest score would be winner. Each rider had to ride his horse to a complete standstill before the judge would award a score.

It was a great contest, with the first cowboy getting bucked off after four minutes of riding. Will, Tye, and the cowboy from the Circle C rode their horses to a standstill, but Will won the contest. He had ridden with reckless abandonment, spurring his horse at every jump and even riding with one hand in the air for a part of the ride.

Rebecca watched with her heart in her throat as Will rode. Now was not the time for him to get himself hurt.

When the bronc riding was over, Rebecca found Will among several cowhands talking about the rides they had made, the horses that had been ridden, and those that had not. Standing off to one side, she tried unsuccessfully to get his attention. Finally, in frustration she walked into the circle of men, elbowing her way in until she was face-to-face with Will.

"Excuse me, gentlemen, but I need to talk to my husband," she said, taking him by the arm and ushering him away to the laughs and jeers of the men.

Will allowed himself to be led reluctantly from the group. He was puzzled by Rebecca's behavior. She had never acted like this before, and he wondered what could possibly be wrong.

"Where are we going?" he asked, noticing she was leading him away from the crowd to a secluded place behind the barn.

"We're getting away from the crowd," she said. "We've been so busy the last week getting ready for this that we haven't had a moment to ourselves, and there's something I've got to tell ya."

Hearing the seriousness in her voice, Will was alarmed. "Is there anything wrong?" He asked, concern in his voice.

Seeing the worry on his face, Rebecca laughed. "No, darling, nothing is wrong. In fact everything is wonderful."

"Then what is it?" He asked.

"Calm down," Rebecca said. "I've got something to tell ya, and I want it to be just right."

Will cocked an eyebrow, looking intently at her as he waited for her to go on.

Smiling, she walked up to him and wrapped her arms around his waist. Leaning her head against his chest, she asked, "Are you happy, Will?"

The question took him by surprise, and it took him a moment to answer.

"Of course I'm happy. I've got ya, this ranch, a great partner. What else could a man ask for?

"A baby," Rebecca said, looking into his face.

It took a moment for Will to realize the implication of what she had said.

"A baby! Is that what yer sayin'? We're havin' a baby?"

Rebecca searched his face. "Do you want a baby?"

The shock was still evident on his face as he answered. "Of course I want a baby. I want a whole house full of babies. Six boys and six girls, and I want all the girls to look just like ya."

Rebecca laughed. "How about we start with one and see where it goes from there."

"That's fine with me," Will said. "When did ya find out?"

"I've been pretty sure for about a month, but I knew for sure last week. I've just been waiting for the right time to tell ya."

He pulled her tight against him. " I love ya, Becky. I'll always love ya."

She smiled as she clung to him, tears of joy running down her cheek.

His face was pressed against her cheek so strongly, she almost didn't hear him whisper his request. "If it's a boy, can we name him Tye?"

Laughing, she pulled away from him. "I couldn't think of a better name."

They stood there holding each other, oblivious to the people around them.

Will felt as if his heart would burst. He now had everything a man could ask for. With Tye and Rebecca's help, he would build something that would last, something that would be here for future generations of Paxtons. He would lay the foundation for them to build on. He looked around him and pictured Paxtons in the future, raising cattle, working the land. But what made him smile was his mind's picture of future Paxtons riding the horses. He could see his son as he gave him pointers and watched him ride the rough broncs to a standstill. He felt the pride he knew he would feel when that day came. He kissed Rebecca one more time. Then, taking her by the arm, he started back to the house. He couldn't wait to tell Tye.

Epilogue

At the turn of the century Texas continued its growth as an agricultural state, but it also strove to remove the stigma of being a backwoods state with nothing but ruffians, outcasts, and wild Indians.

Austin was now the state capitol. It also was the center for business.

Houston had established itself as the port of trade, and cotton was a major export for Texas, supplying many of the world markets and helping establish the United States once again as a leader in the cotton industry.

Cattle were still a major part of Texas's growth, only now it wasn't the large cattle drives that were making history but the building of cattle empires. The King Ranch was now established in the southern part of the state. The XIT Ranch had been established with the building of the state capitol. The Matador was being operated by Mudro McKenzie, and the Scottish syndicate that owned the ranch was well pleased. Many other ranches had been started on the vast plains of this magnificent state, some to succeed, some doomed to failure. But when one failed, there was always someone willing to step in and try again. It was this determination that built Texas and kept it proud.

Texas was the number one state in oil production. Railroads were spreading all over the state, bringing economic prosperity to all corners. It was the beginning of the progressive era for the cattle state known as Texas, and those willing to take the risks and put forth the effort reaped the benefits.

Will Paxton and Tye Garrett never held back but continued to build and strengthen their holdings. The Rafter TP was thriving. Cotton and sheep had proven to be more lucrative than cattle, not to say that cattle had not played a large part in the building of the ranch nor would they ever be replaced. Both Will and Tye devoted most of their time and energies into building strong herds. They began by crossing the rangy longhorns with the Herefords. The results of their labor had produced more pounds of beef on the same amount of range. They had continued their cross-breeding, researching different breeds of cattle to cross with their herds and importing the best bulls they could. But both Will's and Tye's first loves were the horses.

They had built a reputation for producing some of the best horse flesh to come out of Texas. With the eastern markets Tye had opened up, as well as the western ranches that bought their stock, they had more requests for horses than they could fill.

Pedro was still responsible for the daily care of the horse herds. Now in his seventies, Pedro worked alongside his sons and grandsons to insure that the stock was well cared for. Juanita still worked in the kitchen, helping with the daily cooking to feed the twenty or more ranch hands now employed by the Rafter TP.

Rowdy had been ranch foreman for twenty-five years now, looking after the day-to-day operation of the ranch and managing the hundred thousand-plus acres that made up the Rafter TP. Now in his sixties, he would not consider retirement.

Will was in his late fifties and Tye in his late sixties, yet both worked from sunup to sundown. Even though neither rode the rough stock any more, their most enjoyable moments were spent sitting by the large fireplace in the main house and reminiscing about the horses they'd ridden or a bad one that had been ridden by one of the hands.

Rebecca, as beautiful in her later years as she had been in her youth, loved to listen to the two of them talk and even joined in the conversation, mainly to keep the facts accurate and not allow their imaginations to embellish the stories beyond the point of credibility.

She spent most of her time now working with the accounts of the ranch. She had turned over the sheep operation to Ringo, who had become the best hand with sheep. Preferring the quiet solitude to the everyday workings of the ranch, she now had more than four thousand of the woollies running in the broken hills on the westernmost region of the ranch.

Will's dream of a son came true, but only after two daughters were born first. Even though he had tried his best to turn Katie Lynn, named after Rebecca's mother, and Corie Jo into the boys he wanted, both had married and moved from the ranch. Katie lived in Dallas with her husband, an attorney in his father's law firm. Corie, who lived in Austin, came often to the ranch. Her husband was part owner in the local newspaper and was well on his way to a successful career.

Tye Paxton came along late in Will and Rebecca's life. Will was in his early forties and Rebecca in her middle thirties when he was born, surprising them both.

While Will and Rebecca doted on their only male child, it was Tye Garrett who seemed the proudest of his namesake. Having never married again, but having devoted his life to the ranch, he took young Tye, whom he nicknamed Boots, under his wing, teaching him the things he would have taught his own son.

Will and Rebecca often wondered if Boots didn't sometimes regard Tye as a parent rather than his godfather, but they did not interfere in the relationship. As far as they could see, Boots was getting the best of all worlds.

On his sixteenth birthday, Tye led him down to the corral and presented him with a two-year-old dapplegray colt, the best of the young stock on the ranch. As Will and Rebecca looked on, Tye moved the young horse into the bucking chute and placed Boots' saddle on its back, then motioned for Boots to climb on.

It was Boots' first time on an untried horse. He had ridden many of the horses on the ranch and been thrown on several occasions, but both Will and Tye had forbidden him to break the young colts, leaving that job to the hired hands. Now, with both Will and Rebecca's consent, Boots was about to try his first true bronc.

As the young horse bolted from the chute, Boots gripped the saddle tightly with his knees, trying to remember the instructions his dad and Tye had given him. The gray planted his front feet in the ground and bunched his knees, then shot skyward, clearing the ground by a good six feet. Boots hung on the reins and gripped with his knees, bracing himself for the impact to come.

He managed to ride the young horse through six more leaps before a twisting lunge unseated him and sent him crashing to the earth. He got up slowly from the ground, smiling as he straightened up.

"Can I try him again?" he asked, looking first at his father then to Tye.

Rebecca had been standing with her fist held to her mouth, watching her son ride. She felt relief flood through her as he stood up and dusted himself off. She opened her mouth to protest when he made his request but instantly closed it, shutting off the words she wanted to speak. She knew she would accomplish nothing by denying him his wish.

Two hands herded the colt back into the chute, and Boots hurriedly climbed the rails to take his place in the saddle.

Will put his arm around Rebecca, his mind wandering back to a day many years ago when Rebecca first told him she was pregnant. He remembered how he had thought of the day when he would see his son ride the rough stock. Things had changed. The days of breaking horses the rough way were about gone. Now they broke most horses slowly, training them with more patience. Some exhibitions were still being held, and Will was reading more and more about the wild west shows that were being held around the country. He didn't know if it was something that would take hold or not, but it sounded exciting.

Boots made his second ride, managing to ride longer. But in the end he ended up plowing up the dirt in the large corral.

"I think it's time we taught this boy to ride broncs," Tye said as Will came into the corral to talk to Boots.

Will looked at his son. The look of excitement and anticipation in his eyes reminded him of someone he had known long ago. Smiling, he said, "I think you're right. There's nothing wrong with knowing how to stay aboard a rank one. When do you think we should start? How about after the spring gather? We'll have more time then." He smiled at Tye without Boots seeing him.

"But Dad, that's a month away. Can't we start now?" Boots asked, his voice pleading.

Will and Tye laughed, each recalling another youngster who was eager to ride the wild broncs.

"All right, Tye," Will answered, reverting back to his son's given name. "We'll start in the morning. I know what it's like to want to ride. I hope this country doesn't become so tame that there's no more rough stock to ride. It would be a shame to see the desire to climb on the back of one more bronc die because there are no more broncs to be ridden."

The young man looked at his father. Seeing the sadness that came into his eyes, he spoke softly. "Don't worry, Dad. As long as there are Paxtons on this earth, there will always be broncs to ride."

Father and son looked at each other, and both smiled. One was thinking about the past, the other about the future.

ISBN 1-888952-09-1

6 10529 00009 4